英美海洋文学
教 程

SELECTED READINGS OF
BRITISH AND AMERICAN SEA LITERATURE

主 编 王松林 芮渝萍
副主编 徐 燕
编 者 白玉凤 李 莉 唐燕琼 应素芳 张 陟

上海交通大学出版社
SHANGHAI JIAO TONG UNIVERSITY PRESS

内容提要

本书以海洋文学为专题,选编了英美文学中具有代表性的海洋文学作品,包括诗歌、小说、戏剧和散文,注重反映不同时期人与大海的关系。全书由作家简介、作品选读、注释等内容构成,并提供了阅读参考书目和网络资源推荐,便于学生及文学爱好者进一步研修。

本书可作为高校英语专业、海洋大学相关专业通识课或专业选修课的教材,也可作为外国文学爱好者的有益读物。

图书在版编目(CIP)数据

英美海洋文学教程 / 王松林,芮渝萍主编 . — 上海:
上海交通大学出版社,2021.12
ISBN 978 - 7 - 313 - 25791 - 8

Ⅰ. 英…　Ⅱ. ①王… ②芮…　Ⅲ. ①英国文学—文学研究—教材 ②文学研究—美国—教材　Ⅳ. ①I561.06
②I712.06

中国版本图书馆 CIP 数据核字(2021)第 265407 号

英美海洋文学教程
YING-MEI HAIYANG WENXUE JIAOCHENG

主　　编:王松林　芮渝萍
出版发行:上海交通大学出版社　　　地　　址:上海市番禺路 951 号
邮政编码:200030　　　　　　　　　　电　　话:021 - 64071208
印　　刷:上海天地海设计印刷有限公司　经　　销:全国新华书店
开　　本:787mm×1092mm　1/16　　印　　张:19.75
字　　数:442 千字
版　　次:2021 年 12 月第 1 版　　　　印　　次:2021 年 12 月第 1 次印刷
书　　号:ISBN 978 - 7 - 313 - 25791 - 8
定　　价:58.00 元

英美海洋文学流变述略
（代序）

众所周知，地球表面积的 71% 被海洋覆盖。人类生命源自海洋，人类的文明起源于海洋。面对大海的浩瀚、神秘和凶险，人类的先民对大海抱有深深的敬畏并因此产生了丰富而充满智慧的遐想。海洋于是成为早期人类口头文学的最主要题材之一。从早期的神话和史诗到后来的海洋文学书写，我们可以发现人类的海洋意识经历了漫长的变化过程。

一

在希腊神话中，海神波塞冬（Poseidon）是个复杂的形象。波塞冬与天王宙斯（Zeus）、地王哈得斯（Hades）本是三兄弟。当初他们抽签划分势力范围，结果宙斯得了天空，哈得斯获得大地，波塞冬得到大海和湖泊。三兄弟看似平分天下，但宙斯自视天神，居心巨测，动辄威胁要把大地和大海拉起吊在奥林匹斯山上。性格像大海那样桀骜不驯的波塞冬对此极为不满。传说中的波塞冬经常驾驭烈马金车在海面狂奔，掀起巨浪表达自己的愤怒。他发怒时还会用手中的三叉戟搅起海啸，震得地动山摇。爱琴海附近的希腊渔民和水手对他极为崇拜，认为海上的惊涛骇浪和地震引发的海啸是波塞冬内心不平的表现。当然，波塞冬也有宁静温和的时候，此时海面风平浪静，人们可见海豚成群，逐游戏耍。由此看来，古希腊神话中的海神性格具有双重性，荷马史诗将他称为"大地和大海的震撼者"及"野马的驯服者和船只的救星"。根据《伊利亚特》的记载，在特洛伊战争中海神波塞冬偏袒希腊人，帮助希腊人打败了特洛伊人。在《奥德赛》中，经历过特洛伊十年鏖战的英雄奥德修斯（Odysseus）在回家途中来到波塞冬之子独眼巨人波吕斐摩斯（Polyphemus）居住的西西里岛。为补充给养，奥德修斯和他的手下与独眼巨人发生冲突，逃生过程中奥德修斯设计弄瞎了波吕斐摩斯的眼睛。波塞冬知道后发誓报复，他唤起巨浪和大风，将奥德修斯的船只吹离了回家的航线，致使他连遭不测。总的看来，希腊神话中的海神脾气暴躁、好战好斗、心胸狭隘、报复心强，稍后的古希腊文学中，大海的形象仍以暴虐、冷漠为主要特征。

虽然大海险象丛生、暴虐无常，但人们还是表达了征服大海的愿望和对美好生活的憧憬。在希腊神话中，英雄赫拉克勒斯（Heracles）和忒修斯（Theseus）力斩海怪，普罗米修斯（Prometheus）教人们掌握航海知识，奥德修斯历经十年漂泊抵御住了海妖的诱惑终归故乡。这些与海洋相关的神话和传说曲折地反映了远古时代恶劣的生存环境以及人们渴望征服大海的梦想。这一梦想将在以后人类有关海洋的书写中以不同的方式不断重现。古希腊杰出的政治家、军事家地米斯托克利（Themistocles，前524—前460年）很早就预言：谁控制了海洋,谁就控制了一切。可以说,从古希腊开始人们就渴望认识大海,征服大海。

童年时代的人类是自然神论者,人类对自然充满敬畏,人类眼中的大海既有兽性的一面,也有神性和人性的一面。现代西方文学作品中的大海依然保留了这种双重性品格:她既凶险神秘又充满美感和浪漫;她既挑战人的勇气又像母亲那样给人呵护。受基督教的影响,西方文学中的大海还经常与救赎和再生联系在一起。

大致说来,英语 Sea Literature(海洋文学)含有广义和狭义两层意思。广义上的 Sea Literature 指的是所有与海洋相关的文献(包括航海记录、船只制造技术资料和海洋文学作品);狭义上的 Sea Literature 是指以海洋或海上经历为书写对象、旨在凸显人与海洋的价值关系和审美意蕴的文学作品。换言之,狭义上的海洋文学须兼有海洋性和文学性两大基本属性。但也有学者认为这样的定义还不足以突出海洋文学的内在特质。持这一观点的学者认为,真正意义上的海洋文学应该是作品主题须与海洋的特性密切相关,并给人带来心灵的感动和满足,即作品须令读者在理性、感性和意志方面对海洋产生特殊的兴趣。对海洋文学的这般界定当然有其道理,不过未免显得有些苛刻。我们不妨将海洋文学的定义放宽些,将那些以海洋为题材或根据海上体验写成的反映人类与大海情感关系的文学作品都纳入海洋文学的范畴。一般来说,海洋文学是指以海洋为背景,以海洋、水手、岛屿和船只等作为主要元素,以海洋为题材或根据海上体验写成的展现了人(水手)与大海、人与自我、人与社会(船只或岛屿)、人与人之间关系的文学作品,海洋文学重在体现海洋精神和海洋意识。

二

中古英语时期的英国文学以海洋书写为主。《航海者》("The Seafarer")就是流传下来的最早的古英语诗歌之一,今天我们读到的《航海者》大约是公元 725 年前后的作品,共有124 行,绝大多数普通读者只能通过译本来阅读它。《航海者》讲述了一个水手的孤独和忧郁,他感叹人生短暂,命运无常,第一人称的叙述者有很强的海洋意识,他厌倦了陆地尘世的奢靡生活,更加向往和享受海上的黑夜、冰雹和孤独。诗人笔下的陆地(城市)是现实的、堕落的象征,而海洋则是精神救赎的场所,是老水手逃避尘世生活和走向天国的通道。盎格鲁-撒克逊时代的史诗《贝奥武甫》中的大海黑暗幽深,是海怪的栖身场所,大海的神秘和凶险暗示着大自然的恐怖。贝奥武甫手持利剑潜入海底杀死海怪,为民除害,这象征性地反映了人们希望战胜自然灾害的美好愿望。在很大程度上,史诗中有关大海及海怪的恐怖意象反映了岛国居民的生存焦虑,同时也表明人们试图以大海为参照确立自己的地缘政治和岛国文化身份。英国诗歌之父乔叟(约 1343—1400)的《坎特伯雷故事集》很早就涉及了有关当时商人海上航行及海盗的记录,这表明作者对 14 世纪的英国海上贸易及遭遇的海盗风险有较多的了解。15—17 世纪的航海大发现催生了大量的海洋(航海)文学作品。这一时期,除了神学和宗教著作外,最受欢迎的读物可能就是海外探险游记、航海作品和世界地理著作。1588 年,英国打败西班牙的"无敌舰队",转而成为海上霸主,此后英国海洋文学走向繁荣。16—17 世纪,英国涌现了大量海洋文学作品。不过,与过去有关海上历险的描述有所不同的是,这一时期的海洋书写大多侧重渲染海上(海外)世界的奇幻,比较典型的如托马斯·莫尔(Thomas Moore,1478—1535)的《乌托邦》(1516)和培根的《新大西岛》(1627)。都铎王朝时期,为鼓励海外探险,理查德·伊登(Richard Eden,约 1512—1576)受命翻译西班牙天体学家马丁·科切兹·德·阿尔巴卡(Martín Cortés de Albacar,1510—1582)的《航海艺术》(The Arte of Navigation,1561)一书。《航海艺术》遂成为英语第一部航海手册。文艺复兴时期,以海洋为背景或以海上历险为主题的文学作品频频面世。据说,1609 年发生在百慕大的一次海难就给了莎士比亚创作《暴风雨》的灵感。不过,莎士比亚笔下的大海被赋予了神奇的力量,海上暴风雨在作者的笔下呈现出诗意的色彩,成为检视人们灵魂的极致场所。

自古以来,大海就是诗人灵感的源泉,潮起潮落,波翻浪涌,总能引起诗人内心的强烈共鸣:从斯宾塞的海边恋曲到丁尼生的听涛悼亡,从柯勒律治笔下大海的神秘怪谲到拜伦笔下大海的自由不羁。17 世纪玄学派诗人约翰·邓恩的笔下可见航海科技成果和航海大发现对诗人的影响,他曾发出"没有人是一座孤岛"的感叹。18 世纪的海洋探险和海外殖民在英国文学中留下了深深的烙印。笛福的《鲁滨孙漂流记》是对海上历险和海外殖民的真实记录,但更多的是理性主义时代人们征服自然和挑战自我的意志表达。稍后的斯威夫特写的《格列佛游记》以虚构的海中岛国为参照,对现实世界乃至整个人类都给予了辛辣的讽刺。斯摩莱特的小说几乎都与海洋有关,主要描写英国海军的真实生活,这在英国小说史上开拓了一个新的领域。可以说,他是英国海军军旅小说的创始人。其实,即便在以描写英国风土人情见长的简·奥斯丁笔下,人们也能发现大量有关英国海军军官的描写(如小说《劝导》),足见海洋因素已经渗入英国普通百姓的生活,这也从一个侧面向人们展示了英国海外殖民的影子。斯摩莱特之后,弗雷德里克·马里亚特对英国海军生活做了更细致的描写。马里亚特本人就担任过英国皇家海军上校,他的《海军候补生伊齐先生》(1836)反映了 19 世纪早期拿破仑战争时代的海军生活,笔调诙谐幽默,堪称同时期海洋小说的代表作。小说家狄更斯是马里亚特的好朋友,狄更斯出身于一个有海军背景的家族,虽然他的小说大多描写城市生活,但包含大量的海洋意象及英国海外殖民地的讯息。不仅如此,狄更斯还写有以海难和海上漂流为主题的小说《海上来信》(1860),激发了海上漂流瓶传递音讯的风潮。及至 19 世纪后半叶,"日不落"帝国的势力越加强盛,英国海洋文学也由此达到高潮。

大海在英国浪漫主义诗人笔下是自由的象征。华兹华斯在他的《献给自由的十四行诗》中赞美大海是"自由的女神"。柯勒律治的《古舟子吟》以浪漫主义的手法描写了一个超自然的海上世界,诗人笔下的大海时而泡沫翻滚,时而浓雾弥漫,时而凉风轻拂,时而酷日当头,老水手讲述的故事具有神秘的象征意味,表达了诗人对罪与罚的思考,宣扬了基督教的博爱精神。另一位书写海洋抒情诗的诗人是托马斯·坎贝尔,他的《英格兰水手》是一首歌颂英雄主义和爱国主义的诗歌。第二代浪漫主义诗人更是与大海结下了不解之缘。拜伦一生多次漂洋过海,对大海有着浓厚的感情,他的《查尔德·哈罗尔德游记》和《唐·璜》展现了大海的波涛与人物思想情感的交融,从某种意义上来说,大海成就了诗人拜伦。在《西风颂》中,雪莱将狂风中卷起的海浪比作酒神祭司的万丈魔发在海天之间搅动,想象奇特,气势磅礴,给人强烈的视觉冲击和精神震撼。济慈的长诗《恩狄米昂》中的美少年恩狄米昂为寻求梦中的月亮女神,不惜下地狱入海底,最终实现梦想。济慈从川流不息奔向大海的溪水那里似乎悟出了生命与死亡的真谛,嘱咐友人在自己的墓碑上写上这些字:"这儿埋着一个名字写在水上的人。"19世纪中后期的英国诗人同样写下了大量因大海萌生情愫的优美诗作,如丁尼生的《悼念集》、勃朗宁的《夜间相会》、克里斯蒂娜·罗塞蒂的《大海的面孔》、阿诺德的《多佛海滩》、史文朋的《海上爱情》等。之后,20世纪初的诗人如哈代、布鲁克斯、梅斯菲尔德和豪斯曼等也留下了不少以海洋为意象寄托自己情思的诗篇。特别是被誉为"海洋诗人"的约翰·梅斯菲尔德,他的《海之恋》是脍炙人口的抒情诗。就连短篇小说家凯瑟琳·曼斯菲尔德也写有不少以大海为意象的抒情诗,寄托自己身在异乡的孤独和思乡之情。

19世纪英国的海外扩张还催生了一批描写海上历险或异国情调的新浪漫主义小说家,如吉卜林、康拉德、史蒂文森等,其中不乏专门为儿童创作的海岛历险小说,如巴兰坦的《珊瑚岛》和史蒂文森的《绑架》《金银岛》等。之后,金斯莱的童话《水孩子》和20世纪初詹姆斯·巴利的童话《彼得·潘》也是这一传统的延续。与海洋相关的儿童文学多有成长小说的教谕色彩,旨在培养孩子的自由精神、自主能力、勇气责任以及合作精神。这些精神实际上与水手的优秀品质密切相关。从严格的意义上来说,康拉德是个真正的、富有哲思的海洋小说家。长达20年的海上生涯为他的小说创作提供了丰富的素材。他的许多小说如《青春》《台风》《"水仙号"的黑水手》《阴影线》等都以大海为背景烘托人物的内心世界。譬如,在《阴影线》中,作者通过第一人称叙述者之口表明了大海和船只对人的品格的考验:"我的身体属于海洋,完全属于海和船;海是真正的世界,船则检测着人的男子气概、脾气、勇气、忠诚——和爱。""我"认识到这么一个道理:"一个人要么是海员,要么不是海员,我无疑是海员。"康拉德小说中故事发生的海域几乎遍布全球,艺术视野之开阔令小说家亨利·詹姆斯感叹"无人可与之比肩"。可以说,康拉德是一个以水手的目光来打量世界的小说艺术家。

进入20世纪后,海洋或航海作为一种文学意象,其内涵在英国文学中得到进一步升华。同样是以大海为背景,较之18—19世纪文学作品着重对海上探险本身的描写,20世纪的海洋文学更加倾向以大海(航海)这一意象为隐喻来呈现人物的心路历程。譬如,弗吉尼亚·伍尔夫的《航行》和《到灯塔去》可见主人公泛舟于内心的大海。受特殊地理位置和海洋文化的影响,爱尔兰作家群的笔下尤能体现茫茫大海中人的孤立无助,同时也表现出对这一处境中人的命运的关切。小说家乔伊斯的《尤利西斯》中主人公的内心历程与荷马史诗《奥德赛》有着明显的互文性关系。同样,当代小说家班维尔的《大海》也对人物的心理世界进行了细腻的描写,从亘古不变的大海中作者汲取了丰富的人生哲思。剧作家沁孤的《蹈海骑手》中那不断吞噬生命的大海象征了自然力量和命运的神秘,作者在这个简短的独幕剧中展示了爱尔兰民族在生存的悲剧状态下表现出的人格的尊贵与伟大。大海在叶芝的诗歌中是通往人类心灵和艺术圣地拜占庭的必经之路,诗人这样吟唱:"我扬帆驶过这波涛万顷,来到这神圣之城拜占庭。"

第一次世界大战和第二次世界大战前后,不少以海上军事为题材的小说受到读者的欢迎,较出色的有福利斯特(C. S. Forester,1899—1966)写的有关英国皇家海军军官霍恩伯洛尔(Horatio Hornblower)的11部系列小说和奥布莱恩(Patrick O'Brian,1914—2000)写的有关奥伯雷-马丘林(Aubrey-Maturin)的20部系列小说。两位作家均以拿破仑时代的海战为背景,描写英国皇家海军的战斗故事。奥布莱恩的历史海洋小说尤为读者关注,奥伯雷-马丘林系列小说描述的是皇家海军舰长奥伯雷与随舰军医兼学者马丘林之间的生死情谊。奥布莱恩的大多数小说都名列《纽约时报》畅销书名单之中,特别是他的《怒海争锋》(1969)深受史学家和评论家的好评。小说取材于拿破仑时代一场以少胜多的真实海战,其可贵之处在于作者并不单单着眼于惊心动魄的海战描写,而是细腻地刻画了军人与知识分子间的不同性格和思想的对立及包容。广阔的大海是他们勇气的象征,也是他们宽容之心的象征。2003 年该小说经改编由福克斯公司搬上银幕后,更是好评如潮。奥布莱恩的系列小说被誉为"现代航海史诗"。理查德·休斯(Richard Hughes,1900—1976)是另一位擅长撰写海洋题材的当代小说家,他在《危险航行》(In Hazard,1938)中对暴风雨的描写堪与康拉德的《台风》相媲美。此外,还有蒙赛莱特(Nicholas Monsarrat,1910—1979)的反潜战小说《沧海无情》(The Cruel Sea,1951),其中有关潜艇战的细节描写相当精彩。总的来看,20 世纪下半叶以降,英国海洋文学反映了世界各国海上争霸的局面,英国的海上霸主地位虽然已是辉煌不再,但依然表现出强烈的海权意识。进入 21 世纪后,作家的海洋生态意识日益增强。2013 年,英国《卫报》在"世界水日"(3 月 22 日)发起了一项全球征稿活动,旨在唤醒和提升民众的水危机意识与海洋生态意识。著名作家 A.S.拜厄特(A. S. Byatt,1936)参与了此项活动。她的短篇小说《大海的故事》("Sea Story")以诗意的笔触描述了主人公的漂流瓶在被人类污染的大海上漂浮许久,最终破裂,未能抵达恋人手中的悲伤故事,表达了对海洋生态危机的高度关切。

三

美国文学自殖民地时期甚至更早的土著人的口头文学开始就有大量有关海洋的讲述或书写。在土著印第安人有关世界起源的口头传说中,陆地被认为是从海洋中脱胎而出。此外,他们还有大量关于海上捕鲸或捕鱼的历险故事。殖民地早期的美国文学多半是广义上的文献资料,包括船长的航海日志、牧师的布道词、清教徒的契约等。一般认为,约翰·史密斯船长(Captain John Smith,1580—1631)可能是第一位记录殖民地时期的美国与海洋关系的作家。他于 1607 年在弗吉尼亚建立了詹姆斯镇并率先用英语记录了远渡重洋来北美洲殖民的清教徒的经历。早期清教徒不畏艰辛来到这块"新大陆",首先接受的是海上风暴的洗礼。在他们的眼中,暴虐的海洋是上帝考验他们虔诚信仰的外在力量。

早期美国海洋书写的素材来源大致有二:一是 16 世纪以来,英、法、西、荷等欧洲海上列强的海上探险故事及其在美洲的殖民活动记录,其中不乏诸多有关海难、海盗、鬼船以及与土著人交往的传说;二是有关海上劳工的非人待遇和远洋贩卖黑奴的流传和记录。多年以后,理查德·亨利·达纳(Richard Henry Dana, Jr.,1815—1882)写的《两年水手生涯》(Two Years Before the Mast,1840)记述的就是欧洲劳工前往美国途中在船上受到的惨无人道的待遇的骇人景象。值得注意的是,早期美国文学的主题大多与欧洲有关,风格也受欧洲浪漫主义的影响。譬如,华盛顿·欧文的《见闻札记》中有不少关于美国人在海外的游历(如《航行》),他的《哥伦布及其同伴的发现之旅》(1831)是对欧洲人探险经验的怀念。

真正意义上的美国海洋文学的开创者是詹姆斯·费尼莫尔·库珀。库珀当过商船水手也当过海军军官,故熟知海上恶劣的生存环境和水手的内心世界。他一生创作的 30 多部小说中有 10 余部是海洋小说,如《领航人》《红海盗》《海妖》《海上与岸上》《海狮》等,其中最杰出的是《领航人》(1824)。库珀的海洋小说题材广泛,影响深远,对麦尔维尔和康拉德产生过较大影响。库珀的海洋小说反映了美国人超前的海权意识和海上军事霸权意识。与库珀不同的是,爱伦·坡笔下的海洋笼罩着恐怖的气息,他的诗歌(如《海中之城》)和短篇小说(如《海底漩涡余生记》《南塔克特的亚瑟·戈登·皮姆的故事》等)均把大海描绘得神秘莫测、幽深可怖。爱伦·坡还写有短篇小说《瓶中手稿》,描写了一个去南极探险的青年,在海难中劫后余生,借漂流瓶试图与陆地上的亲人分享自己九死一生经历的故事。同狄更斯的《海上来信》一样,这个故事也引发了美国人用漂流瓶来传递信息的热潮。1851 年,赫尔曼·麦尔维尔发表了小说《白鲸》,标志着美国海洋文学的高潮。虽然麦尔维尔在小说中对捕鲸业的描述并不准确,但这丝毫不影响该小说的地位。小说中那位有强烈意志的亚哈船长对白鲸展开了悲壮的追杀,但最终葬身海底。这暗示了人与大自然(大海)进行愚妄较量的悲剧性结局。捕鲸的历程象征性地呼应了西方文学中一个永恒的"探寻"(quest)母题:故事叙述者以实玛利的内心探寻和船长亚哈的复仇追杀如同两股海浪交织在一起,小说展示的人物的精神世界如大海般波澜壮阔。

如果说《白鲸》依然带有浓郁的海上历险色彩,《白鲸》之后的美国海洋文学书写则明显倾向于借助海洋进行个体心理或民族意识的探究。譬如,朗费罗的诗作《造船》就将美国的形成和发展过程喻成航船的建造,航船在年轻人的领导下无畏地驶向大海;惠特曼诗歌中的大海是生与死的矛盾统一体,是美国南北战争惊涛骇浪的化身。黑人诗人顿巴的海洋诗如《神秘的海洋》《船在夜间过》等均以海洋为意象抒发黑人的艰难处境。大海是女作家凯特·肖邦的小说《觉醒》中的重要意象。涛声阵阵唤醒的是女主人公爱德娜心中的爱情和对自由的渴望。《觉醒》中的大海具有明显的母性特质,大海像母亲那样总是敞开怀抱抚慰心灵受伤的人。同时,小说中的大海还意味着生命的归宿和再生。

美国自然主义时期的文学不乏对海洋的书写。这一阶段的海洋文学从一个侧面反映了美国社会文化变迁的图景。随着工业化时代的到来,蒸汽船取代了帆船成为海上运输的主要工具。南北战争和西进运动期间,美国文学更多地将目光投向蓄奴制、西部开发和政治经济等问题。与此同时,社会达尔文主义的思想在美国社会上广泛传播,这直接催生了美国的海外扩张意识(尤其是海疆意识)。这一时期,美国政治家开始有了海洋战略意识,其中最主要的代表性人物就是阿尔弗雷德·赛耶·马汉(Alfred Thayer Mahan,1840—1914)。马汉的《海权对历史的影响》(又称《海权论》,1890)被誉为近代制海权理论的奠基之作。虽然这本书不是文学作品,但在一定程度上引发了此后美国海洋文学对海疆和海权问题的关注。譬如,第一次世界大战之后美国旅行小说家弗雷德里克·奥布莱恩(Frederick O'Brian,1869—1932)的"波利尼西亚三部曲"(《南海白影》《南海上的神秘岛》《太阳环礁》)虽然描写的是太平洋群岛的奇风异俗,但是也蕴含了美国的海洋殖民意识和帝国想象。

当然,自然主义思潮对美国文学更直接的影响在于,它促进了作家对生存和人性这两大主题的深度思考。不少小说家将帆船时代水手之间形成的兄弟情谊与工业化时代人们各自为"适者生存"而进行的残酷斗争进行比较。最能反映这一冲突的是小说家史蒂芬·克莱恩的小说《海上扁舟》和杰克·伦敦的小说《海狼》。前者暗示了置身于茫茫大海中的人类的渺小与无助,同时也说明了合作精神的重要性;后者笔下的海狼拉森统治下的"魔鬼"号船纯粹是一个残酷的自然主义世界的缩影。将自然主义的手法运用于戏剧创作的杰出代表是尤金·奥尼尔。奥尼尔有过六年海上生活经历,他创作了大量海洋戏剧作品,主要有《东航卡迪夫》(1916)、《归途迢迢》(1917)、《天边外》(1918)、《加勒比人的月亮》(1918)、《安娜·克里斯蒂》(1921)、《长夜漫漫路迢迢》(1941)等。值得注意的是,奥尼尔笔下的大海已不再是传统自然主义作家笔下那个冷漠无情的世界。相反,大海是一个自由的精神家园。在一首名为《大海的呼唤》(1912)的诗中,奥尼尔将大海喻为自己心灵的归宿:"经过黑夜风雨飘摇/我拉紧了操帆索/高声唱起船夫曲/手握舵轮有多亲切/强劲的信风迎面扑/于是回到大海,弟兄们/又回到了大海/我喜欢停泊在异国海岸/又回到了大海。"奥尼尔颇具自传色彩的剧作《长夜漫漫路迢迢》的主人公埃德蒙在皎洁的月光下,迎着海风,站在甲板上,触景生情:"脚下海水翻滚,泡沫飞溅,头上桅杆风帆高扬,月光下皎洁一片。美景满目、风帆悦耳,令人陶醉,蓦然间怡然自得、心驰神往。⋯⋯我顿感自由无比!我整个身心都融入大海,与白帆、浪花、美景、风声,与帆船、与星空融为一体!"这番富有诗意的感受最能体现奥尼尔对大海的浓浓深情。

继奥尼尔之后,另一位对大海抱有深厚情感的作家是海明威。海明威写有不少以海洋为题材的小说,如《海变》(1931)、《有的和没有的》(1937)、《过河入林》(1950)、《海流中的岛屿》(1970)等,但堪称海洋文学杰作的是《老人与海》(1952)。在古巴老渔民圣地亚哥的眼中,人与大海的关系并不是自然主义小说中的那种敌对关系,而是休戚相关、生死与共的和谐关系。在谈到《老人与海》的创作意图时,海明威说:"我试图塑造一位真正的老人、一个真正的孩子、一片真正的海、一条真正的鱼和真正的鲨鱼。如果我能将他们塑造得十分出色和真实,他们将意味许多东西。"我们发现,老人圣地亚哥把海洋及海洋生物都当作有灵性和有尊严的生命来对待。他对小鸟、海鸥、海龟、海豚、马林鱼等或抱有怜悯之情,或抱有敬畏之心。通过圣地亚哥对海洋以及海洋生物的态度,海明威对人类中心主义进行了批评,表达了超前的海洋生态意识。这种对海洋的生态伦理关怀在当代著名文学家、生态学家和环境保护主义者雷切尔·卡森那里得到了最充分的体现。"海洋三部曲"《在海风的下面》(1941)、《我们周围的海洋》(1951)、《海的边缘》(1955)奠定了卡森海洋传记作家和科普作家的地位。卡森的海洋科普作品语言充满诗意,叙述引人入胜。《我们周围的海洋》曾获1952年美国国家图书奖并被拍成电影;影片获得奥斯卡最佳纪录片奖,被誉为"海的诗史"。大海是卡森一生迷恋的对象,她临终前给好友多萝西·弗里曼写过一封信,表达了她对大海的眷恋之情:"[我]最终归于大海——归于神圣的大洋,归于大洋里的海流,仿佛永远流动的时间之河,由始及终,由死到生。"另一位具有海洋生态意识的美国当代小说家是彼得·马修森(Peter Matthiessen),他的代表作是1975年出版的《遥远的龟岛》(Far Tortuga)。这部小说讲述的是一个惊心动魄的捕海龟船葬身加勒比海的历险故事,展示了人与海龟、大海及自我的内在关系,旨在唤醒人们的海洋生态意识。

四

海洋文学是一种有自身独特品格的文学类型。从人类文明和文学的起源来看,人类文明的诞生与海洋密切相关,大海是人类想象力的重要源泉,它激发了人类的无限遐想和哲思。文学创作与航海有共通之处,它们都是身体和心灵的历险。从西方文学和文化传统来看,西方神话、史诗和《圣经》中的大海意象已沉淀为西方文学与文化的精神内核。古英语诗歌的大海是孤独、绝望和放逐的场所,也是自由、浪漫和精神救赎之所在。现代(主义)文学中的大海是自我发现及与"他者"接触的空间,具有浓郁的象征色彩。从研究的范式来看,海洋文学研究具有跨学科特性,涉及海洋史、海洋文化、海洋生态、海洋政治、海洋贸易、海洋军事、民族国家身份等问题。大海的流动性、连接性和移动性特征表明,大海在全球化和去(欧洲)中心化的进程中起着关键作用。由是观之,大海是现代性生产的重要发源地,海洋文学与文化研究是通往现代性研究的重要路径。

21世纪是海洋的世纪。海洋是21世纪人类社会可持续发展的宝贵财富和最后空间。然而,我们必须清楚地意识到,在不少人眼中大海一直是取之不尽用之不竭的宝藏,人们理所当然地认为人与大海的关系是主宰与被主宰、索取与被索取的关系。长期以来,这种对大海的占有欲和控制意识反映在人类有关海洋的各类书写中,其中也包括文学作品。然而,值得欣慰的是,文学家似乎比政治家、经济学家和普通百姓更早更清醒地意识到,若是一味向大海索取和无限地开发大海,人类必将遭到大自然的惩罚。本书在选材时就特别注意文学作品中传达的海洋生态伦理意识。我们认为,文学作品记录的是人类的心路历程。文学家眼中的大海不仅是创作灵感的源泉,而且是一面反观自我的镜子,正如法国诗人波德莱尔所言:"[大海]有时风平浪静,水面/成为映照我的绝望的巨大镜子。"

王松林

2021 年 12 月 1 日

前　言

本书是国内第一部以英美海洋文学为专题的读本。在选材上，本书力求做到系统全面，融英美海洋文学作品精华于一炉，反映出英美海洋文学的历史概貌。

本书的选材有三个方面的考虑。首先考虑了英国和美国海洋文学作品入选的比重。英国海洋文学源远流长，从古代史诗到文艺复兴时期的诗歌与戏剧，再到 18 世纪的海洋历险故事和 19 世纪的浪漫主义诗歌与新浪漫主义小说，一直到 20 世纪的现代主义文学，都可见到大量以大海为主要意象的作品，反映了人们海洋意识的变化过程。在篇幅上，考虑到英国海洋文学传统悠久，故入选篇目较多。而美国海洋文学历史相对较短，故入选篇目少些，但这并不意味着美国海洋文学的匮乏。其次考虑了英美海洋文学作品样式的多样性，包括诗歌、小说、戏剧和散文。在作家作品的取舍上，考虑到阅读的相对完整性，海洋抒情短诗入选较多。有些重要作家的作品，如奥布莱恩的海上军事题材小说和奥尼尔的戏剧，囿于篇幅只好割爱。最后充分考虑了海洋文学的历史流变问题，注重选取不同时期反映人与大海关系的代表性作品。譬如，就美国海洋文学而言，自库珀开创美国海洋文学以来，美国海洋文学历经了以麦尔维尔为代表的浪漫主义海洋文学书写、以克莱恩和杰克·伦敦为代表的自然主义海洋文学书写、以奥尼尔和海明威为代表的现代主义海洋文学书写，一直到以雷切尔·卡森为代表的生态主义海洋文学书写，表现出非凡的成就。本书收录了这些代表性作家的代表作品。

在编写体例上，本书由作家作品简介、作品选读和注释等内容构成，同时还为读者提供了拓展阅读书目和网站资源推介，便于学生和海洋文学爱好者进一步研修。本书可作为高等院校英语专业、海洋大学（学院）相关专业通识课或专业选修课的教科书或参考书，也可作为外国文学爱好者的有益读物。

本书由宁波大学"英语海洋文学与文化研究"课题组成员通力协作完成。王松林负责全书理念的设计和统稿，芮渝萍负责美国海洋文学部分的选材编注，徐燕为书稿的整理和编写做了大量的工作。白玉凤、李莉、唐燕琼、应素芳、张陟、邵琦、刘珂、陈岑、吴琳华、王亚妮、刘浩、朱慧琳、王霁雯等参与了本书的编写工作。本书的序言是对英美海洋文学的一个鸟瞰，希望对读者有所裨益。由于编者水平有限，时间较仓促，谬误在所难免，希望读者批评指正，以便再版时修正。

Contents

I. "The Seafarer"

《航海者》("The Seafarer")是流传下来的最早的古英语诗歌之一,今天的读者绝大数只能通过译本来阅读。盎格鲁-撒克逊时期的诗歌留存至今的十分稀少,主要见于 10 世纪末和 11 世纪初的四份手稿中,分别为《〈贝奥武甫〉手稿》("The Beowulf Manuscript")、《朱尼乌斯手稿》("The Junius Manuscript")、《韦尔切利手稿》("The Vercelli Book")以及记录了本诗的《埃克塞特诗集》("Exeter Book")。《航海者》的手抄本现存于英国埃克塞特大教堂收藏的《埃克塞特诗集》中,这是一部现存最丰富的古英语诗集,收录了大约自公元 904 年以来的盎格鲁-撒克逊时期的诗歌,由 11 世纪的利奥弗里克大主教(Bishop Leofric)捐赠给埃克塞特大教堂。今天我们读到的《航海者》的版本大约是公元 725 年前后的作品,共有 124 行。和同时期大多数口头流传的文学作品一样,该诗作者的真实身份不详。直到 19 世纪,这首诗才引起人们的关注,并逐渐得到赞赏。《航海者》和另一首著名的古英语诗歌《流浪者》("The Wanderer")被看成盎格鲁-撒克逊时期口头文学的经典。

这首诗描述了一位航海者的悲叹、渴望和对上帝的赞美与尊崇。诗歌的内容大致由两部分组成。在第一部分,航海者以第一人称视角回忆自己此前作为船头守夜人的航海经历:极端恶劣的天气、凶险的海上环境及与世隔绝的生活,令他饱尝了形影相吊与饥寒交迫之苦。譬如,在诗歌的第五到十三行,他回想起了海上的孤独与艰辛:汹涌翻腾的海浪不断冲袭着悬崖,独自坐在船头焦急地守候,天气严寒,铁链如冰,风霜冻僵了双足。然而,尽管内心充满孤独和痛苦,尽管陆地上的"亲人"不理解航海者的艰辛和凄楚,老水手仍然执意要回到大海,不愿像城里人那样享受安逸、奢侈的陆地生活。可以看出,老水手有强烈的陆地—海洋二分对立的意识。他多次将海上与陆地上的生活和环境进行对比,陆地上人声鼎沸,人们举办着宴会,酣饮着美酒,享受着琴乐,而航海者只能与冷漠咆哮的海浪声、发出死亡之音的海鸟的叫声和尖锐刺耳的老鹰的叫声终日为伴,偶尔听到的天鹅的歌声于他而言,已是难得的乐趣与慰藉。诗歌的第一部分用了大量笔墨描绘了主人公与大海之间这种爱恨交织的关系。到了第二部分,诗中加入了基督教元素,展现了大海与救赎和再生之间的联系,主人公期待再次开启的海上之旅具有象征色彩,他想象自己的灵魂与大海一起漫游,希望通过出海来摆脱陆地上的各种物质诱惑,逃离这个堕落的世界。

不少学者认为,《航海者》的后半部系后人所加,融入了基督教的思想。也有些学者认为,诗的后半部分和前半部分可以视作一体,它是原诗的自然发展,航海者感到尘世间人情冷淡,生活无依无靠,命运不济,所以希望最终投入上帝的怀抱,享受永恒的幸福和关爱。其实,不管何种解释,这首诗都体现了日耳曼文化和基督教教义的混合。但总的来说,《航海者》最精彩的内容还是诗的前半部分对凶险的大海的描写。今天看来,一方面,《航海者》表现了盎格鲁-撒克逊人不畏艰险的精神,充分显示出渺小、孤独的生命个体与大自然(大海)进行激烈搏斗的意志;另一方面,《航海者》的叙述者具有很强的陆地—海洋意识。老水手厌倦了尘世的奢靡生活,他更加向往和享受海上的黑夜、冰雹和孤独。老水手眼中的陆地(城市)是现实的、尘世的象征,而海洋则是浪漫的、历练生命的精神场所,海洋也成为老水手逃避尘世生活、走向天国的通道。换言之,这首古老的诗歌蕴含了作为岛民的盎格鲁-撒克逊人朴素的海洋观念,这一观念将在英国海洋文学中不断得到衍生、丰富和发展。

由于《航海者》原稿为古英语,一般读者难以看懂,为了方便读者理解,我们采用了著名古英语文学学者伯顿·拉菲尔(Burton Raffel)的现代英语译本。

The Seafarer

This tale is true, and mine. It tells
How the sea tookme, swept me back
And forth in sorrow and fear and pain,
Showed me suffering in a hundred ships,
In a thousand ports, and in me. It tells　　　　5
Of smashing surf when I sweated in the cold
Of an anxious watch, perched① in the bow②
As it dashed under cliffs. My feet were cast
In icy bands, bound with frost,
With frozen chains, and hardship groaned　　　　10
Around my heart. Hunger tore
At my sea-weary soul. No man sheltered
On the quiet fairness③ of earth can feel
How wretched I was, drifting through winter
On an ice-cold sea, whirled in sorrow,　　　　15
Alone in a world blown clear of④ love,

---

① perched:坐在……边沿。
② bow:船头。
③ quiet fairness:fairness 此处是"美好"的意思,quiet fairness 此处指陆地上一片安定美好,不像航海者所在的海上这般险象环生,环境艰苦。
④ clear of:清除,此处指海上世界是一个没有爱的世界。

Hung with icicles①. The hailstorms② flew.

The only sound was the roaring sea,

The freezing waves. The song of the swan

Might serve for pleasure, the cry of the sea-fowl,   20

The death-noise of birds instead of laughter,

The mewing③ of gulls instead of mead④.

Storms beat on the rocky cliffs and were echoed

By icy-feathered terns⑤ and the eagle's screams;

No kinsman could offer comfort there,   25

To a soul left drowning in desolation.

And who could believe, knowing but

The passion of cities, swelled proud with wine

And no taste of misfortune, how often, how wearily,

I put myself back on the paths of the sea.   30

Night would blacken; it would snow from the north;

Frost bound the earth and hail would fall,

The coldest seeds. And how my heart

Would begin to beat, knowing once more

The salt waves tossing and the towering⑥ sea!   35

The time for journeys would come and my soul

Called me eagerly out, sent me over

The horizon, seeking foreigners' homes⑦.

But there isn't a man on earth so proud,

So born to greatness, so bold with his youth,   40

Grown so brave, or so graced by God,

That he feels no fear as the sails unfurl⑧,

Wondering what Fate has willed and will do.

No harps ring in his heart, no rewards,

No passion for women, no worldly pleasures,   45

① icicles:冰柱。
② hailstorm:冰雹。
③ mewing:海鸟叫声。
④ mead:蜂蜜酒。
⑤ tern:燕鸥。
⑥ tossing and towering:汹涌翻腾的(海浪)。
⑦ foreigners' homes:指航行去往一个陌生的国度。
⑧ unfurl:展开,此处指扬帆启航。

Nothing, only the ocean's heave;

But longing wraps itself around him.

Orchards① blossom, the towns bloom,

Fields grow lovely as the world springs fresh,

And all these admonish that willing mind   50

Leaping to journeys, always set

In thoughts traveling on a quickening tide.

So summer's sentinel②, the cuckoo, sings

In his murmuring voice, and our hearts mourn

As he urges. Who could understand,   55

In ignorant ease, what we others suffer

As the paths of exile stretch endlessly on?

And yet my heart wanders away,

My soul roams with the sea, the whales'

Home, wandering to the widest corners   60

Of the world, returning ravenous③ with desire,

Flying solitary, screaming, exciting me

To the open ocean, breaking oaths

On the curve of a wave.

Thus the joys of God

Are fervent with life, where life itself   65

Fades quickly into the earth. The wealth

Of the world neither reaches to Heaven nor remains.

No man has ever faced the dawn

Certain which of Fate's three threats

Would fall: illness, or age, or an enemy's   70

Sword, snatching the life from his soul.

The praise the living pour on the dead

Flowers from reputation: plant

An earthly life of profit reaped

Even from hatred and rancor④, of bravery   75

Flung in the devil's face, and death

---

① orchards:果园。
② sentinel:哨兵。
③ ravenous:贪婪的。
④ rancor:深仇大恨。

Can only bring you earthly praise

And a song to celebrate a place

With the angels, life eternally blessed

In the hosts of Heaven.

The days are gone   80

When the kingdoms of earth flourished in glory;

Now there are no rulers, no emperors,

No givers of gold, as once there were,

When wonderful things were worked among them

And they lived in lordly magnificence.   85

Those powers havevanished, those pleasures are dead.

The weakest survives and the world continues,

Kept spinning by toil①. All glory is tarnished.

The world's honor ages and shrinks.

Bent like the men whomould it. Their faces   90

Blanch② as time advances, their beards

Wither and they mourn the memory of friends.

The sons of princes, sown in the dust.

The soul stripped of its flesh knows nothing

Of sweetness or sour, feels no pain,   95

Bends neither its hand nor its brain. A brother

Opens his palms and pours down gold

On his kinsman's grave, strewing his coffin

With treasures intended for Heaven, but nothing

Golden shakes the wrath of God   100

For a soul overflowing with sin, and nothing

Hidden on earth rises to Heaven.

We all fear God. He turns the earth,

He set it swinging firmly in space,

Gave life to the world and light to the sky.   105

Death leaps at③ the fools who forget their God.

He who lives humbly has angels from Heaven

To carry him courage and strength and belief.

---

① toil：辛劳。

② blanch：变得苍白。

③ leaps at：向……扑去，此处指死亡会降临到忘记上帝的愚人身上。

A man must conquer pride, not kill it,

Be firm with his fellows, chaste for himself,   110

Treat all the world as the world deserves,

With love or with hate but never with harm,

Though an enemy seek to scorch① him in hell,

Or set the flames of a funeral pyre②

Under his lord. Fate is stronger   115

And God mightier than any man's mind.

Our thoughts should turn to where our home is,

Consider the ways of coming there,

Then strive for sure permission for us

To rise to that eternal joy,   120

That life born in the love of God

And the hope of Heaven. Praise the Holy

Grace of Him who honored us,

Eternal, unchanging creator of earth. Amen.

▶扩展阅读

1. Crossley-Holland, K. Ed. & Trans. *The Anglo-Saxon World: An Anthology*. Oxford: Oxford University Press, 2009.

2. Liuzza, R. M. Ed. & Trans. *Old English Literature: Critical Essays*. New Haven: Yale University Press, 2002.

3. O'Neill, M. Ed. *The Cambridge History of English Poetry*. Cambridge: Cambridge University Press, 2010.

4. Greenfield, S. B. & Galder, D. G. Eds. *A New Critical History of Old English Literature*. New York: New York University Press, 1996.

▶学习参考网站

1. http://www.anglo-saxons.net/hwaet/? do＝get&type＝text&id＝Sfr

2. https://www.usask.ca/english/seafarer/split.htm

3. https://www.cs.mcgill.ca/～rwest/wikispeedia/wpcd/wp/a/Anglo-Saxon_literature.htm

【王松林　刘　浩　编注】

---

① scorch:烧焦。
② pyre:(火葬用的)柴堆。

2. "Beowulf"

贝奥武甫（Beowulf），公元 7—8 世纪之交开始流传于民间的盎格鲁-撒克逊同名史诗中的主人公，曾与水怪、火龙等搏斗。公元 5 世纪中叶，盎格鲁、撒克逊、哥特三个日耳曼部落开始从丹麦以及现在的荷兰一带迁入不列颠。在盎格鲁-撒克逊时代给我们留下的古英语文学作品中，最重要的一部是长篇叙事诗《贝奥武甫》（"Beowulf"），全诗共 3 182 行，被认为是英国的民族史诗。早在 6—7 世纪，《贝奥武甫》就以口头形式流传于日耳曼民族聚居的北欧沿海；8 世纪初形成文字；10 世纪末，一位不知名的僧侣在前人的文字基础上加以整理修改，最后形成今天的文本。

史诗讲述了盖世英雄贝奥武甫降魔除怪的故事，主要情节分三部分：贝奥武甫力战怪物格兰道尔、贝奥武甫大战格兰道尔之母和贝奥武甫战火龙。丹麦国王赫罗斯加建造了宏大的宫殿鹿厅，每日在此宴乐赏赐部属，欢声笑语引来了可怕的怪物格兰道尔。夜幕降临，格兰道尔潜入鹿厅残忍地屠杀了国王的士兵，之后遁入自己占据的沼泽地，留给清晨的鹿厅一片悲伤和哭号。从此，整整 12 年里，这怪物总是隔三差五地夜袭鹿厅，致使雄伟的大厅空空荡荡。丹麦人的领袖蒙受耻辱，陷入无限悲伤。恶魔的暴行传到耶阿特王国，年轻的贝奥武甫自告奋勇带领 14 名武士乘快船跨越大海驰援丹麦。当晚贝奥武甫安排人马在鹿厅设下埋伏，格兰道尔果然又来作恶。贝奥武甫徒手与恶魔交战，凭借着自己的神力重创恶魔，并扭下了他的一只臂膀，格兰道尔逃回他的老巢，贝奥武甫初战告捷。翌日，鹿厅大摆宴席庆祝胜利，英雄得到了极大的犒赏。宴会结束后，安然无忧的人们进入了梦乡，不料不幸再次降临。格兰道尔的母亲潜入鹿厅为儿子报仇。她抓走了赫罗斯加最为恩宠的一名扈从，并抢走了格兰道尔血污的臂膀。翌晨，贝奥武甫得到消息，即刻赶到鹿厅，并带领人马循迹追至妖母盘踞的黑暗的深潭。贝奥武甫潜入凶险的水中，与女妖展开一场恶战，最终将其杀死，并取下了格兰道尔的首级。鹿厅迎来了又一次的庆祝酒宴，赫罗斯加对英雄无限感激，赏赐了无数的金银财宝。贝奥武甫带着胜利的喜悦和国王的馈赠登上了返航的船只，临别时双方发誓今后同仇敌忾，互相照应。回国几年之后，贝奥武甫做了耶阿特人的国王，成功地治理国家五十个春秋。这时国内出现了一条火龙，火龙趁着黑夜胡作非为，喷吐火焰烧毁房屋，毁灭生灵。国王贝奥武甫此时已是一位老人，但是他依然决定亲自讨伐恶龙。在毒龙盘踞的石窟前一场恶战开始了。酣战之中，贝奥武甫的宝剑砸断了，火龙尖利的毒牙咬住了他的脖子。但是，在一名勇士的帮助下，贝奥武甫用短剑斩断了毒龙的脖子，终于杀死了邪恶的仇敌。然而,贝奥武甫身受致命伤,不久即丧命。全诗以贝奥武甫的葬礼为结局。

《贝奥武甫》反映的是5—6世纪时北欧各部落的生活情景。怪物恶魔乃远古邪恶的精灵造就,盘踞在人迹罕至的沼泽湖泊之中或悬崖峭壁之下,具有非凡的破坏力,这似乎反映了当时人们对于大自然的敬畏之情。英雄贝奥武甫也是一个具有神力的人,他是恶魔的天敌,肩负着拯救人民于水火的重任,这反映了人们战胜自然的美好愿望。值得注意的是,大海在诗篇中多以神秘阴险、暗藏杀机的形象出现,是妖魔鬼怪的庇护所,比如选段中贝奥武甫儿时嬉戏遭遇海怪的场景、格兰道尔之母栖身的黑暗深潭等,象征着大自然给人们带来的灾难和令人恐惧的力量。以下为诗中的两个选段。选段"Feast at Heorot"描述了贝奥武甫初到丹麦,受到国王的款待,席间有好勇不服气之士挑衅,引出一段贝奥武甫大海中显神力的描述;选段"Beowulf Fights Grendel's Mother"描述了贝奥武甫追踪至深潭大战母妖的经过。史诗原稿为古英语,现藏于大英图书馆。为了方便读者的理解,本书选用了1995年诺贝尔文学奖得主、爱尔兰诗人谢默斯·希尼(Seamus Heaney)的现代英语译本,选段末尾圆括号内标注有原稿中的起止行号,诗行按照原文每10行做出标记,方便读者阅读和查阅资料。

▶选段1

Feast at Heorot①

Then a bench was cleared in that banquet hall	491
so the Geats② could have room to be together	
and the party sat, proud in their bearing,	
strong and stalwart. An attendant stood by	
with a decorated pitcher, pouring bright	
helpings of mead. And the minstrel sang,	
filling Heorot with his head-clearing voice,	
gladdening that great rally of Geats and Danes③.	
From where he crouched at the king's feet,	
Unferth, a son of Ecglaf's, spoke	500
contrary words. Beowulf's coming,	
his sea-braving, made him sick with envy:	

---

① Heorot:即 hart,鹿厅。鹿是王权的象征。原稿没有小标题,这里是译者加上去的。下同。

② Geats:耶阿特人。这里指贝奥武甫及其随从。耶阿特人的领地在今斯堪的纳维亚半岛南端。史诗中耶阿特人还被称作 War-Geats、Sea-Geats 和 Weather-Geats。

③ Danes:丹麦人。史诗中还被称作 Bright-Danes、Spear-Danes、Ring-Danes、South-Danes、West-Danes、Shieldings(希尔德的子民)、Victory-Shieldings 和 Ingwins。文中丹麦部落领地在今英格兰,其他部落领地位置可参见"参考阅读"条目1第97页地图。

he could not brook or abide the fact

that anyone else alive under heaven

might enjoy greater regard than he did：

"Are you the Beowulf who took on Breca①

in a swimming match on the open sea，

risking the water just to prove that you could win?

It was sheer vanity made you venture out

on the main deep. And no matter who tried，　　　　510

friend or foe，to deflect the pair of you，

neither would back down：the sea-test obsessed you.

You waded in，embracing water，

taking its measure，mastering currents，

riding on the swell. The ocean swayed，

winter went wild in the waves，but you vied

for seven nights；and then he outswam you，

came ashore the stronger contender.

He was cast up safe and sound one morning

among the Heatho-Reams②，then made his way　　　520

to where he belonged in Bronding③ country，

home again，sure of his ground

in strongroom and bawn④. So Breca made good

his boast upon you and was proved right.

No matter，therefore，how you may have fared

in every bout and battle until now，

this time you'll be worsted；no one has ever

outlasted an entire night against Grendel⑤."

Beowulf，Ecgtheow's⑥ son，replied：

"Well，friend Unferth，you have had your say　　　530

about Breca and me. But it was mostly beer

that was doing the talking. The truth is this：

---

① Breca：布雷克，是下文中布朗丁部落的杰出勇士。

② Heatho-Reams：希塞里姆海湾，在今挪威。

③ Brondings：布朗丁部落。该部落辖区在瑞典人和耶阿特人辖区之间。

④ strongrooms and bawn：此处意为"坚固的堡垒"。

⑤ Grendel：格兰道尔。前文介绍说，自从该隐残杀了自己的兄弟亚伯，永恒的神就严惩了他的后裔，把他驱逐到荒无人烟的边鄙，从此那里孳生了大批妖孽。格兰道尔就是这样的妖孽。

⑥ Ecgtheow：艾克塞奥。贝奥武甫的父亲，耶阿特部落前国王雷塞尔的女婿。

when the going was heavy in those high waves,
I was the strongest swimmer of all.
We'd been children together and we grew up
daring ourselves to outdo each other,
boasting and urging each other to risk
our lives on the sea. And so it turned out.
Each of us swam holding a sword,
a naked, hard-proofed blade for protection   540
against the whale-beasts. But Breca could never
move out farther or faster from me
than I could manage to move from him.
Shoulder to shoulder, we struggled on
for five nights, until the long flow
and pitch of the waves, the perishing cold,
night falling and winds from the north
drove us apart. The deep boiled up
and its wallowing sent the sea-brutes wild.
My armor helped me to hold out;   550
my hard-ringed chain-mail, hand-forged and linked,
a fine, close-fitting filigree of gold,
kept me safe when some ocean creature
pulled me to the bottom. Pinioned fast
and swathed in its grip, I was granted one
final chance: my sword plunged
and the ordeal was over. Through my own hands,
the fury of battle had finished off the sea-beast.
"Time and again, foul things attacked me,
lurking and stalking, but I lashed out,   560
gave as good as I got with my sword.
My flesh was not for feasting on,
there would be no monsters gnawing and gloating
over their banquet at the bottom of the sea.
Instead, in the morning, mangled and sleeping
the sleep of the sword, they slopped and floated
like the ocean's leavings. From now on
sailors would be safe, the deep-sea raids

were over for good. Light came from the east,
bright guarantee of God, and the waves 570
went quiet; I could see headlands
and buffeted cliffs. Often, for undaunted courage,
fate spares the man it has not already marked.
However it occurred, my sword had killed
nine sea-monsters. Such night dangers
and hard ordeals I have never heard of
nor of a man more desolate in surging waves.
But worn out as I was, I survived,
came through with my life. The ocean lifted
and laid me ashore, I landed safe 580
on the coast of Finland. ..."

(line 491 - line 581)

▶选段 2

Beowulf Fights Grendel's Mother

Beowulf, son of Ecgtheow, spoke; 1383
"Wise sir, do not grieve. It is always better
to avenge dear ones than to indulge in mourning.
For every one of us, living in this world
means waiting for our end. Let whoever can
win glory before death. When a warrior is gone,
that will be his best and only bulwark.
So arise, my lord, and let us immediately 1390
set forth on the trail of this troll-dam.
I guarantee you: she will not get away,
not to dens under ground nor upland groves
nor the ocean floor. She'll have nowhere to flee to.
Endure your troubles today. Bear up
and be the man I expect you to be."
With that the old lord① sprang to his feet
and praised God for Beowulf's pledge.

---

① the old lord:这里指丹麦国王赫罗斯加(Hrothgar)。

Then a bit and halter were brought for his horse

with the plaited mane. The wise king mounted   1400

the royal saddle and rode out in style

with a force of shield-bearers. The forest paths

were marked all over with the monster's tracks，

her trail on the ground wherever she had gone

across the dark moors，dragging away

the body of that thane，Hrothgar's best

counselor and overseer of the country.

So the noble prince proceeded undismayed

up fells and screes①，along narrow footpaths

and ways where they were forced into single file，   1410

ledges on cliffs above lairs of water-monsters.

He went in front with a few men，

good judges of the lie of the land，

and suddenly discovered the dismal wood，

mountain trees growing out at an angle

above gray stones：the bloodshot water

surged underneath. It was a sore blow

to all of the Danes，friends of the Shieldings②，

a hurt to each and every one

of that noble company when they came upon   1420

Aeschere's head at the foot of the cliff.

Everybody gazed as the hot gore

kept wallowing up and an urgent war-horn

repeated its notes：the whole party

sat down to watch. The water was infested

with all kinds of reptiles. There were writhing sea-dragons

and monsters slouching on slopes by the cliff，

serpents and wild things such as those that often

surface at dawn to roam the sail-road

and doom the voyage. Down they plunged，   1430

lashing in anger at the loud call

---

①   fells and screes：陡峭的山崖。

②   Shieldings：希尔德的子民，诗中丹麦人的另一种称呼，因其最初的部落首领 Shield 而得名。

of the battle-bugle. An arrow from the bow
of the Geat chief got one of them
as he surged to the surface: the seasoned shaft
stuck deep in his flank and his freedom in the water
got less and less. It was his last swim.
He was swiftly overwhelmed in the shallows,
prodded by barbed boar-spears,
cornered, beaten, pulled up on the bank,
a strange lake-birth, a loathsome catch   1440
men gazed at in awe.

          Beowulf got ready,
donned① his war-gear, indifferent to death;
his mighty, hand-forged, fine-webbed mail
would soon meet with the menace underwater.
It would keep the bone-cage of his body safe:
no enemy's clasp could crush him in it,
no vicious armlock choke his life out.
To guard his head he had a glittering helmet
that was due to be muddied on the mere bottom
and blurred in the upswirl. It was of beaten gold,   1450
princely headgear hooped and hasped
by a weapon-smith who had worked wonders
in days gone by and adorned it with boar-shapes;
since then it had resisted every sword.
And another item lent by Unferth
at that moment of need was of no small importance:
the brehon② handed him a hilted weapon,
a rare and ancient sword named Hrunting.
The iron blade with its ill-boding patterns
had been tempered in blood. It had never failed   1460
the hand of anyone who hefted it in battle,
anyone who had fought and faced the worst
in the gap of danger. This was not the first time

---

① donned：穿上，戴上。
② brehon：古爱尔兰法官。

it had been called to perform heroic feats.
When he lent that blade to the better swordsman，
Unferth，the strong-built son of Ecglaf，
could hardly have remembered the ranting speech
he had made in his cups. He was not man enough
to face the turmoil of a fight under water
and the risk to his life. So there he lost   1470
fame and repute. It was different for the other
rigged out in his gear，ready to do battle.
Beowulf，son of Ecgtheow，spoke：
"Wisest of kings，now that I have come
to the point of action，I ask you to recall
what we said earlier：that you，son of Halfdane①
and gold-friend to retainers，that you，if I should fall
and suffer death while serving your cause，
would act like a father to me afterward.
If this combat kills me，take care   1480
of my young company，my comrades in arms.
And be sure also，my beloved Hrothgar，
to send Hygelac② the treasures I received.
Let the lord of the Geats gaze on that gold，
let Hrethel's③ son take note of it and see
that I found a ring-giver of rare magnificence
and enjoyed the good of his generosity.
And Unferth is to have what I inherited：
to that far-famed man I bequeath my own
sharp-horned，wave-sheened wonder-blade.   1490
With Hrunting I shall gain glory or die."
After these words，the prince of the Weather-Geats
was impatient to be away and plunged suddenly：
without more ado，he dived into the heaving
depths of the lake. It was the best part of a day
before he could see the solid bottom.

---

① Halfdane：先王哈夫丹，赫罗斯加的父亲，育有三儿一女。
② Hygelac：海格拉克，耶阿特人的国王，贝奥武甫的舅舅。
③ Hrethel：雷塞尔，海格拉克的父亲，贝奥武甫的外公。

Quickly the one① who haunted those waters,

who had scavenged and gone her gluttonous rounds

for a hundred seasons, sensed a human

observing her outlandish lair from above.   1500

So she lunged and clutched and managed to catch him

in her brutal grip; but his body, for all that,

remained unscathed: the mesh of the chain-mail

saved him on the outside. Her savage talons

failed to rip the web of his war-shirt.

Then once she touched bottom, that wolfish swimmer

carried the ring-mailed prince to her court

so that for all his courage he could never use

the weapons he carried; and a bewildering horde

came at him from the depths, droves of sea-beasts   1510

who attacked with tusks and tore at his chain-mail

in a ghastly onslaught. The gallant man

could see he had entered some hellish turn-hole

and yet the water there did not work against him

because the hall-roofing held off

the force of the current; then he saw firelight,

a gleam and flare-up, a glimmer of brightness.

The hero observed that swamp-thing from hell,

the tarn-hag in all her terrible strength,

then heaved his war-sword and swung his arm: 1520

the decorated blade came down ringing

and singing on her head. But he soon found

his battle-torch extinguished; the shining blade

refused to bite. It spared her and failed

the man in his need. It had gone through many

hand-to-hand fights, had hewed the armor

and helmets of the doomed, but here at last

the fabulous powers of that heirloom failed.

Hygelac's kinsman kept thinking about

his name and fame: he never lost heart.   1530

---

① the one: 这里指格兰道尔的母亲。

Then, in a fury, he flung his sword away.
The keen, inlaid, worm-loop-patterned steel
was hurled to the ground: he would have to rely
on the might of his arm. So must a man do
who intends to gain enduring glory
in a combat. Life doesn't cost him a thought.
Then the prince of War-Geats, warming to this fight
with Grendel's mother, gripped her shoulder
and laid about him in a battle frenzy:
he pitched his killer opponent to the floor   1540
but she rose quickly and retaliated,
grappled him tightly in her grim embrace.
The sure-footed fighter felt daunted,
the strongest of warriors stumbled and fell.
So she pounced upon him and pulled out
a broad, whetted knife: now she would avenge
her only child. But the mesh of chain-mail
on Beowulf's shoulder shielded his life,
turned the edge and tip of the blade.
The son of Ecgtheow would have surely perished   1550
and the Geats lost their warrior under the wide earth
had the strong links and locks of his war-gear
not helped to save him: holy God
decided the victory. It was easy for the Lord,
the Ruler of Heaven, to redress the balance
once Beowulf got back up on his feet.
Then he saw a blade that boded well,
a sword in her armory, an ancient heirloom
from the days of the giants①, an ideal weapon,
one that any warrior would envy,   1560
but so huge and heavy of itself
only Beowulf could wield it in a battle.
So the Shielding's hero hard-pressed and enraged,
took a firm hold of the hilt and swung

---

① the giants：巨人族，希腊神话中常与天神作战的种族。

the blade in an arc, a resolute blow

that bit deep into her neck-bone

and severed it entirely, toppling the doomed

house of her flesh; she fell to the floor.

The sword dripped blood, the swordsman was elated.

A light appeared and the place brightened   1570

the way the sky does when heaven's candle

is shining clearly. He inspected the vault:

with sword held high, its hilt raised

to guard and threaten, Hygelac's thane

scouted by the wall in Grendel's wake.

Now the weapon was to prove its worth.

The warrior determined to take revenge

for every gross act Grendel had committed—

and not only for that one occasion

when he'd come to slaughter the sleeping troops,   1580

fifteen of Hrothgar's house-guards

surprised on their benches and ruthlessly devoured,

and as many again carried away,

a brutal plunder. Beowulf in his fury

now settled that score: he saw the monster

in his resting place, war-weary and wrecked,

a lifeless corpse, a casualty

of the battle in Heorot. The body gaped

at the stroke dealt to it after death:

Beowulf cut the corpse's head off.   1590

Immediately the counselors keeping a lookout

with Hrothgar, watching the lake water,

saw a heave-up and surge of waves

and blood in the backwash. They bowed gray heads,

spoke in their sage, experienced way

about the good warrior, how they never again

expected to see that prince returning

in triumph to their king. It was clear to many

that the wolf of the deep had destroyed him forever.

The ninth hour of the day arrived.   1600

The brave Shieldings abandoned the cliff-top
and the king went home; but sick at heart,
staring at the mere, the strangers held on.
They wished, without hope, to behold their lord,
Beowulf himself.

              Meanwhile, the sword
began to wilt into gory icicles
to slather and thaw. It was a wonderful thing,
the way it all melted as ice melts
when the Father eases the fetters off the frost
and unravels the water-ropes, He who wields power   1610
over time and tide: He is the true Lord.
The Geat captain saw treasure in abundance
but carried no spoils from those quarters
except for the head and the inlaid hilt
embossed with jewels; its blade had melted
and the scrollwork on it burned, so scalding was the blood
of the poisonous fiend who had perished there.
Then away he swam, the one who had survived
the fall of his enemies, flailing to the surface.
The wide water, the waves and pools,   1620
were no longer infested once the wandering fiend
let go of her life and this unreliable world.
The seafarers' leader made for land,
resolutely swimming, delighted with his prize,
the mighty load he was lugging to the surface.
His thanes advanced in a troop to meet him,
thanking God and taking great delight
in seeing their prince back safe and sound.
Quickly the hero's helmet and mail-shirt
were loosed and unlaced. The lake settled,   1630
clouds darkened above the bloodshot depths.
With high hearts they headed away
along footpaths and trails through the fields,
roads that they knew, each of them wrestling
with the head they were carrying from the lakeside cliff,

men kingly in their courage and capable

of difficult work. It was a task for hour

to hoist Grendel's head on a spear

and bear it under strain to the bright hall.

But soon enough they neared the place，   1640

fourteen Geats in fine fettle，

striding across the outlying ground

in a delighted throng around their leader.

In he came then，the thanes' commander，

the arch-warrior，to address Hrothgar：

his courage was proven，his glory was secure.

Grendel's head was hauled by the hair，

dragged across the floor where the people were drinking，

a horror for both queen and company to behold.

They stared in awe. It was an astonishing sight.   1650

（line 1383 – line 1650）

▶扩展阅读

1. Donoghue，D. Ed. *Beowulf：A Verse Translation（A Norton Critical Version）*. New York：W. W. Norton & Company，2002.

2. Newton，S. *The Origins of Beowulf and the Pre-Viking Kingdom of East Anglia*. Woodbridge，Suffolk， England：Boydell & Brewer Ltd，1993.

3. Orchard，A. *A Critical Companion to Beowulf*. Cambridge：D. S. Brewer，2003.

4. Tolkien，J. R. R. *Beowulf：the Monsters and the Critics*. London：Oxford University Press，1958.

5. 陈才宇，译. 英国早期文学经典文本. 杭州：浙江大学出版社，2007.

▶学习参考网站

1. http：//en.wikipedia.org/wiki/Beowulf

2. http：//www.heorot.dk/beowulf-on-steorarume_front-page.html

3. http：//commons.wikimedia.org/wiki/Category：Beowulf

【徐　燕　编注】

3. William Shakespeare: The Tempest

威廉·莎士比亚（William Shakespeare，1546—1616）是英国著名的剧作家、诗人，一生著有 37 部戏剧、154 首十四行诗和 2 首长诗。1564 年，莎士比亚出身于英国埃文河畔斯特拉特福镇一个富有的羊毛商人家庭，在那里他度过了自己的童年时光，在当地的文法学校上了六年学。后来父亲陷入债务，莎士比亚就辍学在家，帮助父亲维持全家生计。1582 年，莎士比亚结婚，妻子比他大八岁，婚后育有一男两女。也许是为了养家糊口，1587 年，莎士比亚离开家乡来到伦敦。适逢戏剧蓬勃发展，莎士比亚从杂工做起，渐渐进入了戏剧圈，出演一些小角色，并开始戏剧创作。莎士比亚的戏剧创作可分为四个阶段：

第一阶段（1590—1594）以改写前人的故事为主，模仿的痕迹较重，但语言清新优美，题材多是青春爱情戏，也有历史剧。主要作品有《亨利六世》（*King Henry VI*）、《驯悍记》（*The Taming of the Shrew*）和《罗密欧与朱丽叶》（*Romeo and Juliet*）。

第二阶段（1595—1600）是创作的成熟时期，这一时期的莎士比亚无论是在知识、智力、政治领悟力方面，还是在戏剧技巧、创造力、人物刻画和遣词造句等方面都有了长足的进步。创作速度也相当惊人，5 年创作了 12 部戏，并且绝大多数都是相传至今的经典，主要有《仲夏夜之梦》（*A Midsummer Night's Dream*）、《威尼斯商人》（*The Merchant of Venice*）、《第十二夜》（*Twelfth Night*，or *What You Will*）、《亨利四世》（*King Henry IV*）、《亨利五世》（*King Henry V*）等。据说他所有的十四行诗也完成于这个时期。

第三阶段（1601—1607）基本上都是悲剧，其四大悲剧《哈姆雷特》（*Hamlet*）、《奥赛罗》（*Othello*）、《李尔王》（*King Lear*）和《麦克白》（*Macbeth*）就是这个时期的产物，这与当时英国复杂的社会矛盾有关。伊丽莎白女王一世在位的最后几年王朝发生了叛乱，叛乱头目被斩首，莎士比亚的恩主也以叛国的罪名被新王詹姆斯一世逮捕。这些直接影响到作者的创作，谋杀、贪欲、背叛、忘恩负义和犯罪等主题弥漫在每一部作品中。

第四阶段（1608—1612）的作品都有一种"和解"的意味，就好像一位阅世已深的老人，已经磨灭了轻浮凌厉之气，复归于平和之境，比如《暴风雨》（*The Tempest*）、《辛伯林》（*Cymbeline*，*King of Britain*）和《冬天的故事》（*The Winter's Tale*）等。与前一阶段紧张激烈的谋杀复仇主题不同，这一时期的作品中尽管也有风暴、背叛、忘恩负义、邪恶等，但是随着时间的推移，最终都以沉冤得雪、宽容谅解、悔过自新和大团圆结局收场。有论者说这反映了莎翁从喧闹的伦敦回到平静的乡镇后人生观的改变，也是作者渐入老年心态的必然结果。1611 年,莎士比亚回到故乡斯特拉特福,五年后去世,葬于斯特拉特福教堂。

　　莎士比亚与海洋的关系主要体现在《暴风雨》上,当然他的其他作品中也有诸多以海洋为意象的比喻。《暴风雨》是莎士比亚晚年的作品,也是其唯一以大海为全剧背景的作品。猛烈的海上风暴、惊慌失措的水手、沉没的船只、海难的劫后余生等典型的情节给《暴风雨》打上了鲜明的海洋文学的烙印。普罗斯彼罗(Prospero)本是米兰的合法公爵,因沉溺于自己的魔法研究而疏忽了世俗的事务,结果被亲弟弟安东尼奥(Antonio)篡位,连同幼小的女儿米兰达(Miranda)一起被驱逐出国。那不勒斯的国王阿隆索(Alonso)也参与了这场政治阴谋,成为帮凶。为了掩人耳目,篡位者把普罗斯彼罗和米兰达送到几海里之外的一条没有绳索、没有帆、没有樯的旧船上,任由他们向着狂暴的海洋哭泣。但是善良的枢密大臣贡萨洛(Gonzalo)暗中留下了粮食和衣物,他们因而没有饿死,后来流落到了一个海上荒岛并生存了下来。12 年过去了,机缘巧合,篡位的仇人们参加国王阿隆索的女儿在非洲举行的婚礼,在返航途中经过此岛附近,而研究魔法多年的普罗斯彼罗决定好好利用这个机会惩罚仇人。于是他制造了一场暴风雨,把国王的航船打了个七零八落,船上的人员全部落水。但是米兰的合法公爵并没有置仇人于死地,而是让他们吃了苦头之后再给以言辞教训。剧末,那不勒斯国王为自己的行为忏悔,普罗斯彼罗与之和解,公主米兰达将嫁给阿隆索的儿子费迪南(Ferdinand)。惊心动魄的海上风暴既是故事发生的场所,也隐喻了主要人物普罗斯彼罗的人生突变和内心的愤怒。《暴风雨》以大海为背景,描写的是深邃复杂的人性问题。作者借助奇特的想象来推动剧情的发展,阿里尔(Ariel)和卡利班(Caliban)就是这样想象出来的精灵与丑八怪。《暴风雨》以狂暴的海上风暴开始,却归于诗意的平和宁静。著名学者梁实秋认为,"技术的圆熟,文字的老练,声调的自然,以及全剧之静穆严肃的气息,很明显地表示这部戏必是莎士比亚的思想艺术臻于烂熟时的作品"。《暴风雨》全剧共五幕,本选段出自第五幕和尾声。

Dramatis Personae in This Scene：

　　Alonso，King of Naples

　　Sebastian，his Brother

　　Prospero，the right Duke of Milan

　　Antonio，his Brother，the usurping Duke of Milan

　　Ferdinand，Son to the King of Naples

　　Gonzalo，an honest old counselor

　　Adrian and Francisco，lords

　　Caliban，a savage and deformed Slave

　　Trinculo，a Jester

　　Stephano，a drunken Butler

　　Master of a Ship

　　Boatswain

Miranda，Daughter to Prospero

Ariel，an airy Spirit

▶ Act 5, Scene 1: Before the Cell of Prospero

[*Enter Prospero in his magic robes*；*and ARIEL.*]

Prospero：　　Now does my project gather to a head：

My charms crack not；my spirits obey，and time

Goes upright with his carriage. How's the day?

Ariel：　　On the sixth hour；at which time，my lord，

You said our work should cease.

Prospero：　　I did say so，

When first I rais'd the tempest. Say，my spirit，

How fares the King and 's followers?

Ariel：　　Confin'd together

In the same fashion as you gave in charge；

Just as you left them：all prisoners，sir，

In the line-grove① weather-fends your cell；

They cannot budge till your release. The king，

His brother，and yours，abide all three distracted，

And the remainder mourning over them，

Brim full of sorrow and dismay；but chiefly

Him you term'd，sir，"the good old lord，Gonzalo"：

His tears run down his beard，like winter's drops

From eaves of reeds；your charm so strongly works them，

That if you now beheld them，your affections

Would become tender.

Prospero：　　Dost thou think so，spirit?

Ariel：　　Mine would，sir，were I human.

Prospero：　　And mine shall.

Hast thou，which art but air，a touch，a feeling

Of their afflictions，and shall not myself，

One of their kind，that relish all as sharply，

Passion as they，be kindlier mov'd than thou art?

---

① line-grove：菩提树林。

Though with their high wrongs I am struck to the quick①,

Yet with my nobler reason 'gainst my fury

Do I take part：the rarer action is

In virtue than in vengeance：② they being penitent，

The sole drift of my purpose doth extend

Not a frown further. Go release them，Ariel.

My charms I'll break，their senses I'll restore，

And they shall be themselves.

Ariel：　　I'll fetch them，sir.

[Exit.]

Prospero：　Ye elves of hills，brooks，standing lakes，and groves；

And ye that on the sands with printless foot

Do chase the ebbing Neptune③，and do fly him

When he comes back；you demi-puppets that

By moonshine do the green sour ringlets make，

Whereof the ewe not bites；and you whose pastime

Is to make midnight mushrooms，that rejoice

To hear the solemn curfew；by whose aid，——

Weak masters though ye be，——I have bedimm'd

The noontide sun，call'd forth the mutinous winds，

And 'twixt the green sea and the azur'd vault

Set roaring war：to the dread rattling thunder

Have I given fire，and rifted Jove's④ stout oak

With his own bolt：the strong-bas'd promontory

Have I made shake；and by the spurs pluck'd up

The pine and cedar：graves at my command

Have wak'd their sleepers，op'd，and let them forth

By my so potent art. But this rough magic

---

①　struck to the quick：痛心疾首。

②　The rare action is in virtue than in vengeance：德行比报仇更为神圣。所以下一句普罗斯彼罗表示"他们既已忏悔，我就不愿再追究了"。

③　Neptune：［罗神］尼普顿（海神）。此处代指海潮。

④　Jove：［罗神］朱庇特。

I here abjure①; and, when I have requir'd
Some heavenly music,—which even now I do,—
To work mine end upon their senses that
This airy charm is for, I'll break my staff,
Bury it certain fathoms in the earth,
And deeper than did ever plummet sound
I'll drown my book.②

[*Solemn music*]

[*Re-enter Ariel: after him, Alonso, with frantic gesture, attended by Gonzalo; Sebastian and Antonio in like manner, attended by Adrian and Francisco: they all enter the circle which Prospero had made, and there stand charmed: which Prospero observing, speaks.*]

A solemn air, and the best comforter
To an unsettled fancy, cure thy brains,
Now useless, boil'd within thy skull! There stand,
For you are spell-stopp'd.
Holy Gonzalo, honourable man,
Mine eyes, even sociable to the show of thine,
Fall fellowly drops. The charm dissolves apace;
And as the morning steals upon the night,
Melting the darkness, so their rising senses
Begin to chase the ignorant fumes that mantle
Their clearer reason. —O good Gonzalo!
My true preserver, and a loyal sir
To him thou follow'st, I will pay thy graces
Home, both in word and deed. —Most cruelly
Didst thou, Alonso, use me and my daughter:
Thy brother was a furtherer③ in the act; —
Thou'rt pinch'd for 't now, Sebastian. —Flesh and blood,
You, brother mine, that entertain'd ambition,
Expell'd remorse and nature, who, with Sebastian, —
Whose inward pinches therefore are most strong, —

---

① abjure:发誓放弃。

② ... bury it certain fathoms in the earth, and deeper than did ever plummet sound I'll drown my book:深深埋在土里,并且把我的魔法书沉到不曾测到过的更深的海底。

③ furtherer:帮凶。

Would here have kill'd your king; I do forgive thee,

Unnatural though thou art! Their understanding

Begins to swell, and the approaching tide

Will shortly fill the reasonable shores

That now lie foul and muddy. Not one of them

That yet looks on me, or would know me. —Ariel,

Fetch me the hat and rapier in my cell:—

[Exit Ariel]

I will discase me, and myself present,

As I was sometime Milan. —Quickly, spirit;

Thou shalt ere long① be free.

[Ariel re-enters, singing, and helps to attire Prospero.]

Ariel: Where the bee sucks, there suck I:

In a cowslip's bell I lie;

There I couch when owls do cry.

On the bat's back I do fly

After summer merrily:

Merrily, merrily shall I live now

Under the blossom that hangs on the bough.

Prospero: Why, that's my dainty Ariel! I shall miss thee;

But yet thou shalt have freedom; —so, so, so②.—

To the king's ship, invisible as thou art:

There shalt thou find the mariners asleep

Under the hatches; the master and the boatswain

Being awake, enforce them to this place,

And presently, I prithee.

Ariel: I drink the air before me, and return

Or ere your pulse twice beat.

[Exit]

Gonzalo: All torment, trouble, wonder and amazement

Inhabits here. Some heavenly power guide us

Out of this fearful country!

Prospero: Behold, sir king,

---

① ere long:不久,很快。

② so, so, so:普罗斯彼罗在整理衣服或者已经穿戴整齐,满意地说"好,好,好"。

The wrongèd Duke of Milan, Prospero.

For more assurance that a living prince

Does now speak to thee, I embrace thy body;

And to thee and thy company I bid

A hearty welcome.

Alonso:　　Whe'er thou be'st he or no[1],

Or some enchanted trifle to abuse me,

As late I have been, I not know: thy pulse

Beats, as of flesh and blood; and, since I saw thee,

Th' affliction of my mind amends, with which,

I fear, a madness held me: this must crave, —

An if this be at all[2] —a most strange story.

Thy dukedom I resign, and do entreat

Thou pardon me my wrongs. —But how should Prospero

Be living and be here?

Prospero:　　First, noble friend,

Let me embrace thine age; whose honour cannot

Be measur'd or confin'd.

Gonzalo:　　Whether this be

Or be not, I'll not swear.[3]

Prospero:　　You do yet taste

Some subtleties o' the isle, that will not let you

Believe things certain. —Welcome, my friends all: —

[*Aside to Sebastian and Antonio*]

But you, my brace of

lords, were I so minded,

I here could pluck his highness' frown upon you,

And justify you traitors: at this time

I will tell no tales.[4]

Sebastian:　　[*Aside*] The devil speaks in him.

Prospero:　　No.

For you, most wicked sir, whom to call brother

---

① Whe'er thou be'st he or no:你究竟是不是他。

② An if this be at all:如果这一切是真的。

③ Whether this be or be not, I'll not swear:这究竟是真还是假,我不敢说。

④ at this time I will tell no tales:现在我却不愿告发。

	Would even infect my mouth, I do forgive
	Thy rankest fault; all of them; and require
	My dukedom of thee, which, perforce, I know
	Thou must restore.①
Alonso:	If thou beest Prospero,
	Give us particulars of thy preservation;
	How thou hast met us here, whom three hours since
	Were wrack'd upon this shore; where I have lost, —
	How sharp the point of this remembrance is! —
	My dear son Ferdinand.
Prospero:	I am woe for't, sir.
Alonso:	Irreparable is the loss, and patience
	Says it is past her cure.
Prospero:	I rather think
	You have not sought her help; of whose soft grace,
	For the like loss I have her sovereign aid,
	And rest myself content.
Alonso:	You the like loss!
Prospero:	As great to me, as late; and, supportable
	To make the dear loss, have I means much weaker
	Than you may call to comfort you, for I
	Have lost my daughter.
Alonso:	A daughter?
	O heavens! that they were living both in Naples,
	The king and queen there! That they were, I wish
	Myself were mudded in that oozy bed
	Where my son lies. When did you lose your daughter?
Prospero:	In this last tempest. I perceive, these lords
	At this encounter do so much admire
	That they devour their reason, and scarce think

---

① ... require my dukedom of thee, which, perforce, I know thou must restore:我要你交还我的国土,我知道你是非交不可的。 perforce:necessarily,必需的。

Their eyes do offices of truth[①], their words

Are natural breath; but, howsoe'er you have

Been justled from your senses, know for certain

That I am Prospero, and that very duke

Which was thrust forth of Milan; who most strangely

Upon this shore, where you were wrack'd, was landed

To be the lord on 't. No more yet of this;

For 'tis a chronicle of day by day,

Not a relation for a breakfast nor

Befitting this first meeting. Welcome, sir:

This cell's my court: here have I few attendants

And subjects none abroad: pray you, look in.

My dukedom since you have given me again,

I will requite you with as good a thing;

At least bring forth a wonder, to content ye

As much as me my dukedom.

[*The entrance of the Cell opens, and discovers Ferdinand and Miranda playing at chess.*]

Miranda:	Sweet lord, you play me false.
Ferdinand:	No, my dearest love,
	I would not for the world.
Miranda:	Yes, for a score of kingdoms you should wrangle,
	And I would call it fair play.
Alonso:	If this prove
	A vision of the island, one dear son
	Shall I twice lose.
Sebastian:	A most high miracle!
Ferdinand:	Though the seas threaten, they are merciful:
	I have curs'd them without cause.

[*Kneels to Alonso.*]

Alonso:	Now all the blessings
	Of a glad father compass[②] thee about!
	Arise, and say how thou cam'st here.

---

①　their eyes do offices of truth: 他们所见为实。

②　compass: 拥抱。

Miranda:	O, wonder!
	How many goodly creatures are there here!
	How beauteous mankind is! O brave new world
	That has such people in 't!
Prospero:	'Tis new to thee.
Alonso:	What is this maid, with whom thou wast at play?
	Your eld'st acquaintance cannot be three hours:
	Is she the goddess that hath sever'd① us,
	And brought us thus together?
Ferdinand:	Sir, she is mortal;
	But by immortal Providence she's mine.
	I chose her when I could not ask my father
	For his advice, nor thought I had one. She
	Is daughter to this famous Duke of Milan,
	Of whom so often I have heard renown,
	But never saw before; of whom I have
	Receiv'd a second life: and second father
	This lady makes him to me.
Alonso:	I am hers:
	But, O! how oddly will it sound that I
	Must ask my child forgiveness!
Prospero:	There, sir, stop:
	Let us not burden our remembrances with
	A heaviness that's gone.②
Gonzalo:	I have inly wept,
	Or should have spoke ere this. Look down, you gods,
	And on this couple drop a blessed crown;
	For it is you that have chalk'd forth the way③
	Which brought us hither.
Alonso:	I say, Amen, Gonzalo!
Gonzalo:	Was Milan thrust from Milan, that his issue④

---

① sever'd：severed，分割开，使割离。

② Let us not burden our remembrances with a heaviness that's gone：我们不可再以过去的烦恼来回忆。

③ chalk'd forth the way：mark the path(as with a piece of chalk)，指路（像用粉笔灰做记号）。

④ issue：后代子孙。

Should become kings of Naples? O, rejoice

Beyond a common joy, and set it down

With gold on lasting pillars. In one voyage

Did Claribel① her husband find at Tunis②,

And Ferdinand, her brother, found a wife

Where he himself was lost; Prospero his dukedom

In a poor isle; and all of us ourselves,

When no man was his own.

Alonso：[*To Ferdinand and Miranda*]

　　　　Give me your hands：

　　　　Let grief and sorrow still embrace his heart

　　　　That doth not wish you joy!

Gonzalo：　　Be it so. Amen!

　　[*Re-enter Ariel, with the Master and Boatswain amazedly following.*]

　　　　O look, sir! look, sir! Here are more of us.

　　　　I prophesied, if a gallows were on land,

　　　　This fellow could not drown. —Now, blasphemy③,

　　　　That swear'st grace o'erboard, not an oath on shore?

　　　　Hast thou no mouth by land? What is the news?

Boatswain：　The best news is that we have safely found

　　　　Our king and company：the next, our ship,—

　　　　Which but three glasses④ since we gave out split,—

　　　　Is tight and yare, and bravely rigg'd as when

　　　　We first put out to sea.

Ariel：[*Aside to Prospero*]

　　　　Sir, all this service

　　　　Have I done since I went.

Prospero：[*Aside to Ariel*]

　　　　My tricksy spirit!

Alonso：　　These are not natural events; they strengthen

　　　　From strange to stranger —Say, how came you hither?

---

① Claribel：那不勒斯国王新出嫁的女儿。

② Tunis：突尼斯，位于非洲大陆最北端。

③ blasphemy：blasphemer，亵渎神灵者。

④ glasses：小时。这里以古时计时的玻璃沙漏代指时间。

Boatswain: If I did think, sir, I were well awake,

I'd strive to tell you. We were dead of sleep,

And,—how, we know not,—all clapp'd under hatches,

Where, but even now, with strange and several noises

Of roaring, shrieking, howling, jingling chains,

And mo① diversity of sounds, all horrible,

We were awak'd; straightway, at liberty:

Where we, in all her trim, freshly beheld

Our royal, good, and gallant ship; our master

Cap'ring to eye her②: on a trice, so please you,

Even in a dream, were we divided from them,

And were brought moping hither.

Ariel: [*Aside to Prospero*]

Was't well done?

Prospero: [*Aside to Ariel*]

Bravely, my diligence.

Thou shalt be free.

Alonso: This is as strange a maze as e'er men trod;

And there is in this business more than nature

Was ever conduct of: some oracle

Must rectify our knowledge.

Prospero: Sir, my liege,

Do not infest your mind with beating on

The strangeness of this business: at pick'd leisure③,

Which shall be shortly, single I'll resolve you,—

Which to you shall seem probable—of every

These happen'd accidents; till when, be cheerful

And think of each thing well. —[*Aside to Ariel*] Come hither, spirit;

Set Caliban and his companions free;

Untie the spell.

[*Exit Ariel*]

How fares my gracious sir ④?

---

① mo:同现代英语中的 more。

② Cap'ring to eye her: dancing with joy at the sight of her, 看到她喜出望外的样子。

③ pick'd leisure:找个空闲的时间。

④ How fares my gracious sir? 我的陛下您好吗?

There are yet missing of your company

Some few odd lads that you remember not.

[*Re-enter Ariel*, *driving in Caliban*, *Stephano*, *and Trinculo*, *in their stolen apparel*.]

Stephano：　Every man shift for all the rest，and let no man take care for himself，

for all is but fortune. —Coragio! bully-monster, Coragio①!

Trinculo：　If these be true spies which I wear in my head，here's a goodly sight.

Caliban：　O Setebos②，these be brave spirits indeed.

How fine my master is! I am afraid

He will chastise me.

Sebastian：　Ha，ha!

What things are these，my lord Antonio?

Will money buy them?

Antonio：　Very like；one of them

Is a plain fish，and，no doubt，marketable.

Prospero：　Mark but the badges③ of these men，my lords，

Then say if they be true. —This mis-shapen knave—

His mother was a witch；and one so strong

That could control the moon，make flows and ebbs，

And deal in her command without her power.

These three have robb'd me；and this demi-devil，—

For he's a bastard one，—had plotted with them

To take my life：two of these fellows you

Must know and own；this thing of darkness I

Acknowledge mine.

Caliban：　I shall be pinch'd to death.

Alonso：　Is not this Stephano，my drunken butler?

Sebastian：　He is drunk now：where had he wine?

Alonso：　And Trinculo is reeling-ripe：where should they

Find this grand liquor that hath gilded them?

---

① Every man shift for all the rest，and let no man take care for himself，for all is but fortune. —Coragio! bully-monster, Coraggio! 每人都要管别人，人人都别管自己，因为一切都是命运。——勇敢! 蠢怪物，勇敢! Stephano 仍在醉态中，故说话语无伦次。谚语：Every man for himself and god for us all.人人为自己，上帝为大家。因为是醉话，所以这里词语颠倒了。

② Setebos：莎士比亚虚构的神。1999 年人类发现天卫十九，采用此名。文中可译为"神啊""天哪"等。

③ badges：仆人们佩戴在衣服上以识别其主人的徽章。Stephano 和 Trinculo 衣服上的徽章表明他们是阿隆索的人。

	How cam'st thou in this pickle?①
Trinculo:	I have been in such a pickle since I saw you last that, I fear me,
	will never out of my bones. I shall not fear fly-blowing.
Sebastian:	Why, how now, Stephano!
Stephano:	O! touch me not: I am not Stephano, but a cramp.
Prospero:	You'd be king o' the isle, sirrah?
Stephano:	I should have been a sore one, then.②
Alonso:	This is as strange a thing as e'er I look'd on. [*Pointing to Caliban*]
Prospero:	He is as disproportioned in his manners
	As in his shape. —Go, sirrah, to my cell;
	Take with you your companions: as you look
	To have my pardon, trim it handsomely.
Caliban:	Ay, that I will; and I'll be wise hereafter,
	And seek for grace. What a thrice-double ass
	Was I, to take this drunkard for a god,
	And worship this dull fool!
Prospero:	Go to; away!
Alonso:	Hence, and bestow your luggage where you found it.
Sebastian:	Or stole it, rather.
	[*Exeunt Caliban, Stephano, and Trinculo.*]
Prospero:	Sir, I invite your Highness and your train
	To my poor cell, where you shall take your rest
	For this one night; which—part of it—I'll waste
	With such discourse as, I not doubt, shall make it
	Go quick away; the story of my life
	And the particular accidents gone by
	Since I came to this isle: and in the morn
	I'll bring you to your ship, and so to Naples,
	Where I have hope to see the nuptial

---

① in this pickle: in this sorry state, 醉成这个样子。pickle: 盐卤;腌泡。(但是 Trinculo 的回答接着 pickle 这个词的第二层意思说"泡在水里",即"烂醉如泥"或"泡在马尿里"。)

② I should have been a sore one, then: 那么我也一定是个恶王。a sore one 系双关语,既可指"一个浑身酸疼的王",又可指"一个凶恶的王"。

	Of these our dear-belov'd solemnized;
	And thence retire me to my Milan, where
	Every third thought shall be my grave.
Alonso:	I long
	To hear the story of your life, which must
	Take the ear strangely.
Prospero:	I'll deliver all;
	And promise you calm seas, auspicious gales,
	And sail so expeditious that shall catch
	Your royal fleet far off. — [*Aside to Ariel*]
	My Ariel, chick,
	That is thy charge: then to the elements
	Be free, and fare thou well! —Please you, draw near.

[*Exeunt*]

▶Epilogue

[*Spoken by Prospero*]

Now my charms are all overthrown,

And what strength I have's mine own;

Which is most faint; now 'tis true,

I must be here confin'd by you,

Or sent to Naples. Let me not,

Since I have my dukedom got,

And pardon'd the deceiver, dwell

In this bare island by your spell:

But release me from my bands

With the help of your good hands①.

Gentle breath② of yours my sails

Must fill, or else my project fails,

Which was to please. Now I want

Spirits to enforce, art to enchant;

And my ending is despair,

---

① your good hands: 观众的鼓掌声。

② gentle breath: 赞美的话,也可理解为"哨子声"(航海中,水手们常在无风的时候吹口哨以招风)。

Unless I be reliev'd by prayer,

Which pierces so that it assaults

Mercy itself, and frees all faults.

As you from crimes would pardon'd be,

Let your indulgence set me free.

▶扩展阅读

1. Cartelli，T. "After 'The Tempest:' Shakespeare, Postcoloniality, and Michelle Cliff's New, New World Miranda". *Contemporary Literature*，36 (1)：82-102. 1995.

2. Graff，G. & Phelan，J. *The Tempest：A Case Study in Critical Controversy*，London：MacMillan，2000.

3. Malone，E. *An Account of the Incidents, from Which the Title and Part of the Story of Shakespeare's "Tempest" Were Derived；And Its True Date Ascertained*. London：C. and R. Baldwin，1808.

4. Wells，S. *The Cambridge Companion to Shakespeare Studies*. Cambridge：Cambridge University Press，1986.

5. Wells，S. & Stanton，S. Ed. *The Cambridge Companion to Shakespeare on Stage*. Cambridge：Cambridge University Press，2002.

6. Yates，F. A. *Shakespeare's Last Plays：A New Approach*. London：Routledge & Kegan Paul，1975.

▶学习参考网站

1. http：//www.shakespeare-navigators.com/tempest/

2. http：//www.speak-the-speech.org/thetempestpage.htm

3. http：//records.viu.ca/～johnstoi/eng366/lectures/tempest.htm

4. http：//webenglishteacher.com/tempest.html

【徐 燕 编注】

4. Daniel Defoe: Robinson Crusoe

丹尼尔·笛福（Daniel Defoe，1660?—1731），英国小说家、报刊撰稿人，写过讽刺诗和大量政论小册子，代表作《鲁滨孙漂流记》。他出身于英国伦敦的一个小商人家庭，信奉不同于国教的长老会。笛福原姓福（Foe），1703年后自称笛福（Defoe）。笛福没有受过大学古典文学教育，仅接受过中等教育。他早年经商，经营过内衣、烟酒业等，曾到过欧洲大陆的许多国家；1692年经商破产转而以其他方式谋生。他反对封建专制，主张发展资本主义工商业，善于写政论和讽刺诗，曾因讽刺政府入狱。1683年，笛福曾被海盗俘虏。

笛福一生追求冒险与刺激，他的经历可以说毫不逊色于其小说《鲁滨孙漂流记》（Robinson Crusoe）中的主人公鲁滨孙。笛福在59岁时开始小说创作，他的小说从一个侧面反映了18世纪英国海外扩张的历史。《鲁滨孙漂流记》就是最具代表性的一部海上和荒岛历险小说。小说题材取自苏格兰水手亚历山大·塞尔柯克的历险及作者本人被海盗俘虏的经历，1719年小说发表后随即赢得读者的欢迎。此后，他创作了大量海上历险及传奇故事，如《辛格尔顿船长》（Captain Singleton，1720）、《摩尔·费兰德斯》（Moll Flanders，1722）、《杰克上校》（Colonel Jack，1722）和《罗克萨娜》（Roxana：The Fortunate Mistress，1724）等。此外，他还发表了若干传记、游记及几部有关经商的书。笛福是英国启蒙时期现实主义小说的奠基人，被后人尊称为"英国小说之父"。

笛福的小说大多与海洋有关，小说传承了文艺复兴时期西班牙流浪汉小说的格调。小说中的主人公往往出身卑微却拥有超人的聪明才智，能在不利的环境中克服重重困难，靠机智和个人奋斗而获得成功。笛福善于描写人物，他的主人公一般充满活力且不信天命。故事情节大多由主人公自述，这样的叙事技巧让小说阅读者在阅读时倍感亲切。其小说细节逼真，语言自然，使读者犹如身临其境。

《鲁滨孙漂流记》是笛福的代表作。这部小说问世一年之内竟连出了四版。小说从初版至今，已出了几百版，几乎译成了世界上所有的语言，至今仍被世界各国读者广为阅读。小说讲述了一个在海难中逃生的水手在一个荒岛上如何战胜险恶的自然环境，终于获救回到英国的故事。这是一部历险小说，鲁滨孙在岛上艰难、惊险的经历是该小说的重点。小说主人公鲁滨孙出身于一个体面的商人家庭，他的父亲常常教育他要知足常乐，要满足于现状，不要出海。但海外的新世界像一块巨大的磁铁一样强烈地吸引着他。鲁滨孙渴望航海，一心一意想要去海外闯荡。他多次瞒着父亲出海。第一次航行即遭不幸，船只因遇到大风浪而沉没,他历尽千辛万苦才得以保命。第二次出海去非洲经商,很幸运地小赚了一笔钱。第三次出海被摩尔人俘获而当了奴隶,后偷了主人的小船而逃脱,途中被一艘葡萄牙货船救走。船到巴西后,鲁滨孙买了一个庄园,做了庄园主。他不甘心于这样发财致富,又再次出海,到非洲贩卖奴隶。船在途中遇到风暴触礁,船上其他人员全部遇难,唯有鲁滨孙幸存下来,只身漂流到一个荒芜的孤岛上。在孤立无援中,鲁滨孙克服了最初到荒岛时的悲观绝望情绪,凭着顽强的毅力开始了征服大自然的斗争。他修建住所、种植粮食、驯养家畜、制造器具、缝制衣服,把荒岛改造成了可居之处。在与大自然的搏斗中,鲁滨孙表现出了非凡的毅力。在荒岛上,鲁滨孙被大海包围,孤立无援。鲁滨孙坚韧不拔的精神、改造自然的毅力和战胜孤独的勇气,是这部小说历久弥新的艺术魅力所在。以下选自小说第四章,讲述鲁滨孙落难荒岛,一无所有,折回遇难船骸寻找物品,并在荒岛上寻找安全住处的过程,从中可见其务实理性的商人品格。

▶Chapter 4

First Weeks on the Island

When I waked it was a broad day, the weather clear, and the storm abated, so that the sea did not rage and swell as before. But that which surprised me most was, that the ship was lifted off in the night from the sand where she lay by the swelling of the tide, and was driven up almost as far as the rock which I at first mentioned, where I had been so bruised by the wave dashing me against it. This being within about a mile from the shore where I was, and the ship seeming to stand upright still, I wished myself on board, that at least I might save some necessary things for my use.

When I came down from my apartment in the tree, I looked about me again, and the first thing I found was the boat, which lay, as the wind and the sea had tossed her up, upon the land, about two miles on my right hand. I walked as far as I could upon the shore to have got to her; but found a neck or inlet of water between me and the boat which was about half a mile broad; so I came back for the present, being more intent upon getting at the ship, where I hoped to find something for my present subsistence.

A little after noon I found the sea very calm, and the tide ebbed so far out that I could come within a quarter of a mile of the ship. And here I found a fresh renewing of my grief; for I saw evidently that if we had kept on board we had been all safe—that is to say, we had all got safe on shore, and I had not been so miserable as to be left entirely destitute of all comfort and company as I now was. This forced tears to my eyes again; but as there was little relief in that, I resolved, if possible, to get to the ship; so I pulled off my clothes—for the weather was hot to extremity—and took the water. But when I came to the ship my difficulty was still greater to know how to get on board; for, as she lay aground, and high out of the water, there was nothing within my reach to lay hold of. I swam round her twice, and the second time I spied a small piece of rope, which I wondered I did not see at first, hung down by the fore-chains so low, as that with great difficulty I got hold of it, and by the help of that rope I got up into the forecastle of the ship. Here I found that the ship was bulged, and had a great deal of water in her hold, but that she lay so on the side of a bank of hard sand, or, rather earth, that her stern lay lifted up upon the bank, and her head low, almost to the water. By this means all her quarter was free, and all that was in that part was dry; for you may be sure my first work was to search, and to see what was spoiled and what was free. And, first, I found that all the ship's provisions were dry and untouched by the water, and being very well disposed to eat, I went to the bread room and filled my pockets with biscuit, and ate it as I went about other things, for I had no time to lose. I also found some rum① in the great cabin, of which I took a large dram, and which I had, indeed, need enough of to spirit me for what was before me. Now I wanted nothing but a boat to furnish myself with many things which I foresaw would be very necessary to me.

It was in vain to sit still and wish for what was not to be had; and this extremity roused my application. We had several spare yards, and two or three large spars of wood, and a spare topmast or two in the ship; I resolved to fall to work with these, and I flung as many of them overboard as I could manage for their weight, tying every one with a rope, that they might not drive away. When this was done I went down the ship's side, and pulling them to me, I tied four of them together at both ends as well as I could, in the form of a raft, and laying two or three short pieces of plank upon them crossways, I found I could walk upon it very well, but that it was not able to bear any great weight, the pieces being too light. So I went to work, and with a carpenter's saw② I cut a spare topmast into three lengths, and added them to my raft, with a great deal of labour and pains. But the hope of furnishing myself with necessaries encouraged me to go beyond what I should have been able to have done upon another occasion.

My raft was now strong enough to bear any reasonable weight. My next care was what to load it with, and how to preserve what I laid upon it from the surf of the sea; but I was not long considering this. I first laid all the planks or boards upon it that I could get, and having considered well what I most wanted, I got three of the seamen's chests③, which I had broken open, and emptied, and lowered them down upon my raft; the first of these I

---

① rum:朗姆酒(糖蜜酒),其名源自西印度群岛原住民用语 rumbullion 一词的词首 rum,意指"兴奋"或"骚动"。以盛产甘蔗闻名的西印度群岛是朗姆酒的故乡。朗姆酒的特色在于风味醇厚,适合与可乐、果汁等各式非酒精饮料搭配使用,是调制鸡尾酒的主要基酒之一。

② saw:锯。

③ seamen's chests:海员的大箱子。

filled with provisions—viz. bread, rice, three Dutch cheeses[1], five pieces of dried goat's flesh (which we lived much upon), and a little remainder of European corn, which had been laid by for some fowls which we brought to sea with us, but the fowls were killed. There had been some barley and wheat together; but, to my great disappointment, I found afterwards that the rats had eaten or spoiled it all. As for liquors, I found several, cases of bottles belonging to our skipper[2], in which were some cordial waters; and, in all, about five or six gallons of rack. These I stowed by themselves, there being no need to put them into the chest, nor any room for them. While I was doing this, I found the tide begin to flow, though very calm; and I had the mortification to see my coat, shirt, and waistcoat, which I had left on the shore, upon the sand, swim away. As for my breeches, which were only linen, and open-kneed, I swam on board in them and my stockings. However, this set me on rummaging for clothes, of which I found enough, but took no more than I wanted for present use, for I had other things which my eye was more upon—as, first, tools to work with on shore. And it was after long searching that I found out the carpenter's chest, which was, indeed, a very useful prize to me, and much more valuable than a shipload of gold would have been at that time. I got it down to my raft, whole as it was, without losing time to look into it, for I knew in general what it contained.

My next care was for some ammunition[3] and arms. There were two very good fowling-pieces in the great cabin, and two pistols. These I secured first, with some powder-horns and a small bag of shot, and two old rusty swords. I knew there were three barrels of powder in the ship, but knew nowhere our gunner had stowed them; but with much search I found them, two of them dry and good, the third had taken water. Those two I got to my raft with the arms. And now I thought myself pretty well freighted, and began to think how I should get to shore with them, having neither sail, oar, nor rudder; and the least capful of wind would have overset all my navigation.

I had three encouragements—1st, a smooth, calm sea; 2ndly, the tide rising, and setting in to the shore; 3rdly, what little wind there was blew me towards the land. And thus, having found two or three broken oars belonging to the boat—and, besides the tools which were in the chest, I found two saws, an axe, and a hammer; with this cargo I put to sea. For a mile or thereabouts my raft went very well, only that I found it drive a little distant from the place where I had landed before; by which I perceived that there was some indraft of the water, and consequently I hoped to find some creek or river there, which I

---

① Dutch cheeses:荷兰奶酪。荷兰是世界上最大的奶酪出口国,荷兰的奶酪世界闻名。

② skipper:船长。

③ ammunition:弹药。

might make use of as a port to get to land with my cargo.

As I imagined, so it was. There appeared before me a little opening of the land, and I found a strong current of the tide set into it; so I guided my raft as well as I could, to keep in the middle of the stream.

But here I had like to have suffered a second shipwreck, which, if I had, I think verily would have broken my heart; for, knowing nothing of the coast, my raft ran aground at one end of it upon a shoal, and not being aground at the other end, it wanted but a little that all my cargo had slipped off towards the end that was afloat, and to fallen into the water. I did my utmost, by setting my back against the chests, to keep them in their places, but could not thrust off the raft with all my strength; neither durst I stir from the posture I was in; but holding up the chests with all my might, I stood in that manner near half-an-hour, in which time the rising of the water brought me a little more upon a level; and a little after, the water still-rising, my raft floated again, and I thrust her off with the oar I had into the channel, and then driving up higher, I at length found myself in the mouth of a little river, with land on both sides, and a strong current of tide running up. I looked on both sides for a proper place to get to shore, for I was not willing to be driven too high up the river: hoping in time to see some ships at sea, and therefore resolved to place myself as near the coast as I could.

At length I spied a little cove on the right shore of the creek, to which with great pain and difficulty I guided my raft, and at last got so near that, reaching ground with my oar, I could thrust her directly in. But here I had like to have dipped all my cargo into the sea again; for that shore lying pretty steep—that is to say sloping—there was no place to land, but where one end of my float, if it ran on shore, would lie so high, and the other sink lower, as before, that it would endanger my cargo again. All that I could do was to wait till the tide was at the highest, keeping the raft with my oar like an anchor, to hold the side of it fast to the shore, near a flat piece of ground, which I expected the water would flow over; and so it did. As soon as I found water enough—for my raft drew about a foot of water—I thrust her upon that flat piece of ground, and there fastened or moored her, by sticking my two broken oars into the ground, one on one side near one end, and one on the other side near the other end; and thus I lay till the water ebbed away, and left my raft and all my cargo safe on shore.

My next work was to view the country, and seek a proper place for my habitation, and where to stow my goods to secure them from whatever might happen. Where I was, I yet knew not; whether on the continent or on an island; whether inhabited or not inhabited; whether in danger of wild beasts or not. There was a hill not above a mile from me, which rose up very steep and high, and which seemed to overtop some other hills, which lay as in a ridge from it northward. I took out one of the fowling-pieces, and one of the pistols, and a horn of powder; and thus armed, I travelled for discovery up to the top of that hill, where, after I had with great labour and difficulty got to the top, I saw any fate, to my great affliction—viz. that I was in an island environed every way with the sea: no land to be seen except some rocks, which lay a great way off; and two small islands, less than this, which lay about three leagues to the west.

I found also that the island I was in was barren, and, as I saw good reason to believe, uninhabited except by wild beasts, of whom, however, I saw none. Yet I saw abundance of fowls, but knew not their kinds; neither when I killed them could I tell what was fit for food, and what not. At my coming back, I shot at a great bird which I saw sitting upon a tree on the side of a great wood. I believe it was the first gun that had been fired there since the creation of the world. I had no sooner fired, than from all parts of the wood there arose an innumerable number of fowls, of many sorts, making a confused screaming and crying, and every one according to his usual note, but not one of them of any kind that I knew. As for the creature I killed, I took it to be a kind of hawk, its colour and beak resembling it, but it had no talons or claws more than common. Its flesh was carrion, and fit for nothing.

Contented with this discovery, I came back to my raft, and fell to work to bring my cargo on shore, which took me up the rest of that day. What to do with myself at night I knew not, nor indeed where to rest, for I was afraid to lie down on the ground, not knowing but some wild beast might devour me, though, as I afterwards found, there was really no need for those fears.

However, as well as I could, I barricaded myself round with the chest and boards that I had brought on shore, and made a kind of hut for that night's lodging. As for food, I yet saw not which way to supply myself, except that I had seen two or three creatures like hares run out of the wood where I shot the fowl.

I now began to consider that I might yet get a great many things out of the ship which would be useful to me, and particularly some of the rigging and sails, and such other things as might come to land; and I resolved to make another voyage on board the vessel, if possible. And as I knew that the first storm that blew must necessarily break her all in pieces, I resolved to set all other things apart till I had got everything out of the ship that I could get. Then I called a council—that is to say in my thoughts—whether I should take back the raft; but this appeared impracticable: so I resolved to go as before, when the tide was down; and I did so, only that I stripped before I went from my hut, having nothing on but my chequered shirt, a pair of linen drawers, and a pair of pumps on my feet.

I got on board the ship as before, and prepared a second raft; and, having had experience of the first, I neither made this so unwieldy, nor loaded it so hard, but yet I brought away several things very useful to me; as first, in the carpenters stores I found two or three bags full of nails and spikes, a great screw-jack, a dozen or two of hatchets, and, above all, that most useful thing called a grindstone①. All these I secured, together with several things belonging to the gunner, particularly two or three iron crows, and two barrels of musket bullets, seven muskets, another fowling-piece, with some small quantity of powder more; a large bagful of small shot, and a great roll of sheet-lead; but this last was so heavy, I could not hoist it up to get it over the ship's side. Besides these things, I took all the men's clothes that I could find, and a spare fore-topsail, a hammock②, and some bedding; and with this I loaded my second raft, and brought them all safe on shore, to my very great comfort.

I was under some apprehension, during my absence from the land, that at least my provisions might be devoured on shore: but when I came back I found no sign of any visitor; only there sat a creature like a wild cat upon one of the chests, which, when I came towards it, ran away a little distance, and then stood still. She sat very composed and unconcerned, and looked full in my face, as if she had a mind to be acquainted with me. I presented my gun at her, but, as she did not understand it, she was perfectly unconcerned at it, nor did she offer to stir away; upon which I tossed her a bit of biscuit, though by the way, I was not very free of it, for my store was not great: however, I spared her a bit, I say, and she went to it, smelled at it, and ate it, and looked (as if pleased) for more; but I thanked her, and could spare no more: so she marched off.

Having got my second cargo on shore—though I was fain to open the barrels of powder, and bring them by parcels, for they were too heavy, being large casks—I went to work to make me a little tent with the sail and some poles which I cut for that purpose: and into this tent I brought everything that I knew would spoil either with rain or sun; and I piled all the empty chests and casks up in a circle round the tent, to fortify it from any sudden attempt, either from man or beast.

When I had done this, I blocked up the door of the tent with some boards within, and an empty chest set up on end without; and spreading one of the beds upon the ground, laying my two pistols just at my head, and my gun at length by me, I went to bed for the first time, and slept very quietly all night, for I was very weary and heavy; for the night before I had slept little, and had laboured very hard all day to fetch all those things from the ship, and to get them onshore.

I had the biggest magazine of all kinds now that ever was laid up, I believe, for one

---

① grindstone:磨。

② hammock:吊床。

man: but I was not satisfied still, for while the ship sat upright in that posture, I thought I ought to get everything out of her that I could; so every day at low water I went on board, and brought away something or other; but particularly the third time I went I brought away as much of the rigging as I could, as also all the small ropes and rope-twine I could get, with a piece of spare canvas, which was to mend the sails upon occasion, and the barrel of wet gunpowder. In a word, I brought away all the sails, first and last; only that I was fain to cut them in pieces, and bring as much at a time as I could, for they were no more useful to be sails, but as mere canvas only.

But that which comforted me more still, was, that last of all, after I had made five or six such voyages as these, and thought I had nothing more to expect from the ship that was worth my meddling with—I say, after all this, I found a great hogshead of bread, three large runlets of rum, or spirits, a box of sugar, and a barrel of fine flour; this was surprising to me, because I had given over expecting any more provisions, except what was spoiled by the water. I soon emptied the hogshead of the bread, and wrapped it up, parcel by parcel, in pieces of the sails, which I cut out; and, in a word, I got all this safe on shore also.

The next day I made another voyage, and now, having plundered the ship of what was portable and fit to hand out, I began with the cables. Cutting the great cable into pieces, such as I could move, I got two cables and a hawser on shore, with all the ironwork I could get; and having cut down the spritsail-yard, and the mizen-yard, and everything I could, to make a large raft, I loaded it with all these heavy goods, and came away. But my good luck began now to leave me; for this raft was so unwieldy, and so overladen, that, after I had entered the little cove where I had landed the rest of my goods, not being able to guide it so handily as I did the other, it overset, and threw me and all my cargo into the water. As for myself, it was no great harm, for I was near the shore; but as to my cargo, it was a great part of it lost, especially the iron, which I expected would have been of great use to me; however, when the tide was out, I got most of the pieces of the cable ashore, and some of the iron, though with infinite labour; for I was fain to dip for it into the water, a work which fatigued me very much. After this, I went every day on board, and brought away what I could get.

I had been now thirteen days on shore, and had been eleven times on board the ship, in which time I had brought away all that one pair of hands could well be supposed capable to bring; though I believe verily, had the calm weather held, I should have brought away the whole ship, piece by piece. But preparing the twelfth time to go on board, I found the wind began to rise: however, at low water I went on board, and though I thought I had rummaged the cabin so effectually that nothing more could be found, yet I discovered a locker with drawers in it, in one of which I found two or three razors, and one pair of large scissors, with some ten or a dozen of good knives and forks: in another I found about thirty-six pounds value in money—some European coin, some Brazil, some pieces of eight, some gold, and some silver.

I smiled to myself at the sight of this money: "O drug!" said I, aloud, "what art thou good for? Thou art not worth to me—no, not the taking off the ground; one of those knives is worth all this heap; I have no manner of use for thee—e'en remain where thou art, and go to the bottom as a creature whose life is not worth saying." However, upon second thoughts I took it away; and wrapping all this in a piece of canvas, I began to think of making another raft; but while I was preparing this, I found the sky overcast, and the wind began to rise, and in a quarter of an hour it blew a fresh gale from the shore. It presently occurred to me that it was in vain to pretend to make a raft with the wind offshore; and that it was my business to be gone before the tide of flood began, otherwise I might not be able to reach the shore at all. Accordingly, I let myself down into the water, and swam across the channel, which lay between the ship and the sands, and even that with difficulty enough, partly with the weight of the things I had about me, and partly the roughness of the water; for the wind rose very hastily, and before it was quite high water it blew a storm.

But I had got home to my little tent, where I lay, with all my wealth about me, very secure. It blew very hard all night, and in the morning, when I looked out, behold, no more ship was to be seen! I was a little surprised, but recovered myself with the satisfactory reflection that I had lost no time, nor abated any diligence, to get everything out of her that could be useful to me; and that, indeed, there was little left in her that I was able to bring away, if I had had more time. I now gave over any more thoughts of the ship, or of anything out of her, except what might drive on shore from her wreck; as, indeed, divers pieces of her afterwards did; but those things were of small use to me.

My thoughts were now wholly employed about securing myself against either savages, if any should appear, or wild beasts, if any were in the island; and I had many thoughts of the method how to do this, and what kind of dwelling to make—whether I should make me a cave in the earth, or a tent upon the earth; and, in short, I resolved upon both; the manner and description of which, it may not be improper to give an account of.

I soon found the place I was in was not fit for my settlement, because it was upon a low, moorish ground, near the sea, and I believed it would not be wholesome, and more particularly because there was no fresh water near it; so I resolved to find a more healthy and more convenient spot of ground.

I consulted several things in my situation, which I found would be proper for me: 1st, health and fresh water, I just now mentioned; 2ndly, shelter from the heat of the sun;

3rdly, security from ravenous creatures, whether man or beast; 4thly, a view to the sea, that if God sent any ship in sight, I might not lose any advantage for my deliverance, of which I was not willing to banish all my expectation yet.

In search of a place proper for this, I found a little plain on the side of a rising hill, whose front towards this little plain was steep as a house-side, so that nothing could come down upon me from the top. On the one side of the rock there was a hollow place, worn a little way in, like the entrance or door of a cave but there was not really any cave or way into the rock at all.

On the flat of the green, just before this hollow place, I resolved to pitch my tent. This plain was not above a hundred yards broad, and about twice as long, and lay like a green before my door; and, at the end of it, descended irregularly every way down into the low ground by the seaside. It was on the N.N.W. side of the hill; so that it was sheltered from the heat every day, till it came to a W. and by S. sun, or thereabouts, which, in those countries, is near the setting.

Before I set up my tent I drew a half-circle before the hollow place, which took in about ten yards in its semi-diameter from the rock, and twenty yards in its diameter from its beginning and ending.

In this half-circle I pitched two rows of strong stakes, driving them into the ground till they stood very firm like piles, the biggest end being out of the ground above five feet and a half, and sharpened on the top. The two rows did not stand above six inches from one another.

Then I took the pieces of cable which I had cut in the ship, and laid them in rows, one upon another, within the circle, between these two rows of stakes, up to the top, placing other stakes in the inside, leaning against them, about two feet and a half high, like a spur to a post; and this fence was so strong, that neither man nor beast could get into it or over it. This cost me a great deal of time and labour, especially to cut the piles in the woods, bring them to the place, and drive them into the earth.

The entrance into this place I made to be, not by a door, but by a short ladder to go over the top; which ladder, when I was in, I lifted over after me; and so I was completely fenced in and fortified, as I thought, from all the world, and consequently slept secure in the night, which otherwise I could not have done; though, as it appeared afterwards, there was no need of all this caution from the enemies that I apprehended danger from.

Into this fence or fortress, with infinite labour, I carried all my riches, all my provisions, ammunition, and stores, of which you have the account above; and I made a large tent, which to preserve me from the rains that in one part of the year are very violent there, I made double—one smaller tent within, and one larger tent above it; and covered the uppermost with a large tarpaulin[①], which I had saved among the sails.

And now I lay no more for a while in the bed which I had brought on shore, but in a hammock, which was indeed a very good one, and belonged to the mate of the ship. Into this tent I brought all my provisions, and everything that would spoil by the wet; and having thus enclosed all my goods, I made up the entrance, which till now I had left open, and so passed and repassed, as I said, by a short ladder.

When I had done this, I began to work my way into the rock, and bringing all the earth and stones that I dug down out through my tent, I laid them up within my fence, in the nature of a terrace, so that it raised the ground within about a foot and a half; and thus I made me a cave, just behind my tent, which served me like a cellar to my house.

It cost me much labour and many days before all these things were brought to perfection; and therefore I must go back to some other things which took up some of my thoughts. At the same time it happened, after I had laid my scheme for the setting up my tent, and making the cave, that a storm of rain falling from a thick, dark cloud, a sudden flash of lightning happened, and after that a great clap of thunder, as is naturally the effect of it. I was not so much surprised with the lightning as I was with the thought which darted into my mind as swift as the lightning itself—Oh, my powder! My very heart sank within me when I thought that, at one blast, all my powder might be destroyed; on which, not my defence only, but the providing my food, as I thought, entirely depended. I was nothing near so anxious about my own danger, though, had the powder took fire, I should never have known who had hurt me.

Such impression did this make upon me, that after the storm was over I laid aside all my works, my building and fortifying, and applied myself to make bags and boxes, to separate the powder, and to keep it a little and a little in a parcel, in the hope that, whatever might come, it might not all take fire at once; and to keep it so apart that it should not be possible to make one part fire another. I finished this work in about a fortnight; and I think my powder, which in all was about two hundred and forty pounds weight, was divided in not less than a hundred parcels. As to the barrel that had been wet, I did not apprehend any danger from that; so I placed it in my new cave, which, in my fancy, I called my kitchen; and the rest I hid up and down in holes among the rocks, so that no wet might come to it, marking very carefully where I laid it.

In the interval of time while this was doing, I went out once at least every day with my gun, as well to divert myself as to see if I could kill anything fit for food; and, as near as I could, to acquaint myself with what the island produced. The first time I went out, I

---

① tarpaulin: 篷帆布,(防水)油布。

presently discovered that there were goats in the island, which was a great satisfaction to me; but then it was attended with this misfortune to me—viz. that they were so shy, so subtle, and so swift of foot, that it was the most difficult thing in the world to come at them; but I was not discouraged at this, not doubting but I might now and then shoot one, as it soon happened; for after I had found their haunts a little, I laid wait in this manner for them: I observed if they saw me in the valleys, though they were upon the rocks, they would run away, as in a terrible fright; but if they were feeding in the valleys, and I was upon the rocks, they took no notice of me; from whence I concluded that, by the position of their optics, their sight was so directed downward that they did not readily see objects that were above them; so afterwards I took this method—I always climbed the rocks first, to get above them, and then had frequently a fair mark.

The first shot I made among these creatures, I killed a she-goat, which had a little kid by her, which she gave suck to, which grieved me heartily; for when the old one fell, the kid stood stock still by her, till I came and took her up; and not only so, but when I carried the old one with me, upon my shoulders, the kid followed me quite to my enclosure; upon which I laid down the dam, and took the kid in my arms, and carried it over my pale, in hopes to have bred it up tame; but it would not eat; so I was forced to kill it and eat it myself. These two supplied me with flesh a great while, for I ate sparingly, and saved my provisions, my bread especially, as much as possibly I could.

Having now fixed my habitation, I found it absolutely necessary to provide a place to make a fire in, and fuel to burn: and what I did for that, and also how I enlarged my cave, and what conveniences I made, I shall give a full account of in its place; but I must now give some little account of myself, and of my thoughts about living, which, it may well be supposed, were not a few.

I had a dismal prospect of my condition; for as I was not cast away upon that island without being driven, as is said, by a violent storm, quite out of the course of our intended voyage, and a great way, viz. some hundreds of leagues, out of the ordinary course of the trade of mankind, I had great reason to consider it as a determination of Heaven, that in this desolate place, and in this desolate manner, I should end my life. The tears would run plentifully down my face when I made these reflections; and sometimes I would expostulate with myself why Providence should thus completely ruin His creatures, and render them so absolutely miserable; so without help, abandoned, so entirely depressed, that it could hardly be rational to be thankful for such a life.

But something always returned swift upon me to check these thoughts, and to reprove me; and particularly one day, walking with my gun in my hand by the seaside, I was very pensive upon the subject of my present condition, when reason, as it were, expostulated with me the other way, thus: "Well, you are in a desolate condition, it is true; but, pray remember, where are the rest of you? Did not you come, eleven of you in the boat? Where are the ten? Why were they not saved, and you lost? Why were you singled out? Is it better to be here or there?" And then I pointed to the sea. All evils are to be considered with the good that is in them, and with what worse attends them. Then it occurred to me again, how well I was furnished for my subsistence, and what would have been my case if it had not happened (which was a hundred thousand to one) that the ship floated from the place where she first struck, and was driven so near to the shore that I had time to get all these things out of her; what would have been my case, if I had been forced to have lived in the condition in which I at first came on shore, without necessaries of life, or necessaries to supply and procure them? "Particularly," said I, aloud (though to myself), "what should I have done without a gun, without ammunition, without any tools to make anything, or to work with, without clothes, bedding, a tent, or any manner of covering?" and that now I had all these to sufficient quantity, and was in a fair way to provide myself in such a manner as to live without my gun, when my ammunition was spent: so that I had a tolerable view of subsisting, without any want, as long as I lived; for I considered from the beginning how I would provide for the accidents that might happen, and for the time that was to come, even not only after my ammunition should be spent, but even after my health and strength should decay.

I confess I had not entertained any notion of my ammunition being destroyed at one blast—I mean my powder being blown up by lightning; and this made the thoughts of it so surprising to me, when it lightened and thundered, as I observed just now.

And now being about to enter into a melancholy relation of a scene of silent life, such, perhaps, as was never heard of in the world before, I shall take it from its beginning, and continue it in its order. It was by my account the 30th of September, when, in the manner as above said, I first set foot upon this horrid island; when the sun, being to us in its autumnal equinox[①], was almost over my head; for I reckoned myself, by observation, to be in the latitude of nine degrees twenty-two minutes north of the line.

After I had been there about ten or twelve days, it came into my thoughts that I should lose my reckoning of time for want of books, and pen and ink, and should even forget the Sabbath days[②]; but to prevent this, I cut with my knife upon a large post, in capital letters—and making it into a great cross, I set it up on the shore where I first landed—"I came on shore here on the 30th September 1659."

---

① equinox：二分时刻，昼夜平分时（指春分或秋分）。
② Sabbath days：安息日（犹太教徒及某些基督教徒以星期六为安息日，基督教徒大都以星期日为安息日）。

Upon the sides of this square post I cut every day a notch with my knife, and every seventh notch was as long again as the rest, and every first day of the month as long again as that long one; and thus I kept my calendar, or weekly, monthly, and yearly reckoning of time.

In the next place, we are to observe that among the many things which I brought out of the ship, in the several voyages which, as above mentioned, I made to it, I got several things of less value, but not at all less useful to me, which I omitted setting down before; as, in particular, pens, ink, and paper, several parcels in the captain's, mate's, gunner's and carpenter's keeping; three or four compasses[①], some mathematical instruments, dials, perspectives, charts, and books of navigation, all which I huddled together, whether I might want them or no; also, I found three very good *Bibles*, which came to me in my cargo from England, and which I had packed up among my things; some Portuguese books also; and among them two or three Popish prayer-books[②], and several other books, all which I carefully secured. And I must not forget that we had in the ship a dog and two cats, of whose eminent history I may have occasion to say something in its place; for I carried both the cats with me; and as for the dog, he jumped out of the ship of himself, and swam on shore to me the day after I went on shore with my first cargo, and was a trusty servant to me many years; I wanted nothing that he could fetch me, nor any company that he could make up to me; I only wanted to have him talk to me, but that would not do. As I observed before, I found pens, ink, and paper, and I husbanded them to the utmost; and I shall show that while my ink lasted, I kept things very exact, but after that was gone I could not, for I could not make any ink by any means that I could devise.

And this put me in mind that I wanted many things notwithstanding all that I had amassed together; and of these, ink was one; as also a spade, pickaxe, and shovel, to dig or remove the earth; needles, pins, and thread; as for linen, I soon learned to want that without much difficulty.

This want of tools made every work I did go on heavily; and it was near a whole year before I had entirely finished my little pale, or surrounded my habitation. The piles, or stakes, which were as heavy as I could well lift, were a long time in cutting and preparing in the woods, and more, by far, in bringing home; so that I spent sometimes two days in cutting and bringing home one of those posts, and a third day in driving it into the ground; for which purpose I got a heavy piece of wood at first, but at last bethought myself of one of the iron crows; which, however, though I found it, made driving those posts or piles very

---

① compass：指南针。
② Popish prayer-books：天主教祈祷书。

laborious and tedious work. But what need I have been concerned at the tediousness of anything I had to do, seeing I had time enough to do it in? nor had I any other employment, if that had been over, at least that I could foresee, except the ranging the island to seek for food, which I did, more or less, every day.

I now began to consider seriously my condition, and the circumstances I was reduced to; and I drew up the state of my affairs in writing, not so much to leave them to any that were to come after me—for I was likely to have but few heirs—as to deliver my thoughts from daily poring over them, and afflicting my mind; and as my reason began now to master my despondency, I began to comfort myself as well as I could, and to set the good against the evil, that I might have something to distinguish my case from worse; and I stated very impartially, like debtor and creditor, the comforts I enjoyed against the miseries I suffered, thus:—

Evil: I am cast upon a horrible, desolate island, void of all hope of recovery.

Good: But I am alive; and not drowned, as all my ship's company were.

Evil: I am singled out and separated, as it were, from all the world, to be miserable.

Good: But I am singled out, too, from all the ship's crew, to be spared from death; and He that miraculously saved me from death can deliver me from this condition.

Evil: I am divided from mankind—a solitaire; one banished from human society.

Good: But I am not starved, and perishing on a barren place, affording no sustenance.

Evil: I have no clothes to cover me.

Good: But I am in a hot climate, where, if I had clothes, I could hardly wear them.

Evil: I am without any defence, or means to resist any violence of man or beast.

Good: But I am cast on an island where I see no wild beasts to hurt me, as I saw on the coast of Africa; and what if I had been shipwrecked there?

Evil: I have no soul to speak to or relieve me.

Good: But God wonderfully sent the ship in near enough to the shore, that I have got out as many necessary things as will either supply my wants or enable me to supply myself, even as long as I live.

Upon the whole, here was an undoubted testimony that there was scarce any condition in the world so miserable but there was something negative or something positive to be thankful for in it; and let this stand as a direction from the experience of the most miserable of all conditions in this world: that we may always find in it something to comfort ourselves from, and to set, in the description of good and evil, on the credit side of the account.

Having now brought my mind a little to relish my condition, and given over looking out to sea, to see if I could spy a ship—I say, giving over these things, I begun to apply myself to arrange my way of living, and to make things as easy to me as I could.

I have already described my habitation, which was a tent under the side of a rock, surrounded with a strong pale of posts and cables: but I might now rather call it a wall, for I raised a kind of wall up against it of turfs, about two feet thick on the outside; and after some time (I think it was a year and a half) I raised rafters from it, leaning to the rock, and thatched or covered it with boughs of trees, and such things as I could get, to keep out the rain; which I found at some times of the year very violent.

I have already observed how I brought all my goods into this pale, and into the cave which I had made behind me. But I must observe, too, that at first this was a confused heap of goods, which, as they lay in no order, so they took up all my place; I had no room to turn myself: so I set myself to enlarge my cave, and work farther into the earth; for it was a loose sandy rock, which yielded easily to the labour I bestowed on it: and so when I found I was pretty safe as to beasts of prey, I worked sideways, to the right hand, into the rock; and then, turning to the right again, worked quite out, and made me a door to come out on the outside of my pale or fortification. This gave me not only egress and regress①, as it was a back way to my tent and to my storehouse, but gave me room to store my goods.

And now I began to apply myself to make such necessary things as I found I most wanted, particularly a chair and a table; for without these I was not able to enjoy the few comforts I had in the world; I could not write or eat, or do several things, with so much pleasure without a table: so I went to work. And here I must needs② observe, that as reason is the substance and origin of the mathematics, so by stating and squaring everything by reason, and by making the most rational judgment of things, every man may be, in time, master of every mechanic art. I had never handled a tool in my life; and yet, in time, by labour, application, and contrivance, I found at last that I wanted nothing but I could have made it, especially if I had had tools. However, I made abundance of things, even without tools; and some with no more tools than an adze and a hatchet, which perhaps were never made that way before, and that with infinite labour. For example, if I wanted a board, I had no other way but to cut down a tree, set it on an edge before me, and hew it flat on either side with my axe, till I brought it to be thin as a plank, and then dub it smooth with my adze. It is true, by this method I could make but one board out of a whole tree; but this I had no remedy for but patience, any more than I had for the prodigious deal of time and labour which it took me up to make a plank or board: but my time or labour was little worth, and so it was as well employed one way as another.

However, I made me a table and a chair, as I observed above, in the first place; and

---

① egress and regress：在物权法中，该词组意指一个人，比如说租户，有留下和归还某一财物的权利。

② must needs：是古旧英语用法，后接动词，现已不通用，意为"不可避免或情不自禁地做某事"（cannot avoid or help doing something）。needs 在这里作副词，意为"必须"（of necessity）。

this I did out of the short pieces of boards that I brought on my raft from the ship. But when I had wrought out some boards as above, I made large shelves, of the breadth of a foot and a half, one over another all along one side of my cave, to lay all my tools, nails and ironwork on; and, in a word, to separate everything at large into their places, that I might come easily at them. I knocked pieces into the wall of the rock to hang my guns and all things that would hang up; so that, had my cave been to be seen, it looked like a general magazine of all necessary things; and had everything so ready at my hand, that it was a great pleasure to me to see all my goods in such order, and especially to find my stock of all necessaries so great.

And now it was that I began to keep a journal of every day's employment; for, indeed, at first I was in too much hurry, and not only hurry as to labour, but in too much discomposure of mind; and my journal would have been full of many dull things; for example, I must have said thus: "30th. —After I had got to shore, and escaped drowning, instead of being thankful to God for my deliverance, having first vomited, with the great quantity of salt water which had got into my stomach, and recovering myself a little, I ran about the shore wringing my hands and beating my head and face, exclaiming at my misery, and crying out, 'I was undone, undone! ' till, tired and faint, I was forced to lie down on the ground to repose, but durst not sleep for fear of being devoured."

Some days after this, and after I had been on board the ship, and got all that I could out of her, yet I could not forbear getting up to the top of a little mountain and looking out to sea, in hopes of seeing a ship; then fancy at a vast distance I spied a sail, please myself with the hopes of it, and then after looking steadily, till I was almost blind, lose it quite, and sit down and weep like a child, and thus increase my misery by my folly.

But having gotten over these things in some measure, and having settled my household staff and habitation, made me a table and a chair, and all as handsome about me as I could, I began to keep my journal; of which I shall here give you the copy (though in it will be told all these particulars over again) as long as it lasted; for having no more ink, I was forced to leave it off.

▶扩展阅读

1. Byrd, M. Ed. *Daniel Defoe: A Collection of Critical Essays*. New York: Prentice Hall, 1976.

2. Novak, E. M. *Daniel Defoe: Master of Fictions: His Life and Ideas*. Oxford: Oxford University Press, 2001.

3. Richetti, J. *Life of Daniel Defoe: A Critical Biography*. Oxford: Blackwell Publishers, 2005.

4. Watt, I. *Myths of Modern Individualism*. New York: Cambridge University Press, 1994.

5. Zimmerman, E. *Defoe and the Novel*. Los Angeles: University of California Press, 1975.

▶学习参考网站

1. http：// en.wikipedia.org/wiki/Daniel_Defoe

2. http：// www.online-literature.com/defoe/

3. http：// homepage.newschool.edu/het // profiles/defoe.htm

4. http：// www.davidsemporium.co.uk/_SIXTEEN.html

5. http：// www.gradesaver.com/robinson-crusoe/

【应素芳　编注】

5. Tobias George Smollett:
The Adventures of Roderick Random

托比亚斯·乔治·斯摩莱特（Tobias George Smollett，1721—1771），英国小说家，以行医和写作为生，曾写过诗和书信体小说。斯摩莱特于 1721 年出生在苏格兰的丹巴顿郡，幼年丧父，青年时代就读于格拉斯哥大学，成为外科医生学徒，1739 年来到伦敦。1740 年，他以外科医生助手的身份加入海军远征队，参加了英国与西班牙争夺美洲殖民地的战争；1744 年定居伦敦，不久之后就将注意力从医学转移到写作。丰富的生活阅历为他提供了艺术创作的素材。他的作品包括戏剧、诗歌、政治讽刺和欧洲游记。他还是一位新闻工作者、编辑和译者，著有 6 部长篇小说，2 部戏剧，编辑和撰写的非虚构作品多达 70 卷，还翻译过大量的文学作品，其中包括 35 卷本《伏尔泰全集》。斯摩莱特的主要成就还是小说，他著有《蓝登传》(*The Adventures of Roderick Random*，1748)、《佩里格林·皮克尔传》(*The Adventures of Peregrine Pickle*，1751)、《菲迪南伯爵》(*The Adventures of Ferdinand Count Fathom*，1753)、《朗斯洛·格里弗爵士》(*The Life and Adventures of Sir Launcelot Greaves*，1760)和《亨佛利·克林克历险记》(*The Expedition of Humphry Clinker*，1771)等。与菲尔丁和理查逊一样，斯摩莱特是在 18 世纪英国小说发展过程中起到极其重要作用的人物。斯摩莱特的小说既具有很强的写实成分，又带有很强烈的主观色彩。其作品社会批判倾向鲜明，继承了流浪汉小说的传统，讽刺辛辣，人物漫画化。他的小说语言简洁，动作性强，非常个性化。他在作品中引进苏格兰、威尔士、爱尔兰等各种方言及专业术语。尤其令人叫绝的是他根据亲身经历收集的有着海军语言特征的词语，这些词语为情节的发展和人物的塑造起到了画龙点睛的作用。斯摩莱特与同时代的小说家相比，他的不同之处在于他更彻底地撕去了 18 世纪英国社会漂亮、伪善的外衣，把卑鄙、残忍、腐朽、惨不忍睹的黑暗面完全暴露在读者面前，并对其进行无情的鞭挞。他对军舰上污秽不堪的病区及伤员所受的折磨的描写极为真实，让人感到惊骇。这种接近自然主义的写实手法是当时现实主义的新发展。斯摩莱特对于英国文学，特别是对 18 世纪英国现实主义小说的发展有着独特的贡献。

斯摩莱特的小说几乎都与海洋有关，他的小说以大海为背景，描写海军的真实生活，他在表现海军生活方面开拓了一个新的领域。从某种意义上说，他是英国海军生活小说的创始人。斯摩莱特的处女作《蓝登传》是根据斯摩莱特本人的经历写成的自传体作品，是一部典型的流浪汉小说。主人公蓝登出身于苏格兰的绅士家庭，因不堪其祖父的暴虐，蓝登的父亲在他很小的时候便离家出走。在没有父爱的环境中长大后,蓝登带上一名侍从到伦敦谋生。经过努力,他获得医师资格,当上海军医生助理,在海上经历过种种磨难,一度沦为奴仆并爱上主人的侄女。在爱而不得的打击下,他返回伦敦,却因债务缠身而被关进监狱。后来,叔父将他救出,两人一起四处流浪,在西班牙他遇见了早年离家出走现已身为富豪的父亲。蓝登从此过上了衣食无忧的绅士生活。《蓝登传》最具吸引力的情节是那些大胆揭露军舰上水兵遭受非人待遇的章节。蓝登被强征到舰队上当兵,见证了船长的残酷和专横与军医的冷漠,还目睹了底舱里一个气闷和污秽的小医务室中水兵们病死的可怕情景。《蓝登传》以大海为背景,通过描述水兵海上生活的艰辛和军官对水兵的虐待,将资本主义海外殖民的血腥一面和丑恶本质暴露无遗。

以下选段出自《蓝登传》的第二十七章,主要讲述了医生离开后,欧克姆船长上船,带来一位新医生麦克贤,船长命人把伤病海员召集到上层甲板以做检查,扬言"我的船上是没有病号的",由此导致了全船伤病海员大量死亡。选段细致而真实地描写了海军长官的残酷无情和水手们的悲惨生活,尤其是军医麦克贤的草菅人命。

▶Chapter 27

I acquire the friendship of the surgeon, who procures a warrant for me, and makes me a present of clothes—a battle between a midshipman and me—the surgeon leaves the ship—the captain comes on board with another surgeon—a dialogue between the captain and Morgan—the sick are ordered to be brought upon the quarter-deck and examined—the consequences of that order—a madman accuses Morgan, and is set at liberty by command of the captain, whom he instantly attacks and pummels without mercy.

While I was busied with my friend in this practice, the doctor chanced to pass by the place where we were, and stopping to observe me, appeared very well satisfied with my method of application; and afterwards sent for me to his cabin, where, having examined me touching my skill in surgery, and the particulars of my fortune, interested himself so far in my behalf, as to promise his assistance in procuring a warrant for me, seeing I had been already found qualified at Surgeon's hall, for the station I now filled on board; and this he the more cordially engaged in, when he understood I was nephew to lieutenant Bowling, for whom he expressed a particular regard. — In the mean time, I could learn from his discourse, that he did not intend to go to sea again with captain Oakhum, having, as he thought, been indifferently used by him during the last voyage.

While I lived tolerably easy, in expectation of preferment, I was not altogether without mortifications, which I not only suffered from the rude insults of the sailors, and petty officers, among whom I was known by the name of *Loblolly Boy*[①]; but also from the disposition of Morgan, who, though friendly in the main, was often very troublesome with his pride, which expected a good deal of submission from me, and delighted in recapitulating the favours I had received at his hands.

About six weeks after my arrival on board, the surgeon bidding me follow him into his cabin, presented a warrant to me, by which I was appointed surgeon's third mate on board the Thunder. —This he had procured by his interest at the Navy-Office; as also another for himself, by virtue of which he was removed into a second rate. I acknowledged his kindness in the strongest terms my gratitude could suggest, and professed my sorrow at the prospect of losing such a valuable friend, to whom I hoped to have recommended myself still further, by my respectful and diligent behaviour. —But his generosity rested not here; —for, before he left the ship, he made me a present of a chest and some clothes, that enabled me to support the rank to which he had raised me. —I found my spirit revive with my good fortune; and now I was an officer, resolved to maintain the dignity of my station, against all opposition or affronts; nor was it long before I had occasion to exert my resolution; my old enemy the midshipman (whose name was Crampley) entertaining an implacable animosity against me, for the disgrace he had suffered on my account, had since that time taken all opportunities of reviling and ridiculing me, when I was not entitled to retort his bad usage. —And even after I had been rated on the books, and mustered as surgeon's mate, did not think fit to restrain his insolence. —In particular, being one day present, while I dressed a wound in a sailor's leg, he began to sing a song, which I thought highly injurious to the honour of my country, and therefore signified my resentment, by observing, that the Scots always laid their account in finding enemies among the ignorant, insignificant and malicious. —This unexpected piece of assurance enraged him to such a degree, that he lent me a blow on the face, which I verily thought had demolished my cheekbone; I was not slow in returning the obligation, and the affair began to be very serious, when by accident Mr. Morgan, and one of the master's mates, coming that way, interposed, and inquiring into the cause, endeavored to promote a reconciliation; but finding us both exasperated to the uttermost, and bent against accommodation, they advised us, either to leave our difference undecided till we should have an opportunity of terminating it on shore, like gentlemen, or else chuse a proper place on board, and bring it to an issue by boxing. This last expedient was greedily embraced; and being forthwith conducted to the ground proposed, we stript in a moment, and began a very furious contest, in which I soon found myself inferior to my

---

① loblolly boy: loblolly 原指船上医生多以流质食物作为药物治病（现已不存在这种用法），此处的 loblolly boy 意为"船上外科医生的助手"。

antagonist, not so much in strength and agility, as in skill, which he had acquired in the school at Hockley in the Hole①, and Tottenham-Court②. —Many cross-buttocks③ did I sustain, and pegs④ on the stomach without number, till at last, my breath being quite gone, as well as my vigour wasted, I grew desperate, and collecting all my spirits in one effort, threw in at once head, hands, and feet with such violence, that I drove my antagonist three paces backward into the main hatch-way, down which he fell, and pitching upon his head and right shoulder, remained without sense and motion—Morgan looking down, and seeing him lie in that condition, cried, "Upon my conscience, as I am a Christian sinner (look you) I believe his battles are all offer; but I take you all to witness that there was no treachery in the case, and that he has suffered by the chance of war." —So saying, he descended to the deck below, to examine into the situation of my adversary; and left me very little pleased with my victory, as I found myself not only terribly bruised, but likewise in danger of being called to account for the death of Crampley: But this fear vanished when my fellow-mate, having by bleeding him in the jugular, brought him to himself, and assured himself of the state of his body, called up to me, to be under no concern, for the midshipman had received no other damage than as pretty a luxation of the *os humeri*⑤, as one would desire to see on a summer's day. —Upon this information, I crawled down to the cockpit, and acquainted Thomson with the affair, who, providing himself with bandages, & c. necessary for the occasion, went up to assist Mr. Morgan in the reduction of the dislocation. —When this was successfully performed, they wished me joy of the event of the combat; and the Welchman, after observing, that in all likelihood, the ancient Scots and Britons were the same people, bid me "Praise Cot for putting mettle in my pelly, and strength in my limbs to support it". —I acquired such reputation by this recounter (which lasted twenty minutes) that every body became more cautious in his behaviour towards me; though Crampley with his arm in a sling, talked very high, and threatened to seize the first opportunity of retrieving on shore, the honour he had lost by an accident, from which I could justly claim no merit.

About this time, captain Oakhum, having received sailing orders, came on board, and brought along with him a surgeon of his own country, who soon made us sensible of the loss we suffered in the departure of doctor Atkins; being grossly ignorant, and intolerably assuming, false, vindictive, and unforgiving; a merciless tyrant to his inferiors, an abject sycophant to those above him. In the morning after the captain came on board, our first

---

① Hockley in the Hole:指克拉肯韦尔格林附近一个有名的公共娱乐场所,该场所有斗熊、斗牛、拳击等竞技活动。约翰·盖伊的《乞丐歌剧》(*The Beggar's Opera*)中的人物 Peachum 夫人曾以此来指代获得勇气的地方。

② Tottenham-Court:指托特纳姆法院路,此地和拳击有关。

③ cross-buttocks:在摔跤和拳击中使用的跨臀部抛出的传统招式。

④ pegs:此处指用力的一拳。

⑤ os humeri:【医】肱骨。humeri 是复数形式,其单数形式为 humerus。此处意为肱骨脱臼。

mate, according to custom, went to wait on him with a sick list, which when this grim commander had perused, he cried with a stern countenance, "Blood and oons![①] sixty-one sick people on board of my ship! —Harkee you, sir, I'll have no sick in my ship, by G—d." The Welchman replied, he should be very glad to find no sick people on board; but while it was otherwise, he did no more than his duty in presenting him with a list. —"You and your list may be d—n'd, (said the captain, throwing it at him) I say, there shall be no sick in this ship while I have the command of her." —Mr. Morgan being nettled at this treatment, told him, his indignation ought to be directed to Got Almighty, who visited his people with distempers, and not to him, who contributed all in his power towards their cure. The Bashaw[②] not being used to such behaviour in any of his officers, was enraged to fury at this satirical insinuation, and stamping with his foot, called him insolent scoundrel, threatening to have him pinioned to the deck, if he should presume to utter another syllable. But the blood of Caractacus being thoroughly heated, disdained to be restricted by such a command, and began to manifest itself in, "Captain Oakhum, I am a gentleman of birth and parentage (look you) and peradventure, I am moreover—." Here his harangue was broke off by the captain's steward, who being Morgan's countryman, hurried him out of the cabin before he had time to exasperate his master to a greater degree, which would certainly have been the case; for the indignant Welchman, could hardly be hindered by his friend's arguments and intreats, from re-entering the presence chamber, and defying captain Oakhum to his teeth. —He was, however, appeased at length, and came down to the birth, where finding Thomson and me at work preparing medicines, he bid us leave off our labour and go to play, for the captain, by his sole word and power and command, had driven sickness a pegging to the evil, and there was no more malady on board. So saying, he drank off a gill of brandy, sighed grievously three times, poured forth an ejaculation of "Got bless my heart, liver, and lungs!" and then began to sing a Welch song with great earnestness of visage, voice and gesture. —I could not conceive the meaning of this singular phenomenon, and saw by the looks of Thomson, who at the same time, shook his head, that he suspected poor Cadwallader's brains were unsettled. He perceiving our amazement, told us, he would explain the mystery; but at the same time, bid us take notice, that he had lived boy, bachelor, married man and widower, almost forty years, and in all that time, there was no man nor mother's son in the whole world, who durst use him so ill as captain Oakhum had done. Then he acquainted us with the dialogue that passed between them, as I have already related it; and had no sooner finished this narration, than he received a message from the

---

① Blood and oons:此处是委婉语,其完整的表达是"Christ's blood and wounds"。

② Bashaw:是土耳其语 pasha 的变体形式,这里表示"小暴君"。亨利·菲尔丁在其《里斯本航海日记》(*The Journal of a Voyage to Lisbon*,1755)中多次使用了 bashaw 一词来形容船上残暴的指挥官。

surgeon, to bring the sick-list to the quarter-deck, for the captain had ordered all the patients thither to be reviewed. —This inhuman order shocked us extremely, as we knew it would be impossible to carry some of them on the deck, without imminent danger of their lives; but as we likewise knew it would be to no purpose for us to remonstrate against it, we repaired to the quarter-deck in a body, to see the extraordinary muster; Morgan observing by the way, that the captain was going to send to the other world, a great many evidences to testify against himself. When we appeared upon deck, the captain bid the doctor, who stood bowing at his right hand, look at these lazy, lubberly sons of bitches, who were good for nothing no board, but to eat the king's provision, and encourage idleness in the skulker. — The surgeon grinned approbation, and taking the list, began to examine the complaints of each as they could crawl to the place appointed. —The first who came under his cognizance, was a poor fellow just feed of a fever, which had weakened him so much, that he could hardly stand. —Mr. Macshane (for that was the doctor's name) having felt his pulse, protested he was as well as any man in the world; and the captain delivered him over to the boatswain's mate, with orders that he should receive a round dozen at the gangway immediately, for counterfeiting himself sick when he was not; —but before the discipline could be executed, the man dropt down on the deck, and had well nigh perished under the hands of the executioner. —The next patient to be considered, laboured under a quartan ague①, and being then, in his interval of health, discovered no other symptoms of distemper, than a pale meager countenance, and emaciated body; upon which, he was declared fit for duty, and turned over to the boatswain; —but being resolved to disgrace the doctor, died upon the forecastle next day, during his cold fit. —The third complained of a pleuritic stitch②, and spitting of blood, for which doctor Mackshane prescribed exercise at the pump to promote expectoration; but whether this was improper for one in his situation, or that it was used to excess, I know not, but in less than half an hour, he was suffocated with a deluge of blood that issued from his lungs. —A fourth, with much difficulty climbed to the quarter-deck, being loaded with a monstrous ascites③ or dropsy, that invaded his chest so much, he could scarce fetch his breath; but his disease being interpreted into fat, occasioned by idleness and excess of eating, he was ordered, with a view to promote perspiration and enlarge his chest, to go aloft immediately: It was in vain for this unwieldy wretch, to allege his utter incapacity, the boatswain's driver④ was commanded to whip him up with a cat and nine tails: The smart of this application made him exert himself so much,

---

① quartan ague:【医】三日疟。
② pleuritic stitch:【医】肋膜性缝合。
③ ascites:【医】腹水。
④ the boatswain's driver:通常指执行水手长任何有关处罚命令的人。

that he actually arrived at the foot-hook-shrouds[①], but when the enormous weight of his body had nothing else to support it than his weakened arms, either out of spite or necessity, he quitted his hold, and plumped into the sea, where he must have been drowned, had not a sailor who was in a boat along-side, saved his life, by keeping him afloat, till he was hoisted on board by a tackle —It would be tedious and disagreeable to describe the fate of every miserable object that suffered by the inhumanity and ignorance of the captain and surgeon, who so wantonly sacrificed the lives of their fellow-creatures. Many were brought up in the height of fevers, and rendered delirious by the presence of their inspectors; and others, who were ordered to their duty, languished a few days at work, among their fellows, and then departed without any ceremony. —On the whole, the number of sick was reduced to less than a dozen; and the authors of this reduction were applauding themselves for the service they had done to their king and country, when the boatswain's mate informed his honour, that there was a man below lashed to his hammock by the leased; affirming, he had been so maltreated only for a grudge Mr. Morgan bore to him, and that he was as much in his senses as any man aboard. —The captain hearing this, darted a severe look at the Welchman, and ordered the man to be brought up immediately: Upon which, Morgan protested with great fervency, that the person in question was as mad as a March-hare; and begged for the love of Cot, they would at least keep his arms pinioned during his examination, to prevent him from doing mischief. —This request the commander granted for his own sake, and the patient was produced, who insisted upon his being in his right wits with such calmness and strength of argument, that every body present was inclined to believe him, except Morgan, who affirmed there was no trusting to appearances; for he himself had been so much imposed upon by his behaviour two days before, that he had actually unbound him with his own hands, and had well nigh been murdered for his pains: this was confirmed by the evidence of one of the waiters, who declared, he had pulled this patient from the doctor's mate, whom he had gotten down and almost strangled. —To this the man answered, that the witness was a creature of Morgan's, and was suborned to give his testimony against him by the malice of the mate, whom the defendant had affronted, by discovering to the people on board, that Mr. Morgan's wife kept a gin-shop in Rag Fair.[②]—This anecdote produced a laugh at the expense of the Welchman, who shaking his head with some emotion, said, "Ay, ay, 'tis no matter, —Cot knows, it is an arrant falsehood." —Captain Oakhum, without any further hesitation, ordered the fellow to be unfettered; at the same time, threatening to make Morgan exchange situations with him for his spite; but the Briton no sooner heard the

---

① foot-hook-shrouds：现在的通常用法是"futtock shrouds"，意为"连接上下桅的铁索"。

② Rag Fair：位于罗斯玛丽巷(现在的皇家铸币厂街)，是一个出售低俗物品的肮脏之地。

decision in favour of the madman, than he got up the mizen-shrouds, crying to Thomson and me to get out of his reach, for we should see him play the devil with a vengeance. We did not think fit to disregard this caution, and accordingly got up on the poop, whence we beheld the maniac (as soon as he was released) fly at the captain like a fury, crying, "I'll let you know, you scoundrel, that I am commander of this vessel" —and pummel him without mercy. The surgeon, who went to the assistance of his patron, shared the same fate; and it was with the utmost difficulty, that he was mastered at last, after having done great execution among those who opposed him.

▶扩展阅读

1. Bourgeois, S. *Nervous Juyces and the Feeling Heart: The Growth of Sensibility in the Novels of Tobias Smollett*. New York: Peter Lang Inc., 1986.

2. Douglas, A. *Uneasy Sensations: Smollett and the Body*. Chicago: The University of Chicago Press, 1995.

3. Kelly, L. Ed. *Tobias Smollett: The Critical Heritage*. London: Routledge, 1987.

4. Rousseau, G. S. *Tobias Smollett: Essays of Two Decades*. Edinburgh: T. & T. Clark, 1982.

5. Fasick, L. & Spector, R. D. "Smollett's Women: A Study in an Eighteenth-Century Masculine Sensibility". *South Atlantic Review*, 60 (4):149, 1994.

▶学习参考网站

1. http://www.enotes.com/literary-criticism/smollett-tobias-george
2. http://www.novelguide.com/a/discover/ewb_14/ewb_14_06028.html
3. http://www.booksfromscotland.com/Authors/Tobias-Smollett
4. http://en.wikisource.org/wiki/Smollett,_Tobias_George_(DNB00)

【邵 琦 编注】

6. Samuel Taylor Coleridge: "The Rime of the Ancient Mariner"

　　塞缪尔·泰勒·柯勒律治（Samuel Taylor Coleridge，1772—1834），英国诗人、评论家，英国浪漫主义文学的奠基人之一。柯勒律治 1772 年出生于英格兰德文郡，他的父亲是一名牧师，也是当地一所文法学校的校长。8 岁那年父亲去世，之后他被送去慈善学校基督医院学习，在那里度过了孤独的少年时代。1791 年柯勒律治考入剑桥大学学习，1793 年弃学从军，但因不适应军队的严格训练，于 1794 年退伍，同年返回剑桥大学学习，但最终没能获得学位。在大学期间，他结识了诗人罗伯特·骚塞（Robert Southey，1774—1843），两人曾计划在美国建立一个"大同社会"，但最终未能付诸实践。1795 年柯勒律治搬到英格兰西部湖区居住，与威廉·华兹华斯（William Wordsworth，1770—1850）相识，这成为他文学道路上的一个重要转折点。他与华兹华斯、骚塞被称为"湖畔派诗人"（Lake Poets）。柯勒律治的文学生涯大致可划分为四个阶段：

　　一是创作前期（1794—1796），这一时期他一度热衷于政治革命，曾到安格尔西岛宣传"大同社会"理念。1795 年柯勒律治在布利斯托举办了婚礼，而且把蜜月安排在海滨小镇克利文顿，那里可远眺海峡，海岸步道激发了他的创作灵感。这一时期的诗作多为友情诗或"谈话诗"，主要作品有《风瑟》（"The Eolian Harp"，1795）、《杂诗》（"Poems on Various Subjects"，1796）及与骚塞合写的剧本《罗伯斯庇尔的失败》（*The Fall of Robespierre*，1794）。

　　二是创作黄金期（1797—1801），这一时期柯勒律治和华兹华斯结为密友，两人经常在风景如画的湖区海滨山脚下边，散步谈诗论艺。柯勒律治还曾于 1798 年远航去德国，途中记录了许多海上逸事。他大部分传世名篇都是在这一阶段完成的，诗歌类型主要是象征诗和神秘诗。主要作品有《忽必烈汗》（"Kubla Khan"，1797）、《古舟子咏》（"The Rime of the Ancient Mariner"，1798）和《克里斯特贝尔》（"Christabel"，1797—1800），这三部诗作被称为"魔幻三杰作"；此外他还与华兹华斯合著了《抒情歌谣集》（*Lyrical Ballads*，1798）。

　　三是转型积累期（1802—1810），这期间柯勒律治开始独自环湖旅行。1803 年柯勒律治远航去了海滨城市朴次茅斯，随后经直布罗陀海峡到达马耳他，之后又航行至西西里岛。当时海上私掠猖獗，英国商船屡遭敌对国家私掠船的掠夺，远航时常需皇家海军舰队护航。庞大的船队航行阵列一度引起了柯勒律治对海洋的研究兴趣，但好友华兹华斯的弟弟约翰·华兹华斯（John Wordsworth，1772—1805）航海失事遇难的消息令他对海洋顿生恐惧，随后他去了罗马,转乘美国航船回到了英国,途中还因遇西班牙私掠船遗失了大部分的创作资料。这一阶段他的游历较丰富但创作不多,《悲戚颂》("Dejection: An Ode", 1802)是这一时期的主要作品。

四是创作晚期(1811—1834),柯勒律治的文学批评讲学生涯也是从这一时期开始的。除诗歌创作外,他还撰写了许多哲学、神学和文学理论著作,代表作品有《文学传记》(*Biographia Literaria*, 1817)、《俗人的布道》(*Layman Sermons*, 1816—1817)、《柯氏莎士比亚论集》(*Coleridge's Shakespearean Criticism*, 1818)和《反省指南》(*Aids to Reflections*, 1825)等。他晚年常在海滨度假,1834年病逝。柯勒律治的作品想象力丰富,语言朴素;他的诗学理论分析深刻,见解独到,这些都奠定了他在英国文学史上的重要地位。

柯勒律治曾多次远航,并常年居住于湖畔海滨之地,他的海洋诗歌想象奇特,色彩瑰丽,充满幻觉和诡谲的意象,折射出柯勒律治作为英国浪漫主义代表"诗人"和"神学家"重叠的身影。《古舟子咏》是其最著名的传世之作,这是一首以中世纪歌谣体写成的叙事长诗。最初华兹华斯和柯勒律治计划共同完成,后来华兹华斯放弃了共同创作,由柯勒律治一人完成。故事创作的灵感源于柯勒律治朋友的一个奇异而荒诞的梦,华兹华斯以船长乔治·歇尔弗柯的《环球航行——南海记》("Voyage round the World by the Way of the Great South Sea", 1726)为原题材,在此基础上作了某些变更。这首诗写一位老水手在航行途中杀死了一只信天翁,因而受到了南极精灵的报复,同船的两百名水手全部丧生。因两个幽灵的打赌,老水手免于一死,但却要忍受两百具尸体怨恨目光的折磨,直到他祝福另一个小生物——水蛇之后,精灵才原谅了他。之后在死人的共同努力下,老水手侥幸回到故乡,但是他必须向别人讲述自己的痛苦经历才能减轻痛苦从而生活下去。该诗通过对罪与罚的因果关系的探讨,宣扬一切生物皆由上帝创造,应该相互爱护。这一思想虽然神秘却有明显的生态主义特征。诗歌叙事节奏明快,节律简朴明朗,同时还结合了当时流行的哥特式传奇的凄厉气氛和超自然因素,向读者展现了一个奇幻的航海故事。这首诗在创作中梦幻与现实交错,意象情景交融,神秘、诡谲、恐怖、朦胧以及它的音乐性,无不给读者以强烈的美感。以下选段是《古舟子咏》中的前三部分,讲述了老水手不顾好生之德杀死了信天翁,随后老水手及其同伴遭遇了一系列的厄运,幽灵的骰子决定了众水手的死亡和老水手的幸存。

The Rime of the Ancient Mariner

▶Part 1

It is an ancient mariner,
And he stopped one of three.
—"By thy long grey beard and glittering eye,
Now wherefore stopp'st thou me?

The Bridegroom's doors are opened wide,

And I am next of kin；
The guests are met，the feast is set：
May'st hear the merry din."

He holds him with his skinny hand，
"There was a ship," quoth he.
"Hold off! unhand me，grey-beard loon!"
Eftsoons his hand dropt he.

He holds him with his glittering eye—
The Wedding-Guest stood still，
And listens like a three-years' child：
The Mariner hath his will.

The Wedding-Guest sat on a stone：
He cannot choose but hear；
And thus spake on that ancient man，
The bright-eyed Mariner.

"The ship was cheered，the harbour cleared，
Merrily did we drop
Below the kirk，below the hill，
Below the lighthouse top.

The sun came up upon the left，
Out of the sea came he!
And he shone bright，and on the right
Went down into the sea.

Higher and higher every day，
Till over the mast at noon—"
The Wedding-Guest here beat his breast，
For he heard the loud bassoon.

The bride hath paced into the hall，
Red as a rose is she；
Nodding their heads before her goes
The merry minstrelsy.

The Wedding-Guest he beat his breast，
Yet he cannot choose but hear；

And thus spake on that ancient man,
The bright-eyed Mariner.

"And now the STORM-BLAST came, and he
Was tyrannous and strong:
He struck with his o'ertaking wings,
And chased us south along.

With sloping masts and dipping prow,
As who pursued with yell and blow
Still treads the shadow of his foe,
And forward bends his head,
The ship drove fast, loud roared the blast,
And southward aye we fled.

And now there came both mist and snow,
And it grew wondrous cold:
And ice, mast-high, came floating by,
As green as emerald.

And through the drifts the snowy clifts
Did send a dismal sheen:
Nor shapes of men nor beasts we ken—
The ice was all between.

The ice was here, the ice was there,
The ice was all around:
It cracked and growled, and roared and howled,
Like noises in a swound!

At length did cross an Albatross,
Thorough the fog it came;
As if it had been a Christian soul,
We hailed it in God's name.

It ate the food it ne'er had eat,
And round and round it flew.
The ice did split with a thunder-fit;
The helmsman steered us through!

And a good south wind sprung up behind;

The Albatross did follow,
And every day, for food or play,
Came to the mariner's hollo!

In mist or cloud, on mast or shroud,
It perched for vespers nine;
Whiles all the night, through fog-smoke white,
Glimmered the white Moon-shine."

"God save thee, ancient Mariner!
From the fiends, that plague thee thus! —
Why look'st thou so?" —With my cross-bow
I shot the ALBATROSS.

▶ Part 2

The Sun now rose upon the right:
Out of the sea came he,
Still hid in mist, and on the left
Went down into the sea.

And the good south wind still blew behind,
But no sweet bird did follow,
Nor any day for food or play
Came to the mariners' hollo!

And I had done an hellish thing,
And it would work 'em woe:
For all averred, I had killed the bird
That made the breeze to blow.
Ah wretch! said they, the bird to slay,
That made the breeze to blow!

Nor dim nor red, like God's own head,
The glorious Sun uprist:
Then all averred, I had killed the bird
That brought the fog and mist.
'Twas right, said they, such birds to slay,
That bring the fog and mist.

The fair breeze blew, the white foam flew,
The furrow followed free;
We were the first that ever burst
Into that silent sea.

Down dropt the breeze, the sails dropt down,
'Twas sad as sad could be;
And we did speak only to break
The silence of the sea!

All in a hot and copper sky,
The bloody Sun, at noon,
Right up above the mast did stand,
No bigger than the Moon.

Day after day, day after day,
We stuck, nor breath nor motion;
As idle as a painted ship
Upon a painted ocean.

Water, water, every where,
And all the boards did shrink;
Water, water, every where,
Nor any drop to drink.

The very deep did rot: O Christ!
That ever this should be!
Yea, slimy things did crawl with legs
Upon the slimy sea.

About, about, in reel and rout
The death-fires① danced at night;
The water, like a witch's oils②,
Burnt green, and blue and white.

And some in dreams assured were
Of the Spirit that plagued us so;

---

① death fire：即水手所说的圣爱尔莫之火，也就是海面上的磷光。相传这种磷光出现，船上就会有人死亡。

② witch's oils：西方迷信，女巫要在大锅里熬煮毒虫，借熬出的毒油才能作法。

Nine fathom deep he had followed us[①]
From the land of mist and snow.

And every tongue，through utter drought，
Was withered at the root；
We could not speak，no more than if
We had been choked with soot.

Ah! well a-day! what evil looks
Had I from old and young!
Instead of the cross，the Albatross
About my neck was hung.

▶**Part 3**

There passed a weary time. Each throat
Was parched，and glazed each eye.
A weary time! a weary time!
How glazed each weary eye，
When looking westward，I beheld
A something in the sky.

At first it seemed a little speck，
And then it seemed a mist；
It moved and moved，and took at last
A certain shape，I wist.

A speck，a mist，a shape，I wist!
And still it neared and neared：
As if it dodged a water-sprite，
It plunged and tacked and veered.

With throats unslaked，with black lips baked，
We could nor laugh nor wail；
Through utter drought all dumb we stood!
I bit my arm，I sucked the blood，
And cried，A sail! a sail!

---

① Nine fathom deep he had followed us：这里指的是南极精灵。它很爱那死去的信天翁，信天翁被无辜射死，南极精灵便约了几个鬼伴，在船下九英寻深处一直跟踪，伺机为屈死的信天翁报仇。

With throats unslaked, with black lips baked,
Agape they heard me call:
Gramercy! they for joy did grin,
And all at once their breath drew in,
As they were drinking all.

See! see! (I cried) she tacks no more!
Hither to work us weal;
Without a breeze, without a tide,
She steadies with upright keel!

The western wave was all a-flame
The day was well nigh done!
Almost upon the western wave
Rested the broad bright Sun;
When that strange shape drove suddenly
Betwixt us and the Sun.

And straight the Sun was flecked with bars,
(Heaven's Mother send us grace!)
As if through a dungeon-grate he peered
With broad and burning face.

Alas! (thought I, and my heart beat loud)
How fast she nears and nears!
Are those *her* sails that glance in the Sun,
Like restless gossamers!

Are those *her* ribs through which the Sun
Did peer, as through a grate?
And is that Woman all her crew?
Is that a DEATH? and are there two?
Is DEATH that woman's mate?

Her lips were red, *her* looks were free,
Her locks were yellow as gold:
Her skin was as white as leprosy,

The Night-Mare LIFE-IN-DEATH[①] was she,
Who thicks man's blood with cold.

The naked hulk alongside came,
And the twain were casting dice;
"The game is done! I've won! I've won!"
Quoth she, and whistles thrice.
The Sun's rim dips; the stars rush out:
At one stride comes the dark;
With far-heard whisper, o'er the sea.
Off shot the spectre-bark.

We listened and looked sideways up!
Fear at my heart, as at a cup,
My life-blood seemed to sip!
The stars were dim, and thick the night,
The steersman's face by his lamp gleamed white;
From the sails the dew did drip—
Till clomb above the eastern bar
The horned Moon, with one bright star
Within the nether tip[②].

One after one, by the star-dogged Moon
Too quick for groan or sigh,
Each turned his face with a ghastly pang,
And cursed me with his eye.

Four times fifty living men,
(And I heard nor sigh nor groan)
With heavy thump, a lifeless lump,
They dropped down one by one.

The souls did from their bodies fly, —
They fled to bliss or woe!
And every soul, it passed me by,

---

① LIFE-IN-DEATH:诗人把"死中生"写成生与死糅合一起的形象,红唇金发而皮肤病态苍白,用以代表死亡,预示老水手今后要过一种生不如死的人生。

② with one bright star within the nether tip:水手们迷信,认为月牙儿下面出现一颗星是不祥之兆,必将发生大不幸之事。

Like the whizz of my CROSS-BOW!

▶扩展阅读

1. Ashto，R. *The Life of Samuel Taylor Coleridge*. Oxford：Blackwell，1996.

2. Byatt，A. S. *Unruly Times：Wordsworth and Coleridge in Their Time*. London：Vintage，1997.

3. Ford，J. *Coleridge on Dreaming*. London：Cambridge University Press，1998.

4. Hill，J. S. *A Coleridge Companion*. London：Macmillan Press，1983.

5. Perry，S. *Samuel Taylor Coleridge*. Shanghai：Shanghai Foreign Language Education Press，2009.

▶学习参考网站

1. http：// en.wikipedia.org/wiki/Samuel_Taylor_Coleridge

2. http：// www.online-literature.com/coleridge/

3. http：// www.poets.org/poet.php/prmPID/292

4. http：// www.literaryhistory.com/19thC/COLERIDGE.htm

5. http：// classicauthors.net/Coleridge/

【李　莉　编注】

7. Frederick Marryat: Mr. Midshipman Easy

弗雷德里克·马里亚特（Frederick Marryat，1792—1848），英国小说家，1792 年生于伦敦，父亲是国会议员，也是当时英国在格林纳达岛的殖民代理人；他母亲是一名德国后裔。马里亚特幼时因不喜欢学校的老师和校长曾多次逃学。他 14 岁时就加入英国皇家海军，由此开始了人生中的航海生涯。在历时 25 年漫长的远航经历中，马里亚特曾到过世界很多地方，还参加了许多战役，战绩卓著。他的海上生涯大致可分成三个阶段：一是作为一名海军候补生在英国舰队服役的时期（1806—1809）；二是由海军中尉晋升为海军中校的时期（1810—1819），其间他在圣赫勒拿岛附近巡航以防止拿破仑逃跑，也曾巡航至百慕大；三是升任上校的时期（1820—1830），1820 年他获悉拿破仑死讯后，赶赴圣赫勒拿岛并成功绘制了拿破仑的遗像。之后，马里亚特参加了第一次英缅战争，还奉命驻守了百慕大地区（1820—1830）。他的后期海上生活主要是在大西洋的群岛间执行搜寻任务。

　　孤独的航海生活令他逐渐对航海产生了厌倦，他转而从事小说创作。1829 年他的第一部小说《海军军官》（*The Naval Officer*）问世；次年他便以海军上校军衔引退，全身心投入小说创作，开始了人生的另一个重要阶段。他的文学创作主要分为两个时期：一是创作高峰期（1830—1839）。退役后的马里亚特曾任《大都会》（*The Metropolitan*）杂志的编辑，其间曾在美国和加拿大生活了两年。这一时期的作品具有鲜明的时代特征，反映的是家庭成员关系和社会身份地位等问题，但故事多半根据马里亚特的海上见闻写成。小说主人公通常是一些爱惹麻烦的年轻人，在冒险（特别是航海历险）的过程中不断成熟。他的主要作品有《傻子彼得》（*Peter Simple*，1834）、《忠实的雅各布》（*Jacob Faithful*，1834）、《海军候补生易齐先生》（*Mr. Midshipman Easy*，1836）、《海盗》（*The Pirate*，1836）、《幽灵船》（*The Phantom Ship*，1839）和《美国日记》（*Diary in America*，1939）等。这些海洋小说后来深受康拉德和海明威的喜爱。二是创作转型期（1840—1848）。这一时期马里亚特回到了伦敦，与克拉克森·斯坦菲尔德、赛缪尔·罗杰斯以及查尔斯·狄更斯等作家交往甚密，由于成就突出他还被授予了"皇家学会会员"的称号。也正是在这一时期，马里亚特开始了儿童文学创作。这一时期的作品主题大多以海难遭遇、荒岛或丛林历险为主，主要作品有《马斯特曼·雷迪》（*Masterman Ready*，1841）、《加拿大定居者》（*Settlers in Canada*，1844）、《任务》（*The Mission*，1845）、《新森林的孩子们》（*The Children of the New Forest*，1847）。马里亚特于 1848 年病逝，他的最后一部鲁滨孙式的小说《小野人》（*The Little Savage*，1848）后来由其儿子弗兰西斯·塞缪尔·马里亚特(Francis Samuel Marryat)完成。马里亚特的作品情节曲折,文笔流畅幽默,人物形象惟妙惟肖,尤其是他铺设紧张事件的技巧在当时几乎无人可及,他的作品亦被后人视为海洋小说的典范。

马里亚特写过许多海洋历险小说,他的个人航海经历也可在其作品中窥见一斑。在他的小说中,海洋既是检阅主人公品格的理想场所,又是自然美的化身。《海军候补生易齐先生》是马里亚特最优秀、最畅销的作品,描述的是19世纪早期拿破仑战争时代的海军生活。小说以作者自己的航海冒险经历和真实历史事件为素材,对海上战役、法国监狱以及海军候补生的生活进行了生动的描写。小说主人公杰克·易齐家境富裕,备受宠爱,在父亲的影响下,自幼信奉人人平等的哲学,且随时为捍卫这一观点与他人辩论,后在其父亲朋友的游说下开始了皇家海军生活。他在船上经历了一系列的冒险,目睹了军舰上的残酷及有悖他生活信念的海军等级制度,并逐渐接受了权威和等级的概念。在小说中,马里亚特塑造了一群幽默风趣的人物,虽说表现手法稍显粗糙,但人物刻画的生动性丝毫不逊于狄更斯。这部小说的最大特点是其语言的轻松和幽默。作者通过第三人称的叙述手法,以讽刺幽默的口吻描写了军舰上的生活,每一个场景读来都令人忍俊不禁。不过,马里亚特在作品中对"人人平等"和"等级社会"这两个截然不同的观点却并未表明自己的立场。以下选段摘自《海军候补生易齐先生》第一部分第十章,描述了主人公初次登上甲板,目睹军舰上水兵恃强凌弱的情景。

▶**Chapter 10**

Showing How Jack Transgresses Against His Own Philosophy

When Jack Easy had gained the deck, he found the sun shining gaily, a soft air blowing from the shore, and the whole of the rigging[①] and every part of the ship loaded with the shirts, trousers, and jackets of the seamen, which had been wetted during the heavy gale, and were now hanging up to dry; all the wet sails were also spread on the booms or triced up in the rigging, and the ship was slowly forging through the blue water. The captain and first-lieutenant[②] were standing on the gangway in converse, and the majority of the officers were with their quadrants[③] and sextants[④] ascertaining the latitude at noon. The decks were white and clean, the sweepers had just laid by their brooms, and the men were busy coiling down the ropes. It was a scene of cheerfulness, activity, and order, which lightened his heart after the four days of suffering, close air, and confinement, from which he had just

---

① the rigging:船缆。
② first-lieutenant:海军中尉。
③ quadrants:航海四分仪。
④ sextants:航海六分仪。

emerged.

The captain, who perceived him, beckoned to him, asked him kindly how he felt; the first lieutenant also smiled upon him, and many of the officers, as well as his messmates, congratulated him upon his recovery. The captain's steward came up to him, touched his hat, and requested the pleasure of his company to dinner in the cabin. Jack was the essence of politeness, took off his hat, and accepted the invitation. Jack was standing on a rope which a seaman was coiling down; the man touched his hat and requested he would be so kind as to take his foot off. Jack took his hat off his head in return, and his foot off the rope. The master touched his hat, and reported twelve o'clock to the first lieutenant—the first lieutenant touched his hat, and reported twelve o'clock to the captain—the captain touched his hat, and told the first lieutenant to make it so. The officer of the watch touched his hat, and asked the captain whether they should pipe to dinner—the captain touched his hat and said, "If you please."

The midshipman received his orders, and touched his hat, which he gave to the head boatswain's mate①, who touched his hat, and then the calls whistled cheerily.

"Well," thought Jack, "politeness seems to be the order of the day, and every one has an equal respect for the other." Jack stayed on deck; he peeped through the ports, which were open, and looked down into the deep blue wave; he cast his eyes aloft, and watched the tall spars sweeping and tracing with their points, as it were, a small portion of the clear sky, as they acted in obedience to the motion of the vessel; he looked forward at the range of carronades② which lined the sides of the deck, and then he proceeded to climb one of the carronades, and lean over the hammocks to gaze on the distant land.

"Young gentleman, get off those hammocks," cried the master, who was officer of the watch, in a surly tone. Jack looked round.

"Do you hear me, sir? I'm speaking to you," said the master again.

Jack felt very indignant, and he thought that politeness was not quite so general as he supposed.

It happened that Captain Wilson was upon deck.

"Come here, Mr. Easy," said the captain; "it is a rule in the service, that no one gets on the hammocks, unless in case of emergency—I never do—nor the first lieutenant—nor any of the officers or men—therefore, upon the principle of equality, you must not do it either."

"Certainly not, sir," replied Jack, "but still I do not see why that officer in the shining

---

① boatswain's mate：副水手长。

② carronade：(旧时一种装在船上宜于近距离射击的)臼炮。

hat should be so angry, and not speak to me as if I were a gentleman, as well as himself."

"I have already explained that to you, Mr. Easy."

"Oh, yes, I recollect now, it's zeal; but this zeal appears to me to be the only unpleasant thing in the service. It's a pity, as you said, that the service cannot do without it."

Captain Wilson laughed, and walked away; and shortly afterwards, as he turned up and down the deck with the master, he hinted to him that he should not speak so sharply to a lad who had committed such a trifling error through ignorance. Now Mr. Smallsole, the master, who was a surly sort of a personage, and did not like even a hint of disapprobation of his conduct, although very regardless of the feeling of others, determined to pay this off on Jack, the very first convenient opportunity. Jack dined in the cabin, and was very much pleased to find that every one drank wine with him, and that everybody at the captain's table appeared to be on an equality. Before the dessert had been on the table five minutes, Jack became loquacious on his favourite topic; all the company stared with surprise at such an unheard-of doctrine being broached on board of a man-of-war; the captain argued the point, so as to controvert, without too much offending, Jack's notions, laughing the whole time that the conversation was carried on.

It will be observed, that this day may be considered as the first in which Jack really made his appearance on board, and it also was on this first day that Jack made known, at the captain's table, his very peculiar notions. If the company at the captain's table, which consisted of the second lieutenant, purser, Mr. Jolliffe, and one of the midshipmen, were astonished at such heterodox opinions being started in the presence of the captain, they were equally astonished at the cool, good-humoured ridicule with which they were received by Captain Wilson. The report of Jack's boldness, and every word and opinion that he had uttered (of course much magnified) was cirulated that evening through the whole ship; it was canvassed in the gun-room by the officers, it was descanted upon by the midshipmen as they walked the deck; the captain's steward held a levee abreast of the ship's funnel, in which he narrated this new doctrine. The sergeant of marines gave his opinion in his berth that it was damnable. The boatswain talked over the matter with the other warrant officers, till the grog was all gone, and then dismissed it as too dry a subject; and it was the general opinion of the ship's company, that as soon as they arrived at Gibraltar Bay[①], our hero would bid adieu to the service, either by being sentenced to death by a court-martial, or by being dismissed, and towed on shore on a grating. Others, who had more of the wisdom of the serpent, and who had been informed by Mr. Sawbridge that our hero was a lad who would inherit a large property, argued differently, and considered that Captain Wilson had

---

① Gibraltar Bay:(英国直属殖民地)直布罗陀湾。

very good reason for being so lenient—and among them was the second lieutenant. There were but four who were well inclined towards Jack—to wit, the captain, the first lieutenant, Mr. Jolliffe, the one-eyed master's mate, and Mephistopheles, the black, who, having heard that Jack had uttered such sentiments, loved him with all his heart and soul.

We have referred to the second lieutenant, Mr. Asper. This young man had a very high respect for birth, and particularly for money, of which he had very little. He was the son of an eminent merchant who, during the time that he was a midshipman, had allowed him a much larger sum for his expenses than was necessary or proper; and, during his career, he found that his full pocket procured him consequence, not only among his own messmates, but also with many of the officers of the ships that he sailed in. A man who is able and willing to pay a large tavern bill will always find followers—that is, to the tavern; and lieutenants did not disdain to dine, walk arm in arm, and be "hail fellow well met"[①] with a midshipman, at whose expense they lived during the time they were on shore. Mr. Asper had just received his commission and appointment, when his father became a bankrupt, and the fountain was dried up from which he had drawn such liberal supplies. Since that, Mr. Asper had felt that his consequence was gone: he could no longer talk about the service being a bore, or that he should give it up; he could no longer obtain that deference paid to his purse, and not to himself; and he had contracted very expensive habits, without having any longer the means of gratifying them. It was therefore no wonder that he imbibed a great respect for money; and, as he could no longer find the means himself, he was glad to pick up anybody else at whose cost he could indulge in that extravagance and expense to which he had been so long accustomed, and still sighed for. Now, Mr. Asper knew that our hero was well supplied with money, as he had obtained from the waiter the amount of the bill paid at the Fountain, and he had been waiting for Jack's appearance on deck to become his very dearest and most intimate friend. The conversation in the cabin made him feel assured that Jack would require and be grateful for support, and he had taken the opportunity of a walk with Mr. Sawbridge, to offer to take Jack in his watch. Whether it was that Mr. Sawbridge saw through the design of Mr. Asper, or whether he imagined that our hero would be better pleased with him than with the master, considering his harshness of deportment; or with himself, who could not, as first lieutenant, overlook any remission of duty, the offer was accepted, and Jack Easy was ordered, as he now entered upon his duties, to keep watch under Lieutenant Asper.

But not only was this the first day that Jack may be said to have appeared in the service, but it was the first day in which he had entered the midshipman's berth, and was made acquainted with his messmates.

---

① hail fellow well met (with): 与……一见如故。

We have already mentioned Mr. Jolliffe, the master's mate, but we must introduce him more particularly. Nature is sometimes extremely arbitrary, and never did she show herself more so than in insisting that Mr. Jolliffe should have the most sinister expression of countenance that ever had been looked upon.

He had suffered martyrdom with the small-pox, which probably had contracted his lineaments: his face was not only deeply pitted, but scarred, with this cruel disorder. One eye had been lost, and all eyebrows had disappeared—and the contrast between the dull, sightless opaque orb on one side of his face, and the brilliant, piercing little ball on the other, was almost terrifying. His nose had been eaten away by the disease till it formed a sharp but irregular point: part of the muscles of the chin were contracted, and it was drawn in with unnatural seams and puckers. He was tall, gaunt, and thin, seldom smiled, and when he did, the smile produced a still further distortion.

Mr. Jolliffe was the son of a warrant officer. He did not contract this disease until he had been sent out to the West Indies①, where it swept away hundreds. He had now been long in the service, with little or no chance of promotion. He had suffered from indigence, from reflections upon his humble birth, from sarcasms on his appearance. Every contumely had been heaped upon him at one time or another, in the ships in which he served; among a crowd he had found himself desolate—and now, although no one dared treat him to his face with disrespect, he was only respected in the service from a knowledge of his utility and exemplary performance of his duties—he had no friends or even companions. For many years he had retired within himself, he had improved by reading and study, had felt all the philanthropy of a Christian, and extended it towards others. Silent and reserved, he seldom spoke in the berth, unless his authority, as caterer, was called for; all respected Mr. Jolliffe, but no one liked, as a companion, one at whose appearance the very dogs would bark. At the same time every one acknowledged his correct behaviour in every point, his sense of justice, his forbearance, his kindness, and his good sense. With him life was indeed a pilgrimage, and he wended his way in all Christian charity and all Christian zeal.

In all societies, however small they may be, provided that they do but amount to half a dozen, you will invariably meet with a bully. And it is also generally the case that you will find one of that society who is more or less the butt. You will discover this even in occasional meetings, such as a dinner-party, the major part of which have never met before.

Previous to the removal of the cloth, the bully will have shown himself by his dictatorial manner, and will also have selected the one upon whom he imagines that he can best practise. In a midshipman's berth this fact has become almost proverbial, although now

① the West Indies:西印度群岛。

perhaps it is not attended with that disagreeable despotism which was permitted at the time that our hero entered the service.

The bully of the midshipman's berth of H. M. sloop *Harpy* was a young man about seventeen, with light, curly hair, and florid countenance, the son of the clerk in the dockyard at Plymouth, and his name was Vigors.

The butt was a pudding-face Tartar-physiognomied[①] boy of fifteen, whose intellects, with fostering, if not great, might at least have been respectable, had he not lost all confidence in his own powers from the constant jeers and mockeries of those who had a greater fluency of speech without perhaps so much real power of mind. Although slow, what he learned he invariably retained. This lad's name was Gossett. His father was a wealthy yeoman of Lynn, in Norfolk. There were at the time but three other midshipmen in the ship, of whom it can only be said that they were like midshipmen in general, with little appetite for learning, but good appetites for dinner, hating everything like work, fond of everything like fun, fighting—a l'outrance[②]—one minute, and sworn friends the next— with general principles of honour and justice, but which were occasionally warped according to circumstances; with all the virtues and vices so heterogeneously jumbled and heaped together, that it was almost impossible to ascribe any action to its true motive, and to ascertain to what point their vice was softened down into almost a virtue, and their virtues from mere excess degenerated into vice. Their names were O'Connor, Mills, and Gascoigne. The other shipmates of our hero it will be better to introduce as they appear on the stage.

After Jack had dined in the cabin he followed his messmates Jolliffe and Gascoigne down into the midshipmen's berth.

"I say, Easy," observed Gascoigne, "you are a devilish free and easy sort of a fellow, to tell the captain that you considered yourself as great a man as he was."

"I beg your pardon," replied Jack, "I did not argue individually, but generally, upon the principles of the rights of man."

"Well," replied Gascoigne, "it's the first time I ever heard a middy do such a bold thing; take care your rights of man don't get you in the wrong box—there's no arguing on board of a man-of-war. The captain took it amazingly easy, but you'd better not broach that subject too often."

"Gascoigne gives you very good advice, Mr. Easy," observed Jolliffe; "allowing that your ideas are correct, which it appears to me they are not, or at least impossible to be acted upon, there is such a thing as prudence, and however much this question may be canvassed

---

① a pudding-face Tartar-physiognomied：面孔扁圆呆板，像鞑靼人的面相。

② a l'outrance：【法】你死我活的，死而后已的。

on shore, in his Majesty's service it is not only dangerous in itself, but will be very prejudicial to you."

"Man is a free agent," replied Easy.

"I'll be shot if a midshipman is," replied Gascoigne, laughing, "and that you'll soon find."

"And yet it was the expectation of finding that equality that I was induced to come to sea."

"On the first of April, I presume," replied Gascoigne. "But are you really serious?"

Hereupon Jack entered into a long argument, to which Jolliffe and Gascoigne listened without interruption, and Mesty with admiration: at the end of it, Gascoigne laughed heartily and Jolliffe sighed.

"From whence did you learn all this?" inquired Jolliffe.

"From my father, who is a great philosopher, and has constantly upheld these opinions."

"And did your father wish you to go to sea?"

"No, he was opposed to it," replied Jack, "but of course he could not combat my rights and free-will."

"Mr. Easy, as a friend," replied Jolliffe, "I request that you would as much as possible keep your opinions to yourself: I shall have an opportunity of talking to you on the subject, and will then explain to you my reasons."

As soon as Mr. Jolliffe had ceased, down came Mr. Vigors and O'Connor, who had heard the news of Jack's heresy.

"You do not know Mr. Vigors and Mr. O'Connor," said Jolliffe to Easy.

Jack, who was the essence of politeness, rose and bowed, at which the others took their seats, without returning the salutation. Vigors had, from what he had heard and now seen of Easy, thought he had somebody else to play upon, and without ceremony he commenced.

"So, my chap, you are come on board to raise a mutiny here with your equality—you came off scot free at the captain's table; but it won't do, I can tell you, even in the midshipman's berth some must knock under, and you are one of them."

"If, sir," replied Easy, "you mean by knock under, that I must submit, I can assure you that you are mistaken. Upon the same principle that I would never play the tyrant to those weaker than myself, so will I resent oppression if attempted."

"Damme, but he's a regular sea lawyer already: however, my boy, we'll soon put your mettle to the proof."

"Am I then to infer that I am not on an equality with my messmates?" replied Jack, looking at Jolliffe. The latter was about to answer him, but Vigors interrupted.

"Yes, you are on an equality as far as this—that you have an equal right to the berth, if you are not knocked out of it for insolence to your masters; that you have an equal share to pay for the things purchased for the mess, and an equal right to have your share, provided you can get it; you have an equal right to talk, provided you are not told to hold your tongue. The fact is, you have an equal right with every one else to do as you can, get what you can, and say what you can, always provided that you can do it; for here the weakest goes to the wall①, and that is midshipmen's berth equality. Now, do you understand all that; or will you wait for a practical illustration?"

"I am then to infer that the equality here is as much destroyed as it even will be among savages, where the strong oppress the weak, and the only law is club law—in fact, much the same as it is at a public or large school on shore?"

"I suspect you are right for once. You were at a public school: how did they treat you there?"

"As you propose treating people here—'the weakest went to the wall.'"

"Well, then, a nod's as good as a wink to a blind horse, that's all, my hearty," said Vigors.

But the hands being turned up, "Shorten sail" put an end to the altercation for the present.

As our hero had not yet received orders to go to his duty, he remained below with Mesty.

"By de powers, Massa Easy, but I lub you with my hole soul," said Mesty.

"By Jasus, you really tark fine, Massa Easy; dat Mr. Vigor—nabber care for him, wouldn't you like him—and sure you would," continued the black, feeling the muscle of Jack's arm. "By the soul of my fader, I'd bet my week's allowance on you anyhow. Nabber be 'fraid, Massa Easy."

"I am not afraid," replied Jack; "I've thrashed bigger fellows than he;" and Jack's assertion was true. Mr. Bonnycastle never interfered in a fair fight, and took no notice of black eyes, provided the lessons were well said. Jack had fought and fought again, until he was a very good bruiser, and although not so tall as Vigors, he was much better built for fighting. A knowing Westminster boy would have bet his half-crown upon Jack, had he seen him and his anticipated adversary.

The constant battles which Jack was obliged to fight at school had been brought forward by Jack against his father's arguments in favour of equality, but they had been overruled by

---

① the weakest goes to the wall: 弱者受排挤。

Mr. Easy's pointing out that the combats of boys had nothing to do with the rights of man.

As soon as the watch was called, Vigors, O'Connor, Gossett, and Gascoigne, came down from the berth. Vigors, who was strongest in the berth, except Jolliffe, had successively had his superiority acknowledged, and, when on deck, he had talked of Easy's impertinence, and his intention of bringing him to his senses. The others, therefore, came down to see the fun.

"Well, Mr. Easy," observed Vigors, as he came into the berth, "you take after your name, at all events; I suppose you intend to eat the king's provision, and do nothing."

Jack's mettle was already up.

"You will oblige me, sir, by minding your own business," replied Jack.

"You impudent blackguard, if you say another word I'll give you a good thrashing, and knock some of your equality out of you."

"Indeed," replied Jack, who almost fancied himself back at Mr. Bonnycastle's; "we'll try that."

Whereupon Jack very coolly divested himself of his upper garments, neckerchief, and shirt, much to the surprise of Mr. Vigors, who little contemplated such a proof of decision and confidence, and still more to the delight of the other midshipmen, who would have forfeited a week's allowance to see Vigors well thrashed. Vigors, however, knew that he had gone too far to retreat; he therefore prepared for action; and, when ready, the whole party went out into the steerage to settle the business.

Vigors had gained his assumed authority more by bullying than fighting; others had submitted to him without a sufficient trial; Jack, on the contrary, had won his way up in school by hard and scientific combat: the result, therefore, may easily be imagined. In less than a quarter of an hour Vigors, beaten dead, with his eyes closed, and three teeth out, gave in; while Jack, after a basin of water, looked as fresh as ever, with the exception of a few trifling scratches.

The news of this victory was soon through the ship; and before Jack had resumed his clothes, it had been told confidentially by Sawbridge to the captain.

"So soon!" said Captain Wilson, laughing; "I expected that a midshipman's berth would do wonders; but I did not expect this, yet awhile. This victory is the first severe blow to Mr. Easy's equality, and will be more valuable than twenty defeats. Let him now go to his duty: he will soon find his level."

▶扩展阅读

1. Buster, A. *Captain Marryat*. Los Angeles: University of California Library, 1980.

2. Marryat, F. *Life and Letters of Captain Marryat*. London: R. Bentley & Son, 1872.

3. Pocock，T. *Captain Marryat：Seaman，Writer，and Adventurer*. London：Chatham，2000.

4. Sadleir，M. *Excursion in Victorian Bibliography*. London：Chaundy & Cox，1922.

5. Warner，O. *Captain Marryat：A Rediscovery*. London：Constable，1953.

▶学习参考网站

1. http：//en.wikipedia.org/wiki/Frederick_Marryat

2. http：//www.kirjasto.sci.fi/fmarryat.htm

3. http：//www.focusdep.com/biographies/Frederick/Marryat

4. http：//www.fantasticfiction.co.uk/m/frederick-marryat/

【王松林　编注】

8. Robert Michael Ballantyne: *The Coral Island*

  罗伯特・迈克尔・巴兰坦（Robert Michael Ballantyne，1825—1894），苏格兰作家，1825 年出身于爱丁堡印刷出版界的名门望族。16 岁时去往加拿大，在著名的哈德逊湾公司工作了六年。出于工作需要，他经常要到偏远的地区同土著印第安人做皮毛生意，历尽艰险。巴兰坦于是将自己在北美荒野的经历和思乡之情以书信的形式向家人叙述，这可以说是他写作生涯的开端。1847 年巴兰坦回到苏格兰，第二年出版处女作《哈德逊湾》(*Hudson's Bay*，or *Life in the Wilds of North America*，又名《北美荒野生活录》)。1856 年他弃商从文。1857 年《珊瑚岛》(*The Coral Island*)问世，作者对南太平洋风光的描写吸引了无数的读者，巴兰坦因此一举成名。但是，小说中大量关于椰子壳的细节描写却严重失真，这一失误促使作者开始身体力行以获取第一手资料。譬如，为了创作小说《救火》(*Fighting the Flames*，1867)，巴兰坦特意做了一段时间的伦敦消防员；为了创作反映矿工生活的小说《在深处》(*Deep Down*，1868)，他和康沃尔的锡矿工人同吃同住。可以说，巴兰坦的写作力求真实可信。他的作品涵盖的地理范围十分广泛，北国的冰川世界，南太平洋的热带风光，神秘的印第安部落，凶险的海上世界等无不在他的笔下呈现出来。他的作品涉猎面广，有对陆地和海洋动物（如狮子、大猩猩、野牛、鲸、海象等）捕猎的描述，也有关于船只、水手、大海、湖泊、河流、沼泽及北美大草原、安第斯山脉、食人岛等的绮丽风光的描写，更有迷失丛林、陷身海底等引人入胜的故事情节的叙述。巴兰坦给读者（尤其是青少年读者）创造了一个又一个神秘而精彩的想象世界。他有着惊人的创造力，一生共有近百部文学作品问世。在 1967 年出版的一本关于巴兰坦的传记中，作者埃里克・奎尔(Eric Quayle)曾评论道，几乎所有的年轻人都读过巴兰坦的历险故事，今天的父辈在听到这个 19 世纪作家的名字时，脑海中一定会浮现出那个弥漫着芬芳青春气息的珊瑚岛。值得一提的是，巴兰坦不仅是个小说家，还是个成功的艺术家，曾多次在苏格兰皇家学院展出自己的画作。巴兰坦晚年居住伦敦郊外的哈罗，1894 年因劳累过度前往意大利罗马疗养，最终在那里逝世，享年 69 岁。

  时至今日，巴兰坦渐渐淡出了读者的视线，只有《珊瑚岛》还为青少年读者所喜爱。因为威廉・戈尔丁的《蝇王》的缘故，《珊瑚岛》在评论家们眼里又有了新的意义。《珊瑚岛》描写了三个少年在南太平洋珊瑚岛上的经历。主人公拉尔夫从小热爱大自然，特别向往遥远神秘的珊瑚岛。他 15 岁时征得父亲的同意，乘船周游世界。船遇到暴风雨而失事，他和两个好友杰克和彼得金漂到珊瑚岛上,开始了一段难忘的历险生活。岛上奇特的生物景观、美妙的热带风光迷住了三个孩子,他们凭借自己的聪明才智在岛上获取食物,制造小船,探索海底世界,但他们很快发现生活并不像表面那么和平宁静,食人者的暴行使他们深感震惊和愤怒,他们不惜一切代价,勇敢机智地向受害者伸出了援救之手。最后三个少年终于找到机会,踏上了归乡之途。作品对人物性格的刻画细腻生动、栩栩如生。少年热爱生活、勇于探索、乐于助人的风貌给人留下了深刻的印象。作者写作语言亲切、朴素、生动,故事娓娓道来,深受少年读者的喜爱。海洋在这部小说中有着极为重要的作用,故事情节起于航程,归于航程,这中间的过程则是故事展开的空间。作者笔下的南太平洋海域风光旖旎,景色宜人,一切植物自然生长,没有污染,没有破坏;蔚蓝的海水清澈见底,这里是鱼儿们安全的栖身之所,也是孩子们水中嬉戏的天堂。三个少年互相关心,分工合作,团结一致,在岛上生活得非常惬意。小说虚拟的这种梦幻般的世界是以大海为背景来展开的。作者笔下的海洋和自然美景成为陶冶人物性情的场所。巴兰坦笔下的大海纯净、清澈、有着天然的亲和力。金灿灿的热带阳光、碧蓝的海水烘托了天真无邪的少年形象,带给读者美好的感受。以下选段出自《珊瑚岛》第五、七、十三、十六章,分别讲述了惊魂甫定的拉尔夫、彼得金和杰克落难珊瑚岛后一系列有趣的经历。

▶Chapter 5

(*Morning, and cogitations connected therewith—We luxuriate in the sea, try our diving powers, and make enchanting excursions among the coral groves at the bottom of the ocean— The wonders of the deep enlarged upon.*)

What a joyful thing it is to awaken on a fresh, glorious morning, and find the rising sun staring into your face with dazzling brilliancy! to hear the birds twittering in the bushes, and to hear the murmuring of a rill, or the soft, hissing ripples as they fall upon the seashore! At any time, and in any place, such sights and sounds are most charming; but more especially are they so when one awakens to them, for the first time, in a novel and romantic situation, with the soft, sweet air of a tropical climate mingling with the fresh smell of the sea, and stirring the strange leaves that flutter overhead and around one, or ruffling the plumage of the stranger birds that fly inquiringly around as if to demand what business we have to intrude uninvited on their domains. When I awoke on the morning after the shipwreck, I found myself in this most delightful condition; and as I lay on my back upon my bed of leaves, gazing up through the branches of the cocoa-nut trees into the clear blue sky, and watched the few fleecy clouds that passed slowly across it, my heart expanded more and more with an exulting gladness, the like of which I had never felt before. While I meditated, my thoughts again turned to the great and kind Creator of this beautiful world, as they had done on the previous day when I first beheld the sea and the coral reef, with the mighty waves dashing over it into the calm waters of the lagoon.

While thus meditating, I naturally bethought me of my *Bible*, for I had faithfully kept the promise which I gave at parting to my beloved mother—that I would read it every morning; and it was with a feeling of dismay that I remembered I had left it in the ship. I was much troubled about this. However, I consoled myself with reflecting that I could keep the second part of my promise to her—namely, that I should never omit to say my prayers. So I rose quietly lest I should disturb my companions, who were still asleep, and stepped aside into the bushes for this purpose.

On my return I found them still slumbering, so I again lay down to think over our situation. Just at that moment I was attracted by the sight of a very small parrot, which Jack afterwards told me was called a paroquet. It was seated on a twig that overhung Peterkin's head, and I was speedily lost in admiration of its bright-green plumage, which was mingled with other gay colours. While I looked I observed that the bird turned its head slowly from side to side and looked downwards, first with the one eye and then with the other. On glancing downwards I observed that Peterkin's mouth was wide open, and that this remarkable bird was looking into it. Peterkin used to say that I had not an atom of fun in my composition, and that I never could understand a joke. In regard to the latter, perhaps he was right; yet I think that, when they were explained to me, I understood jokes as well as most people. But in regard to the former, he must certainly have been wrong, for this bird seemed to me to be extremely funny; and I could not help thinking that if it should happen to faint, or slip its foot, and fall off the twig into Peterkin's mouth, he would perhaps think it funny too! Suddenly the paroquet bent down its head and uttered a loud scream in his face. This awoke him, and with a cry of surprise, he started up, while the foolish bird flew precipitately away.

"Oh, you monster!" cried Peterkin, shaking his fist at the bird. Then he yawned, and rubbed his eyes, and asked what o'clock it was.

I smiled at this question, and answered that, as our watches were at the bottom of the sea, I could not tell, but it was a little past sunrise.

Peterkin now began to remember where we were. As he looked up into the bright sky, and snuffed the scented air, his eyes glistened with delight, and he uttered a faint "Hurrah!" and yawned again. Then he gazed slowly round, till, observing the calm sea through an opening in the bushes, he started suddenly up as if he had received an electric shock, uttered a vehement shout, flung off his garments, and rushing over the white sands, plunged into the water. The cry awoke Jack, who rose on his elbow with a look of grave surprise; but this was followed by a quiet smile of intelligence on seeing Peterkin in the water. With an energy that he only gave way to in moments of excitement, Jack bounded to his feet, threw off his clothes, shook back his hair, and with a lion-like spring, dashed over the sands and plunged into the sea with such force as quite to envelop Peterkin in a shower of spray. Jack was a remarkably good swimmer and diver, so that after his plunge we saw no sign of him for nearly a minute, after which he suddenly emerged, with a cry of joy, a good many yards out from the shore. My spirits were so much raised by seeing all this that I, too, hastily threw off my garments and endeavoured to imitate Jack's vigorous bound; but I was so awkward that my foot caught on a stump, and I fell to the ground. Then I slipped on a stone while running over the sand and nearly fell again, much to the amusement of Peterkin, who laughed heartily and called me a "slow coach"; while Jack cried out, "Come along, Ralph, and I'll help you!" However, when I got into the water I managed very well; for I was really a good swimmer and diver too. I could not, indeed, equal Jack, who was superior to any Englishman I ever saw; but I infinitely surpassed Peterkin, who could only swim a little, and could not dive at all.

While Peterkin enjoyed himself in the shallow water and in running along the beach, Jack and I swam out into the deep water and occasionally dived for stones. I shall never forget my surprise and delight on first beholding the bottom of the sea. As I have before stated, the water within the reef was as calm as a pond; and as there was no wind, it was quite clear from the surface to the bottom, so that we could see down easily even at a depth of twenty or thirty yards. When Jack and I dived into shallower water we expected to have found sand and stones, instead of which we found ourselves in what appeared really to be an enchanted garden. The whole of the bottom of the lagoon, as we called the calm water within the reef, was covered with coral of every shape, size, and hue. Some portions were formed like large mushrooms; others appeared like the brain of a man, having stalks or necks attached to them; but the most common kind was a species of branching coral, and some portions were of a lovely pale-pink colour, others were pure white. Among this there grew large quantities of seaweed of the richest hues imaginable, and of the most graceful forms; while innumerable fishes—blue, red, yellow, green, and striped—sported in and out amongst the flower-beds of this submarine garden, and did not appear to be at all afraid of our approaching them.

On darting to the surface for breath after our first dive, Jack and I rose close to each other.

"Did you ever in your life, Ralph, see anything so lovely?" said Jack as he flung the spray from his hair.

"Never," I replied. "It appears to me like fairy realms. I can scarcely believe that we are not dreaming."

"Dreaming!" cried Jack. "Do you know, Ralph, I'm half-tempted to think that we really are dreaming! But if so, I am resolved to make the most of it and dream another dive; so here goes—down again, my boy!"

We took the second dive together, and kept beside each other while under water; and I was greatly surprised to find that we could keep down much longer than I ever recollect having done in our own seas at home. I believe that this was owing to the heat of the water, which was so warm that we afterwards found we could remain in it for two and three hours at a time without feeling any unpleasant effects such as we used to experience in the sea at home. When Jack reached the bottom, he grasped the coral stems and crept along on his hands and knees, peeping under the seaweed and among the rocks. I observed him, also, pick up one or two large oysters and retain them in his grasp, as if he meant to take them up with him; so I also gathered a few. Suddenly he made a grasp at a fish with blue and yellow stripes on its back, and actually touched its tail, but did not catch it. At this he turned towards me and attempted to smile; but no sooner had he done so than he sprang like an arrow to the surface, where, on following him, I found him gasping and coughing and spitting water from his mouth. In a few minutes he recovered, and we both turned to swim ashore.

"I declare, Ralph," said he, "that I actually tried to laugh under water!"

"So I saw," I replied; "and I observed that you very nearly caught that fish by the tail. It would have done capitally for breakfast, if you had."

"Breakfast enough here," said he, holding up the oysters as we landed and ran up the beach. —"Hallo, Peterkin! Here you are, boy! split open these fellows while Ralph and I put on our clothes. They'll agree with the cocoa-nuts excellently, I have no doubt."

Peterkin, who was already dressed, took the oysters and opened them with the edge of our axe, exclaiming, "Now, that's capital! There's nothing I'm so fond of."

"Ah! that's lucky," remarked Jack. "I'll be able to keep you in good order now, Master Peterkin. You know you can't dive any better than a cat. So, sir, whenever you behave ill you shall have no oysters for breakfast."

"I'm very glad that our prospect of breakfast is so good," said I, "for I'm very hungry."

"Here, then, stop your mouth with that, Ralph," said Peterkin, holding a large oyster to my lips. I opened my mouth and swallowed it in silence, and really it was remarkably good.

We now set ourselves earnestly about our preparations for spending the day. We had no difficulty with the fire this morning as our burning-glass was an admirable one; and while we roasted a few oysters and ate our cocoa-nuts, we held a long, animated conversation about our plans for the future. What those plans were, and how we carried them into effect, the reader shall see hereafter.

▶Chapter 7

(Jack's ingenuity—We get into difficulties about fishing, and get out of them by a method which gives us a coldbath—Horrible encounter with a shark.)

For several days after the excursion related in the last chapter we did not wander far from our encampment, but gave ourselves up to forming plans for the future and making our present abode comfortable.

There were various causes that induced this state of comparative inaction. In the first place, although everything around us was so delightful, and we could without difficulty obtain all that we required for our bodily comfort, we did not quite like the idea of settling down here for the rest of our lives, far away from our friends and our native land. To set energetically about preparations for a permanent residence seemed so like making up our minds to saying *adieu* to home and friends for ever that we tacitly shrank from it, and put off our preparations, for one reason and another, as long as we could. Then there was a little uncertainty still as to there being natives on the island, and we entertained a kind of faint hope that a ship might come and take us off. But as day after day passed, and neither savages nor ships appeared, we gave up all hope of an early deliverance, and set diligently to work at our homestead.

During this time, however, we had not been altogether idle. We made several experiments in cooking the cocoa-nut, most of which did not improve it. Then we removed our goods and took up our abode in the cave, but found the change so bad that we returned gladly to the bower. Besides this, we bathed very frequently, and talked a great deal—at least Jack and Peterkin did; I listened. Among other useful things, Jack, who was ever the most active and diligent, converted about three inches of the hoop-iron into an excellent knife. First, he beat it quite flat with the axe; then he made a rude handle, and tied the hoop-iron to it with our piece of whip-cord, and ground it to an edge on a piece of sandstone. When it was finished he used it to shape a better handle, to which he fixed it with a strip of his cotton handkerchief—in which operation he had, as Peterkin pointed out, torn off one of Lord Nelson's[①] noses. However, the whip-cord, thus set free, was used by Peterkin as a fishing-line. He merely tied a piece of oyster to the end of it. This the fish were allowed to swallow, and then they were pulled quickly ashore. But as the line was very short and we had no boat, the fish we caught were exceedingly small.

One day Peterkin came up from the beach, where he had been angling, and said in a

---

① Lord Nelson:指英国海军上将纳尔逊勋爵,他在 1805 年的特拉法加战役中打败了拿破仑的法国舰队使英国方面取得决定性胜利,但他本人也在本次战役中因受重伤而亡。

very cross tone, "I'll tell you what, Jack, I'm not going to be humbugged with catching such contemptible things any longer. I want you to swim out with me on your back, and let me fish in deep water!"

"Dear me, Peterkin!" replied Jack; "I had no idea you were taking the thing so much to heart, else I would have got you out of that difficulty long ago. Let me see"; and Jack looked down at a piece of timber, on which he had been labouring, with a peculiar gaze of abstraction which he always assumed when trying to invent or discover anything.

"What say you to building a boat?" he inquired, looking up hastily.

"Take far too long," was the reply; "can't be bothered waiting. I want to begin at once!"

Again Jack considered. "I have it!" he cried. "We'll fell a large tree and launch the trunk of it in the water, so that when you want to fish you've nothing to do but to swim out to it."

"Would not a small raft do better?" said I.

"Much better; but we have no ropes to bind it together with. Perhaps we may find something hereafter that will do as well, but in the meantime let us try the tree."

This was agreed on; so we started off to a spot, not far distant, where we knew of a tree that would suit us which grew near the water's edge. As soon as we reached it Jack threw off his coat, and wielding the axe with his sturdy arms, hacked and hewed at it for a quarter of an hour without stopping. Then he paused, and while he sat down to rest I continued the work. Then Peterkin made a vigorous attack on it; so that when Jack renewed his powerful blows, a few minutes' cutting brought it down with a terrible crash.

"Hurrah! Now for it!" cried Jack. "Let us off with its head!"

So saying, he began to cut through the stem again at about six yards from the thick end. This done, he cut three strong, short poles or levers from the stout branches, with which to roll the log down the beach into the sea; for, as it was nearly two feet thick at the large end, we could not move it without such helps. With the levers, however, we rolled it slowly into the sea.

Having been thus successful in launching our vessel, we next shaped the levers into rude oars or paddles, and then attempted to embark. This was easy enough to do; but after seating ourselves astride the log, it was with the utmost difficulty we kept it from rolling round and plunging us into the water. Not that we minded that much; but we preferred, if possible, to fish in dry clothes. To be sure, our trousers were necessarily wet, as our legs were dangling in the water on each side of the log; but as they could be easily dried, we did not care. After half-an-hour's practice, we became expert enough to keep our balance pretty steadily. Then Peterkin laid down his paddle, and having baited his line with a whole oyster, dropped it into deep water.

"Now, then, Jack," said he, "be cautious; steer clear o' that seaweed. There! that's it; gently, now—gently. I see a fellow at least a foot long down there coming to — Ha! that's it! Oh bother! he's off!"

"Did he bite?" said Jack, urging the log onwards a little with his paddle.

"Bite? Ay! he took it into his mouth, but the moment I began to haul he opened his jaws and let it out again."

"Let him swallow it next time," said Jack, laughing at the melancholy expression of Peterkin's visage.

"There he's again!" cried Peterkin, his eyes flashing with excitement. "Look out! Now, then! No! Yes! No! Why, the brute won't swallow it!"

"Try to haul him up by the mouth, then!" cried Jack. "Do it gently."

A heavy sigh and a look of blank despair showed that poor Peterkin had tried and failed again.

"Never mind, lad," said Jack in a voice of sympathy; "we'll move on and offer it to some other fish." So saying, Jack plied his paddle; but scarcely had he moved from the spot when a fish with an enormous head and a little body darted from under a rock and swallowed the bait at once.

"Got him this time—that's a fact!" cried Peterkin, hauling in the line. "He's swallowed the bait right down to his tail, I declare! Oh, what a thumper①!"

As the fish came struggling to the surface we leaned forward to see it, and overbalanced the log. Peterkin threw his arms round the fish's neck, and in another instant we were all floundering in the water!

A shout of laughter burst from us as we rose to the surface, like three drowned rats, and seized hold of the log. We soon recovered our position, and sat more warily; while Peterkin secured the fish, which had well-nigh escaped in the midst of our struggles. It was little worth having, however. But, as Peterkin remarked, it was better than the snouts② he had been catching for the last two or three days; so we laid it on the log before us, and having re-baited the line, dropped it in again for another.

Now, while we were thus intent upon our sport, our attention was suddenly attracted by a ripple on the sea, just a few yards away from us. Peterkin shouted to us to paddle in that direction, as he thought it was a big fish and we might have a chance of catching it. But Jack, instead of complying, said, in a deep, earnest tone of voice, which I never before

---

① thumper:〈口〉巨人；大家伙。
② snouts：口鼻部（指上文提到的咬饵但关键时刻又吐出来的鱼嘴）。

heard him use, "Haul up your line, Peterkin; seize your paddle. Quick—it's a shark!"

The horror with which we heard this may well be imagined; for it must be remembered that our legs were hanging down in the water, and we could not venture to pull them up without upsetting the log. Peterkin instantly hauled up the line, and grasping his paddle, exerted himself to the utmost, while we also did our best to make for shore. But we were a good way off, and the log being, as I have before said, very heavy, moved but slowly through the water. We now saw the shark quite distinctly swimming round and round us, its sharp fin every now and then protruding above the water. From its active and unsteady motions, Jack knew it was making up its mind to attack us; so he urged us vehemently to paddle for our lives, while he himself set us the example. Suddenly he shouted, "Look out! there he comes!" and in a second we saw the monstrous fish dive close under us and turn half-over on his side. But we all made a great commotion with our paddles, which, no doubt, frightened it away for that time, as we saw it immediately after circling round us as before.

"Throw the fish to him!" cried Jack in a quick, suppressed voice; "we'll make the shore in time yet if we can keep him off for a few minutes."

Peterkin stopped one instant to obey the command, and then plied his paddle again with all his might. No sooner had the fish fallen on the water than we observed the shark to sink. In another second we saw its white breast rising; for sharks always turn over on their sides when about to seize their prey, their mouths being not at the point of their heads like those of other fish, but, as it were, under their chins. In another moment his snout rose above the water; his wide jaws, armed with a terrific double row of teeth, appeared; the dead fish was engulfed, and the shark sank out of sight. But Jack was mistaken in supposing that it would be satisfied. In a very few minutes it returned to us, and its quick motions led us to fear that it would attack us at once.

"Stop paddling!" cried Jack suddenly. "I see it coming up behind us. Now, obey my orders quickly. Our lives may depend on it. Ralph—Peterkin—do your best to balance the log. Don't look out for the shark. Don't glance behind you. Do nothing but balance the log."

Peterkin and I instantly did as we were ordered, being only too glad to do anything that afforded us a chance or a hope of escape, for we had implicit confidence in Jack's courage and wisdom. For a few seconds, that seemed long minutes to my mind, we sat thus silently; but I could not resist glancing backward, despite the orders to the contrary. On doing so, I saw Jack sitting rigid like a statue, with his paddle raised, his lips compressed, and his eyebrows bent over his eyes, which glared savagely from beneath them down into the water.

I also saw the shark, to my horror, quite close under the log, in the act of darting towards Jack's foot. I could scarce suppress a cry on beholding this. In another moment the shark rose. Jack drew his leg suddenly from the water and threw it over the log. The monster's snout rubbed against the log as it passed, and revealed its hideous jaws, into which Jack instantly plunged the paddle and thrust it down its throat. So violent was this act that Jack rose to his feet in performing it; the log was thereby rolled completely over, and we were once more plunged into the water. We all rose, spluttering and gasping, in a moment.

"Now, then, strike out for shore!" cried Jack. —"Here, Peterkin, catch hold of my collar, and kick out with a will!"

Peterkin did as he was desired, and Jack struck out with such force that he cut through the water like a boat; while I, being free from all encumbrance, succeeded in keeping up with him. As we had by this time drawn pretty near to the shore, a few minutes more sufficed to carry us into shallow water; and finally, we landed in safety, though very much exhausted, and not a little frightened, by our terrible adventure.

▶Chapter 13

(*Notable discovery at the spouting cliffs—The mysterious green monster explained—We are thrown into unutterable terror by the idea that Jack is drowned—The diamond cave*.)

"Come, Jack," cried Peterkin one morning about three weeks after our return from our long excursion, "let's be jolly to-day, and do something vigorous. I'm quite tired of hammering and bammering, hewing and screwing, cutting and butting[1] at that little boat of ours, that seems as hard to build as Noah's Ark[2]. Let us go on an excursion to the mountain-top, or have a hunt after the wild ducks, or make a dash at the pigs. I'm quite flat—flat as bad ginger-beer—flat as a pancake; in fact, I want something to rouse me—to toss me up, as it were. Eh! what do you say to it?"

"Well," answered Jack, throwing down the axe with which he was just about to proceed towards the boat, "if that's what you want, I would recommend you to make an excursion to the waterspouts. The last one we had to do with tossed you up a considerable height; perhaps the next will send you higher—who knows? —if you're at all reasonable or moderate in your expectations!"

"Jack, my dear boy," said Peterkin gravely, "you are really becoming too fond of

---

① hammering and bammering, hewing and screwing, cutting and butting:敲敲打打,砍砍拧拧,凿凿接接。这些都是自制小船的一系列动作。双声叠韵,形容彼得金对这一活动的厌倦心理。

② Noah's Ark:诺亚方舟。《圣经·创世纪》中记载,远古时期大地上连降暴雨 40 多天,世界一片汪洋,地球上的一切生物都处于毁灭的边缘。诺亚造了一艘大船即"诺亚方舟"带家人逃难,途中将世界上每种干净的生物都带了一对,这就发展成为今天的人类和生物界。

jesting. It's a thing I don't at all approve of; and if you don't give it up, I fear that, for our mutual good, we shall have to part."

"Well, then, Peterkin," replied Jack with a smile, "what would you have?"

"Have?" said Peterkin. "I would have nothing. I didn't say I wanted to have; I said that I wanted to do."

"By the bye," said I, interrupting their conversation, "I am reminded by this that we have not yet discovered the nature of yon[①] curious appearance that we saw near the waterspouts on our journey round the island. Perhaps it would be well to go for that purpose."

"Humph!" ejaculated Peterkin, "I know the nature of it well enough."

"What was it?" said I.

"It was of a mysterious nature, to be sure!" said he with a wave of his hand, while he rose from the log on which he had been sitting and buckled on his belt, into which he thrust his enormous club.

"Well, then, let us away to the waterspouts," cried Jack, going up to the bower for his bow and arrows. —"And bring your spear, Peterkin; it may be useful."

We now, having made up our minds to examine into this matter, sallied forth eagerly in the direction of the waterspout rocks, which, as I have before mentioned, were not far from our present place of abode. On arriving there we hastened down to the edge of the rocks and gazed over into the sea, where we observed the pale-green object still distinctly visible, moving its tail slowly to and fro in the water.

"Most remarkable!" said Jack.

"Exceedingly curious!" said I.

"Beats everything!" said Peterkin. —"Now, Jack," he added, "you made such a poor figure in your last attempt to stick that object that I would advise you to let me try it. If it has got a heart at all, I'll engage to send my spear right through the core of it; if it hasn't got a heart, I'll send it through the spot where its heart ought to be."

"Fire away, then, my boy," replied Jack with a laugh.

Peterkin immediately took the spear, poised it for a second or two above his head, then darted it like an arrow into the sea. Down it went straight into the centre of the green object, passed quite through it, and came up immediately afterwards, pure and unsullied, while the mysterious tail moved quietly as before!

"Now," said Peterkin gravely, "that brute is a heartless monster; I'll have nothing more to do with it."

---

① yon:〈古〉〈方〉在那边;远处。

"I'm pretty sure now," said Jack, "that it is merely a phosphoric light; but I must say I'm puzzled at its staying always in that exact spot."

I also was much puzzled, and inclined to think with Jack that it must be phosphoric light, of which luminous appearance we had seen much while on our voyage to these seas. "But," said I, "there is nothing to hinder us from diving down to it, now that we are sure it is not a shark."

"True," returned Jack, stripping off his clothes. "I'll go down, Ralph, as I'm better at diving than you are. —Now, then, Peterkin, out o' the road!" Jack stepped forward, joined his hands above his head, bent over the rocks, and plunged into the sea. For a second or two the spray caused by his dive hid him from view; then the water became still, and we saw him swimming far down in the midst of the green object. Suddenly he sank below it, and vanished altogether from our sight! We gazed anxiously down at the spot where he had disappeared for nearly a minute, expecting every moment to see him rise again for breath; but fully a minute passed and still he did not reappear. Two minutes passed! and then a flood of alarm rushed in upon my soul when I considered that, during all my acquaintance with him, Jack had never stayed under water more than a minute at a time—indeed, seldom so long.

"Oh Peterkin!" I said in a voice that trembled with increasing anxiety, "something has happened. It is more than three minutes now." But Peterkin did not answer; and I observed that he was gazing down into the water with a look of intense fear mingled with anxiety, while his face was overspread with a deadly paleness. Suddenly he sprang to his feet and rushed about in a frantic state, wringing his hands, and exclaiming, "Oh Jack! Jack! He is gone! It must have been a shark, and he is gone for ever!"

For the next five minutes I know not what I did; the intensity of my feelings almost bereft me of[①] my senses. But I was recalled to myself by Peterkin seizing me by the shoulders and staring wildly into my face, while he exclaimed, "Ralph! Ralph! perhaps he has only fainted! Dive for him, Ralph!"

It seemed strange that this did not occur to me sooner. In a moment I rushed to the edge of the rocks, and without waiting to throw off my garments, was on the point to spring into the waves when I observed something black rising up through the green object. In another moment Jack's head rose to the surface, and he gave a wild shout, flinging back the spray from his locks, as was his wont after a dive. Now we were almost as much amazed at seeing him reappear, well and strong, as we had been at first at his non-appearance; for, to the best of our judgment, he had been nearly ten minutes under water—perhaps longer—and it

---

① bereft of:丧失。

required no exertion of our reason to convince us that this was utterly impossible for mortal man to do and retain his strength and faculties. It was, therefore, with a feeling akin to superstitious awe that I held down my hand and assisted him to clamber up the steep rocks. But no such feeling affected Peterkin. No sooner did Jack gain the rocks and seat himself on one, panting for breath, than he threw his arms round his neck and burst into a flood of tears. "Oh Jack! Jack!" said he, "where were you? What kept you so long?"

After a few moments Peterkin became composed enough to sit still and listen to Jack's explanation, although he could not restrain himself from attempting to wink every two minutes at me in order to express his joy at Jack's safety. I say he attempted to wink, but I am bound to add that he did not succeed; for his eyes were so much swollen with weeping that his frequent attempts only resulted in a series of violent and altogether idiotical contortions of the face, that were very far from expressing what he intended. However, I knew what the poor fellow meant by it; so I smiled to him in return, and endeavoured to make believe that he was winking.

"Now, lads," said Jack when we were composed enough to listen to him, "yon green object is not a shark; it is a stream of light issuing from① a cave in the rocks. Just after I made my dive, I observed that this light came from the side of the rock above which we are now sitting; so I struck out for it, and saw an opening into some place or other that appeared to be luminous within. For one instant I paused to think whether I ought to venture. Then I made up my mind and dashed into it; for you see, Peterkin, although I take some time to tell this, it happened in the space of a few seconds, so that I knew I had wind enough in me to serve to bring me out o' the hole and up to the surface again. Well, I was just on the point of turning—for I began to feel a little uncomfortable in such a place—when it seemed to me as if there was a faint light right above me. I darted upwards, and found my head out of water. This relieved me greatly, for I now felt that I could take in air enough to enable me to return the way I came. Then it all at once occurred to me that I might not be able to find the way out again; but on glancing downwards, my mind was put quite at rest by seeing the green light below me streaming into the cave, just like the light that we had seen streaming out of it, only what I now saw was much brighter.

"At first I could scarcely see anything as I gazed around me, it was so dark; but gradually my eyes became accustomed to it, and I found that I was in a huge cave, part of the walls of which I observed on each side of me. The ceiling just above me was also visible, and I fancied that I could perceive beautiful, glittering objects there; but the farther end of the cave was shrouded in darkness. While I was looking around me in great wonder, it came

---

① issue from：由······产生；传下；从······流出。

into my head that you two would think I was drowned; so I plunged down through the passage again in a great hurry, rose to the surface, and—here I am!"

When Jack concluded his recital of what he had seen in this remarkable cave, I could not rest satisfied[①] till I had dived down to see it; which I did, but found it so dark, as Jack had said, that I could scarcely see anything. When I returned we had a long conversation about, it, during which I observed that Peterkin had a most lugubrious expression on his countenance.

"What's the matter, Peterkin?" said I.

"The matter?" he replied. "It's all very well for you two to be talking away like mermaids about the wonders of this cave; but you know I must be content to hear about it, while you are enjoying yourselves down there like mad dolphins. It's really too bad!"

"I'm very sorry for you, Peterkin—indeed I am," said Jack; "but we cannot help you. If you would only learn to dive—"

"Learn to fly, you might as well say!" retorted Peterkin in a very sulky tone.

"If you would only consent to keep still," said I, "we would take you down with us in ten seconds."

"Hum!" returned Peterkin; "suppose a salamander was to propose to you 'only to keep still' and he would carry you through a blazing fire in a few seconds, what would you say?"

We both laughed and shook our heads, for it was evident that nothing was to be made of Peterkin in the water. But we could not rest satisfied till we had seen more of this cave; so, after further consultation, Jack and I determined to try if we could take down a torch with us, and set fire to it in the cavern. This we found to be an undertaking of no small difficulty, but we accomplished it at last by the following means: First, we made a torch of a very inflammable nature out of the bark of a certain tree, which we cut into strips, and after twisting, cemented together with a kind of resin or gum, which we also obtained from another tree; neither of which trees, however, was known by name to Jack. This, when prepared, we wrapped up in a great number of plies of cocoa-nut cloth, so that we were confident it could not get wet during the short time it should be under water. Then we took a small piece of the tinder, which we had carefully treasured up lest we should require it, as before said, when the sun should fail us; also, we rolled up some dry grass and a few chips, which, with a little bow and drill, like those described before, we made into another bundle and wrapped it up in cocoa-nut cloth. When all was ready we laid aside our garments, with the exception of our trousers, which, as we did not know what rough scraping against the rocks we might be subjected to, we kept on.

---

① rest satisfied:心满意足。

Then we advanced to the edge of the rocks—Jack carrying one bundle, with the torch; I the other, with the things for producing fire.

"Now don't weary for us, Peterkin, should we be gone some time," said Jack. "We'll be sure to return in half-an-hour at the very latest, however interesting the cave should be, that we may relieve your mind."

"Farewell!" said Peterkin, coming up to us with a look of deep but pretended solemnity, while he shook hands and kissed each of us on the cheek—"farewell! And while you are gone I shall repose my weary limbs under the shelter of this bush, and meditate on the changefulness of all things earthly, with special reference to the forsaken condition of a poor shipwrecked sailor-boy!" So saying, Peterkin waved his hand, turned from us, and cast himself upon the ground with a look of melancholy resignation, which was so well feigned that I would have thought it genuine had he not accompanied it with a gentle wink. We both laughed, and springing from the rocks together, plunged head first into the sea.

We gained the interior of the submarine cave without difficulty, and on emerging from the waves, supported ourselves for some time by treading water, while we held the two bundles above our heads. This we did in order to let our eyes become accustomed to the obscurity. Then, when we could see sufficiently, we swam to a shelving rock, and landed in safety. Having wrung the water from our trousers, and dried ourselves as well as we could under the circumstances, we proceeded to ignite the torch. This we accomplished without difficulty in a few minutes; and no sooner did it flare up than we were struck dumb with the wonderful objects that were revealed to our gaze. The roof of the cavern just above us seemed to be about ten feet high, but grew higher as it receded into the distance until it was lost in darkness. It seemed to be made of coral, and was supported by massive columns of the same material. Immense icicles[①] (as they appeared to us) hung from it in various places. These, however, were formed, not of ice, but of a species of limestone, which seemed to flow in a liquid form towards the point of each, where it became solid. A good many drops fell, however, to the rock below, and these formed little cones, which rose to meet the points above. Some of them had already met, and thus we saw how the pillars were formed, which at first seemed to us as if they had been placed there by some human architect to support the roof. As we advanced farther in we saw that the floor was composed of the same material as the pillars, and it presented the curious appearance of ripples such as are formed on water when gently ruffled by the wind. There were several openings on either hand in the walls that seemed to lead into other caverns, but these we did not explore at this time. We also observed that the ceiling was curiously marked in many places, as if it were the

---

① icicles：冰锥。

fretwork of a noble cathedral[①]; and the walls, as well as the roof, sparkled in the light of our torch, and threw back gleams and flashes as if they were covered with precious stones. Although we proceeded far into this cavern, we did not come to the end of it; and we were obliged to return more speedily than we would otherwise have done, as our torch was nearly expended. We did not observe any openings in the roof, or any indications of places whereby light might enter; but near the entrance to the cavern stood an immense mass of pure-white coral rock, which caught and threw back the little light that found an entrance through the cave's mouth, and thus produced, we conjectured, the pale-green object which had first attracted our attention. We concluded, also, that the reflecting power of this rock was that which gave forth the dim light that faintly illumined the first part of the cave.

Before diving through the passage again we extinguished the small piece of our torch that remained, and left it in a dry spot—conceiving that we might possibly stand in need of it if, at any future time, we should chance to wet our torch while diving into the cavern. As we stood for a few minutes after it was out, waiting till our eyes became accustomed to the gloom, we could not help remarking the deep, intense stillness and the unutterable gloom of all around us; and as I thought of the stupendous dome above, and the countless gems that had sparkled in the torchlight a few minutes before, it came into my mind to consider how strange it is that God should make such wonderful and exquisitely beautiful works never to be seen at all—except, indeed, by chance visitors such as ourselves.

I afterwards found that there were many such caverns among the islands of the South Seas, some of them larger and more beautiful than the one I have just described.

"Now, Ralph, are you ready?" said Jack in a low voice, that seemed to echo up into the dome above.

"Quite ready."

"Come along, then," said he; and plunging off the ledge of the rock into the water, we dived through the narrow entrance. In a few seconds we were panting on the rocks above, and receiving the congratulations of our friend Peterkin.

▶ Chapter 16

(*The boat launched—We visit the coral reef—The great breaker that never goes down—Coral insects—The way in which coral islands are made—The boats sail—We tax our ingenuity to form fish-hooks—Some of the fish we saw—And a monstrous whale—Wonderful shower of little fish—Waterspouts.*)

---

① fretwork of a noble cathedral: 宏伟大教堂的精细浮雕。

It was a bright, clear, beautiful morning when we first launched our little boat and rowed out upon the placid waters of the lagoon. Not a breath of wind ruffled the surface of the deep. Not a cloud spotted the deep-blue sky. Not a sound that was discordant broke the stillness of the morning, although there were many sounds—sweet, tiny, and melodious— that mingled in the universal harmony of nature. The sun was just rising from the Pacific's ample bosom, and tipping the mountain-tops with a red glow. The sea was shining like a sheet of glass, yet heaving with the long, deep swell that, all the world round, indicates the life of Ocean; and the bright seaweeds and the brilliant corals shone in the depths of that pellucid① water, as we rowed over it, like rare and precious gems. Oh, it was a sight fitted to stir the soul of man to its profoundest depths! and if he owned a heart at all, to lift that heart in adoration and gratitude to the great Creator of this magnificent and glorious universe!

At first, in the strength of our delight, we rowed hither and thither② without aim or object. But after the effervescence of our spirits was abated, we began to look about us and to consider what we should do.

"I vote that we row to the reef," cried Peterkin.

"And I vote that we visit the islands within the lagoon," said I.

"And I vote we do both," cried Jack; "so pull away, boys!"

As I have already said, we had made four oars; but our boat was so small that only two were necessary. The extra pair were reserved in case any accident should happen to the others. It was therefore only needful that two of us should row, while the third steered by means of an oar—and relieved the rowers occasionally.

First we landed on one of the small islands and ran all over it, but saw nothing worthy of particular notice. Then we landed on a larger island, on which were growing a few cocoa-nut trees. Not having eaten anything that morning, we gathered a few of the nuts and breakfasted. After this we pulled straight out to sea, and landed on the coral reef.

This was indeed a novel and interesting sight to us. We had now been so long on shore that we had almost forgotten the appearance of breakers, for there were none within the lagoon. But now, as we stood beside the foam-crested billow of the open sea, all the enthusiasm of the sailor was awakened in our breasts; and as we gazed on the widespread ruin of that single magnificent breaker that burst in thunder at our feet, we forgot the Coral Island behind us, we forgot our bower and the calm repose of the scented woods, we forgot all that had passed during the last few months, and remembered nothing but the storms, the

---

① pellucid:透明的;清澈的。

② hither and thither:到处;忽此忽彼。

calms, the fresh breezes, and the surging billows of the open sea.

This huge, ceaseless breaker, to which I have so often alluded, was a much larger and more sublime object than we had at all imagined it to be. It rose many yards above the level of the sea, and could be seen approaching at some distance from the reef. Slowly and majestically it came on, acquiring greater volume and velocity as it advanced, until it assumed the form of a clear watery arch, which sparkled in the bright sun. On it came with resistless and solemn majesty, the upper edge lipped gently over, and it fell with a roar that seemed as though the heart of Ocean were broken in the crash of tumultuous water, while the foam-clad coral reef appeared to tremble beneath the mighty shock!

We gazed long and wonderingly at this great sight, and it was with difficulty we could tear ourselves away from it. As I have once before mentioned, this wave broke in many places over the reef and scattered some of its spray into the lagoon; but in most places the reef was sufficiently broad and elevated to receive and check its entire force. In many places the coral rocks were covered with vegetation—the beginning, as it appeared to us, of future islands. Thus, on this reef, we came to perceive how most of the small islands of those seas are formed. On one part we saw the spray of the breaker washing over the rocks, and millions of little, active, busy creatures continuing the work of building up this living rampart①. At another place, which was just a little too high for the waves to wash over it, the coral insects were all dead; for we found that they never did their work above water. They had faithfully completed the mighty work which their Creator had given them to do, and they were now all dead. Again, in other spots the ceaseless lashing of the sea had broken the dead coral in pieces, and cast it up in the form of sand. Here sea-birds had alighted, little pieces of seaweed and stray bits of wood had been washed up, seeds of plants had been carried by the wind, and a few lovely blades of bright green had already sprung up, which, when they died, would increase the size and fertility of these emeralds of Ocean. At other places these islets had grown apace②, and were shaded by one or two cocoa-nut trees, which grew literally in the sand, and were constantly washed by the ocean spray—yet, as I have before remarked, their fruit was most refreshing and sweet to our taste.

Again, at this time Jack and I pondered the formation of the large coral islands. We could now understand how the low ones were formed; but the larger islands cost us much consideration, yet we could arrive at no certain conclusion on the subject.

Having satisfied our curiosity, and enjoyed ourselves during the whole day in our little boat, we returned, somewhat wearied, and withal rather hungry, to our bower.

---

① rampart:堡礁;壁垒。
② grow apace:迅速增长;飞速传播。

"Now," said Jack, "as our boat answers so well we will get a mast and sail made immediately."

"So we will!" cried Peterkin as we all assisted to drag the boat above high-water mark. "We'll light our candle and set about it this very night. Hurrah, my boys, pull away!"

As we dragged our boat, we observed that she grated heavily on her keel; and as the sands were in this place mingled with broken coral rocks, we saw portions of the wood being scraped off.

"Hallo!" cried Jack on seeing this, "that won't do. Our keel will be worn off in no time at this rate."

"So it will," said I, pondering deeply as to how this might be prevented. But I am not of a mechanical turn naturally, so I could conceive no remedy save that of putting a plate of iron on the keel; but as we had no iron, I knew not what was to be done. "It seems to me, Jack," I added, "that it is impossible to prevent the keel being worn off thus."

"Impossible?" cried Peterkin. "My dear Ralph, you are mistaken; there is nothing so easy."

"How?" I inquired in some surprise.

"Why, by not using the boat at all!" replied Peterkin.

"Hold your impudent tongue, Peterkin!" said Jack as he shouldered the oars. "Come along with me, and I'll give you work to do. In the first place, you will go and collect cocoa-nut fibre, and set to work to make sewing-twine with it—"

"Please, captain," interrupted Peterkin, "I've got lots of it made already—more than enough, as a little friend of mine used to be in the habit of saying every day after dinner."

"Very well," continued Jack; "then you'll help Ralph to collect cocoa-nut cloth and cut it into shape, after which we'll make a sail of it. I'll see to getting the mast and the gearing; so let's to work."

And to work we went right busily, so that in three days from that time we had set up a mast and sail, with the necessary rigging, in our little boat. The sail was not, indeed, very handsome to look at, as it was formed of a number of oblong patches of cloth; but we had sewed it well by means of our sail-needle, so that it was strong, which was the chief point. —Jack had also overcome the difficulty about the keel by pinning to it a false keel. This was a piece of tough wood, of the same length and width as the real keel, and about five inches deep. He made it of this depth because the boat would be thereby rendered not only much more safe, but more able to beat against the wind—which, in a sea where the trade-winds[1] blow so long and so steadily in one direction, was a matter of great importance. This piece of

---

[1] trade-wind: (吹向赤道的)信风。

wood was pegged very firmly to the keel; and we now launched our boat with the satisfaction of knowing that when the false keel should be scraped off we could easily put on another,—whereas, should the real keel have been scraped away, we could not have renewed it without taking our boat to pieces, which Peterkin said made his "marrow quake to think upon".

The mast and sail answered excellently; and we now sailed about in the lagoon with great delight, and examined with much interest the appearance of our island from a distance. Also, we gazed into the depths of the water, and watched for hours the gambols of the curious and bright-coloured fish among the corals and seaweed. Peterkin also made a fishing-line; and Jack constructed a number of hooks, some of which were very good, others remarkably bad. Some of these hooks were made of iron-wood—which did pretty well, the wood being extremely hard—and Jack made them very thick and large. Fish there are not particular. Some of the crooked bones in fish-heads also answered for this purpose pretty well. But that which formed our best and most serviceable hook was the brass finger-ring belonging to Jack. It gave him not a little trouble to manufacture it. First he cut it with the axe, then twisted it into the form of a hook. The barb took him several hours to cut. He did it by means of constant sawing with the broken penknife. As for the point, an hour's rubbing on a piece of sandstone made an excellent one.

It would be a matter of much time and labour to describe the appearance of the multitudes of fish that were day after day drawn into our boat by means of the brass hook. Peterkin always caught them—for we observed that he derived much pleasure from fishing—while Jack and I found ample amusement in looking on, also in gazing down at the coral groves, and in baiting the hook. Among the fish that we saw, but did not catch, were porpoises[①] and swordfish, whales and sharks. The porpoises came frequently into our lagoon in shoals[②], and amused us not a little by their bold leaps into the air and their playful gambols in the sea. The swordfish were wonderful creatures—some of them apparently ten feet in length, with an ivory spear six or eight feet long projecting from their noses. We often saw them darting after other fish, and no doubt they sometimes killed them with their ivory swords. Jack remembered having heard once of a swordfish attacking a ship, which seemed strange indeed; but as they are often in the habit of attacking whales, perhaps it mistook the ship for one. This swordfish ran against the vessel with such force that it drove its sword quite through the thick planks; and when the ship arrived in harbour, long afterwards, the sword was found still sticking in it!

---

① porpoise:鼠海豚(尤指大西洋鼠海豚)。

② shoal:浅滩。

Sharks did not often appear; but we took care never again to bathe in deep water without leaving one of our number in the boat, to give us warning if he should see a shark approaching. As for the whales, they never came into our lagoon; but we frequently saw them spouting in the deep water beyond the reef. I shall never forget my surprise the first day I saw one of these huge monsters close to me. We had been rambling about on the reef during the morning, and were about to re-embark in our little boat to return home, when a loud blowing sound caused us to wheel rapidly round. We were just in time to see a shower of spray falling, and the flukes or tail of some monstrous fish disappear in the sea a few hundred yards off. We waited some time to see if he would rise again. As we stood, the sea seemed to open up at our very feet; an immense spout of water was sent with a snort high into the air, and the huge, blunt head of a sperm-whale rose before us. It was so large that it could easily have taken our little boat, along with ourselves, into its mouth! It plunged slowly back into the sea, like a large ship foundering, and struck the water with its tail so forcibly as to cause a sound like a cannon-shot.

We also saw a great number of flying-fish, although we caught none; and we noticed that they never flew out of the water except when followed by their bitter foe the dolphin, from whom they thus endeavoured to escape. But of all the fish that we saw, none surprised us so much as those that we used to find in shallow pools after a shower of rain; and this not on account of their appearance, for they were ordinary-looking and very small, but on account of their having descended in a shower of rain! We could account for them in no other way, because the pools in which we found these fish were quite dry before the shower, and at some distance above high-water mark. Jack, however, suggested a cause which seemed to me very probable. We used often to see waterspouts in the sea. A waterspout is a whirling body of water, which rises from the sea like a sharp-pointed pillar. After rising a good way, it is met by a long tongue, which comes down from the clouds; and when the two have joined, they look something like an hour-glass. The waterspout is then carried by the wind— sometimes gently, sometimes with violence—over the sea, sometimes up into the clouds; and then, bursting asunder[①], it descends in a deluge. This often happens over the land as well as over the sea; and it sometimes does much damage, but frequently it passes gently away. Now, Jack thought that the little fish might perhaps have been carried up in a waterspout, and so sent down again in a shower of rain. But we could not be certain as to this point, yet we thought it likely.

During these delightful fishing and boating excursions we caught a good many eels, which we found to be very good to eat. We also found turtles among the coral rocks, and

---

① burst asunder:裂成碎片。

made excellent soup in our iron kettle. Moreover，we discovered many shrimps and prawns[①]，so that we had no lack of variety in our food；and，indeed，we never passed a week without making some new and interesting discovery of some sort or other，either on the land or in the sea.

▶扩展阅读

1. Golding，W. *Lord of the Flies*. London：Faber and Faber，1954.

2. Kermode，F. *Puzzles and Epiphanies*，London：Routledge and Kegan Paul，1962.

3. Quayle，E. *Ballantyne the Brave：A Victorian Writer and His Family*. Chester Springs，PA：Dufour Edition，Inc.，1967.

4. Quayle，E. *R. M. Ballantyne：a bibliography of first editions*. London：Dawsons，1968.

5. Siegl，K. *The Robinsonade Tradition in Robert Michael Ballantyne's the Choral Island and William Golding's the Lord of the Flies*，New York：Edwin Mellen Press，1996.

▶学习参考网站

1. http：//en.wikipedia.org/wiki/The_Coral_Island

2. http：//librivox.org/the-coral-island-by-r-m-ballantyne/

【徐 燕 编注】

---

① prawn：大虾；对虾。

9. Joseph Conrad: Youth

　　约瑟夫·康拉德（Joseph Conrad，1857—1924），英国小说家，1857 年出生于波兰，父亲因策划反抗沙俄起义被捕而遭流放，母亲和年幼的康拉德被迫同行，但由于气候恶劣父母不久身亡。1874 年，康拉德来到法国马赛，开始了他长达 20 年的海上生涯。1878 年，康拉德作为一艘英国商船上的伙计第一次踏上英国领土，但此时的他还不懂英语。在接下来的 16 年里，康拉德在英国的商船上经历了无数次远航，足迹几乎遍及世界各地。康拉德的海上生涯大致分为四个时期：一是在法国马赛做普通水手的时期（1874—1878）；二是成为英国水手，由伙计晋升为船长的时期（1880—1886）；三是他的东方航行时期（1886—1889）；四是他的刚果之行（1890—1891）。1890 年康拉德前往刚果，一路上目睹了殖民者对当地人民的奴役，这令他非常愤怒。非洲之行是他从水手转为作家的一个重要转折点。此后 30 年里康拉德一直致力于小说创作。

　　康拉德的文学创作大致可以分为四个时期：一是创作初期（1894—1896），这一时期的小说主要以马来群岛为故事背景，小说有较明显的模仿痕迹，艺术手法相对粗糙，但小说的材料非常新奇，显露出浓郁的海上生活和丛林生活气息，主要作品有《奥迈耶的痴梦》（*Almayer's Folly*，1895）和《海隅逐客》（*An Outcast of the Island*，1896）。这两部小说与晚期小说《救援》（*Rescue*，1920）并称为"马来小说三部曲"。

　　二是创作成熟期（1897—1911），绝大部分优秀的作品都是在这一时期完成的。康拉德在此期间表现出惊人的创造力，小说视野广阔，艺术手法娴熟，故事背景涉及海洋、丛林和城市，人物活动的地域范围遍布欧、亚、非、拉美等世界各地，小说主题触及文化、政治、道德、人性等方方面面的问题。主要作品有《"水仙"号上的黑水手》（*The Nigger of the "Narcissus"*，1897）、《吉姆爷》（*Lord Jim*，1900）、《青春》（*Youth*，1902）、《黑暗的中心》（*Heart of Darkness*，1902）、《走投无路》（*The End of the Tether*，1902）、《台风》（*Typhoon*，1902）、《诺斯托罗莫》（*Nostromo*，1904）、《间谍》（*The Secret Agent*，1907）、《在西方的眼睛下》（*Under Western Eyes*，1911）。

　　三是创作过渡期（1912—1918），这一时期的作品质量参差不齐，有短篇小说集《陆海之间》（*Twixt Land and Sea*，1912）、《在潮汐之间》（*Within the Tides*，1915），长篇小说《机缘》（*Chance*，1914）、《胜利》（*Victory*，1915）及中篇小说《阴影线》（*The Shadow Line*，1917）。

　　四是创作晚期（1919—1924），这一时期的主要作品有《金箭》（*The Arrow of Gold*，

1919)、《救援》和《流浪者》(*Rover*,1923)。除小说外,康拉德还书写了四部散文集:《大海如镜》(*The Mirror of the Sea*,1902)、《个人记录》(*Personal Record*,1912)、《文学与人生札记》(*Notes on Life and Letters*,1921)和《晚年文集》(*Last Essays*,1925,去世后出版)。1924年8月康拉德死于心脏病。康拉德的作品对人性的弱点和"道德的失败"进行了细察,批评家利维斯(Frank Raymond Leavis)称康拉德是英国文学"伟大传统"的继承者。

康拉德写有大量与大海有关的小说和散文,他的海洋小说通常以大海为背景烘托人物的内心世界,充满人生哲思。可以说,康拉德是一个以水手的目光来看待世界的小说家。《青春》是一部自传体小说,是作者根据自己在"巴勒斯坦"号(Palestine)船上担任二副时的真实经历写成的。1881年,"巴勒斯坦"号在开往曼谷的途中历尽艰险,遭遇迷航并漏水,最后船上运载的煤自燃爆炸,船员们不得不弃船逃生。《青春》描述的正是这样一场惊心动魄的海上历险。年轻水手马洛在一次东方航行中遭遇了狂风暴雨,一条破旧不堪的运煤帆船先是漏水,继而煤发生自燃爆炸起火,最终导致船只毁灭。年轻的主人公与其他水手一道与风浪和火灾进行了殊死搏斗,小说渲染了"奋斗不息,死而后已"(Do or Die)的激情和拼搏精神。在叙事手法上,作者采用了典型的康拉德式的"框架叙事"模式。故事讲述的虽然是叙述者本人马洛年轻时的激情,但故事叙述者则是人到中年的马洛。回首往事,他对年轻时抱有的激情和梦幻欣赏不已,同时又流露出历经磨难后中年人理想的幻灭以及由此而生的自嘲和怀旧心理。《青春》以大海为背景,讴歌了英国商船社长期以来形成的职业道德(work ethics),是对工作责任心和激情的歌颂,但更多的是一首哀叹昔日道德精神不再的挽歌。以下选段取自《青春》,描写了"朱迪亚"号船自燃爆炸后,主人公面对海上火光冲天的壮观景象时的内心感受。

We had fair breezes, smooth water right into the tropics, and the old *Judea*[①] lumbered along in the sunshine. When she went eight knots[②] everything cracked aloft, and we tied our caps to our heads; but mostly she strolled on at the rate of three miles an hour. What could you expect? She was tired—that old ship. Her youth was where mine is—where yours is—you fellows who listen to this yarn; and what friend would throw your years and your weariness in your face? We didn't grumble at her. To us aft, at least, it seemed as though we had been born in her, reared in her, had lived in her for ages, had never known any other ship. I would just as soon have abused the old village church at home for not being a cathedral.

And for me there was also my youth to make me patient. There was all the East before me, and all life, and the thought that I had been tried in that ship and had come out pretty

---

① Judea:地名,朱迪亚(古巴勒斯坦的南部地区,包括今巴勒斯坦的南部地区和约旦的西南部地区)源自希伯来语"Judah",属古犹太王国的领地,意为"值得赞美的地方",因为此处对古犹太人而言意味着生命的重生。"朱迪亚"号船在海中最终沉没,有一定的宗教象征意义。

② eight knots:8节。节,航速和流速单位(1节＝1海里/小时)。

well. And I thought of men of old who, centuries age, went that road in ships that sailed no better, to the land of palms, and spices, and yellow sands, and of brown nations ruled by kings more cruel than Nero[①] the Roman, and more splendid than Solomon[②] the Jew. The old bark lumbered on, heavy with her age and the burden of her cargo, while I lived the life of youth in ignorance and hope. She lumbered on through an interminable procession of days; and the fresh gilding flashed back at the setting sun, seemed to cry out over the darkening sea the words painted on her stern, "*Judea, London. Do or Die.*"[③]

Then we entered the Indian Ocean and steered northerly for Java Head[④]. The winds were light. Weeks slipped by. She crawled on, do or die, and people at home began to think of posting us as overdue.

One Saturday evening, I being off duty, the men asked me to give them an extra bucket of water or so—for washing clothes. As I did not wish to screw on the fresh-water pump so late, I went forward whistling, and with a key in my hand to unlock the forepeak scuttle, intending to serve the water out of a spare tank we kept there.

The smell down below was as unexpected as it was frightful. One would have thought hundreds of paraffin-lamps has been flaring and smoking in that hole for days. I was glad to get out. The man with me coughed and said, "Funny smell, sir." I answered negligently, "It's good for the health they say," and walked aft.

The first thing I did was to put my head down the square of the midship ventilator. As I lifted the lid a visible breath, something like a thin fog, a puff of faint haze, rose from the opening. The ascending air was hot, and had a heavy, sooty, paraffin smell. I gave one sniff, and put down the lid gently. It was no use choking myself. The cargo was on fire.

Next day she began to smoke in earnest. You see it was to be expected, for though the coal was of a safe kind, that cargo had been so handled, so broken up with handling, that it looked more like smithy coal than anything else. Then it had been wetted—move than once. It rained all the time we were taking it back from the hulk, and now with this long passage it got heated, and there was another case of spontaneous combustion.

The captain called us into the cabin. He had a chart spread on the table, and looked unhappy. He said, "The coast of West Australia is near, but I mean to proceed to our destination. It is the hurricane month, too; but we will just keep her head for Bangkok, and

---

① Nero:尼禄,古罗马皇帝,以残暴、专制、荒淫出名。

② Solomon:所罗门(? —932BC),以色列国王,以智慧著称,大卫(David)和芭示示芭(Bathsheba)之子,加强国防,以武力维持其统治,使犹太达到鼎盛时期。

③ do or die:"奋斗不息,死而后已",这是"朱迪亚"号船的铭文,源自丁尼生(Alfred Tennyson)的诗歌 *Charge of the Light Brigade*:Theirs not to make reply,/Theirs not to reason why,/Theirs but to do and die. 年轻的马洛拥有"奋斗不息,死而后已"这一信念,富有工作热情和强盛的责任心,其形象是典型的维多利亚时期人们工作精神的写照。

④ Java Head:爪哇岬,位于印度尼西亚。

fight the fire. No more putting back anywhere, if we all get roasted. We will try first to strife this 'ere damned combustion by want of air."

We tried. We battened down everything, and still she smoked. The smoke kept coming out through imperceptible crevices; it forced itself through bulk-heads and covers; it oozed here and there and everywhere in slender threads, in an invisible film, in an incomprehensible manner. It made its way into the cabin, into the forecastle; it poisoned the sheltered places on the deck, it could be sniffed as high as the main yard. It was clear that if the smoke came out the air came in. This was disheartening. This combustion refused to be stifled.

We resolved to try water, and took the hatches off. Enormous volumes of smoke, whitish, yellowish, thick, greasy, misty, choking, ascended as high as the trucks. All hands cleared out aft. Then the poisonous cloud blew away, and we went back to work in a smoke that was to thicker now than that of an ordinary factory chimney.

We rigged the force-pump, got the hose along, and by and by it burst. Well, it was as old as the ship—a prehistoric hose, and past repair. Then we pumped with the feeble head-pump, drew water with buckets, and in this way managed in time to pour lots of Indian Ocean into the main hatch. The bright stream flashed in sunshine, fell into a layer of white crawling smoke, and vanished on the black surface of coal. Steam ascended mingling with the smoke. We poured salt water as into a barrel without a bottom. It was our fate to pump in that ship, to pump out of her, to pump into her; and after keeping water out of her to save ourselves from being drowned, we frantically poured water into her to save ourselves from being burnt.

And she crawled on, do or die, in the serene weather. The sky was a miracle of purity, a miracle of azure. The sea was polished, was blue, was pellucid, was sparkling like a precious stone, extending on all sides, all round to the horizon—as if the whole terrestrial globe had been one jewel, one colossal sapphire, a single gem fashioned into a planet. And on the lustre of the great calm waters the Judea glided imperceptibly, enveloped in languid and unclean vapours, in a lazy cloud that drifted to leeward, light and slow; a pestiferous cloud defiling the splendour of sea and sky.

All this time of course we saw no fire. The cargo smouldered at the bottom somewhere. Once Mahon[①], as we were working side by side, said to me with a queer smile: "Now, if she only would spring a tidy leak—like that time when we first left the Channel—it would put a stopper on this fire. Wouldn't it?" I remarked irrelevantly, "Do you remember the

---

① Mahon:马洪,"朱迪亚"号船上的大副。他坚持自己的名字应该念作"Mann"(曼恩),这一读音令人联想到 man(男子汉)。

rates?"

We fought the fire and sailed the ship too as carefully as though nothing had been the matter. The steward cooked and attended on us. Of the other twelve men, eight worked while four rested. Everyone took his turn, captain included. There was equality, and if not exactly fraternity, then a deal of good feeling. Sometimes a man, as he dashed a bucketful of water down the hatchway, would yell out, "Hurrah for Bangkok!" and the rest laughed. But generally we were taciturn and serious—and thirsty. Oh! How thirsty! And we had to be careful with the water. Strict allowance.[①] The ship smoked, the sun blazed...Pass me the bottle.[②]

We tried everything. We even made an attempt to dig down to the fire. No good, of course. No man could remain more than a minute below. Mahon, who went first, fainted there, and the man who went to fetch him out did likewise. We lugged them out on deck. Then I leaped down to show how easily it could be done. They had learned wisdom by that time, and contend themselves by fishing for me with a chain-hook tied to a broom handle, I believe. I did not offer to go and fetch up my shovel, which was left down below.

Things began to look bad. We put the long-boat into the water. The second boat was ready to swing out. We had also another, a 14-foot thing, on davits aft, where it was quite safe.

Then, behold, the smoke suddenly decreased. We redoubled our efforts to flood the bottom of the ship. In two days there was no smoke at all. Everybody was on the broad grin. This was on a Friday. On Saturday no work, but sailing the ship of course, was done. The men washed their clothes and their faces for the first time in a fortnight, and has a special dinner given them. They spoke of spontaneous combustion with contempt, and implied *they* were the boys to put out combustion. Somehow we all felt as though we each had inherited a large fortune. But a beastly smell of burning hung about the ship. Captain Beard had hollow eyes and sunken cheeks. I had never noticed so much before how twisted and bowed he was. He and Mahon prowled soberly about hatches and ventilators, sniffing. It struck me suddenly poor Mahon was a very, very old chap. As to me, I was as pleased and proud as though I had helped to win a great naval battle. Oh, Youth!

The night was fine. In the morning a homeward-bound ship passed us hull down—the first we had seen for months; but we were nearing the land at last, Java Head being about

---

① But generally we were taciturn and ...to be careful with the water. Strict allowance.: 不过通常我们总是沉默、严肃……而且口渴。啊,多么口渴! 我们又不敢随便用水。有严格的限制。这几句话的意思是指"朱迪亚"号一再出事,船上储存的淡水已很有限,对船员饮水,不得不采取严格的限制。

② Pass me the bottle: 把酒瓶递过来。叙述者马洛在讲述中不时回到讲述现场,与听众做交流。这是典型的康拉德式小说叙述方式。这一手法令小说的时空来回切换。

190 miles off, and nearly due north.

Next day it was my watch on deck from eight to twelve. At breakfast the captain observed, "It's wonderful how that smell hangs about the cabin." About ten, the mate being on the poop, I stepped down on the main-deck for a moment. The carpenter's bench stood abaft the mainmast: I leaned against it sucking at my pipe, and the carpenter, a young chap, came to talk to me. He remarked, "I think we have done very well, haven't we?" and then I perceived with annoyance the fool was trying to tilt the bench. I said curtly, "Don't, Chips," and immediately became aware of a queer sensation, of an absurd delusion, —I seemed somehow to be in the air. I heard all round me like a pent-up breath released—as if a thousand giants simultaneously had said Phoo! —and felt a dull concussion which made my ribs ache suddenly. No doubt about it—I was in the air, and my body was describing a short parabola. But short as it was, I had time to think several thoughts in, as far as I can remember, the following order: "This can't be the carpenter—What is it?—Some accident—Submarine volcano?—Coals, gas!—By Jove! We are being blown up—Everybody's dead—I am falling into the after-hatch—I see fire in it."

The coal-dust suspended in the air of the hold had glowed dull-red at the moment of the explosion. In the twinkling of an eye, in an infinitesimal fraction of a second since the first tilt of the bench, I was sprawling full length on the cargo. I picked myself up and scrambled out. It was quick like a rebound. The deck was a wilderness of smashed timber, lying crosswise like trees in a wood after a hurricane; an immense curtain of soiled rags waved gently before me—it was the mainsail blown to strips. I thought. The masts will be toppling over directly; and to get out of the way bolted on all-fours towards the poop-ladder. The first person I saw was Mahon, with eyes like saucers, his mouth open, and the long white hair standing straight on end round his head like a silver halo. He was just about to go down when the sight of the main-deck stirring, heaving up, and changing into splinters before his eyes, petrified his on the top step. I stared at him in unbelief, and he stared at me with a queer kind of shocked curiosity. I did not know that I had no hair, no eye-brows, no eyelashes, that my young moustache was burnt off, that my face was black, one cheek laid open, my nose cut, and my chin bleeding. I had lost my cap one of my slippers, and my shirt was torn to rags. Of all this I was not aware. I was amazed to see the ship still afloat, the poop-deck whole—and, most of all, to see anybody alive. Also the peace of the sky and the serenity of the sea were distinctly surprising. I suppose I expected to see them convulsed with horror... Pass me the bottle.

There was a voice hailing the ship from somewhere—in the air, in the sky—I couldn't tell. Presently I saw the captain—and he was mad. He asked me eagerly, "Where's the cabin-table?" and to hear such a question was a frightful shock. I had just been blown up, you understand, and vibrated with that experience, —I wasn't quite sure whether I was alive. Mahon began to stamp with both feet and yelled at him, "Good God! Don't you see the deck's blown out of her?" I found my voice, and stammered out as if conscious of some gross neglect of duty, "I don't know where the cabin-table is." It was like an absurd dream.

Do you know what he wanted next? Well, he wanted to trim the yards. Very placidly, and as if lost in thought, he insisted on having the foreyard squared. "I don't know if there's anybody alive," said Mahon, almost tearfully. "Surely," he said, gently, "there will be enough left to square the foreyard."

The old chap, it seems, was in his own berth winding up the chronometers, when the shock sent him spinning. Immediately it occurred to him—as he said afterwards—that the ship had struck something, and he ran out into the cabin. There, he saw, the cabin-table had vanished somewhere. The deck being blown up, it had fallen down into the lazarette of course. Where we had our breakfast that morning he saw only a great hole in the floor. This appeared to him so awfully mysterious, and impressed him so immensely, that what he saw and heard after he got on deck were mere trifles in comparison. And, mark, he noticed directly the wheel deserted and his barque off her course—and his only thought was to get that miserable, stripped, undecked, smouldering shell of a ship back again with her head pointing at her port of destination. Bangkok! That's what he was after. I tell you this quiet, bowed, bandy-legged, almost deformed little man was immense in the singleness of his ides and in his placid ignorance of our agitation. He motioned us forward with a commanding gesture, and went to take the wheel himself.

Yes; that was the first thing we did—trim the yards of that wreck! No one was killed, or even disabled, but everyone was more or less hurt. You should have seen them! Some were in rags, with black faces, like coal-heavers, like sweeps, and had bullet heads that seemed closely cropped, but were in fact singed to the skin. Others, of the watch below, awakened by being shot out from their collapsing bunks, shivered incessantly, and kept on groaning even as we went about our work. But they all worked. That crew of Liverpool hard cases had in them the right stuff. It's my experience they always have. It is the sea that gives it—the vastness, the loneliness surrounding their dark stolid souls. Ah! Well! We stumbled, we crept, we fell, we barked our shins on the wreckage, we hauled. The masts stood, but we did not know how much they might be charred down below. It was nearly calm, but a long swell ran from the west and made her roll. They might go at any moment. We looked at them with apprehension. One could not foresee which way they would fall. Then we retreated aft and looked about us. The deck was a tangle of planks on edge, of planks on end, of splinters, of ruined woodwork. The masts rose from that chaos like big trees above a matted undergrowth. The interstices of that mass or wreckage were full of something whitish, sluggish, stirring—of something that was like a greasy fog. The smoke of the invisible fire was coming up again, was trailing, like a poisonous thick mist in some valley choked with dead wood. Already lazy wisps were beginning to curl upwards amongst the mass of splinters. Here and there a piece of timber, stuck uprigh, resembled a post. Half of a fife-rail had been shot through the foresail, and the sky made a patch of glorious blue in the ignobly soiled canvas. A portion of several boards holding together had fallen across the rail, and one end protruded overboard, like a gangway leading upon nothing, like a gangway leading over the deep sea, leading to death—as if inviting us to walk the plank[①] at once and be done with our ridiculous troubles. And still the air, the sky—a ghost, something invisible was hailing the ship.

Someone had the sense to look over, and there was the helmsman, who had impulsively jumped overboard, anxious to come back. He yelled and swam lustily like a merman, keeping up with the ship. We threw him a rope, and presently he stood amongst us streaming with water and very crestfallen. The captain had surrendered the wheel, and apart, elbow on rail and chin in hand, gazed at the sea wistfully. We asked ourselves, What next? I thought, Now, this is something I like. This is great. I wonder what will happen. O youth!

Suddenly Mahon sighted a steamer far astern. Captain Beard said, "We may do something with her yet." We hoisted two flags, which said in the international language of the sea, "On fire. Want immediate assistance." The steamer grew bigger rapidly, and by and by spoke with two flags on her foremast, "I am coming to your assistance."

In half an hour she was abreast, to windward, within hail, and rolling slightly, with her engines stopped. We lost our composure, and yelled all together with excitement, "We've been blown up". A man in a white helmet, on the bridge, cried, "Yes! All right! All right!" and he nodded his head, and smiled, and made soothing motions with his hand as though at a lot of frightened children. One of the boats dropped in the water, and walked towards us upon the sea with her long oars. Four Calashes pulled a swinging stroke. This was my first sight of Malary seamen. I've known them since, but what struck me then was their unconcern: they came alongside, and even the bowman standing up and holding to our main-chains with the boat-hook did not deign to lift his head for a glance. I thought people who had been blown up deserved more attention.

A little man, dry like a chip and agile like a monkey, clambered up. It was the mate of the steamer. He gave one look, and cried, "O boys—you had better quit."

We were silent. He talked apart with the captain for a time, —seemed to argue with

---

① walk the plank:走跳板。"走跳板"是海盗残害俘虏的一种方法,即蒙着俘虏的双眼,强迫他在一条伸出舷外的跳板上行走而掉落在海里。

him. Then they went away together to the steamer.

When our skipper came back we learned that the steamer was the *Somerville*, Captain Nash, from West Australia to Singapore *via* Batavia with mails, and that the agreement was she should tow us to Anjer or Batavia, if possible, where we could extinguish the fire by scuttling, and then proceed on our voyage—to Bangkok! The old man seemed excited. "We will do it yet," he said to Mahon, fiercely. He shook his fist at the sky. Nobody else said a word.

At noon the steamer began to tow. She went ahead slim and high, and what was left of the *Judea* followed at the end of seventy fathom of tow-rope, —followed her swiftly like a cloud of smoke with mast-heads protruding above. We went aloft to furl the sails. We coughed on the yards, and were careful about the bunts. Do you see the lot of us there, putting a neat furl on the sails of that ship doomed to arrive nowhere? There was not a man who didn't think that at any moment the masts would topple over. From aloft we could not see the ship for smoke, and they worked carefully, passing the gaskets with even turns. "Harbour furl...aloft there!"[①] cried Mahon from below.

You understand this? I don't think one of those chaps expected to get down in the usual way. When we did I heard them saying to each other, "Well, I thought we would come down overboard, in a lump...sticks and all...blame me if I didn't." "That's what I was thinking to myself," would answer wearily another battered and bandaged scarecrow. And, mind, these were men without the drilled-in habit of obedience. To an onlooker they would be a lot of profane scallywages without a redeeming point. What made them do it...what made them obey me when I, thinking consciously how fine it was, made them drop the bunt of the foresail twice to try and do it better? What? They had no professional reputation...no examples, no praise. It wasn't a sense of duty; they all knew well enough how to shirk, and laze, and dodge...when they had a mind to it...and mostly they had. Was it the two pounds ten a-month that sent them there? They didn't think their pay half good enough. No; it was something in them, something inborn and subtle and everlasting. I don't say positively that the crew of a French or German merchantman wouldn't have done it, but I doubt whether it would have been done in the same way. There was a completeness in it, something solid like a principle, and masterful like an instinct...a disclosure of something secret...of that hidden something, that gift of good or evil that makes racial difference, that shapes the late of nations.

It was that night at ten that, for the first time since we had been fighting it, we saw

---

① Harbour furl...aloft there!：进港收帆……你们在上面的人！"进港收帆"是航海的术语，意谓把船帆卷起，用绳索捆扎好，像进港一般。

the fire. The speed of the towing had fanned the smouldering destruction. A blue gleam appeared forward, shining below the wreck of the deck. It wavered in patches, it seemed to stir and creep like the light of a glowworm! I saw it first, and told Mahon. "Then the game's up", he said. "We had better stop this towing, or she will burst out suddenly fore and apt before we can clear out." We set up a yell; rang bells to attract their attention; they towed on. At last Mahon and I had to crawl forward and cut the rope with an axe. There was no time to cast off the lashings. Red tongues could be seen licking the wilderness of splinters under our feet as we made our way back to the poop.

Of course they very soon found out in the steamer that the rope was gone. She gave a loud blast of her whistle, her lights were seen sweeping in a wide circle, and she came up ranging close along-side, and stopped. We were all in a tight group on the poop looking at her. Every man had saved a little bundle or a bag. Suddenly a conical flame with a twisted top shot up forward and threw upon the black sea a circle of light, with the two vessels side by side and heaving gently in its centre. Captain Beard had been sitting on the gratings still and mutes for hours, but now he rose slowly and advanced in front of us, to the mizzen-shrouds. Captain Nash hailed: "Come along! Look sharp. I have mail-bags on board. I will take you and your boats to Singapore."

"Thank you! No!" said our skipper. "We must see the last of the ship."

"I can't stand by any longer," shouted the other. "Mails—you know."

"Ay! Ay! We are all right."

"Very well! I'll report you in Singapore...Good-bye!"

He waved his hand. Our men dropped their bundles quietly. The steamer moved ahead, and passing out of the circle of light, vanished at once from our sight, dazzled by the fire which burned fiercely. And then I knew that I would see the East first as commander of a small boat. I thought it fine; and the fidelity to the old ship was fine. We should see the last of her. Oh, the glamour of youth! Oh, the fire of it, more dazzling than the flames of the burning ship, throwing a magic light on the wide earth, leaping audaciously to the sky, presently to be quenched by time, more cruel, more pitiless, more bitter than the sea—and like the flames of the burning ship surrounded by an impenetrable night.

The old man warned us in his gentle and inflexible way that it was part of our duty to save for the under-writers as much as we could of the ship's gear. Accordingly we went to work aft, while she blazed forward to give us plenty of light. We lugged out a lot of rubbish. What didn't we save? An old barometer fixed with an absurd quantity of screws nearly cost me my life: a sudden rush of smoke came upon me, and I just got away in time. There were various stories, bolts of canvas, coils of rope; the poop looked like a marine bazaar, and the boats were lumbered to the gunwales. One would have thought the old man wanted to take as much as he could of his first command with him. He was very, very quiet, but off his balance evidently. Would you believe it? He wanted to take a length of old stream-cable and a kedge-anchor with him in the long-boat. We said, "Ay, ay, sir," deferentially, and on the quiet let the things slip overboard. The heavy medicine-chest went that way, two bags of green coffee, tins of paint...fancy, paint! ...a whole lot of things. Then I was ordered with two hands into the boats to make a stowage and get them ready against the time it would be proper for us to leave the ship.

We put everything straight, stepped the long-boat's mast for our skipper, who was to take charge of her, and I was not sorry to sit down for a moment. My face felt raw, every limb ached as if broken, I was aware of all my ribs, and would have sworn to a twist in the backbone. The boats, fast astern, lay in a deep shadow, and all around I could see the circle of the sea lighted by the fire. A gigantic flame arose forward straight and clear. It flared fierce, with noises like the whirr of wings, with rumbles as of thunder. There were cracks, detonations, and from the cone of flame the sparks flew upwards, as man is born to trouble, to leaky ships, and to ships that burn.

What bothered me was that the ship, lying broadside to the swell and to such wind as there was...a mere breath...the beats would not keep astern where they were safe, but persisted, in a pig-headed way boats have, in getting under the counter and then swinging alongside. They were knocking about dangerously and coming near the flame, while the ship rolled on them, and, of course, there was always the danger of the masts going over the side at any moment. I and my two boat-keepers kept them off as best we could, with oars and boat-hooks; but to be constantly at it became exasperating, since there was no reason why we should not leave at once. We could not see those on board, nor could we imagine what caused the delay. The boat-keepers were swearing feebly, and I had not only my share of the work but also had to keep at it two men who showed a constant inclination to lay themselves down and let things slide.

At last I hailed, "On deck there," and someone looked over. "We're ready here," I said. The head disappeared, and very soon popped up again. "The captain says, All right, sir, and to keep the boats well clear of the ship."

Half an hour passed. Suddenly there was a frightful racket, rattle, clanking of chain, hiss of water, and millions of sparks flew up into the shivering column of smoke that stood leaning slightly above the ship. The cat-heads had burned away, and the two red-hot anchors had gone to the bottom, tearing out after them two hundred fathom of red-hot chain. The ship trembled, the mass of flame swayed as if ready to collapse, and the fore top-gallant-mast fell. It darted down like an arrow of fire, shot under, and instantly leaping up within an oar's-length of the boats, floated quietly, very black on the luminous sea.

I hailed the deck again. After some time a man in an unexpectedly cheerful but also muffled tone, as though he had been trying to speak with his mouth shut, informed me "coming directly, sir," and vanished. For a long time I heard nothing but the whirr and roar of the fire. There were also whistling sounds. The boats jumped, tugged at the painters, ran at each other playfully. Knocked their sides together, or, do what we would, swung in a bunch against the ship's side. I couldn't stand it any longer, and swarming up a rope, clambered aboard over the stern.

It was as bright as day. Coming up like this, the sheet of fire facing me was a terrifying sight, and the heat seemed hardly bearable at first. On a settee cushion dragged out of the cabin Captain Beard, his legs drawn up and one arm under his head, slept with the light playing on him. Do you know what the rest were busy about? They were sitting on deck right aft, round an open case, eating bread and cheese and drinking bottled stout.

On the background of flames twisting in fierce tongues above their heads they seemed at home like salamanders, and looked like a band of desperate pirates. The fire sparkled in the whites of their eyes, gleamed on patches of white skin seen through the torn shirts. Each had the marks as of a battle about him...bandaged heads, tied-up arms, a strip of dirty rag round a knee...and each man had a bottle between his legs and a chunk of cheese in his hand. Mahon got up. With his handsome and disreputable head, his hooked profile, his long white beard, and with an uncorked bottle in his hand, he resembled one of those reckless sea-robbers of old making merry amidst violence and disaster. "The last meal on board," he explained solemnly. "We had nothing to eat all day, and it was no use leaving all this." He flourished the bottle and indicated the sleeping skipper. "He said he couldn't swallow anything, so I got him to lie down," he went on; and as I stared, "I don't know whether you are aware, young fellow, the man had no sleep to speak of for days—and there will be dam' little sleep in the boats." "There will be no boats by-and-by if you fool about much longer," I said, indignantly. I walked up to the skipper and shook him by the shoulder. At last he opened his eyes, but did not move. "Time to leave her, sir," I said quietly.

He got up painfully, looked at the flames, at the sea sparkling round the ship, and black, black as ink farther away; he looked at the stars shining dim through a thin veil of smoke in a sky black, black as Erebus.

"Youngest first," he said.

And the ordinary seaman, wiping his mouth with the black of his hand, got up, clambered over the taffrail, and vanished. Others followed. One, on the point of going over, stopped short to drain his bottle, and with a great swing of his arm flung it at the fire. "Take this!" he cried.

The skipper lingered disconsolately, and we left him to commune alone for a while with his first command. Then I went up again and brought him away at last. It was time. The ironwork on the poop was hot to the touch.

Then the painter of the long-boat was cut，and the three boats，tied together，drifted clear of the ship. It was just sixteen hours after the explosion when we abandoned her. Mahon had charge of the second boat，and I had the smallest—the 14-foot thing. The long-boat would have taken the lot of us；but the skipper said we must save as much property as we could—for the underwriters—and so I got my first command. I had two men with me，a bag of biscuits，a few tins of meat，and a breaker of water. I was ordered to keep close to the long-boat，that in case of bad weather we might be taken into her.

And do you know what I thought?[1] I thought I would part company as soon as I could. I wanted to have my first command all to myself. I wasn't going to sail in a squadron if there were a chance for independent cruising. I would make land by myself. I would beat the other boats. Youth! All youth! The silly，charming，beautiful youth.

But we did not make a start at once. We must see the last of the ship. And so the boats drifted about that night，heaving and setting on the swell. The men dozed，waked，sighed，and groaned. I looked at the burning ship.

Between the darkness of earth and heaven she was burning fiercely upon a disc of purple sea shot by the blood-red play of gleams；upon a disc of water glittering and sinister. A high，clear flame，and immense and lonely flame，ascended from the ocean，and from its summit the black smoke poured continuously at the sky. She burned furiously；mournful and imposing like a funeral pile kindled in the night，surrounded by the sea，watched over by the stars. A magnificent death had come like a grace，like a gift，like a reward to that old ship at the end of her laborious days. The surrender of her weary ghost to the keeping of stars and sea was stirring like the sight of a glorious triumph.[2] The masts fell just before daybreak，and for a moment there was a burst and turmoil of sparks that seemed to fill with flying fire the night patient and watchful，the vast night lying silent upon the sea. At daylight she was only a charred shell，floating still under a cloud of smoke and bearing a glowing mass of coal within.

---

① And do you know what I thought?：注意中年叙述者马洛是以口头叙述的方式向水手们讲述他青年时代的历险故事。叙述者再次把听众带回叙事现场。参见前文注释。

② Between the darkness of earth and heaven she was burning fiercely upon a disc of purple sea shot by the blood-red play of gleams...The surrender of her weary ghost to the keeping of stars and sea was stirring like the sight of a glorious triumph.：在漆黑的天地之间，它烧得好旺——在被血红的、摇曳的火光照耀出一圈紫色的海面上……在一圈亮晃晃又阴森森的水面上。从海里腾起一股明亮的火焰，一团巨大、孤独的火焰；火焰的顶端吐着黑烟，一个劲儿地直向天空冲去。帆船猛烈地燃烧，好不悲壮，就像火葬的积薪在晚上燃烧着。这条辛苦奔波的老船，临终却这样显赫，好像这是老天给它的一种恩惠、一种恩赐、一种嘉奖。它把疲惫不堪的灵魂交出，托付给星象和海洋，就像光荣的凯旋同样激动人心。这是小说中最抒情的一段，年轻的马洛面对海上火光冲天的壮观景象，内心露出激动而浪漫的情怀。这与人到中年因理想幻灭而浪漫不再的马洛形成鲜明对照。

Then the oars were got out，and the boats forming in a line moved round her remains as if in procession—the long-boat leading. As we pulled across her stern a slim dart of fire shot out viciously at us，and suddenly she went down，head first，in a great hiss of steam. The unconsumed stern was the last to sink；but the paint had gone，had cracked，had peeled off，and there were no letters，there was no word，no stubborn device that was like her soul，to flash at the rising sun her creed and her name.

▶扩展阅读

1. Batchelor，J. *The Life of Joseph Conrad：A Critical Biography*. Oxford：Blackwell，1994.

2. Berthoud，J. *Joseph Conrad：The Major Phase*，Cambridge：Cambridge University Press，1979.

3. Knowles，O. & Moore，G. M. Eds. *Oxford Reader's Companion to Conrad*. Oxford：Oxford University Press，2001.

4. Leavis，F. R. *The Great Tradition*，London：Chatto & Windus，1948.

5. Stape，J. H. Ed. *The Cambridge Companion to Joseph Conrad*. Cambridge：Cambridge University Press，2006.

▶学习参考网站

1. http：//www.josephconradsociety.org/

2. http：//en.wikipedia.org/wiki/Youth_(Conrad_story)

3. http：//www.freeonlineresearchpapers.com/man-nature-joseph-conrad-youth

【王松林　编注】

10. Joseph Rudyard Kipling: Captains Courageous

约瑟夫·拉迪亚德·吉卜林（Joseph Rudyard Kipling，1865—1936），是著名诗人、散文家和小说家，英国第一位诺贝尔文学奖获得者。1865 年吉卜林出生于印度孟买，父母都是英国人。他 6 岁时被送回英国接受教育，12 岁时进入专门面向海外服役军人子弟的中学，受到严格的纪律训练，1882 年返回印度，为一家报纸工作。吉卜林花了近 10 年的时间游遍了印度，并根据自己的游历创作了大量诗歌和短篇故事，在文坛上很快脱颖而出。他的早期主要作品有《王者》（*The Man Who Would Be King*，1888）、《山中的平凡故事》（*Plain Tales from the Hills*，1888）和《军营歌谣》（*Barrack-Room Ballads*，1892）等。1889 年，吉卜林长途旅行回到英国，途经缅甸、中国、日本、美国，再横穿大西洋，到达伦敦，途中发表了《漂洋过海》（*From Sea to Sea and Other Sketches*）等。同期创作的诗歌中最著名的是《东西方民谣》（*The Ballad of East and West*，第一句为："Oh, East is East，and West is West，and never the twain shall meet."）。1892 年，吉卜林结婚并随妻回英国，之后他创作了小说《丛林故事》（*The Jungle Book*，1894）、《丛林故事续集》（*The Second Jungle Book*，1895）《勇敢的船长们》（*Captains Courageous*，1897）和诗集《七海》（*The Seven Seas*，1896）等。1897 年吉卜林定居于英国萨塞克斯郡，翌年起，几乎每个冬季都到非洲休假，在那里他收集了儿童文学经典作品《原来如此》（*Just So：Stories for Little Children*，1902）的素材，还创作了小说《基姆》（*Kim*，1901）。1899 年他发表了诗歌《白人的负担》（"The White Man's Burden"）。20 世纪前 10 年，吉卜林在文学上的成就达到顶峰，1907 年他获得了诺贝尔文学奖。直到 19 世纪 30 年代早期，吉卜林不断有新作问世。1936 年 1 月，吉卜林因脑出血逝世。由于吉卜林所生活的年代正值英国海外殖民扩张的全盛时期，他从小被灌输的思想就带有帝国主义色彩，因此他会全力维护英国的"强者"地位，宣扬弱肉强食的"丛林法则"，有些作品流露出高傲与扩张的思想，故而有"帝国诗人"之称。吉卜林一生共创作了 8 部诗集，4 部长篇小说，21 部短篇小说集和历史故事集，以及大量散文、随笔、游记等。他的作品简洁凝练，清新自然，充满异国情调，尤其在短篇小说方面，成就最为突出。诺贝尔授奖词赞扬他具有"观察的能力、新颖的想象、雄浑的思想和杰出的叙事才能"。

经常往返于英、印两国的吉卜林有很多与海洋和海军有关的经历，两者赋予他的作品以

阳刚之气、意志之力和雄浑之风。《勇敢的船长们》是一部典型的海洋小说，集中描写了大海的狂放不羁与喜怒无常、渔民生活的艰难困苦和船长的钢铁意志，体现了"吉卜林法则"（Kipling's Law），即公正、忠诚和独立自主。主人公哈维（Harvey）是纽约一个百万富翁的孩子，乘船去欧洲时，一个巨浪把他抛到海里，后来被救上一艘渔船——"海上"号。船长特鲁普（Disco Troop）精明强悍、明辨是非、嫉恶如仇、乐于助人，总能凭借深广的知识和丰富的经验在茫茫的纽芬兰渔场上找到最理想的停泊地并捕到大量的鱼；他又绝不吝啬，总是愿意帮助船队里其他的人，甚至是漂泊在大海上跟他毫不相干的陌生船只；他对航海技术很差和胡乱进行冒险的船只十分蔑视，但是一旦对方陷入困境，他又会不顾一切地迅速赶去救援。他很自信，也很骄傲，他的自信来自他丰富的经验、广博的知识和敏锐的观察；他虽然骄傲却十分质朴，是一个讨人喜欢的男子。除了船长，"海上"号上还有船长的儿子丹（Dan）和水手梅纽尔（Manuel）、萨尔托斯（Uncle Salters）、隆·杰克（Long Jack）、汤姆·普拉特（Tom Platt）和宾（Penn）等，每个人都勤劳肯干。娇生惯养的哈维在"海上"号上与这样一群人接触，逐渐褪去了身上纨绔子弟的恶习，学会了服从命令和勤奋工作，掌握了航海和捕鱼的本领，最终成长为一名合格的渔民，更成为一个充满生气和活力的青年，赢得了船长特鲁普的喜爱。最后哈维回到了家人身边，他的父亲惊喜地发现自己的儿子完全变了一个人。这部小说既有对大海细致而精彩的描写，也有对船上艰苦生活的真切描绘。小说中的大海磨炼了主人公的品质，教会了人们许多生存的法则。《勇敢的船长们》是一部有成长小说特征的海洋小说。小说的寓意在于：一个民族犹如一艘航行在大海中的船只，国民是一个群体，必须经受海上暴风雨般严酷的考验和磨难，才能立于世界文明之林而不败。本文选自《勇敢的船长们》第二章，从哈维谩骂船长为贼而吃老拳开始，描述哈维在"海上"号上一天的工作状况和船员之间分工合作的场景，体现了维多利亚时代人们所遵守的"职业准则"。

▶Chapter 2

"I warned ye①，" said Dan, as the drops fell thick and fast on the dark, oiled planking. "Dad ain't noways hasty, but you fair earned it. Pshaw! there's no sense takin' on so." Harvey's shoulders were rising and falling in spasms of dry sobbing. "I know the feeling'. First time dad laid me out was the last—and that was my first trip. Makes ye feel sickish an' lonesome. I know."

"It does," moaned Harvey. "That man's either crazy or drunk, and—and I can't do anything."

"Don't say that to dad," whispered Dan. "He's set ag'in'② all liquor, an'—well, he told me you was the madman. What in creation made you call him a thief? He's my dad."

---

① ye：〈方〉you，你。"海上"号上的每个人都有很重的方言口音，读者要注意辨别。
② set ag'in'：set agasint，反对，憎恶。

Harvey sat up, mopped his nose, and told the story of the missing wad of bills. "I'm not crazy," he wound up. "Only—your father has never seen more than a five-dollar bill at a time, and my father could buy up this boat once a week and never miss it."

"You don't know what the 'We're Here's' worth. Your dad must hey a pile o' money. How did he git it? Dad sez loonies can't shake out a straight yarn.① Go ahead."

"In gold-mines and things, West."

"I've read o' that kind o' business. Out West, too? Does he go around with a pistol on a trick-pony, same ez the circus? They call that the Wild West, and I've heard that their spurs an' bridles was solid silver."

"You are a chump!" said Harvey, amused in spite of himself. "My father hasn't any use for ponies. When he wants to ride he takes his car."

"Haow? Lobster-car?"

"No. His own private car, of course. You've seen a private car some time in your life?"

"Slatin Beeman he hez one," said Dan, cautiously. "I saw her at the Union Depot in Boston, with three niggers hoggin' her run." (Dan meant cleaning the windows.) "But Slatin Beeman he owns 'baout every railroad on Long Island, they say; an' they say he's bought 'baout ha'af Noo Hampshire an' run a line-fence around her, an' filled her up with lions an' tigers an' bears an' buffalo an' crocodiles an' such all. Slatin Beeman he's a millionaire. I've seen his car. Yes?"

"Well, my father's what they call a multi-millionaire; and he has two private cars. One's named for me, the 'Harvey,' and one for my mother, the 'Constance.'"

"Hold on," said Dan. "Dad don't ever let me swear, but I guess you can. 'Fore we go ahead, I want you to say hope you may die if you're lying."

"Of course," said Harvey.

"Thet ain't 'nuff. Say, 'Hope I may die if I ain't speakin' truth.'"

"Hope I may die right here," said Harvey, "if every word I've spoken isn't the cold truth."

"Hundred an' thirty-four dollars an' all?" said Dan. "I heard ye talkin' to dad, an' I ha'af looked you'd be swallered up, same's Jonah."②

Harvey protested himself red in the face. Dan was a shrewd young person along his own lines, and ten minutes' questioning convinced him that Harvey was not lying—much. Besides, he had bound himself by the most terrible oath known to boyhood, and yet he sat, alive, with a red-ended nose, in the scuppers, recounting marvels upon marvels.

---

① Dad sez loonies can't shake out a straight yarn.：我爹说过，疯子讲故事，讲讲就露馅儿了。

② I ha'af looked you'd be swallered up, same's Jonah.：我有点看出来，你跟约拿一样有点理屈词穷了。这句话典出《圣经·约拿书》。先知约拿违背神的旨意，受到神的诘问而答不出话。

"Gosh!" said Dan at last, from the very bottom of his soul, when Harvey had completed an inventory of the car named in his honour. Then a grin of mischievous delight overspread his broad face. "I believe you, Harvey. Dad's made a mistake fer once in his life."

"He has, sure," said Harvey, who was meditating an early revenge.

"He'll be mad clear through. Dad jest hates to be mistook in his judgments." Dan lay back and slapped his thigh. "Oh, Harvey, don't you spile the catch by lettin' on.①"

"I don't want to be knocked down again. I'll get even with him, though."

"Never heard any man ever got even with dad. But he'd knock ye down again sure. The more he was mistook the more he'd do it. But gold-mines and pistols—"

"I never said a word about pistols," Harvey cut in, for he was on his oath.

"Thet's so; no more you did. Two private cars, then, one named fer you an' one fer her; an' two hundred dollars a month pocket-money, all knocked into the scuppers fer not workin' fer ten an' a ha'af a month! It's the top haul o' the season." He exploded with noiseless chuckles.

"Then I was right?" said Harvey, who thought he had found a sympathizer.

"You was wrong; the wrongest kind o' wrong! You take right hold an' pitch in 'longside o' me, or you'll catch it, an' I'll catch it fer backin' you up.② Dad always gives me double helps 'cause I'm his son, an' he hates favourin' folk. 'Guess you're kinder mad at dad. I've been that way time an' again. But dad's a mighty jest man; all the fleet says so."

"Looks like justice, this, don't it?" Harvey pointed to his outraged nose.

"Thet's nothin'. Lets the shore blood outer you. Dad did it for yer health. Say, though, I can't have dealin's with a man that thinks me or dad or any one on the 'We're Here's' a thief. We ain't any common wharf-end crowd by any manner o' means. We're fishermen, an' we've shipped together for six years an' more. Don't you make any mistake on that! I told ye dad don't let me swear. He calls 'em vain oaths, and pounds me; but ef I could say what you said 'baout your pap an' his fixin's, I'd say that 'baout your dollars. I dunno what was in your pockets when I dried your kit, fer I didn't look to see; but I'd say, using the very same words ez you used jest now, neither me nor dad—an' we was the only two that teched you after you was brought aboard—knows anythin' 'baout the money. Thet's my say. Naow?"

The bloodletting had certainly cleared Harvey's brain, and maybe the loneliness of the sea had something to do with it. "That's all right," he said. Then he looked down confusedly. "Seems to me that for a fellow just saved from drowning I haven't been over and above grateful, Dan."

---

① don't you spile the catch by lettin' on.: 你不要把我们说的话捅出去。

② You take right hold an' pitch in 'longside o' me, or you'll catch it, an' I'll catch it fer backin' you up.: 你要掌握正确的时机跟我一起努力干活,否则你会受惩罚,而我也会因为支持你而受连累。

"Well, you was shook up and silly," said Dan. "Anyway, there was only dad an' me aboard to see it. The cook he don't count."

"I might have thought about losing the bills that way," Harvey said, half to himself, "instead of calling everybody in sight a thief Where's your father?"

"In the cabin What d' you want o' him again?"

"You'll see," said Harvey, and he stepped, rather groggily, for his head was still singing, to the cabin steps, where the little ship's clock hung in plain sight of the wheel. Troop, in the chocolate-and-yellow painted cabin, was busy with a note-book and an enormous black pencil, which he sucked hard from time to time.

"I haven't acted quite right," said Harvey, surprised at his own meekness.

"What's wrong now?" said the skipper "Walked into Dan, hev ye?"

"No; it's about you."

"I'm here to listen."

"Well, I—I'm here to take things back," said Harvey, very quickly. "When a man's saved from drowning—" he gulped.

"Ey? You'll make a man yet ef you go on this way."

"He oughtn't begin by calling people names."

"Jest an' right—right an' jest," said Troop, with the ghost of a dry smile.

"So I'm here to say I'm sorry." Another big gulp.

Troop heaved himself slowly off the locker he was sitting on and held out an eleven-inch hand. "I mistrusted 't would do you sights o' good; an' this shows I weren't mistook in my judgments." A smothered chuckle on deck caught his ear. "I am very seldom mistook in my jedgments." The eleven-inch hand closed on Harvey's, numbing it to the elbow. "We'll put a little more gristle to that 'fore we've done with you, young feller; an' I don't think any worse of ye fer anythin' thet's gone by. You wasn't fairly responsible. Go right about your business an' you won't take no hurt."

"You're white," said Dan, as Harvey regained the deck, flushed to the tips of his ears.

"I don't feel it," said he.

"I didn't mean that way. I heard what dad said. When dad allows he don't think the worse of any man, dad's give himself away. He hates to be mistook in his judgments, too. Ho! ho! Once dad has a judgment, he'd sooner dip his colours to the British than change it.[①] I'm glad it's settled right end up. Dad's right when he says he can't take you back. It's all the livin' we make here—fishin'. The men'll be back like sharks after a dead whale in ha'af an

---

① Once dad has a judgment, he'd sooner dip his colours to the British than change it.:我爹一旦有了正确的判断，就算是面对英国人也不会改变立场的。

hour."

"What for?" said Harvey. "Supper, o'course. Don't your stummick tell you? You've a heap to learn."

"'Guess I have," said Harvey, dolefully, looking at the tangle of ropes and blocks overhead.

"She's a daisy," said Dan, enthusiastically, misunderstanding the look. "Wait till our mainsail's bent, an' she walks home with all her salt wet. There's some work first, though." He pointed down into the darkness of the open main-hatch between the two masts.

"What's that for? It's all empty," said Harvey.

"You an' me an' a few more hev got to fill it," said Dan. "That's where the fish goes."

"Alive?" said Harvey.

"Well, no. They're so's to be ruther dead—an' flat—an' salt. There's a hundred hogshead o' salt in the bins; an' we hain't more'n covered our dunnage to now."

"Where are the fish, though?"

"'In the sea, they say; in the boats, we pray,'" said Dan, quoting a fisherman's proverb. "You come in last night with 'about forty of 'em."

He pointed to a sort of wooden pen just in front of the quarter-deck.

"You an' me we'll sluice that out when they're through. 'Send we'll hev full pens to-night! I've seen her down ha'af a foot with fish waitin' to clean, an' we stood to the tables till we was splittin' ourselves instid o' them, we was so sleepy. Yes, they're comin' in now." Dan looked over the low bulwarks at half a dozen dories rowing towards them over the shining, silky sea.

"I've never seen the sea from so low down," said Harvey. "It's fine."

The low sun made the water all purple and pinkish, with golden lights on the barrels of the long swells, and blue and green mackerel shades in the hollows. Each schooner in sight seemed to be pulling her dories towards her by invisible strings, and the little black figures in the tiny boats pulled like clockwork toys.

"They've struck on good," said Dan, between his half-shut eyes. "Manuel hain't room fer another fish. Low ez a lily-pad in still water, ain't he?"

"Which is Manuel? I don't see how you can tell 'em 'way off, as you do."

"Last boat to the south'ard. He f'und you last night," said Dan, pointing. "Manuel rows Portugoosey; ye can't mistake him. East o' him—he's a heap better'n he rows—is Pennsylvania. Loaded with saleratus, by the looks of him. East o' him—see how pretty they string out all along with the humpy shoulders, is Long Jack. He's a Galway man inhabitin' South Boston, where they all live mostly, an' mostly them Galway men are good in a boat. North, away yonder—you'll hear him tune up in a minute—is Tom Platt. Man-o'-war's man he was on the old Ohio—first of our navy, he says, to go around the Horn. He never talks of much else, 'cept when he sings, but he has fair fishin' luck. There! What did I tell you?"

A melodious bellow stole across the water from the northern dory. Harvey heard something about somebody's hands and feet being cold, and then：

"Bring forth the chart, the doleful chart; See where them mountings meet! The clouds are thick around their heads. The mists around their feet."

"Full boat," said Dan, with a chuckle. "If he gives us 'O Captain' it's toppin' full."

The bellow continued：

"And naos to thee, O Capting,

Most earnestly I pray,

That they shall never bury me

In church or cloister grey."

"Double game① for Tom Platt. He'll tell you all about the old Ohio tomorrow.'See that blue dory behind him? He's my uncle, —dad's own brother, —an' ef there's any bad luck loose on the Banks she'll fetch up ag'in' Uncle Salters, sure. Look how tender he's rowin'. I'll lay my wage and share he's the only man stung up today—an' he's stung up good." —"What'll sting him?" said Harvey, getting interested.

"Strawberries, mostly. Punkins, sometimes, an' sometimes lemons an' cucumbers.② Yes, he's stung up from his elbows down. That man's luck's perfectly paralysin'. Now we'll take a-holt o' the tackles an' h'ist 'em in. Is it true, what you told me jest now, that you never done a hand's turn o' work in all your born life? Must feel kinder awful, don't it?"

"I'm going to try to work, anyway," Harvey replied stoutly. "Only it's all dead new."

"Lay a-holt o' that tackle, then. Behind ye!"

Harvey grabbed at a rope and long iron hook dangling from one of the stays of the mainmast, while Dan pulled down another that ran from something he called a "topping-lift," as Manuel drew alongside in his loaded dory.③ The Portuguese smiled a brilliant smile that Harvey learned to know well later, and a short-handled fork began to throw fish into the pen on deck. "Two hundred and thirty-one," he shouted.

"Give him the hook," said Dan, and Harvey ran it into Manuel's hands. He slipped it through a loop of rope at the dory's bow, caught Dan's tackle, hooked it to the stern-becket, and clambered into the schooner.

---

① double game：两个拿手好戏。

② 这句话中出现的 strawberry、punkin、lemon、cucumber 词，此处指各种会刺痛人的海草或海生物，渔民将其戏称为草莓、南瓜、柠檬、黄瓜。渔民们这里说的 punkins，正确的英文表达应该是 pumpkins。

③ 这句话可译为：哈维抓住一根绳和一个从主帆支索上吊下来的长铁钩，丹拉下另一个长铁钩，那是从另一样东西上滑下来的，他把那东西叫作"千斤索"。

"Pull!" shouted Dan; and Harvey pulled, astonished to find how easily the dory rose.

"Hold on; she don't nest in the crosstrees!" Dan laughed; and Harvey held on, for the boat lay in the air above his head.

"Lower away," Dan shouted; and as Harvey lowered, Dan swayed the light boat with one hand till it landed softly just behind the mainmast. "They don't weigh nothin' empty. Thet was right smart fer a passenger. There's more trick to it in a sea-way."

"Ah ha!" said Manuel, holding out a brown hand. "You are some pretty well now? This time last night the fish they fish for you. Now you fish for fish. Eh, wha-at?"

"I'm—I'm ever so grateful," Harvey stammered, and his unfortunate hand stole to his pocket once more, but he remembered that he had no money to offer. When he knew Manuel better the mere thought of the mistake he might have made would cover him with hot, uneasy blushes in his bunk.

"There is no to be thankful for to me!" said Manuel. "How shall I leave you dreeft, dreeft all around the Banks? Now you are a fisherman eh, wha-at? Ouh! Auh!" He bent backward and forward stiffly from the hips to get the kinks out of himself.

"I have not cleaned boat to-day. Too busy. They struck on queek. Danny, my son, clean for me."

Harvey moved forward at once. Here was something he could do for the man who had saved his life.

Dan threw him a swab, and he leaned over the dory, mopping up the slime clumsily, but with great good-will. "Hike out the foot-boards; they slide in them grooves," said Dan. "Swab 'em an' lay 'em down. Never let a foot-board jam. Ye may want her bad some day. Here's Long Jack."

A stream of glittering fish flew into the pen from a dory alongside.

"Manuel, you take the tackle. I'll fix the tables. Harvey, clear Manuel's boat. Long Jack's nestin' on the top of her."

Harvey looked up from his swabbing at the bottom of another dory just above his head.

"Jest like the Injian puzzle-boxes, ain't they?" said Dan, as the one boat dropped into the other.

"Takes to ut like a duck to water," said Long Jack, a grizzly-chinned, long-lipped Galway man, bending to and fro exactly as Manuel had done. Disko in the cabin growled up the hatchway, and they could hear him suck his pencil.

"Wan hunder an' forty-nine an' a half—bad luck to ye, Discobolus!" said Long Jack.

"I'm murderin' meself to fill your pockuts. Slate ut for a bad catch. The Portuguese has bate me."[1]

Whack came another dory alongside, and more fish shot into the pen.

"Two hundred and three. Let's look at the passenger!" The speaker was even larger than the Galway man, and his face was made curious by a purple cut running slantways from his left eye to the right corner of his mouth.

Not knowing what else to do, Harvey swabbed each dory as it came down, pulled out the foot-boards, and laid them in the bottom of the boat.

"He's caught on good," said the scarred man, who was Tom Platt, watching him critically. "There are two ways o' doin' everything. One's fisher-fashion—any end first an' a slippery hitch over all—an' the other's—"

"What we did on the old Ohio!" Dan interrupted, brushing into the knot of men with a long board on legs. "Git out o' here, Tom Platt, an' leave me fix the tables."

He jammed one end of the board into two nicks in the bulwarks, kicked out the leg, and ducked just in time to avoid a swinging blow from the man-o'-war's man.

"An' they did that on the Ohio, too, Danny. See?" said Tom Platt, laughing.

"'Guess they was swivel-eyed, then, fer it didn't git home,[2] and I know who'll find his boots on the main-truck ef he don't leave us alone. Haul ahead! I'm busy, can't ye see?"

"Danny, ye lie on the cable an' sleep all day," said Long Jack. "You're the height av impedence, an' I'm persuaded ye'll corrupt our supercargo in a week."

"His name's Harvey," said Dan, waving two strangely shaped knives, "an' he'll be worth five of any Sou' Boston clam-digger 'fore long." He laid the knives tastefully on the table, cocked his head on one side, and admired the effect.

"I think it's forty-two," said a small voice over-side, and there was a roar of laughter as another voice answered, "Then my luck's turned fer once, 'caze I'm forty-five, though I be stung outer all shape."

"Forty-two or forty-five. I've lost count," the small voice said.

"It's Penn an' Uncle Salters caountin' catch. This beats the circus any day," said Dan. "Jest look at'em!"

"Come in—come in!" roared Long Jack. "It's wet out yondher, children."

"Forty-two, ye said." This was Uncle Salters.

"I'll count again, then," the voice replied meekly.

The two dories swung together and bunted into the schooner's side.

---

[1] 隆杰克说:"一百四十九条半——运气不好,你这个家伙! 我只有杀了我自己再填满你的口袋。你就把这个倒霉的捕获量记下来吧。那个葡萄牙人压倒了我。"

[2] 我猜他们都是斜眼,要不怎么会打不中呢?

"Patience o' Jerusalem!" snapped Uncle Salters, backing water with a splash. "What possest a farmer like you to set foot in a boat beats me. You've nigh stove me all up."

"I am sorry, Mr. Salters. I came to sea on account of nervous dyspepsia. You advised me, I think."

"You an' your nervis dyspepsy be drowned in the Whale-hole," roared Uncle Salters, a fat and tubly little man. "You're comin' down on me ag'in. Did ye say forty-two or forty-five?"

"I've forgotten, Mr. Salters. Let's count."

"Don't see as it could be forty-five. I'm forty-five," said Uncle Salters. "You count keerful, Penn."

Disko Troop came out of the cabin. "Salters, you pitch your fish in naow at once," he said in the tone of authority.

"Don't spile the catch, dad," Dan murmured. "Them two are on'y jest beginnin'."

"Mother av delight! He's forkin' them wan by wan," howled Long Jack, as Uncle Salters got to work laboriously; the little man in the other dory counting a line of notches on the gunwale.

"That was last week's catch," he said, looking up plaintively, his forefinger where he had left off.

Manuel nudged Dan, who darted to the after-tackle, and, leaning far overside, slipped the hook into the stern-rope as Manuel made her fast forward. The others pulled gallantly and swung the boat in—man, fish, and all.

"One, two, four-nine," said Tom Platt, counting with a practised eye. "Forty-seven. Penn, you're it!" Dan let the after-tackle run, and slid him out of the stern on to the deck amid a torrent of his own fish.

"Hold on!" roared Uncle Salters, bobbing by the waist. "Hold on, I'm a bit mixed in my acount."

He had no time to protest, but was hove inboard and treated like "Pennsylvania".

"Forty-one," said Tom Platt. "Beat by a farmer, Salters. An' you such a sailor, too!"

"'T weren't fair caount," said he, stumbling out of the pen; "an' I'm stung up all to pieces."

His thick hands were puffy and mottled purply white.

"Some folks will find strawberry-bottom," said Dan, addressing the newly risen moon, "If they have to dive fer it, seems to me."

"An' others," said Uncle Salters, "eats the fat o' the land in sloth, an' mocks their own blood-kin."

"Seat ye! Seat ye!" a voice Harvey had not heard called from the fo'c'sle. Disko Troop,

Tom Platt, Long Jack, and Salters went forward on the word. Little Penn bent above his square deep-sea reel and the tangled cod-lines; Manuel lay down full length on the deck, and Dan dropped into the hold, where Harvey heard him banging casks with a hammer.

"Salt," he said, returning. "Soon as we're through supper we git to dressing-down[①]. You'll pitch to dad. Tom Platt an' dad they stow together, an' you'll hear 'em arguin'. We're second ha'af, you an' me an' Manuel an' Penn—the youth an' beauty o' the boat."

"What's the good of that?" said Harvey. "I'm hungry."

"They'll be through in a minute. Sniff! She smells good to-night. Dad ships a good cook if he do suffer with his brother. It's a full catch today, ain't it?" He pointed at the pens piled high with cod. "What water did ye hev, Manuel?"

"Twenty-fife fathom," said the Portuguese, sleepily. "They strike on good an' queek. Some day I show you, Harvey."

The moon was beginning to walk on the still sea before the elder men came aft. The cook had no need to cry "second half". Dan and Manuel were down the hatch and at table ere Tom Platt, last and most deliberate of the elders, had finished wiping his mouth with the back of his hand. Harvey followed Penn, and sat down before a tin pan of cod's tongues and sounds, mixed with scraps of pork and fried potato, a loaf of hot bread, and some black and powerful coffee. Hungry as they were, they waited while "Pennsylvania" solemnly asked a blessing. Then they stoked in silence till Dan drew breath over his tin cup and demanded of Harvey how he felt.

"'Most full, but there's just room for another piece."

The cook was a huge, jet-black negro, and, unlike all the negroes Harvey had met, did not talk, contenting himself with smiles and dumb-show invitations to eat more.

"See, Harvey," said Dan, rapping with his fork on the table, "it's jest as I said. The young an' handsome men—like me an' Pennsy an' you an' Manuel—we're second ha'af, an' we eats when the first ha'af are through. They're the old fish; and they're mean an' humpy, an' their stummicks has to be humoured; so they come first, which they don't deserve. Ain't that so, doctor?"

The cook nodded.

"Can't he talk?" said Harvey, in a whisper.

"'Nough to git along. Not much o' anything we know. His natural tongue's kinder curious. Comes from the in'ards of Cape Breton, he does, where the farmers speak home-made Scotch. Cape Breton's full o' niggers whose folk run in there durin' aour war, an' they talk like the farmers—all huffy-chuffy."

---

① dress-down:加工(食物)。此处意为把捕捞回来的鱼杀好洗净盐腌储存。

"That is not Scotch," said "Pennsylvania." "That is Gaelic. So I read in a book."

"Penn reads a heap. Most of what he says is so-'cep' when it comes to a caount o' fish-eh?"

"Does your father just let them say how many they've caught without checking them?" said Harvey.

"Why, yes. Where's the sense of a man lyin' fer a few old cod?"

"Was a man once lied for his catch," Manuel put in. "Lied every day. Fife, ten, twenty-fife more fish than come he say there was."

"Where was that?" said Dan. "None o' aour folk."

"Frenchman of Anguille①."

"Ah! Them West Shore Frenchmen don't acount, anyway. Stands to reason they can't caount. If you run across any of their soft hooks, Harvey, you'll know why," said Dan, with an awful contempt.

"Always more and never less, Every time we come to dress,"

Long Jack roared down the hatch, and the "second ha'af" scrambled up at once.

The shadow of the masts and rigging, with the never-furled riding-sail, rolled to and fro on the heaving deck in the moonlight; and the pile of fish by the stern shone like a dump of fluid silver. In the hold there were tramplings and rumblings where Disko Troop and Tom Platt moved among the salt-bins. Dan passed Harvey a pitchfork, and led him to the inboard end of the rough table, where Uncle Salters was drumming impatiently with a knife-haft. A tub of salt water lay at his feet.

"You pitch to dad an' Tom Platt down the hatch, an' take keer Uncle Salters don't cut yer eye out," said Dan, swinging himself into the hold. "I'll pass salt below."

Penn and Manuel stood knee-deep among cod in the pen, flourishing drawn knives. Long Jack, a basket at his feet and mittens on his hands, faced Uncle Salters at the table, and Harvey stared at the pitchfork and the tub.

"Hi!" shouted Manuel, stooping to the fish, and bringing one up with a finger under its gill and a finger in its eye. He laid it on the edge of the pen; the knife-blade glimmered with a sound of tearing, and the fish, slit from throat to vent, with a nick on either side of the neck, dropped at Long Jack's feet.

"Hi!" said Long Jack, with a scoop of his mittened hand. The cod's liver dropped in the basket. Another wrench and scoop sent the head and offal flying, and the empty fish slid across to Uncle Salters, who snorted fiercely. There was another sound of tearing, the backbone flew over the bulwarks, and the fish, headless, gutted, and open, splashed in the

---

① Anguille:安圭拉岛［拉丁美洲］(在背风群岛中部,17世纪时沦为英国殖民地)。

tub，sending the salt water into Harvey's astonished mouth. After the first yell，the men were silent. The cod moved along as though they were alive，and long ere Harvey had ceased wondering at the miraculous dexterity of it all，his tub was full.

"Pitch!" grunted Uncle Salters，without turning his head，and Harvey pitched the fish by twos and threes down the hatch.

"Hi! Pitch 'em bunchy，" shouted Dan. "Don't scatter! Uncle Salters is the best splitter in the fleet. Watch him mind his book!①"

Indeed，it looked a little as though the round uncle were cutting magazine pages against time. Manuel's body，cramped over from the hips，stayed like a statue; but his long arms grabbed the fish without ceasing. Little Penn toiled valiantly，but it was easy to see he was weak. Once or twice Manuel found time to help him without breaking the chain of supplies，and once Manuel howled because he had caught his finger in a Frenchman's hook. These hooks are made of soft metal，to be rebent after use; but the cod very often get away with them and are hooked again elsewhere; and that is one of the many reasons why the Gloucester boats despise the Frenchmen.

Down below，the rasping sound of rough salt rubbed on rough flesh sounded like the whirring of a grindstone—a steady undertune to the "click-nick" of the knives in the pen; the wrench and schoop of torn heads，dropped liver，and flying offal; the "caraaah" of Uncle Salters's knife scooping away backbones; and the flap of wet，opened bodies falling into the tub.

At the end of an hour Harvey would have given the world to rest; for fresh，wet cod weigh more than you would think，and his back ached with the steady pitching. But he felt for the first time in his life that he was one of a working gang of men，took pride in the thought，and held on sullenly.

"Knife oh!②" shouted Uncle Salters，at last. Penn doubled up，gasping among the fish，Manuel bowed back and forth to supple himself，and Long Jack leaned over the bulwarks. The cook appeared，noiseless as a black shadow，collected a mass of backbones and heads，and retreated.

"Blood-ends for breakfast an' head-chowder，" said Long Jack，smacking his lips.

"Knife oh!" repeated Uncle Salters，waving the flat，curved splitter's weapon.

"Look by your foot，Harve，" cried Dan，below.

Harvey saw half a dozen knives stuck in a cleat in the hatch combing. He dealt these around，taking over the dulled ones.

---

① Uncle Salters is the best splitter in the fleet. Watch him mind his book! 此句意为：萨尔托斯是船队里最好的剖鱼手，瞧他像裁纸一样！

② knife oh：换刀！

"Water!" said Disko Troop.

"Scuttle-butt's for'ard, an' the dipper's alongside. Hurry, Harve," said Dan.

He was back in a minute with a big dipperful of stale brown water which tasted like nectar, and loosed the jaws of Disko and Tom Platt.

"These are cod," said Disko. "They ain't Damarskus figs, Tom Platt, nor yet silver bars. I've told you that every single time sence we've sailed together."

"A matter o' seven seasons," returned Tom Platt, coolly. "Good stowin's good stowin' all the same, an' there's a right an' a wrong way o' stowin' ballast even. If you'd ever seen four hundred ton o' iron set into the—"

"Hi!" With a yell from Manuel the work began again, and never stopped till the pen was empty. The instant the last fish was down, Disko Troop rolled aft to the cabin with his brother; Manuel and Long Jack went forward; Tom Platt only waited long enough to slide home the hatch ere he too disappeared. In half a minute Harvey heard deep snores in the cabin, and he was staring blankly at Dan and Penn.

"I did a little better that time, Danny," said Penn, whose eyelids were heavy with sleep. "But I think it is my duty to help clean."

"Wouldn't hev your conscience fer a thousand quintal," said Dan. "Turn in, Penn. You've no call to do boy's work. Draw a bucket, Harvey. Oh, Penn, dump these in the gurry-butt 'fore you sleep. Kin you keep awake that long?"

Penn took up the heavy basket of fish-livers, emptied them into a cask with a hinged top lashed by the fo'c'sle; then he too dropped out of sight in the cabin.

"Boys clean up after dressin' down, an' first watch in ca'am weather is boy's watch on the 'We're Here'." Dan sluiced the pen energetically, unshipped the table, set it up to dry in the moonlight, ran the red knife-blades through a wad of oakum, and began to sharpen them on a tiny grindstone, as Harvey threw offal and backbones overboard under his direction.

At the first splash a silvery-white ghost rose bolt upright from the oily water and sighed a weird whistling sigh. Harvey started back with a shout, but Dan only laughed. "Grampus," said he. "Beggin' fer fish-heads. They up-eend thet way when they're hungry. Breath on him like the doleful tombs, hain' he?" A horrible stench of decayed fish filled the air as the pillar of white sank, and the water bubbled oilily. "Hain't ye never seen a grampus up-eend before? You'll see 'em by hundreds 'fore ye're through. Say, it's good to hev a boy aboard again. Otto was too old, an' a Dutchy at that. Him an' me we fought consid'ble. ' Wouldn't ha' keered fer thet ef he'd hed a Christian tongue in his head. Sleepy?"

"Dead sleepy," said Harvey, nodding forward.

"'Mustn't sleep on watch. Rouse up an' see ef our anchor-light's bright an' shinin'. You're on watch now, Harve."

"Pshaw! What's to hurt us? Bright's day. Sn-orrr!"

"Jest when things happen[①], dad says. Fine weather's good sleepin', an' 'fore you know, maybe, you're cut in two by a liner, an' seventeen brass-bound officers, all gen'elmen, lift their hand to it that your lights was aout an' there was a thick fog. Harve, I've kinder took to you, but if you nod onct more I'll lay into you with a rope's end."

The moon, who sees many strange things on the Banks, looked down on a slim youth in knickerbockers and a red jersey, staggering around the cluttered decks of a seventy-ton schooner, while behind him, waving a knotted rope, walked, after the manner of an executioner, a boy who yawned and nodded between the blows he dealt.

The lashed wheel groaned and kicked softly, the riding-sail slatted a little in the shifts of the light wind, the windlass creaked, and the miserable procession continued. Harvey expostulated, threatened, whimpered, and at last wept outright, while Dan, the words clotting on his tongue, spoke of the beauty of watchfulness, and slashed away with the rope's end, punishing the dories as often as he hit Harvey. At last the clock in the cabin struck ten, and upon the tenth stroke little Penn crept on deck. He found two boys in two tumbled heaps side by side on the main-hatch, so deeply asleep that he actually rolled them to their berths.

▶扩展阅读

1. Carrington, C. E. *Rudyard Kipling: His Life and Work*. London: Macmillan and Company, 1955.

2. Lycett, A. *Rudyard Kipling*. London: Weidenfeld & Nicolson, 1999.

3. McAveeney, D. *Kipling in Gloucester, the Writing of "Captains Courageous"*. Gloucester, MA: The Curious Traveller Press, 1996.

4. Shanks, E. *Rudyard Kipling, a Study in Literature and Political Ideas*. New York: Doubleday, Doran, 1940.

5. Sullivan, Z. T. *Narratives of Empire: The Fictions of Rudyard Kipling*. Cambridge: Cambridge University Press, 2008.

▶学习参考网站

1. http://www.kipling.org.uk

2. http://www.online-literature.com/kipling/

3. http://nobelprize.org/nobel_prizes/literature/laureates/1907/kipling-bio.html

4. http://www.victorianweb.org/authors/kipling/index.html

【徐　燕　编注】

---

① Jest when things happen:不怕一万,就怕万一。

II. Sir Henry Newbolt: "Drake's Drum"

亨利·纽博尔特（Henry Newbolt，1862—1938），维多利亚时期的著名律师、诗人、批评家、小说家和剧作家。纽博尔特1862年出生于英格兰中部的斯塔福德郡，他的父亲是圣玛丽大教堂的牧师，4岁时，父亲去世，随后他跟随母亲搬到斯塔福德郡南部的沃尔萨尔，与母亲的亲属住在一起。他先后在克利夫顿大学（Clifton College）与牛津大学学习。1887年，纽博尔特毕业以后在伦敦的林肯律师学院（Lincoln's Inn）任律师，直到1899年。

1889年他与来自著名的出版业家庭的玛格丽特·沃斯（Margaret Duck Worth）结婚，婚后，他逐渐进行文学创作，开始写小说和诗歌，作品主题大多与海战有关，宣扬骑士美德、航海精神和爱国精神。他的早期诗作有模仿诗人丁尼生的痕迹。他的第一部作品是在他30岁那年出版的小说《敌手缴获》（*Taken from the Enemy*，1892）。1895年他出版了用无韵体写成的悲剧《莫德雷德》（*Mordred*），剧本中融入了大量有关亚瑟王的传奇故事。但是真正让他声名鹊起的是他那部讴歌海洋和海军的民谣集《海军上将群英颂》（*Admirals All*，1897），而其中最著名的又是《生命的火炬》（"Vitaï Lampada"）和《德雷克的鼓》（"Drake's Drum"）。之后，他还创作了大量与海洋有关的诗歌，如《岛屿之争》（"The Island Race"，1898），《巨轮航行》（"The Sailing of the Long-ships"，1902），《大海之歌》（"Songs of the Sea"，1904）和《舰队之歌》（"Songs of the Fleet"，1910）。第一次世界大战时，纽博尔特服务于英国的战时宣传部，后来，又被任命为通信部部长。因在战时的出色表现，1915年，他被英王授予勋爵称号，又在1922年被授予"荣誉侍从"（Companion of Honor）称号。

《德雷克的鼓》创作于1895年。当时，在海上争霸问题上，俄法两国对英国的战略航路构成严重威胁，各国之间展开了激烈的军备竞赛。在这首诗中，纽博尔特缅怀了为英国战胜西班牙无敌舰队而立下汗马功劳的英国航海家弗朗西斯·德雷克（Sir Francis Drake），并以此来鼓舞英国人的爱国热情和斗志。在诗歌的第一节，诗人设想，德雷克虽然身处遥远的地方，但他整天梦想着普利茅斯港、那里的船只和他手下的水手，一股思乡之情跃然纸上。在第二节中，诗人描写了德雷克的临死遗言：如果祖国遇到危难，他将义无反顾，从天堂回到人间，为保卫祖国尽自己的力量。在第三节中，诗人表示德雷克无论何时何地都会保佑祖国不受敌人侵犯。在这首诗中，诗人运用叠句"An' dreamin' arl the time o' Plymouth Hoe"，旨在通过德雷克对家乡的思念,来激发人们的爱国热情,而"Capten,art tha sleepin' there below?"的反复出现则说明德雷克爱国的英勇形象永远活在人们的心中。叠句的使用起到了烘托爱国主义主题的作用。纽博尔特的诗之所以受到当时读者的喜爱,一方面是因为其诗歌题材符合大英帝国时代大众读者的阅读趣味,另一方面也因为纽博尔特的诗音乐性强,节奏或轻松舒缓或铿锵有力。

▶

Drake's Drum[①]

Drake he's in his hammock[②] an' a thousand miles away[③],

(Capten, art tha sleepin' there below?[④])

Slung[⑤] atween[⑥] the round shot in Nombre Dios Bay[⑦],

An' dreamin' arl the time o' Plymouth Hoe[⑧].

Yarnder[⑨] lumes[⑩] the Island, yarnder lie the ships,

Wi' sailor lads a-dancing' heel-an'-toe[⑪],

An' the shore-lights flashin', an' the night-tide dashin'[⑫],

---

① Drake:德雷克,即 Sir Francis Drake(1540—1596),英国伊丽莎白时代的商船船长、航海家、海盗。他是继麦哲伦之后第一个完成环球航行的英国船长(1577—1580)。伊丽莎白一世在 1581 年赐德雷克皇家爵士头衔。1588 年,在击败当时海上霸王西班牙的无敌舰队(Invincible Armada)时,德雷克发挥了重要作用。1596 年,在袭击并占领巴拿马北侧的迪奥斯港(Nombre de Dios)后,德雷克患病死于海上。他的尸体被装入一个铅皮棺木,遵其遗嘱,在德文郡的波特贝罗(Portobello)被放入大海。德雷克的鼓是他在航海时,随身携带的军鼓。临终前,他吩咐将此鼓送交普利茅斯附近的巴克兰修道院(Buckland Abbey),并发出誓言:日后英国面临危险,有人敲响此鼓的话,他就会重返人间,来保卫自己的祖国。今天此鼓还保存在巴克兰修道院。在历史上,据说有人曾多次听到此鼓发出声响,如 1620 年,当"五月花"号(Mayflower)驶离普利茅斯港前往美国的时候;当纳尔逊将军(Admiral Lord Nelson)成为普利茅斯市荣誉市民的时候;1815 年,当拿破仑被流放到圣赫勒拿岛(St. Helena)经过普利茅斯港时;1914 年,第一次世界大战爆发时。

② hammock:在船上,水手休息用的吊铺。

③ an' a thousand miles away:指德雷克正在 1000 英里外的海底沉睡。

④ Capten,art tha sleepin' there below?:本诗中所用大部分为水手英语。下同。本句应为:Captain, are you sleeping there below? 指德雷克死之前,要求将他的遗体在德文郡外沉入大海。

⑤ slung:sling 的过去式、过去分词。指吊铺的摇晃。

⑥ atween:同 between。

⑦ Nombre Dios Bay:指德雷克的死亡之地,参照注解 1。

⑧ An' dreamin' arl the time o' Plymouth Hoe:and dreaming all the time of Plymouth Hoe. Plymouth Hoe:普利茅斯港口外,伸入大海的一片狭长地带。人们认为德雷克在打败西班牙无敌舰队前,曾在这里打保龄球。这一节诗表明了德雷克在死前的思乡之情。

⑨ Yarnder:in a distance,over there 在远处。

⑩ lume:应为 loom。意为:隐隐约约中出现。

⑪ Wi' sailor lads a-dancing' heel-an'-toe:应为 With sailor lads dancing heel and toe. lads:young men,年轻人。heel and toe:当时一种流行的舞蹈。

⑫ An' the shore-lights flashin', an' the night-tide dashin':应为 And the shore lights flashing,and the night tide dashing.海岸的灯光闪耀,夜晚的潮水奔流。

He sees et arl so plainly as he saw et long ago.①

Drake he was a Devon② man, an' ruled the Devon seas③,
（Capten, art tha' sleepin' there below?）
Roving④ tho' his death fell⑤, he went wi' heart at ease⑥,
A' dreamin' arl the time o' Plymouth Hoe.
"Take my drum to England, hang et by the shore⑦,
Strike et when your powder's runnin' low⑧;
If the Dons⑨ sight Devon⑩, I'll quit the port o' Heaven⑪,
An' drum them up the Channel as we drum'd them long ago⑫."

Drake he's in his hammock till the great Armadas⑬ come,
（Capten, art tha sleepin' there below?）
Slung atween the round shot, listenin' for the drum⑭,
An' dreamin arl the time o' Plymouth Hoe.
Call him on the deep sea, call him up the Sound⑮,
Call him when ye sail to meet the foe⑯;

---

① He sees et arl so plainly as he saw et long ago：应为 He sees it all so plainly as he saw it long ago.如今他平静地看着这一切,如同他很久以前一样。

② Devon：德文郡。德雷克的出生地。

③ an' ruled the Devon seas：该句指德雷克死时,他吩咐将其棺木葬入德文郡的大海,并将随身携带的鼓送交德文郡附近的巴克兰修道院,表明他死后也要保卫家乡不受敌人侵犯。

④ rove：traveling on the sea,在海上航行。

⑤ 该句意思为：德雷克一生在海上航行,直到 1596 年死于海上。tho 应为 through,意为"直到"。

⑥ he went wi' heart at ease：He went with heart at ease.他死的时候,心情平静。

⑦ hang et by the shore：hang it by the shore,以下几句是德雷克死之前的遗言。

⑧ Strike et when your powder's runnin' low.：Strike it when your powder's running low.在弹药快用尽的危急时刻,敲打此鼓。

⑨ Dons：指西班牙人。西班牙人习惯在名字前用 Don 来表示对对方的尊敬。当时,西班牙人是英国主要的海上敌人,所以此处的 Dons 表示英国的敌人。

⑩ If the Dons sight Devon：如果西班牙敌人来到德文郡。

⑪ I'll quit the port o' Heaven：我（Francis Drake）就从天堂来到人间。

⑫ drum 此处指擂鼓进攻的意思。该句指 1588 年英国海军在英吉利海峡大败当时的海上霸主西班牙无敌舰队。

⑬ Armadas：西班牙无敌舰队。

⑭ Slung atween the round shot,listenin' for the drum：slung between the round shot,listening for the drum.德雷克一边躺在吊床上,一边倾听鼓声。

⑮ Sound：指普利茅斯湾（Plymouth Sound）,由流经普利茅斯西部的普利姆河（Plym）和流经东部的泰马河（Tamar）两条河的河口形成,西南邻英吉利海峡,是一个战略要地。

⑯ Call him when ye sail to meet the foe：应为 Call him when you sail to meet your foe. foe：敌人。

Where the old trade's plyin' an' the old flag flyin'[①]

They shall find him ware[②] an' wakin', as they found him long ago![③]

▶扩展阅读

1. Newbolt, M. *The Later Life and Letters of Sir Henry Newbolt*. London: Faber and Faber Limited, 1942.

2. Newbolt, H. *The Idea of an English Association*. Oxford: Oxford University Press, 1928.

3. Newbolt, H. *The Tide of Time in English Poetry*. London: T. Nelson & Sons, Ltd, 1925.

▶学习参考网站

1. http://www.robertfulford.com/newbolt.html

2. http://en.wikiquote.org/wiki/Henry_Newbolt

3. http://www.warpoets.org/conflicts/greatwar/newbolt/

【白玉凤　编注】

---

① Where the old trade's plyin' an' the old flag flyin': Where the old trade is plying and the old flag flying. ply trade: 做生意。

② ware: 〈古〉留神的,警惕的。

③ 最后两句意为:在任何一个经营生意、海船行驶的地方,人们都可以发现德雷克没有睡去,而是时刻保持警惕的状态,正如他们多年前发现的一样。

12. Lord Alfred Tennyson:
"Break, Break, Break"/"Crossing the Bar"

　　阿尔弗雷德·丁尼生（Alfred Tennyson，1809—1892），英国维多利亚时代中期的著名诗人，重视诗的形式完美，音韵和谐，1850 年获得"桂冠诗人"（Poet Laureate）的称号，1884 年被封为男爵。丁尼生出身于林肯郡索姆斯比的一个牧师家庭，在 12 个兄弟姐妹中排行第四。年轻的丁尼生曾在父亲的图书馆阅读大量书籍，8 岁开始写诗。1827 年，他和他的兄弟弗雷德里克及查尔斯出版了《两兄弟诗集》（*Poems by Two Brothers*）。1828 年，丁尼生进入剑桥大学；1829 年他的诗歌《廷巴克图》（"Timbuctoo"）赢得了校长金牌；1830 年，他出版了《抒情诗集》（*Poems Chiefly Lyrical*）。1931 年丁尼生的父亲去世，他未取得学位便离开剑桥大学。第二年他出版了一本小册子，名为《诗歌》，但当时并未被广泛接受。1833 年，丁尼生最亲密的朋友，年仅 22 岁的作家阿瑟·亨利·哈勒姆（Arthur Henry Hallam）突然病逝，在痛失密友及作品受到恶评的双重打击之下，丁尼生近 10 年内未再出版作品。1850 年是丁尼生一生的转折点，他多年来为纪念哈勒姆而作的挽歌集《悼念集》（*In Memoriam*）一问世就大受欢迎。同年 6 月，他与相爱 15 年之久的恋人艾米莉·塞尔伍德（Emily Sellwood）结为伉俪。11 月，由于博得女王的青睐，丁尼生继华兹华斯之后被封为"桂冠诗人"。1853 年起，他定居于怀特岛法令福德（Farringford）的庄园。1892 年 10 月，丁尼生去世，被葬在威斯敏斯特教堂的诗人角。

　　丁尼生的主要诗作有《夏洛特小姐》（"The Lady of Shalott"，1833）、《尤利西斯》（"Ulysses"，1833），长篇叙事诗《公主》（*The Princess*，1847），诗组《悼念集》，《悼惠灵顿公爵之死》（"Ode on the Death of the Duke of Wellington"，1852）、《轻骑兵队的冲锋》（"The Charge of the Light Brigade"，1854）、《莫德》（"Maud"，1855）、《国王叙事诗》（"Idylls of the King"，1859）、《伊诺克·阿登》（"Enoch Arden"，1864）、《过沙洲》（"Crossing the Bar"，1889）等。其中，他的 131 首组诗《悼念集》被视为英国文学史上最优秀的哀歌之一。丁尼生处于英国资本主义大发展的时代，但是他更多地感受到了工业化进程中社会的激烈动荡和价值标准的变化，因而他的作品较多地关注伦理和人生，不时流露出对旧时代秩序的追思和怀念。除了时代因素，他的父亲和挚友的离世深深影响了丁尼生对人生的看法，怀旧、悼亡、对生死问题的探索成了他的诗歌的主题。丁尼生的诗题材广泛、字雕句琢，特别讲求语言形式和音律声韵之美。以下所选两首诗均以大海为意象来抒发诗人的情感，是广为人们吟诵的佳作。

　　《溅吧,溅吧,溅吧》"Break,Break,Break"是丁尼生为哀悼亡友哈勒姆而作。丁尼生和哈勒姆是剑桥大学同学,求学期间两人共同加入了剑桥的"使徒社"(the Society of Apostles),后来哈勒姆还成了丁尼生妹妹的未婚夫。1832 年丁尼生和哈勒姆结伴游历欧洲,翌年哈勒姆因病客死在维也纳,丁尼生悲痛异常,于 1834 年创作了这首诗,1842 年出版。全诗言精而清晰,音律优美,清凄缠绵。break 一词既是模拟海浪拍击岩石发出的声音的拟声词,又有"破碎"之意,象征着诗人的心碎。大海在诗中是一种无法驾驭、具有破坏性的残酷力量,是融生命和死亡为一体的意象。诗中"嬉闹的渔家兄妹""歌唱荡舟的少年水手"和"驶进港口的船舶""沉寂的嗓音""消逝的手"形成了生与死的鲜明对比。"大海在岩石脚下崩裂、美好的日子死了",诗人把对亡友的怀念和痛惜升华为对人生无常的感慨和对生命的怀疑,大海之印象和声音生动地体现了诗人对死亡的深刻感受。

　　《过沙洲》创作于 1889 年。当时丁尼生从奥德沃茨出发,途经英格兰的索伦特海峡,到怀特岛上的法令福德居所,不料在旅途中他大病一场,之后他创作了这首诗。另一个说法是此诗系诗人作于一艘停泊在港口的游船上。这首诗虽不是诗人最后的作品,但丁尼生临终前嘱咐他的儿子哈勒姆·丁尼生将这首《过沙洲》放在他的诗集中的末尾,可见诗人将此诗视作绝唱。全诗共四节,采用传统的 ABAB 韵式。诗歌的形式和内容融为一体,长句短句相济,犹如起伏的海浪,制造出一种涛声阵阵的音效和氛围。在这首为自己而作的挽歌中,诗人将死亡的历程比作"穿过沙洲",而后走向辽阔的海洋,体现了诗人直面死亡的那份平静和乐天知命的情怀。

▶

Break, Break, Break

Break, break, break,
On thy① cold gray stones, O Sea!
And I would② that my tongue could utter
The thoughts that arise in me.

O well for③ the fisherman's boy,
That he shouts with his sister at play④!
O well for the sailor lad⑤,

---

① thy:〈古〉相当于现代英语中的 your,意为"你的"(thou 的所有格)。
② would:wish,但愿。
③ O well for:O it would be well for,但愿……那么么好啊!
④ at play:嬉戏,玩耍。
⑤ the sailor lad:少年水手。

That he sings in his boat on the bay!

And the stately ships go on
To their haven① under the hill;
But O for the touch of a vanished hand②,
And the sound of a voice that is still!

Break, break, break,
At the foot of thy crags, O Sea!
But the tender grace of a day③ that is dead
Will never come back to me.

▶

Crossing the Bar④

Sunset and evening star
And one clear call for me!
And may there be no moaning⑤ of the bar,
When I put out to sea,

But such a tide as moving seems asleep,
Too full for sound and foam⑥,
When that which drew from out the boundless deep
Turns again home.

Twilight⑦ and evening bell,
And after that the dark!
And may there be no sadness of farewell,
When I embark⑧;

---

① haven:港口。
② But O for the touch of a vanished hand:要是能摸到一只消失的手,那该多好啊! 诗人强烈哀悼亡友哈勒姆,希望能再握到他的手。
③ the tender grace of a day:美好的日子。
④ crossing the bar:渡过沙洲,诗中比喻走向死亡。
⑤ moaning:指大海拍击沙洲时,发出类似呻吟的声音。
⑥ Too full for sound and foam:潮涨得太满,以至于大海似乎悄无声息,看不见任何泡沫。
⑦ twilight:黄昏,暮霭中。
⑧ embark:出航,比喻人生之旅的开始。

For though from out our bourne① of Time and Place

The flood may bear me far,

I hope to see my Pilot② face to face

When I have crossed the bar.

▶扩展阅读

1. Martin，R. *Tennyson*：*The Unquiet Heart*. London：Faber and Faber，1979.

2. Shaw，W. D. *Tennyson's Style*. Ithaca：Cornell University Press，1976.

3. Tennyson，H. *Alfred Lord Tennyson*：*A Memoir by His Son*. London：Macmillan，1897.

4. Thorn，M. *Tennyson*. New York：St. Martin's Press，1992.

▶学习参考网站

1. http：//www.blackcatpoems.com/t/alfred_tennyson.html

2. http：//theotherpages.org/poems/poem-st.html♯tennyson

3. http：//www.poetseers.org/the_great_poets/british_poets/alfred_tennyson/library/

4. http：//www.cummingsstudyguides.net/Guides4/Tennyson.html

5. http：//www.victorianweb.org/authors/tennyson/kincaid/ch3a.html

6. http：//en.wikipedia.org/wiki/Break，_Break，_Break

【唐燕琼　编注】

---

① 　bourne：界限，目的地。

② 　pilot：领航员，诗中将上帝喻作人的精神领航员。

13. Mathew Arnold: "Dover Beach"

马修·阿诺德(Mathew Arnold，1822—1888)，英国维多利亚时期杰出的诗人、文学家和社会批评家，生于泰晤士河谷农村，其父曾任拉格比公学(Rugby School)的校长，是著名的教育家、罗马史学者。阿诺德自幼受到良好的教育，于 1841 年进入牛津大学贝利奥尔学院学习，毕业后曾在拉格比公学短期任教，25 岁时任辉格党领袖格兰斯顿勋爵的私人秘书。1849 年，他发表了第一部诗集《迷途浪子》(The Strayed Reveller)。1851 年，29 岁的阿诺德和心仪已久的范妮·露西·威特曼(Fanny Lucy Wightman)结婚，并改任教育督学之职，长达 35 年之久(1851—1886)，其间曾在牛津大学任英诗讲座教授，历时 10 年(1857—1867)，后曾两次到美国讲学，归国后不久突发心脏病猝死。阿诺德任督学期间曾游历欧洲大陆考察各国教育制度，遍访英伦三岛调研社会教育状况，对其所处时代的社会文化生活有深入的了解，正是这种丰富的经验和开阔的视野，成就了阿诺德在文学和评论界的杰出表现。

阿诺德的创作生涯大致分为两个时期：19 世纪 50 年代的诗歌创作和 60—80 年代的文学、社会、宗教、教育等方面的评论。他的主要作品有《被遗弃的人鱼》("The Forsaken Merman"，1849)、《多佛海滩》("Dover Beach"，1851)、《色希斯》("Thyrsis"，1866)、《拉格比教堂》("Rugby Chapel"，1867)、《夜莺》("Philomela"，1853)等抒情诗和《学者吉普赛》("The Scholar Gypsy"，1853)、《邵莱布和罗斯托》("Sohrab and Rustum"，1853)等叙事诗。但是，早在 50 年代中期阿诺德的兴趣就发生了转向。他认为自己的作品色调阴郁，有无法排遣的病态郁结，不能像从前的诗歌一样给人们苦恼的生活带来愉悦，不符合心目中的好诗的要求，因此改弦易辙，先后转战于散文创作和文学、社会、政治、宗教及教育批评等多个领域，并且在每个领域里都硕果累累。其批评论著有《评论一集》(Essay in Criticism，1865)、《评论二集》(Essay in Criticism，1888)、《文化与无政府状态》(Culture and Anarchy，1869)、《文学与教条》(Literature and Dogma，1873)和《上帝与圣经》(God and the Bible，1875)等。

阿诺德从小在泰晤士河畔长大，对海洋有着特殊的感情和深刻的理解。在他的名篇《多佛海滩》中，作者以一种宁静哀婉的曲调，用大海的形象引起比兴，在潮起潮落中反思，表现了诗人面对社会变革、古代文明沦丧和传统道德崩溃时处于精神荒原状态下的苦闷。《多佛海滩》是诗人与新婚妻子 1851 年夏天在多佛海滩欢度蜜月时的随感。诗中忧郁哀愁的格调似乎与这样一个欢愉和美满的时刻有点格格不入。其中一方面是因为阿诺德个人情感的压抑和苦恼所致,阿诺德为了与范妮结婚被迫在范妮父亲的安排下接受了教育督学这个体面的工作,而不得不放弃自己热爱的诗歌创作;另一方面也缘于诗人对维多利亚时期工业迅速发展、物欲膨胀、思想混乱而产生的忧虑。面对社会的信仰危机和精神荒芜,诗人觉得无力回天,只能为之谱写一曲千古悲鸣的绝望之歌。整首诗始以"光明",终以"黑暗"。诗人以其犀利的眼光对时弊给予尖锐的批判,同时流露出一股痛惜扼腕之情。从结构上看,全诗共有四节,每节包括的诗行不等,分别是十四行、六行、八行和九行。诗行长短不一,跨行诗句不断出现,诗歌韵脚和谐,但排列却参差不齐,恰似潮涨潮落,也如思绪绵延,这在形式上更好地揭示了当时社会的动荡和诗人内心的不安。这首诗深刻概括了一个繁华时代背后的精神危机,洞悉了人类内心最深处的孤独和黑暗,因此被誉为维多利亚时代最简练的"诗史"。

Dover Beach

The sea is calm to-night.
The tide is full，the moon lies fair
Upon the straits①；—on the French coast，the light
Gleams，and is gone；the cliffs of England stand，
Glimmering and vast，out in the tranquil bay.
Come to the window，sweet is the night-air!
Only，from the long line of spray②
Where the ebb meets the moon-blanch'd sand③，
Listen! you hear the grating roar④
Of pebbles which the waves suck back，and fling⑤.
At their return，up the high strand，
Begin，and cease，and then again begin，
With tremulous cadence⑥ slow，and bring
The eternal note of sadness in.

---

① the moon lies fair/Upon the straits:皎洁的月亮悬挂在多佛海峡上。the straits:指 the Straits of Dover(多佛海峡),英、法间的海峡,连接英吉利海峡和北海,法国海岸上的灯光与英国海岸仅 20 英里(约 32 公里)之遥,这里是第二次世界大战时重要的海战地点,历史上曾在海峡内发生多次著名海战。
② the long line of spray:浪花飞溅的长长的海岸线。
③ Where the ebb meets the moon-blanch'd sand:和月光所漂白的沙滩相衔接的地方。
④ the grating roar:猛烈的摩擦声响。
⑤ the waves suck back,and fling:水浪把石子卷回去,又抛出。
⑥ cadence:旋律。

Sophocles① long ago

Heard it on the Aegean②, and it brought

Into his mind the turbid ebb and flow

Of human misery; we

Find also in the sound a thought,

Hearing it by this distant northern sea.

The Sea of Faith

Was once, too, at the full, and round earth's shore

Lay like the folds of a bright girdle furl'd③;

But now I only hear

Its melancholy, long, withdrawing roar,

Retreating, to the breath

Of the night-wind down the vast edges drear

And naked shingles④ of the world.

Ah, love, let us be true

To one another! for the world, which seems

To lie before us like a land of dreams,

So various, so beautiful, so new,

Hath⑤ really neither joy, nor love, nor light,

Nor certitude, nor peace, nor help for pain;

And we are here as on a darkling plain

Swept with confused alarms of struggle and flight,

Where ignorant armies clash by night⑥.

▶扩展阅读

1. Allott, K. Ed. *The Poems of Matthew Arnold*. London: Longman Norton, 1965.

2. Collini, S. *Arnold*. Oxford: Oxford University Press, 1988.

---

① Sophocles:索福克勒斯(496BC?—406BC)、埃斯库罗斯(AEschylus)和欧里庇得斯(Euripides)共同被称为古希腊三大悲剧诗人,索福克勒斯一生共写 123 部剧本,主要作品有悲剧《埃阿斯》(*Ajax*,约公元前 442 年)、《安提戈涅》(*Antigone*,约公元前 441 年)和《奥狄浦斯王》(*Oedipus the King*,约公元前 431 年)等。

② the Aegean:爱琴海。关于索福克勒斯听到海潮涨落之声想到人类悲苦的事,见《安提戈涅》第 583—591 行,合唱队把奥狄浦斯一家的命运变迁比作大海的波浪。

③ Lay like the folds of a bright girdle furl'd:(涨潮时,大海将陆地紧紧包围,)就像一条收紧的闪光的腰带。

④ shingles:铺满圆卵石的海滩。

⑤ hath:〈古〉has(have 的第三人称单数形式)。

⑥ ignorant armies clash by night:也许是指 1848 年革命,也许是指法国军队在 1849 年包围罗马之战。

3. Culler，A. D. *Imaginative Reason*：*The Poetry of Matthew Arnold*. New Haven：Yale University Press，1966.

4. Honan，P. *Matthew Arnold*，*a Life*，New York：McGraw-Hill，1981.

5. Pratt，L. R. *Matthew Arnold Revisited*. New York：Twayne Publishers，2000.

6. Tinker，C. B. & Lowry H. F. *The Poetry of Matthew Arnold*：*A Commentary*. New York：Oxford University Press，1940.

▶学习参考网站

1. http：//www.poets.org/poet.php/prmPID/88

2. http：//www.victorianweb.org/authors/arnold/index.html

3. http：//rpo.library.utoronto.ca/poet/7.html

4. http：//www.poetseers.org/the_romantics/matthew_arnold/library/

5. http：//www.iment.com/maida/poetry/arnold.htm

【唐燕琼　编注】

14. John Masefield: "Sea-Fever"

　　约翰·梅斯菲尔德（John Masefield，1878—1967），英国著名的诗人、小说家、剧作家和评论家。他出生于英国赫里福德郡的勒德布里（Ledbury，Hertfordshire），父亲是一名律师。梅斯菲尔德 6 岁时，母亲生下妹妹便去世了，13 岁时，父亲去世，于是他终止学业，离家到海船上当伙计、做水手，开始了他海上漂泊的生涯。在海上旅途中，他阅读了大量书籍并对写作产生了浓厚的兴趣，积累了大量关于海洋的写作素材。1895 年他曾随船航行到美国纽约，在当地一边打零工一边进行创作。1897 年他返回英国，开始给各种杂志写稿，从此走上了文学创作之路。23 岁时，梅斯菲尔德遇到了和他相差 12 岁的康斯坦丝·克罗姆林（Constance Crommelin）。两人结婚后生活幸福，育有一对儿女。1930 年，梅斯菲尔德被授予英国第 22 届"桂冠诗人"的称号。1967 年 5 月 12 日，梅斯菲尔德因坏疽感染逝世，根据他本人的遗愿骨灰安葬在威斯敏斯特教堂的诗人角。

　　梅斯菲尔德一生多才多艺，作品众多，主要以诗歌见长，还写过小说、戏剧和评论，作品题材以大海和英国乡间生活为特色。1902 年他出版了第一本作品集《盐水谣》（*Salt-Water Ballads*），其中的《海之恋》（"Sea-Fever"）是他最著名的抒情短诗之一。他的其他代表作有长篇叙事诗《永恒的宽恕》（*The Everlasting Mercy*，1911）和《狐狸雷纳德》（*Reynard the Fox*，1919），诗歌《背街上的寡妇》（"The Widow in the Bye Street"，1912）、《道伯》（"Dauber"，1913）、《莱特·罗耶》（"Right Royal"，1920）等；小说有《萨德·哈克尔》（*Sard Harker*，1924）、《午夜人》（*The Midnight Folk*，1927）、《黎明的鸟》（*The Bird of Dawning*，1933）等；戏剧有《难河悲剧》（*The Tragedy of Nan*，1909）、《庞培大帝的悲剧》（*The Tragedy of Pompey the Great*，1910）等；文学评论有《威廉·莎士比亚》（*William Shakespeare*，1911）、《约翰·米林顿·辛格》（*John Millington Synge*，1915）、《乔叟》（*Chaucer*，1931）等。

　　约翰·梅斯菲尔德年轻时的海上生涯给他留下了深刻的印象，他的许多诗作的主题都与大海、与水有关，因此，他被誉为"大海的诗人"。这首《海之恋》写于 1900 年，当时年仅 22 岁的梅斯菲尔德因这首诗篇而名震诗坛。其中短短 12 行诗，简洁、凝练的语言营造了一个波浪起伏、白云飘浮的优美的海上画卷。诗人通过描述他对大海魂牵梦萦的眷恋，抒发了他对大海所代表的自由精神的深深渴望与向往，表达了他从尘嚣回归大海、回归大自然的豁达之情。诗中大海的深度展现了诗人对人生的深刻洞察，和对现实的一种超越。从诗的韵律看，全诗押韵，充满了乐感，犹如大海自然波动的韵律，生动地展现了诗中海浪、海风的跌宕起伏和扬帆的大船破浪前行的形象;从形式上看,诗的每一节都用相同的句式展开一个开阔、辽远的大海的境界,海、天、人组成的立体空间展现了诗人对大海的深深眷恋,这律动的大海书写着诗人对永恒、自由的追求和向往,全诗意境优美,洋溢着自由和独立的精神,令人为之振奋。

▶

Sea-Fever

I must down to the seas again，to the lonely sea and the sky，

And all I ask is a tall ship and a star to steer her by①，

And the wheel's kick② and the wind's song and the white sail's shaking③，

And a grey mist on the sea's face，and a grey dawn breaking④.

I must down to the seas again，for the call of the running tide⑤

Is a wild call and a clear call that may not be denied；

And all I ask is a windy day with the white clouds flying，

And the flung spray and the blown spume，and the sea-gulls crying⑥.

I must down to the seas again，to the vagrant gypsy life⑦，

To the gull's way and the whale's way where the wind's like a whetted knife⑧；

And all I ask is a merry yarn from a laughing fellow-rover⑨，

And quiet sleep and a sweet dream when the long trick's over.

▶扩展阅读

1. Dwyer，J. *John Masefield*. New York：Ungar，1987.

2. Hamilton，W. H. *John Masefield：A Critical Study*. London：George Allen and Unwin，1922.

3. Masefield，J. *On the Hill*. London：Heinemann，1949.

4. Smith，C. B. *John Masefield：A Life*. Oxford：Oxford University Press，1978.

5. Spark，M. *John Masefield*. London：Pimlico，1992.

———————————————

① a star to steer her by：指引航程的一点星光。

② the wheel's kick：轮船破浪前行。

③ the white sail's shaking：白帆飘浮摇曳。

④ a grey dawn breaking：黎明破雾而至。

⑤ the call of the running tide：海潮的呼唤。

⑥ the flung spray and the blown spume，and the sea-gulls crying：欢蹦乱跳的浪花,胀鼓鼓的泡沫和海鸥的鸣叫。

⑦ to the vagrant gypsy life：过吉卜赛人般的流浪生活。

⑧ the wind's like a whetted knife：风像利刃一般。

⑨ a merry yarn from a laughing fellow-rover：快乐流浪人的欢乐奇谈。

6. Sternlicht，S. *John Masefield*. Boston：Twayne Publishers，1977.

▶学习参考网站

1. http：∥www.theotherpages.org/poems/poem-mn.html♯masefield

2. http：∥www.poemhunter.com/john-masefield/

3. http：∥en.wikiquote.org/wiki/John_Masefield

4. http：∥www.spartacus.schoolnet.co.uk/Jmasefield.htm

5. http：∥publishingcentral.com/masefield/

6. http：∥www.blupete.com/Literature/Poetry/MasefieldSeaFever.htm

【唐燕琼　编注】

15. John Millington Synge: *Riders to the Sea*

约翰·米林顿·辛格（又译沁孤或辛厄）（John Millington Synge，1871—1909），爱尔兰剧作家，爱尔兰文艺复兴运动代表人物，出身于爱尔兰首府都柏林郊区一个宗教气息浓郁的乡绅家庭，幼年即丧父，跟随母亲长大。辛格自幼体弱多病、性格敏感，却热爱自然，经常独自去野外采集蝴蝶或飞蛾标本。1888年，17岁的辛格赴都柏林三一学院学习盖尔语与爱尔兰历史，毕业后则漫游欧洲，一边学习音乐，一边尝试文学创作。1896年，25岁的辛格在巴黎邂逅大诗人叶芝，遂成好友。据说，叶芝读过辛格的诗作之后，曾劝导辛格应该抛弃巴黎的浮华，去偏僻的海角体验真正的爱尔兰生活，以前人没有讲述过的故事成就自己的诗名。

年轻的辛格听从了叶芝的建议。自1898年起，辛格多次前往偏居于爱尔兰西部的艾兰岛，与岛民同吃同住，从岛上近乎原始的生活中汲取创作的灵感与养分。辛格的几部重要剧作的素材，如《蹈海骑手》（*Riders to the Sea*，1904，又译为《骑马下海的人》）、《圣井》（*The Well of the Saints*，1905）、《西方世界的花花公子》（*The Playboy of the Western World*，1907）均源于他在艾兰岛上的所见所闻。就创作手法而言，辛格善于采用现实主义的手法表现爱尔兰岛民延绵久远的民俗传统与当下孤独艰辛的生活，以荒凉质朴而又悠远深沉的风格触动观众的心灵。1909年，自幼身体羸弱的辛格英年辞世，年仅38岁。辛格的一生虽然短暂，作品数量也颇为有限，但他的剧作却获得了"爱尔兰文艺复兴在戏剧上的最大业绩"的美名，其本人也成了爱尔兰文学史上最重要的剧作家之一。

《蹈海骑手》是一部反映爱尔兰岛民苦难处境的悲剧。四周被大海所困的岛民生活极为艰难，饲养马匹并将马贩卖到对面的岸上换取生活必需品是他们维持生计的主要手段。《蹈海骑手》为独幕剧（one-act play），全剧用词精炼，出场人物中有名有姓的只有四位，分别是老母亲茅利亚、大女儿凯瑟林、小女儿娜拉和儿子巴特莱。剧幕拉开，娜拉返家，请姐姐凯瑟林辨认她所携衣物是否是家中兄弟迈格尔的遗物。两人悄声低语，不愿惊扰年老体衰的茅利亚。巴特莱从外归来，说要出海至集市卖马，茅利亚极力反对，但巴特莱并不从命，茅利亚心中抑郁。凯瑟林发现巴特莱没有带干粮，要茅利亚抄近道送上。茅利亚返回之后，却神色黯然，说自己看到噩兆，有迈格尔的鬼魂跟随在巴特莱马后。想起公公、丈夫和五个儿子已被大海吞噬，最后一个也在劫难逃，茅利亚心中酸楚，神情恍惚。片刻之后，乡邻鱼贯而入，抬进一具尸体——正是被马驹掀入海中溺毙的巴特莱。众人跪伏于巴特莱的尸体旁。恍惚之间，茅利亚平静地缓缓道出一句："托万能的上帝的福，迈格尔在遥远的北方安葬了；巴特莱将安息在上好的棺材里，一定会埋入深深的坟墓。我们还要什么呢？没有一个人是长生不老的，我们应该知足了。"言毕，再度跪下，剧幕徐降，全剧终。

《蹈海骑手》是独幕剧，该剧自上演初始，便好评如潮。我们看到，该剧集中渲染了人与自然搏斗时那种惊心动魄的紧张气氛。剧中既有暴虐无端的大海，又有在大海面前虽然渺小、却镇定达观的人。剧中人物茅利亚堪与悲剧人物俄狄浦斯王相比，她身上体现出一种经典悲剧中的凝重与庄严。如果说不断吞噬生命的大海象征着令人类永远无法认识与把握的神秘的命运，那么茅利亚以一己之身承受命运的次次打击，则更是于谦卑和忍耐中展现了人类生存际遇的尊严与伟大。如此看来，戏剧的场景虽然是在偏居一隅的爱尔兰孤岛之上，但剧中所体现的精神却是属于所有宁愿被摧毁而不愿被打败的、真正的人。

Riders to the Sea

Characters:

Maurya, an old woman
Bartley, her son
Cathleen, her daughter

Nora, a younger daughter
Men and women

[*An island off the West of Ireland. Cottage kitchen, with nets, oilskins, spinning-wheel, some new boards standing by the wall, etc. Cathleen, a girl of about twenty, finishes kneading cake, and puts it down in the pot-oven by the fire; then wipes her hands, and begins to spin at the wheel. Nora, a young girl, puts her head in at the door.*]

Nora: (in a low voice) Where is she?

Cathleen: She's lying down, God help her, and maybe sleeping, if she's able.

[*Nora comes in softly, and takes a bundle from under her shawl.*]

Cathleen: (spinning the wheel rapidly) What is it you have?

Noba: The young priest is after bringing them. It's a shirt and a plain stocking were got off a drowned man in Donegal.

[*Cathleen stops her wheel with a sudden movement, and leans out to listen.*]

Nora: We're to find out if it's Michael's they are; some time herself will be down looking by the sea.

Cathleen: How would they be Michael's, Nora? How would he go the length of that way to the far north?

Nora: The young priest says he's known the like of it. "If it's Michael's they are," says he, "you can tell herself he's got a clean burial by the grace of God, and if they're not his, let no one say a word about them, for she'll be getting her death," says he, "with crying and lamenting."

[*The door which Nora half closed is blown open by a gust of wind.*]

Cathleen: (looking out anxiously) Did you ask him would he stop Bartley going this day with the horses to the Galway① fair?

Nora: "I won't stop him," says he, "but let you not be afraid. Herself does be saying prayers half through the night, and the Almighty God won't leave her destitute," says he, "with no son living."

Cathleen: Is the sea bad by the white rocks, Nora?

Nora: Middling bad, God help us. There's a great roaring in the west, and it's worse it'll be getting when the tide's turned to the wind. [She goes over to the table with the bundle.] Shall I open it now?

Cathleen: Maybe she'd wake up on us, and come in before we'd done. [Coming to the table] It's a long time we'll be, and the two of us crying.

Nora: (goes to the inner door and listens) She's moving about on the bed. She'll be coming in a minute.

Cathleen: Give me the ladder, and I'll put them up in the turf-loft, the way she won't know of them at all, and maybe when the tide turns she'll be going down to see would he be floating from the east.

[*They put the ladder against the gable of the chimney; Cathleen goes up a few steps and hides the bundle in the turf-loft. Maurya comes from the inner room.*]

Maurya: (looking up at Cathleen and speaking querulously) Isn't it turf enough you have for this day and evening?

Cathleen: There's a cake baking at the fire for a short space (throwing down the turf) and Bartley will want it when the tide turns if he goes to Connemara.

[*Nora picks up the turf and puts it round the pot-oven.*]

Maurya: (sitting down on a stool at the fire) He won't go this day with the wind rising from the south and west. He won't go this day, for the young priest will stop him surely.

Nora: He'll not stop him, mother, and I heard Eamon Simon and Stephen Pheety and

---

① Galway,高尔韦,爱尔兰渔港名,爱尔兰西部群岛的贸易中心,有各种定期的牲畜集市。

Colum Shawn saying he would go.

Maurya：Where is he itself?

Nora：He went down to see would there be another boat sailing in the week, and I'm thinking it won't be long till he's here now, for the tide's turning at the green head, and the hooker's tacking from the east.

Cathleen：I hear someone passing the big stones.

Nora：(looking out) He's coming now, and he in a hurry.

Bartley：(comes in and looks round the room; speaking sadly and quietly) Where is the bit of new rope, Cathleen, was bought in Connemara?

Cathleen：(coming down) Give it to him, Nora; it's on a nail by the white boards. I hung it up this morning, for the pig with the black feet was eating it.

Nora：(giving him a rope) Is that it, Bartley?

Maurya：You'd do right to leave that rope, Bartley, hanging by the boards. (Bartley takes the rope) It will be wanting in this place, I'm telling you, if Michael is washed up tomorrow morning, or the next morning, or any morning in the week, for it's a deep grave we'll make him by the grace of God.

Bartley：(beginning to work with the rope) I've no halter the way I can ride down on the mare, and I must go now quickly. This is the one boat going for two weeks or beyond it, and the fair will be a good fair for horses, I heard them saying below.

Maurya：It's a hard thing they'll be saying below if the body is washed up and there's no man in it to make the coffin, and I after giving a big price for the finest white boards you'd find in Connemara.

[*She looks round at the boards.*]

Bartley：How would it be washed up, and we after looking each day for nine days, and a strong wind blowing a while back from the west and south?

Maurya：If it wasn't found itself, that wind is raising the sea, and there was a star up against the moon[①], and it rising in the night. If it was a hundred horses, or a thousand horses you had itself, what is the price of a thousand horses against a son where there is one son only?

Bartley：(working at the halter, to Cathleen) Let you go down each day, and see the sheep aren't jumping in on the rye, and if the jobber comes you can sell the pig with the black feet if there is a good price going.

Maurya：How would the like of her get a good price for a pig?

Bartley：(to Cathleen) If the west wind holds with the last bit of the moon let you and Nora

---

① a star up against the moon：旧时水手和渔民认为，月亮旁有一两颗星星是狂风暴雨即将来临的征兆。

get up weed enough for another cock for the kelp①. It's hard set we'll be from this day with no one in it but one man to work.

Maurya: It's hard set we'll be surely the day you're drown'd with the rest. What way will I live and the girls with me, and I an old woman looking for the grave?

[*Bartley lays down the halter, takes off his old coat, and puts on a newer one of the same flannel.*]

Bartley: (to Nora) Is she coming to the pier?

Nora: (looking out) She's passing the green head and letting fall her sails.

Bartley: (getting his purse and tobacco) I'll have half an hour to go down, and you'll see me coming again in two days, or in three days, or maybe in four days if the wind is bad.

Maurya: (turning round to the fire, and putting her shawl over her head) Isn't it a hard and cruel man won't hear a word from an old woman, and she holding him from the sea?

Cathleen: It's the life of a young man to be going on the sea, and who would listen to an old woman with one thing and she saying it over?

Bartley: (taking the halter) I must go now quickly. I'll ride down on the red mare, and the gray pony'll run behind me. The blessing of God on you.

[*He goes out.*]

Maurya: (crying out as he is in the door) He's gone now, God spare us, and we'll not see him again. He's gone now, and when the black night is falling I'll have no son left me in the world.

Cathleen: Why wouldn't you give him your blessing and he looking round in the door? Isn't it sorrow enough is on everyone in this house without your sending him out with an unlucky word behind him, and a hard word in his ear?

[*Maurya takes up the tongs and begins raking the fire aimlessly without looking round.*]

Nora: (turning towards her) You're taking away the turf from the cake.

Cathleen: (crying out) The Son of God forgive us, Nora, we're after forgetting his bit of bread.

[*She comes over to the fire.*]

Nora: And it's destroyed he'll be going till dark night, and he after eating nothing since

---

① weed enough for another cock for the kelp:因海藻中富含碘,艾兰岛的渔民惯于采集海藻烧灰做肥料。

the sun went up.

Cathleen: (turning the cake out of the oven) It's destroyed he'll be, surely. There's no sense left on any person in a house where an old woman will be talking for ever.

[*Maurya sways herself on her stool*.]

Cathleen: (cutting off some of the bread and rolling it in a cloth, to Maurya) Let you go down now to the spring well and give him this and he passing. You'll see him then and the dark word will be broken, and you can say, "God speed you," the way he'll be easy in his mind.

Maurya: (taking the bread) Will I be in it as soon as himself?

Cathleen: If you go now quickly.

Maurya: (standing up unsteadily) It's hard set I am to walk.

Cathleen: (looking at her anxiously) Give her the stick, Nora, or maybe she'll slip on the big stones.

Nora: What stick?

Cathleen: The stick Michael brought from Connemara.

Maurya: (taking a stick Nora gives her) In the big world the old people do be leaving things after them for their sons and children, but in this place it is the young men do be leaving things behind for them that do be old.

[*She goes out slowly. Nora goes over to the ladder*.]

Cathleen: Wait, Nora, maybe she'd turn back quickly. She's that sorry, God help her, you wouldn't know the thing she'd do.

Nora: Is she gone round by the bush?

Cathleen: (looking out) She's gone now. Throw it down quickly, for the Lord knows when she'll be out of it again.

Nora: (getting the bundle from the loft) The young priest said he'd be passing tomorrow, and we might go down and speak to him below if it's Michael's they are surely.

Cathleen: (taking the bundle) Did he say what way they were found?

Nora: (coming down) "There were two men," says he, "and they rowing round with poteen before the cocks crowed, and the oar of one of them caught the body, and they passing the black cliffs of the north."

Cathleen: (trying to open the bundle) Give me a knife, Nora; the string's perished with the salt water, and there's a black knot on it you wouldn't loosen in a week.

Nora: (giving her a knife) I've heard tell it was a long way to Donegal.

Cathleen: (cutting the string) It is surely. There was a man in here a while ago—the man sold us that knife—and he said if you set off walking from the rocks beyond, it would be seven days you'd be in Donegal.

Nora: And what time would a man take, and he floating?

[*Cathleen opens the bundle and takes out a bit of a stocking. They look at them eagerly.*]

Cathleen: (in a low voice) The Lord spare us, Nora! Isn't it a queer hard thing to say if it's his they are surely?

Nora: I'll get his shirt off the hook the way we can put the one flannel on the other. (She looks through some clothes hanging in the corner) It's not with them, Cathleen, and where will it be?

Cathleen: I'm thinking Bartley put it on him in the morning, for his own shirt was heavy with the salt in it. (Pointing to the corner) There's a bit of a sleeve was of the same stuff. Give me that and it will do.

[*Nora brings it to her and they compare the flannel.*]

Cathleen: It's the same stuff, Nora; but if it is itself, aren't there great rolls of it in the shops of Galway, and isn't it many another man may have a shirt of it as well as Michael himself?

Nora: (who has taken up the stocking and counted the stitches, crying out) It's Michael, Cathleen, it's Michael; God spare his soul and what will herself say when she hears this story, and Bartley on the sea?

Cathleen: (taking the stocking) It's a plain stocking.

Nora: It's the second one of the third pair I knitted, and I put up three score stitches, and I dropped four of them.

Cathleen: (counts the stitches) It's that number is in it. (Crying out) Ah, Nora, isn't it a bitter thing to think of him floating that way to the far north, and no one to keen him but the black hags that do be flying on the sea?

Nora: (swinging herself round, and throwing out her arms on the clothes) And isn't it a pitiful thing when there is nothing left of a man who was a great rower and fisher, but a bit of an old shirt and a plain stocking?

Cathleen: (after an instant) Tell me is herself coming, Nora? I hear a little sound on the path.

Nora: (looking out) She is, Cathleen. She's coming up to the door.

Cathleen: Put these things away before she'll come in. Maybe it's easier she'll be after giving her blessing to Bartley, and we won't let on we've heard anything the time he's on the sea.

Nora: (helping Cathleen to close the bundle) We'll put them here in the corner.

[*They put them into a hole in the chimney corner. Cathleen goes back to the spinning wheel.*]

Nora: Will she see it was crying I was?

Cathleen: Keep your back to the door the way the light'll not be on you.

[*Nora sits down at the chimney corner, with her back to the door. Maurya comes in very slowly, without looking at the girls, and goes over to her stool at the other side of the fire. The cloth with the bread is still in her hand. The girls look at each other, and Nora points to the bundle of bread.*]

Cathleen: (offer spinning for a moment) You didn't give him his bit of bread?

[*Maurya begins to keen softly, without turning round.*]

Cathleen: Did you see him riding down?

[*Maurya goes on keening.*]

Cathleen: (a little impatiently) God forgive you; isn't it a better thing to raise your voice and tell what you seen, than to be making lamentation for a thing that's done? Did you see Bartley, I'm saying to you.

Maurya: (with a weak voice) My heart's broken from this day.

Cathleen: (as before) Did you see Bartley?

Maurya: I seen the fearfulest thing.

Cathleen: (leaves her wheel and looks out) God forgive you; he's riding the mare now over the green head, and the gray pony behind him.

Maurya: (starts, so that her shawl falls back from her head and shows her white tossed hair; with a frightened voice) The gray pony behind him.

Cathleen: (coming to the fire) What is it ails you, at all?

Maurya: (speaking very slowly) I've seen the fearfulest thing any person has seen, since the day Bride Dara seen the dead man with the child in his arms.

Cathleen AND Nora: Uah.

[*They crouch down in front of the old woman at the fire.*]

Nora: Tell us what it is you seen.

Maurya: I went down to the spring-well, and I stood there saying a prayer to myself. Then Bartley came along, and he riding on the red mare with the gray pony behind him. (She puts up her hands, as if to hide something from her eyes.) The Son of God spare us, Nora!

Cathleen: What is it you seen?

Maurya: I seen Michael himself.

Cathleen: (speaking softly) You did not, mother; it wasn't Michael you seen, for his body is after being found in the far north, and he's got a clean burial by the grace of God.

Maurya: (a little defiantly) I'm after seeing him this day, and he riding and galloping. Bartley came first on the red mare; and I tried to say "God speed you," but something choked the words in my throat. He went by quickly; and, "The blessing of God on you," says he, and I could say nothing. I looked up then, and I crying, at the gray pony, and there was Michael upon it—with fine clothes on him, and new shoes on his feet.

Cathleen: (begins to keen) It's destroyed we are from this day. It's destroyed, surely.

Nora: Didn't the young priest say the Almighty God wouldn't leave her destitute with no son living?

Maurya: (in a low voice, but clearly) It's little the like of him knows of the sea... Bartley will be lost now, and let you call in Eamon and make me a good coffin out of the white boards, for I won't live after them. I've had a husband, and a husband's father, and six sons in this house—six fine men, though it was a hard birth I had with every one of them and they coming to the world—and some of them were found and some of them were not found, but they're gone now, the lot of them... There were Stephen, and Shawn, were lost in the great wind, and found after in the Bay of Gregory of the Golden Mouth, and carried up the two of them on the one plank, and in by that door.

[*She pauses for a moment, the girls start as if they heard something through the door that is half-open behind them.*]

Nora: (in a whisper) Did you hear that, Cathleen? Did you hear a noise in the northeast?

Cathleen: (in a whisper) There's someone after crying out by the seashore.

Maurya: (continues without hearing anything) There was Sheamus and his father, and his own father again, were lost in a dark night, and not a stick or sign was seen of them when the sun went up. There was Patch after was drowned out of a curagh[①] that turned over. I was sitting here with Bartley, and he a baby, lying on my two knees, and I seen two women, and three women, and four women coming in, and they crossing themselves, and not saying a word. I looked out then, and there were men coming after them, and they holding a thing in the half of a red sail, and water dripping out of it—it was a dry day, Nora—and leaving a track to the

---

① curagh：艾兰岛与爱尔兰西海岸地区常用的一种小船，用柳条和兽皮制成。

door.

[*She pauses again with her hand stretched out towards the door. It opens softly and old women begin to come in, crossing themselves on the threshold, and kneeling down in front of the stage with red petticoats over their heads*[①].]

Maurya: (half in a dream, to Cathleen) Is it Patch, or Michael, or what is it at all?

Cathleen: Michael is after being found in the far north, and when he is found there how could he be here in this place?

Maurya: There does be a power of young men floating round in the sea, and what way would they know if it was Michael they had, or another man like him, for when a man is nine days in the sea,[②] and the wind blowing, it's hard set his own mother would be to say what man was it.

Cathleen: It's Michael, God spare him, for they're after sending us a bit of his clothes from the far north.

[*She reaches out and hands Maurya the clothes that belonged to Michael. Maurya stands up slowly, and takes them in her hands. Nora looks out.*]

Nora: They're carrying a thing among them and there's water dripping out of it and leaving a track by the big stones.

Cathleen: (in a whisper to the women who have come in) Is it Bartley it is?

One of the women: It is surely, God rest his soul.

[*Two younger women come in and pull out the table. Then men carry in the body of Bartley, laid on a plank, with a bit of a sail over it, and lay it on the table.*]

Cathleen: (to the women, as they are doing so) What way was he drowned?

One of the women: The gray pony knocked him into the sea, and he was washed out where there is a great surf on the white rocks.

[*Maurya has gone over and knelt down at the head of the table. The women are keening softly and swaying themselves with a slow movement. Cathleen and Nora kneel at the other end of the table. The men kneel near the door.*]

Maurya: (raising her head and speaking as if she did not see the people around her) They're all gone now, and there isn't anything more the sea can do to me... I'll

---

① kneeling down in front of the stage with red petticoats over their heads: 这个举动是艾兰岛岛民的一种习俗,表示报丧与哀悼。

② There does be a power of young men floating round in the sea, and what way would they know if it was Michael they had, or another man like him, for when a man is nine days in the sea: 艾兰岛岛民的一种迷信,认为人在海中淹死九天之后尸体会自动浮上来。

have no call now to be up crying and praying when the wind breaks from the south, and you can hear the surf is in the east, and the surf is in the west, making a great stir with the two noises, and they hitting one on the other. I'll have no call now to be going down and getting Holy Water in the dark nights after Samhain, and I won't care what way the sea is when the other women will be keening. (To Nora) Give me the Holy Water, Nora; there's a small sup still on the dresser.

[*Nora gives it to her.*]

Maurya: (drops Michael's clothes across Bartley's feet, and sprinkles the Holy Water over him) It isn't that I haven't prayed for you, Bartley, to the Almighty God. It isn't that I haven't said prayers in the dark night till you wouldn't know what I'd be saying; but it's a great rest I'll have now, and it's time surely. It's a great rest I'll have now, and great sleeping in the long nights after Samhain, if it's only a bit of wet flour we do have to eat, and maybe a fish that would be stinking.

[*She kneels down again, crossing herself, and saying prayers under her breath.*]

Cathleen: (to an old man) Maybe yourself and Eamon would make a coffin when the sun rises. We have fine white boards herself bought, God help her, thinking Michael would be found, and I have a new cake you can eat while you'll be working.

The old man: (looking at the boards) Are there nails with them?

Cathleen: There are not, Colum; we didn't think of the nails.

ANOTHER MAN: It's a great wonder she wouldn't think of the nails, and all the coffins she's seen made already.

Cathleen: It's getting old she is, and broken.

[*Maurya stands up again very slowly and spreads out the pieces of Michael's clothes beside the body, sprinkling them with the last of the Holy Water.*]

Nora: (in a whisper to Cathleen) She's quiet now and easy; but the day Michael was drowned you could hear her crying out from this to the spring-well. It's fonder she was of Michael, and would anyone have thought that?

Cathleen: (slowly and clearly) An old woman will be soon tired with anything she will do, and isn't it nine days herself is after crying and keening, and making great sorrow in the house?

Maurya: (puts the empty cup mouth downwards on the table, and lays her hands together on Bartley's feet) They're all together this time, and the end is come. May the Almighty God have mercy on Bartley's soul, and on Michael's soul, and on the souls of Sheamus and Patch，and Stephen and Shawn（bending her head）；and may He have mercy on my soul，Nora，and on the soul of everyone is left living in the world.

［*She pauses，and the keen rises a little more loudly from the women，then sinks away.*］

Maurya： Michael has a clean burial in the far north，by the grace of the Almighty God. Bartley will have a fine coffin out of the white boards，and a deep grave surely. What more can we want than that? No man at all can be living for ever，and we must be satisfied.

［*She kneels down again，and the curtain falls slowly.*］

—End of Play—

▶扩展阅读

1. Corkery，D. *Synge and Anglo-Irish Literature*：*A Study*. Cork：Cork University Press，1931.

2. Gerstenberger，D. *John Millington Synge*. New York：Twayne，1964.

3. Harmon，M. Ed. *J . M . Synge Centenary Papers*. Dublin：Dolmen Press，1971.

4. Price，A. *Synge and Anglo-Irish Drama*. London：Methuen，1961.

5. Skelton，R. *J . M . Synge and His World*. New York：Viking，1971.

6. 汪义群. 西方现代戏剧流派作品选(第2卷)：象征主义. 北京：中国戏剧出版社，2005.

▶学习参考网站

1. http：// www.theatredatabase.com/20th_century/john_millington_synge_001.html

2. http：// www.theatrehistory.com/irish/synge002.html

3. http：// www.poetry-archive.com/s/synge_john_millington.html

【张　陟　编注】

16. John Banville: The Sea

约翰·班维尔（John Banville，1945），1945 年出生于爱尔兰海港小城韦克斯福德。他父亲是一名汽车修理工，在班维尔三十几岁时就去世了。他母亲是一名家庭主妇。班维尔是家里三个孩子中最小的一个。他曾一度因热衷于美术而放弃了上大学的机会，之后在都柏林的爱尔兰国家航空公司工作过一段时间，在这期间他利用可以享受低折扣机票的机会多次出国旅游，到过欧洲最南端的滨海国家希腊和意大利，也去过美国的港口城市旧金山。

他早年各国旅游的经历及其生活的岛国背景为他以后的创作提供了丰富的灵感和素材。班维尔曾在伦敦住过一年，他的写作生涯就是从那时候开始的。回国后班维尔在《爱尔兰时报》杂志社做过文学编辑，也长期为《纽约时报》副刊撰写书评。1970 年他的第一本作品短篇故事集《朗·莱金》（*Long Lankin*）问世；次年他的第一部小说《夜卵》（*Nightspawn*）出版，之后接连不断地出了十几部小说，受到了评论界的褒奖。他的第一个系列小说包括《哥白尼博士》（*Dr. Copernicus*，1976 年获布莱克纪念奖）、《开普勒》（*Kepler*，1981 年获《卫报》小说奖）、《牛顿信札》（*The Newton Letter：An Interlude*，1982 年被改编搬上了荧屏）和 1986 年出版的《魔鬼梅菲丝特》（*Mefisto*）。这四部重要作品分别以历史上的三位著名科学家哥白尼、开普勒、牛顿以及一位虚构的数学天才加伯利尔·斯万为主人公，探究了作为意识形态的科学与叙事文学之间的深层关系；这四部作品也被称为"科学革命四部曲"。

不久他又发表了另一个被称为"框架三部曲"的小说系列：《证据之书》（*The Book of Evidence*，1989）、《幽灵》（*Ghosts*，1993）和《雅典娜》（*Athena*，1995）。其中《证据之书》入围 1989 年布克奖提名并获 1989 年吉尼斯·皮特航空奖。这三部作品内容关系紧密，故事背景涉及海洋、孤岛和城市，主题同样涉及人类认识和语言局限性之间的联系。此外，班维尔的作品还包括《无法企及》（*The Untouchable*，1997）、《蚀》（*Eclipse*，2000）、《裹尸布》（*Shroud*，2002）和《布拉格画像》（*Prague Pictures：Portrait of a City*，2003）等。2005 年班维尔凭借作品《海》（*The Sea*）获得布克奖（Man Booker Prize）。2011 年，班维尔获得卡夫卡文学奖。他的小说主题涉及面广，创作手法新颖，措辞优美，语言流畅。《波士顿环球报》赞扬他是"当今最伟大的英文作家"，他也被公认为最有可能获得诺贝尔文学奖的爱尔兰作家。

班维尔一直定居在爱尔兰的都柏林，滨海的环境陶冶了他的心境，赋予了他创作的激情与灵感。他的小说不时以大海或孤岛为故事背景来表现人物的内心感受，揭示情节的发展。

在他的作品中,大海和孤岛的意象似乎成了主体意识与语言内化的重要组成部分。《海》是一部散文体式的以第一人称叙述为主的小说。主人公马克斯·莫顿是一名伤感的中年艺术史学家。他的妻子刚刚因罹患癌症去世,为逃离亲人亡故带来的痛苦,逃离死亡逼近时的气息,他重访了儿时生活过的爱尔兰海边小镇。故事情节以叙述者马克斯·莫顿为中心,主要按两条线索发展:一条是他与格雷斯一家的纠葛,另一条则是与妻子安娜和女儿克莱尔的故事。两条线索通过时空转换的手法,使半个世纪以前、妻子生前与现时发生的故事十分巧妙地交织到一起,构成了一幅以忧伤为基调、以爱情为主线、以往事回忆与现实杂糅为框架的画面,读后不禁令人愁怅满怀。这个故事自始至终都由马克斯·莫顿独自讲述完成,他时而生活在现实生活,时而回到半个世纪前;时而生活在妻子安娜在世的过去,时而与女儿谈话回到现实生活。小说故事情节不多,但文体语言相当优美。班维尔运用了娴熟的心理描写技法,并在叙述中加入了对人生和生死观的哲学思考,不仅使叙述者的讲述温婉自然,也激发读者对人生的深层思索。半个世纪夹杂着情与爱、欢乐和哀愁的人生倏然而去,使人不禁感叹时光的流逝,然而亘古不变的是海洋。海洋见证了一切,承载了一切。以下选段出自《海》第一章,叙述主人公马克斯·莫顿与女儿克莱尔重游"雪松"别墅,眼前已物是人非,抚今追昔,往事不断浮现的情景。

▶Chapter 1

THEY DEPARTED, the gods, on the day of the strange tide. All morning under a milky sky the waters in the bay had swelled and swelled, rising to unheard-of heights, the small waves creeping over parched sand that for years had known no wetting save for rain and lapping the very bases of the dunes. The rusted hulk of the freighter that had run aground at the far end of the bay longer ago than any of us could remember must have thought it was being granted a relaunch. I would not swim again, after that day. The seabirds mewled and swooped, unnerved, it seemed, by the spectacle of that vast bowl of water bulging like a blister, lead-blue and malignantly agleam. They looked unnaturally white, that day, those birds. The waves were depositing a fringe of soiled yellow foam along the waterline. No sail married the high horizon. I would not swim, no, nor ever again.

Someone has just walked over my grave. Someone.

The name of the house is the Cedars, as of old. A bristling clump of those trees, monkey-brown with a tarry reek, their trunks nightmarishly tangled, still grows at the left side, facing across an untidy lawn to the big curved window of what used to be the living room but which Miss Vavasour prefers to call, in landladyese, the lounge. The front door is at the opposite side, opening on to a square of oil-stained gravel behind the iron gate that is still painted green, though rust has reduced its struts to a tremulous filigree. I am amazed at how little has changed in the more than fifty years that have gone by since I was last here.

Amazed, and disappointed, I would go so far as to say appalled, for reasons that are obscure to me, since why should I desire change, I who have come back to live amidst the rubble of the past? I wonder why the house was built like that, sideways-on, turning a pebble-dashed windowless white end-wall to the road; perhaps in former time, before the railway, the road ran in a different orientation altogether, passing directly in front of the front door, anything is possible. Miss V. is vague on dates but thinks a cottage was first put up here early in the last century, I mean the century before last, I am losing track of the millennia, and then was added on to haphazardly over the years. That would account for the jumbled look of the place, with small rooms giving on to bigger ones, and windows facing blank walls, and low ceilings throughout. The pitch-pine floors sound a nautical note, as does my spindle-backed swivel chair. I imagine an old seafarer dozing by the fire, landlubbered at last, and the winter gale rattling the window frames. Oh, to be him. To have been him.

When I was here all those years ago, in the time of the gods, the Cedars was a summer house, for rent by the fortnight or the month. During all of June each year a rich doctor and his large, raucous family infested it—we did not like the doctor's loud-voiced children, they laughed at us and threw stones from behind the unbreathable barrier of the gate—and after them a mysterious middle-aged couple came, who spoke to no one, and grimly walked their sausage dog in silence at the same time every morning down Station Road to the strand. August was the most interesting month at the Cedars, for us. The tenants then were different each year, people from England or the Continent, the odd pair of honeymooners whom we would try to spy on, and once even a fit-up troupe of itinerant theatre people who were putting on an afternoon show in the village's galvanized-tin cinema. And then, that year, came the family Grace.

The first thing I saw of them was their motor car, parked on the gravel inside the gate. It was a low-slung, scarred and battered black model with beige leather seats and a big spoked polished wood steering wheel. Books with bleached and dog-eared covers were thrown carelessly on the shelf under the sporty raked back window, and there was a touring map of France, much used. The front door of the house stood wide open, and I could hear voices inside, downstairs, and from upstairs the sound of bare feet running on floorboards and a girl laughing. I had paused by the gate, frankly eavesdropping, and now suddenly a man with a drink in his hand came out of the house. He was short and top-heavy, all shoulders and chest and big round head, with close-cut, crinkled, glittering-black hair with flecks of premature grey in it and a pointed black beard likewise flecked. He wore a loose green shirt unbuttoned and khaki shorts and was barefoot. His skin was so deeply tanned by the sun it had a purplish sheen. Even his feet, I noticed, were brown on the insteps; the majority of fathers in my experience were fish-belly white below the collar-line. He set his tumbler—ice-blue grin and ice cubes and a lemon slice—at a perilous angle on the roof of the car and opened the passenger door and leaned inside to rummage for something under the dashboard. In the unseen upstairs of the house the girl laughed again and gave a wild, warbling cry of mock-panic, and again there was the sound of scampering feet. They were playing chase, she and the voiceless other. The man straightened and took his glass of gin from the roof and slammed the car door. Whatever it was he had been searching for he had not found. As he turned back to the house his eye caught mine and he winked. He did not do it in the way that adults usually did, at once arch and ingratiating. No, this was a comradely, a conspiratorial wink, Masonic, almost, as if this moment that we, two strangers, adult and boy, had shared, although outwardly without significance, without content, even, nevertheless had meaning. His eyes were an extraordinary pale transparent shade of blue. He went back inside then, already talking before he was through the door. "Damned thing," he said, "seems to be..." and was gone. I lingered a moment, scanning the upstairs windows. No face appeared there.

That, then, was my first encounter with the Graces: the girl's voice coming down from on high, the running footsteps, and the man here below with the blue eyes giving me that wink, jaunty, intimate and faintly satanic.

Just now I caught myself at it again, that thin, wintry whistling through the front teeth that I have begun to do recently. *Deedle deedle deedle*, it goes, like a dentist's drill. My father used to whistle like that, am I turning into him? In the room across the corridor Colonel Blunden is playing the wireless. He favours the afternoon talk programmers, the ones in which irate members of the public call up to complain about villainous politicians and the price of drink and other perennial irritants. "Company," he says shortly, and clears his throat, looking a little abashed, his protuberant, parboiled eyes avoiding mine, even though I have issued no challenge. Does he lie on the bed while he listens? Hard to picture him there in his thick grey woolen socks, twiddling his toes, his tie off and shirt collar agape and hands clasped behind that stringy old neck of his. Out of his room he is vertical man itself, from the soles of his much-mended glossy brown brogues to the tip of his conical skull. He has his hair cut every Saturday morning by the village barber, short-back-and-sides, no quarter given, only a hawkish stiff grey crest left on top. His long-lobed leathery ears stick out, they look as if they had been dried and smoked; the whites of his eyes too have a smoky yellow tinge. I can hear the buzz of voices on his wireless but cannot make out what they say. I may go mad here. *Deedle deedle*.

Later that day, the day the Graces came, or the following one, or the one following that, I saw the black car again, recognized it at once as it went bounding over the little humpbacked bridge that spanned the railway line. It is still there, that bridge, just beyond the station. Yes, things endure, while the living lapse. The car was heading out of the village in the direction of the town, I shall call it Ballymore, a dozen miles away. The town is Ballymore[①], this village is Ballyless, ridiculously, perhaps, but I do not care. The man with the beard who had winked at me was at the wheel, saying something and laughing, his head thrown back. Beside him a woman sat with an elbow out of the rolled-down window, her head back too, pale hair shaking in the gusts from the window, but she was not laughing only smiling, that smile she reserved for him, special, tolerant, languidly amused. She wore a white blouse and sunglasses with white plastic rims and was smoking a cigarette. Where am I, lurking in what place of vantage? I do not see myself. They were gone in a moment, the car's sashaying back-end scooting around a bend in the road with a spurt of exhaust smoke. Tall grassed in the ditch, blond like the woman's hair, shivered briefly and returned to their former dreaming stillness.

I walked down Station Road in the sunlit emptiness of afternoon. That beach at the foot of the hill was a fawn shimmer under indigo. At the seaside all is narrow horizontals, the world reduced to a few long straight lines pressed between earth and sky. I approached the Cedars circumspectly. How is it that in childhood everything new that caught my interest had an aura of the uncanny, since according to all the authorities the uncanny is not some now thing but a thing known returning in a different form, become a revenant? So many unanswerables, this the least of them. As I approached I heard a regular rusty screeching sound. A boy of my age was draped on the green gate, his arms hanging limply down from the top bar, propelling himself with one foot slowly back and forth in a quarter circle over the gravel. He had the same straw-pale hair as the woman in the car and the man's unmistakable azure eyes. As I walked slowly past, and indeed I may even have paused, or faltered, rather, he stuck the toe of his plimsoll into the gravel to stop the swimming gate and looked at me with an expression of hostile enquiry. It was the way we all looked at each other, we children, on first encounter. Behind him I could see all the way down the narrow garden at the back of the house to the diagonal row of trees skirting the railway line—they are gone now, those trees, cut down to make way for a row of pastel-colored bungalows like doll's house—and beyond, even, inland, to where the fields rose and their were cows, and tiny bright bursts of yellow that were gorse bushes, and a solitary distant spire, and then the sky, with scrolled white clouds. Suddenly, startlingly, the boy pulled a grotesque face at me, crossing his eyes and letting his tongue loll on his lower lip. I walked on, conscious of his mocking eye following me.

---

① Ballymore 与后面出现的 Ballyless 均为地名，其中 more 意为"多"，less 意为"少"，因此作者谓之可笑（ridiculously）。

Plimsoll. Now, there is a word one does not hear any more, or rarely, very rarely. Originally sailors' footwear, from someone's name, if I recall, and something to do with ships. The Colonel is off to the lavatory again. Prostate trouble, I bet. Going past my door he softens his tread, creaking on tiptoe, out of respect for the bereaved. A stickler for the observances, our gallant Colonel.

I am walking down Station Road.

So much of life was stillness then, when we were young, or so it seems now; a biding stillness; a vigilance. We were waiting in our as yet unfashioned world, scanning the future as the boy and I had scanned each other, like soldiers in the field, watching for what was to come. At the bottom of the hill I stopped and stood and looked three ways, along Strand Road, and back up Station Road, and the other way, toward the tin cinema and the public tennis courts. No one. The road beyond the tennis courts was called the Cliff Walk, although whatever cliffs there may once have been the sea had long ago eroded. It was said there was a church submerged in the sandy was bed down there, intact, with bell tower and bell, that once had stood on a headland that was gone too, brought toppling into the roiling waves one immemorial night of tempest and awful flood. Those were the stories the locals told, such as Duignan the dairyman and deaf Colfer who earned his living selling salvaged golf balls, to make us transients think their tame little seaside village had been of old a place of terrors. The sign over the Strand Café, advertising cigarettes, Navy Cut, with a picture of a bearded sailor inside a lifebuoy, or a ring of rope—was it? —creaked in the sea breeze on its salt-rusted hinges, an echo of the gate at the Cedars on which for all I knew the boy was swinging yet. They creak, this present gate, that post sign, to this day, to this night, in my dreams. I set off along Strand Road. Houses, shops, two hotels—the Golf, the Beach—a granite church, Myler's grocery-cum-post-office-cum-pub, and then the field—the Field—of wooden chalets one of which was our holiday home, my father's, my mother's and mine.

If the people in the car were his parents had they left the boy on his own in the house? And where was the girl, the girl who had laughed? The past beats inside me like a second heart.

The consultant's name was Mr. Todd[1]. This can only be considered a joke in bad taste on the part of polyglot fate. It could have been worse. There is a name De'Ath[2], with that fancy medial capital and apotropaic apostrophe which fool on one. This Todd addressed Anna as Mrs. Morden[3] but called me Max. I was not at all sure I liked the distinction thus made, or the gruff familiarity of his tone. His office, no, his rooms, one says rooms, as one calls him Mister not Doctor, seemed at first sight an eyrie, although they were only on the third

---

① Todd：tod 在德语中意为"死亡"，有暗指庸医之意。

② De'Ath：death，在英语中意为"死亡"，有意无意地在暗示医生的无能。

③ Morden：在德语中意为"谋杀"，暗指医生的治疗不见效，安娜最终被癌症夺去了生命。

floor. The building was a new one, all glass and steel—there was even a glass-and-steel tubular lift shaft, aptly suggestive of the barrel of a syringe, through which the lift rose and fell hummingly like a giant plunger being alternately pulled and pressed—and two walls of his main consulting room were sheets of plate glass from floor to ceiling. When Anna and I were shown in my eyes were dazzled by a blaze of early-autumn sunlight falling down through those vast panes. The receptionist, a blonde blur in a nurse's coat and sensible shoes that squeaked—on such an occasion who would really notice the receptionist? —laid Anna's file on Mr. Todd's desk and squeakingly withdrew. Mr. Todd bade us sit. I could not tolerate the thought of settling myself on a chair and went instead and stood at the glass wall, looking out. Directly below me there was an oak, or perhaps it was a beech, I am never sure of those big deciduous trees, certainly not an elm since they are all dead, but a noble thing, any way, the summer's green of its broad canopy hardly silvered yet with autumn's hoar. Car roofs glared. A young woman in a dark suit was walking away swiftly across the car park, even at that distance I fancied I could hear her high heels tinnily clicking on the tarmac. Anna was palely reflected in the glass before me, sitting very straight on the metal chair in three-quarters profile, being the model patient, with one knee crossed on the other and her joined hands resting on her thigh. Mr. Todd sat sideways at his desk riffling through the documents in her file; the pale-pink cardboard of the folder made me think of those shivery first mornings back at school after the summer holidays, the feel of brand-new schoolbooks and the somehow bodeful smell of ink and pared pencils. How the mind wanders, even on the most concentrated of occasions.

I turned from the glass, the outside become intolerable now.

Mr. Todd was a burly man, not tall or heavy but very broad: one had an impression of squareness. He cultivated a reassuringly old-fashioned manner. He wore a tweed suit with a waistcoat and watch chain, and chestnut-brown brogues that Colonel Blunden would have approved. His hair was oiled in the style of an earlier time, brushed back sternly fro his forehead, and he had a moustache, short and bristly, that gave him a dogged look. I realized with a mild shock that despite these calculatedly venerable effects he could not be much more than fifty. Since when did doctors start being younger than I am? On he wrote, playing for time; I did not blame him, I would have done the same, in his place. At last he put down his pen but still was disinclined to speak, giving the earnest impression of not knowing where to begin or how. There was something studied about his hesitancy, something theatrical. Again, I understand. A doctor must be as good as actor as physician. Anna shifted on her chair impatiently.

"Well, Doctor," she said a little too loudly, putting on the bright, tough tone of one of those film stars of the Forties, "is it the death sentence, or do I get life?"

The room was still. Her sally of wit, surely rehearsed, had fallen flat. I had an urge to rush forward and snatch her up in my arms, fireman-fashion, and carry her bodily out of there. I did not stir. Mr. Todd looked at her in mild, hare-eyed panic, his eyebrows hovering halfway up his forehead.

"Oh, we won't let you go quite yet, Mrs. Modern," he said, showing big grey teeth in an awful smile. "No, indeed we will not."

Another beat of silence followed that. Anna's hands were in her lap, she looked at them, frowning, as if she had not noticed them before. My right knee took fright and set to twitching.

Mr. Todd launched into a forceful disquisition, polished from repeated use, on promising treatments, new drugs, the mighty arsenal of chemical weapons he had at his command; he might have been speaking of magic potions, the alchemist's physic. Anna continued frowning at her hands; she was not listening. At last he stopped and sat gazing at her with the same desperate, leporine look as before, audibly breathing, his lips drawn back in a sort of leer and those teeth on show again.

"Thank you," she said politely in a voice that seemed now to come from very far off. She nodded to herself. "Yes," more remotely still, "thank you."

At that, as if released, Mr. Todd gave his knees a quick smack with two flat palms and jumped to his feet and fairly bustled us to the door. When Anna had gone through he turned to me and gave me a gritty, man-to-man smile, and the handshake, dry, brisk, unflinching, which I am sure he reserves for the spouses at moments such as this.

The carpeted corridor absorbed our footsteps.

The lift, pressed, plunged.

We walked out into the day as if we were stepping on to a new planet, one where no one lived but us.

*

Arrived home, we sat outside the house in the car for a long time, loath of venturing in upon the known, saying nothing, strangers to ourselves and each other as we suddenly were. Anna looked out across the bay where the furled yachts bristled in the glistening sunlight. Her belly was swollen, a round hard lump pressing against the waistband of her skirt, she had said people would think she was pregnant—"At my age!"—and we had laughed, not looking at each other. The gulls that nested in our chimneys had all gone back to sea by now, or migrated, or whatever it is they do. Throughout that drear summer they had wheeled above the rooftops all day long, jeering at our attempts to pretend that all was well, nothing amiss, the world continuous. But there it was, squatting in her lap, the bulge that was big baby De'Ath, burgeoning inside her, biding its time.

At last we went inside, having nowhere else to go. Bright light of midday streamed in at the kitchen window and everything had a glassy, hard-edged radiance as if I were scanning the room through a camera lens. There was an impression of general, tight-lipped awkwardness, of all these homely things—jars on the shelves, saucepans on the stove, that breadboard with its jagged knife—averting their gaze from our all at once unfamiliar, afflicted presence in their midst. This, I realized miserably, this is how it would be from now on, wherever she goes the soundless clapping of the leper's bell[①] preceding her. *How well you look*! they would exclaim, *why, we've never seen you better*! And she with her brilliant smile, putting on a brave face, poor Mrs. Bones[②].

She stood in the middle of the floor in her coat and scarf, hands on her hips, casting about her with a vexed expression. She was still handsome then, high of cheekbone, her skin translucent, paper-fine. I always admired in particular her Attic profile, the nose a line of carven ivory falling sheer from the brow.

"Do you know what it is?" she said with bitter vehemence. "It's inappropriate, that's what it is."

I looked aside quickly for fear my eyes would give me away; one's eyes are always those of someone else, the mad and desperate dwarf crouched within. I knew what she meant. This was not supposed to have befallen her. It was not supposed to have befallen us, we were not that kind of people. Misfortune, illness, untimely death, these things happen to good folk, the humble ones, the salt of the earth, not to Anna, not to me. In the midst of the imperial progress that was our life together a grinning losel had stepped out of the cheering crowd and sketching a parody of a bow had handed my tragic queen the warrant of impeachment.

She put on a kettle of water to boil and fished in a pocket of her coat and brought out her spectacles and put them on, looping the string behind her neck. She began to weep, absent-mindedly, it might be, making no sound. I moved clumsily to embrace her but she drew back sharply.

"For heaven's sake don't fuss!" she snapped. "I'm only dying after all."

The kettle came to the boil and switched itself off and the seething water inside it settled down grumpily. I marveled, not for the first time, at the cruel complacency of ordinary things. But no, not cruel, not complacent, only indifferent, as how could they be otherwise? Henceforth I would have to address things as they are, not as I might imagine them, for this was a new version of reality. I took up the teapot and the sea, making them rattle—my hands were shaking—but she said no, she had changed her mind, it was brandy she wanted, brandy, and a cigarette, she who did not smoke, and rarely drank. She gave me

---

① leper's bell：麻风病人的铃铛。中世纪的欧洲，麻风病人随身带着铃铛，走到哪儿铃声响到哪儿，好让人敬而远之。

② Mrs. Bones：憨豆女士。英美娱乐节目中手持响板（bones），扮傻逗观众一乐的演员。

the dull glare of a defiant child, standing there by the table in her coat. Her tears had stopped. She took off her glasses and dropped them to hang below her throat on their string and rubbed at her eyes with the heels of her hands. I found the brandy bottle and tremblingly poured a measure into a tumbler, the bottle-neck and the rim of the glass chattering against each other like teeth. There were no cigarettes in the house, where was I to get cigarettes? She said it was no matter, she did not really want to smoke. The steel kettle shone, a slow furl of steam at its spout, vaguely suggestive of genie and lamp. Oh, grant me a wish, just the one.

"Take off your coat, at least," I said.

But why at least? What a business it is, the human discourse.

I gave her the glass of brandy and she stood holding it but did not drink. Light from the window behind me shone on the lenses of her spectacles where they hung at her collar bone, giving the eerie effect of another, miniature she standing close in front of her under her chin with eyes cast down. Abruptly she went slack and sat down heavily, extending her arms before her along the table in a strange, desperate-seeming gesture, as if in supplication to some unseen other seated opposite her in judgment. The tumbler in her hand knocked on the wood and splashed out half its contents. Helplessly I contemplated her. For a giddy second the notion seized me that I would never again be able to think of another word to say to her, that we would go on like this, in agonized inarticulacy, to the end. I bent and kissed the pale patch on the crown of her head the size of a sixpence where her dark hair whorled. She turned her face up to me briefly with a black look.

"You smell of hospitals," she said. "That should be me."

I took the tumbler from her hand and put it to my lips and drank at a draught what remained of the scorching brandy. I realized what the feeling was that had been besetting me since I had stepped that morning into the glassy glare of Mr. Todd's consulting rooms. It was embarrassment. Anna felt it as well, I was sure of it. Embarrassment, yes, a panic-stricken sense of not knowing what to say, where to look, how to behave, and something else, too, that was not quite anger but a sort of surly annoyance, a surly resentment at the predicament in which we grimly found ourselves. It was as if a secret had been imparted to us so dirty, so nasty, that we could hardly bear to remain in one another's company yet were unable to break free, each knowing the foul thing that the other knew and bound together by that very knowledge. From this day forward all would be dissembling, there would be no other way to live with death.

Still Anna sat erect there at the table, facing away from me, her arms extended and hands lying inert with palms upturned as if for something to be dropped into them. "Well?" she said without turning. "What now?"

There goes the Colonel, creeping back to his room. That was a long session in the lav.

Strangury, nice word. Mine is the one bedroom in the house which is, as Miss Vavasour puts it with a demure little moue, *en suite*. Also I have a view, or would have were it not for those blasted bungalows at the bottom of the garden. My bed is daunting, a stately, high-built, Italianate affair fit for a Doge, the headboard scrolled and polished like a Stradivarius. I must enquire of Miss V. as to its provenance. This would have been the master bedroom when the Graces were here. In those days I never got further than the downstairs, except in my dreams.

I have just notice today's date. It is a year exactly since that first visit Anna and I were forced to pay Mr. Todd in his rooms. What a coincidence. Or not, perhaps; are there coincidences in Pluto's realm, amidst the trackless wastes of which I wander lost, a lyreless Orpheus[①]? Twelve months, though! I should have kept a diary. My journal of the plague year.

A dream it was that drew me here. In it, I was walking along a country road, that was all. It was in winter, at dusk, or else it was a strange sort of dimly radiant night, the sort of night that there is only in dreams, and a wet snow was falling. I was determinedly on my way somewhere, going home, it seemed, although I did not know what or where exactly home might be. There was open land to my right, flat and undistinguished with not a house or hovel in sight, and to my left a deep line of darkly louring trees bordering the road. The branches were not bare despite the season, and the thick, almost black leaves drooped in masses, laden with snow that had turned to soft, translucent ice. Something had broken down, a car, no, a bicycle, a boy's bicycle, for as well as being the age I am now I was a boy as well, a big awkward boy, yes, and on my way home, it must have been home, or somewhere that had been home, once, and that I would recognize again, when I got there. I had hours of walking to do but I did not mind that, for this was a journey of surpassing but inexplicable importance, one that I must make and was bound to complete. I was calm in myself, quite calm, and confident, too, despite not knowing rightly where I was going except that I was going home. I was alone on the road. The snow which had been slowly drifting down all day was unmarked by tracks of any kind, tyre, boot or hoof, for no one had passed this way and no one would. There was something the matter with my foot, the left one, I must have injured it, but long ago, for it was not painful, though at every step I had to throw it out awkwardly in a sort of half-circle, and this hindered me, not seriously but seriously enough. I felt compassion for myself, that is to say the dreamer that I was felt compassion for the self being dreamed, this poor lummox going along dauntlessly in the snow at fall of day with only the road ahead of him and no promise of homecoming.

---

① Orpheus:奥菲士。希腊神话中色雷斯诗人和歌手,善弹竖琴,弹奏时猛兽俯首,顽石点头,差一点将妻子欧瑞狄柯救出地狱。

That was all there was in the dream. The journey did not end, I arrived nowhere, and nothing happened. I was just walking there, bereft and stalwart, endlessly trudging through the snow and the wintry gloaming. But I woke into the murk of dawn not as I usually do these days, with the sense of having been flayed of yet another layer of protective skin during the night, but with the conviction that something had been achieved, or at least initiated. Immediately then, and for the first time in I do not know how long, I thought of Ballyless and the house there on Station Road, and the Graces, and Chloe Grace, I cannot think way, and it was as if I had stepped suddenly out of the dark into a splash of pale, salt-washed sunlight. It endured only a minute, less than a minute, that happy lightsomeness, but it told me what to do, and where I must go.

I first saw her, Chloe Grace, on the beach. It was a bright, wind-worried day and the Graces were settled in a shallow recess scooped into the dunes by wind and tides to which their somewhat raffish presence lent a suggestion of the proscenium. They were impressively equipped, with a faded length of striped canvas strung between poles to keep chill breezes off, and folding chairs and a little folding table, and a straw hamper as big as a small suitcase containing bottles and vacuum flasks and tins of sandwiches and biscuits; they even had real tea cups, with saucers. This was a part of the beach that was tacitly reserved for residents of the Golf Hotel, the lawn of which ended just behind the dunes, and indignant stares were being directed at these heedlessly interloping villa people with their smart beach furniture and their bottles of wine, stares which the Graces if they noticed them ignored. Mr. Grace, Carlo Grace, Daddy, was wearing shorts again, and a candy-striped blazer over a chest that was bare save for two big tufts of tight curls in the shape of a miniature pair of widespread fuzzy wings. I had never before encountered nor, I think, have I encountered since, anyone so fascinatingly hairy. On his head was clamped a canvas hat like a child's upturned sand bucket. He was sitting on one of the folding chairs, holding a newspaper open before him and at the same time managing to smoke a cigarette, despite the stiff wafts of wind coming in from the sea. The blond boy, the swinger on the gate—it was Myles, I may as well give him his name—was crouched at his father's feet, pouting moodily and delving in the sand with a jagged piece of sea-polished driftwood. Some way behind them, in the shelter of the dune wall, a girl, or young woman, was kneeling on the sand, wrapped in a big red towel, under the cover of which she was trying vexedly to wriggle herself free of what would turn out to be a wet bathing suit. She was markedly pale and soulful of expression, with a long, slender face and very black, heavy hair. I noticed that she kept glancing, resentfully, as it seemed, at the back of Carlo Grace's head. I noticed too that the boy Myles was keeping sidelong watch, in the evident hope, which I shared, that the girl's protective towel would slip. She could hardly be his sister, then.

Mrs. Grace came up the beach. She had been in the sea and was wearing a black swimsuit, tight and darkly lustrous as sealskin, and over it a sort of wraparound skirt made of some diaphanous stuff, held at the waist with a single button and billowing open with each step she took to reveal her bare, tanned, rather thick but shapely legs. She stopped in front of her husband and pushed her white-rimmed sunglasses up into her hair and waited through the beat that he allowed to pass before he lowered the newspaper and looked up at her, lifting his hand that held the cigarette and shading his eyes against the salt-sharpened light. She said something and he put his head on one side and shrugged, and smiled, showing numerous small white even teeth. Behind him the girl, still under the towel, discarded her bathing suit that she had freed herself of at last and, turning her back, sat down on the sand with her legs flexed and made the towel into a tent around herself and rested her forehead on her knees, and Myles drove his stick into the sand with disappointed force.

So there they were, the Graces: Carlo Grace and his wife Constance, their son Myles, the girl or young woman who I was sure was not the girl I had heard laughing in the house that first day, with all their things around them, their folding chairs and tea cups and tumblers of white wine, and Connie① Grace's revealing skirt and her husband's funny hat and newspaper and cigarette, and Myles's stick, and the girl's swimsuit, lying where she had tossed it, limply wadded and stuck along one wet edge with a fringe of sand, like something thrown up drowned out of the sea.

I do not know for how long Chloe had been standing on the dune before she jumped. She may have been there all that time, watching me watching the others. She was first a silhouette, with the sun behind her making a shining helmet of her short-cropped hair. Then she lifted her arms and with her knees pressed together launched herself off the dune wall. The air made the legs of her short balloon briefly. She was barefoot, and landed on her heels, sending up a shower of sand. The girl under the towel—Rose, give her a name too, poor Rosie②—uttered a little shriek of fright. Chloe wobbled, her arms still lifted and her heels in the sand, and it seemed she would fall over or at least sit down hard, but instead she kept her balance, and smiled sideways spitefully at Rose who had sand in her eyes and was making a fish face and shaking her head and blinking. "*Chlo-e*!" Mrs. Grace said, a reproving wail, but Chloe ignored her and came forward and knelt in the sand beside her brother and tried to wrest the stick from him. I was lying on my stomach on a towel with my cheeks propped on my hands, pretending to read a book. Chloe knew I was looking at her and seemed not to care. What age were we, ten, eleven? Say eleven, it will do. Her chest was as

---

① Connie: 对 Constance 的昵称。
② Rosie: 对 Rose 的昵称。

flat as Myles's, her hips were no wider than mine. She wore a white singlet over her shorts. Her sun-bleached hair was almost white. Myles, who had been battling to keep his stick, snatched it free of her grasp at least and hit her with it on the knuckles and she said "Ow!" and struck him in the breastbone with a small, pointed fist.

"Listen to this advertisement," her father said to no one in particular, and read aloud, laughing, from the newspaper. "*Live ferrets required as Venetian blink salesmen. Must be car drivers. Apply box twenty-three.*" He laughed again, and coughed, and, coughing, laughed. "Live ferrets[①]!" he cried. "Oh, my."

How flat all sounds are at the seaside, flat and yet emphatic, like the sound of gunshots heard at a distance. It must be the muffling effect of so much sand. Although I cannot say when I have had occasion to hear a gun or guns being fired.

Mrs. Grace poured wine for herself, tasted it, grimaced, and sat down in a folding chair and crossed one firm leg on the other, her beach shoe dangling. Rose was getting dressed fumblingly under her towel. Now it was Chloe's turn to draw her knees up to her chest—is it a thing all girls do, or did, at least, sitting that way in the shape of a zed fallen over on its front? —and hold her feet in her hands. Myles poked her in the side with his stick. "Daddy," she said with listless irritation, "tell him to stop." Her father went on reading. Connie Grace's dangling shoes was jiggling in time to some rhythm in her head. The sand around me with the sun strong on it gave off its mysterious, catty smell. Out on the bay a white sail shivered and flipped to leeward and for a second the world tilted. Someone away down the beach was calling to someone else. Children. Bathers. A wire-haired ginger dog. The sail turned to windward again and I heard distinctly from across the water the ruffle and snap of the canvas. Then the breeze dropped and for a moment all went still.

They played a game, Chloe and Myles and Mrs. Grace, the children lobbing a ball to each other over their mother's head and she running an leaping to try to catch it, mostly in vain. When she runs her skirt billows behind her and I cannot take my eyes off the tight black bulge at the upside-down apex of her lap. She jumps, grasping air and giving breathless cries and laughing. Her breasts bounce. The sight of her is almost alarming. A creature with so many mounds and scoops of flesh to carry should not cavort like this, she will damage something inside her, some tender arrangement of adipose tissue and pearly cartilage. Her husband has lowered his newspaper and is watching her too, combing his fingers through his beard under his chin and coldly smiling, his lips drawn back a little from those fine small teeth and his nostrils flared wolfishly as if he is trying to catch her scent. His look is one of arousal, amusement and faint contempt; he seems to want to see her fall down in the sand

---

① live ferrets：〈俚〉资深销售商。

and hurt herself; I imagine hitting him, punching him in the exact centre of his hairy chest as Chloe had punched her brother. Already I know these people, am one of them. And I have fallen in love with Mrs. Grace.

Rose comes out of the towel, in red shirt and black slacks, like a magician's assistant appearing from under the magician's scarlet-lined cape, and busies herself in not looking at anything, especially the woman and her children at play.

Abruptly Chloe loses interest in the game and turns aside and flops down in the sand. How well I will come to know these sudden shifts of mood of hers, these sudden sulks. Her mother calls to her to come back and play but she does not respond. She is lying propped on an elbow on her side with her ankles crossed, looking past me narrow-eyed out to sea. Myles does a chimp dance in front of her, flapping his hands under his armpits and gibbering. She pretends to be able to see through him. "Brat," her mother says of her spoilsport daughter, almost complacently, and goes back and sits down on her chair. She is out of breath, and the smooth, sand-colored slope of her bosom heaves. She lifts a hand up high to brush a clinging strand of hair from her damp forehead and I fix on the secret shadow under her armpit, plum-blue, the tint of my humid fantasies for nights to come. Chloe sulks. Myles goes back to delving violently in the sand with his stick. The little waves rise and plash, the ginger dog barks. And my life is changed forever.

But then, at what moment, of all our moments, is life not utterly, utterly changed, until the final, most momentous changes of all?

▶扩展阅读

1. Hand, D. *John Banville: Exploring Fiction*. Dublin: Liffey Press, 2002.

2. Imhofe, R. *John Baville: A Critical Introduction*. Dublin: Wolfhound, 1997.

3. Kenny, J. Dr. *John Banville*. Dublin: Irish Academic Press, 2009.

4. McMinn, J. *Supreme Fiction of John Banville*. Manchester: Manchester University Press, 1999.

5. Peach, L. *The Contemporary Irish Novel: Critical Readings*. New York: Palgrave Macmillan, 2004.

▶学习参考网站

1. http://en.wikipedia.org/wiki/John_Banville

2. http://www.benjaminblackbooks.com/aboutauthor.htm

3. http://www.contemporarywriters.com/authors/?p=auth13

4. http://www.themodernword.com/scriptorium/banville.html

5. http://www.fantasticfiction.co.uk/b/john-banville/

【李　莉　编注】

17. James Fennimore Cooper: The Pilot

詹姆斯·费尼莫尔·库珀（James Fennimore Cooper，1789—1851），美国小说家，开创了美国文学史上三种不同类型的小说，即美国革命历史小说、边疆冒险小说和海上冒险小说。1789 年他生于新泽西州的伯林顿。一年后，他们举家迁至纽约州中部自己开发的库珀镇，库珀在那里生活至 12 岁。之后他离家去耶鲁学习，却在第三年因违反校规被退学。于是他上了一艘商船当水手，随船去欧洲，做了 11 个月的海上航行。1808 年，他加入海军，做见习士官。1809 年，他开始任海军军官，从海军准尉直至升任为海军上尉。1811 年他结婚后退役。这几年的海上生涯为他日后写海洋小说打下了坚实的基础。婚后，库珀和妻子定居威契斯特，在那里听到不少关于独立战争时期的故事，这又为他创作革命历史小说提供了素材。在平静的乡绅生活之余，库珀将注意力转向了写作，并迅速成为美国当时最著名的小说家。

库珀得到广泛认可绝非偶然，他的作品主要有三个特色：其一，他善于将自己的风格和英国文学的传统紧密结合起来，在艺术创作上独辟蹊径。他曾悉心研究过 18 世纪以来的表达艺术，研究过英国文学，对 18 世纪的英国诗人莎士比亚、拜伦等都有过深入的研究。其二，他具有捕捉时代精神的才能，善于把美国的过去和现在提炼成文学的题材。其三，他拥有巧妙处理丰富素材的能力。其作品结构复杂精巧，内容紧张生动，故事情节悬念重重，人物命运瞬息万变，却始终能前后连贯，有条不紊。

库珀一生共创作了 30 余部小说，其中有 10 余部是关于海洋的，他一手开创了美国海洋小说的写作先河，这方面的主要作品有《领航员》（*The Pilot*，1824）、《红海盗》（*The Red Rover*，1828）、《海妖》（*The Water-Witch*，1830）、《海上与岸上》（*Afloat and Ashore*，1844）、《火山口》（*The Crater*，1847）和《海狮》（*The Sea Lions*，1849）。值得一提的是，库珀还是美国第一位杰出的海军历史学家，著有《美国海军成长史》（*The History of the Navy of the United States of America*，1839），以及《美国杰出海军军官们的生活》（*Lives of Distinguished American Naval Officers*，1846）和《奈德·迈尔斯》（*Ned Myers*，1843）等一系列海洋人物传记。库珀的海洋小说涵盖世界地理范围，横跨漫长历史纬度，内容涉及海洋战争、海盗和私掠以及海岛余生等，流传广泛且对后世影响深远。麦尔维尔、康拉德等都在不同场合向库珀表示过敬意。库珀最初创作海洋小说则是由于读到当时盛极一时的历史小说家沃尔特·司各特（Walt Scott，1771—1832）的小说《海盗》（*The Pirate*，1822）。然而，书中对大海和船只的描写令库珀很恼火,他认为司各特对此一无所知,凭自己在海上的经历完全可以写出一部更好的小说。于是,他的第四部作品,也是他的第一部海洋小说《领航员》在1824 年面世,并获得好评。

《领航员》被后世誉为美国第一部海洋小说,它以美国独立战争为时代背景,歌颂了爱国主义情怀。该书主人公领航员的原型是独立战争时期著名的美国海军人物——约翰·保罗·琼斯船长(John Paul Jones,1747—1792)。库珀运用浪漫主义手法,把他描绘成具有神秘色彩的英雄。小说讲述的是独立战争期间,美国国会为了惩戒英国殖民主义者,派遣两艘军舰,远渡重洋,到英国海岸去袭扰,并伺机劫持英国贵族做人质。经历了风暴和海浪的洗礼,以及数场动人心魄的战斗,虽付出了一定的代价,但最终在神秘英雄领航员的引领下,这两艘军舰胜利地返回了祖国。这部小说一经面世立即成为当时最畅销的作品。它打破了旧的思维定式,给读者耳目一新的感觉,也为文学创作注入了新的活力。一方面,作者笔下的大海有着更为复杂的内涵。大海宽广无垠且令人敬畏,它既美丽又危险,静谧温婉中暗藏惊涛骇浪。另一方面,库珀笔下的水手具有鲜明的个性。之前,水兵多以无知或粗野的形象出现在文学作品中,他们只对酒和性感兴趣,是被取笑和愚弄的对象。但是,库珀深知水手们的生存环境和内心世界,他从正面的角度描写水手们的真实情况,突出他们英勇无畏的精神。在他的笔下,大海是一片民主自由的疆域,水手们的个人价值在于他们乘风破浪,驾驭船只的能力,不受出身、文化或肤色影响。正如《领航员》中的主人公,他有着坚毅果敢的性格,冷静睿智的头脑以及高超的领航技术,但也绝非一台冷冰冰的机器,他与爱丽丝之间的感情也为这部铁血铮铮的小说增添了一份柔情。以下选段出自《领航员》第三十三章,描写了美国军舰遭到敌舰追击以及水兵英勇应对的惊险一幕。

▶**Chapter 33**

> "Furious press the hostile squadron[①],
> Furious he repels their rage.
> Loss of blood at length enfeebles;
> Who can war with thousands wage?"
> *Spanish War Song*.

We cannot detain the narrative to detail the scenes which busy wonder, aided by the relation of divers marvelous feats, produced among the curious seamen who remained in the ship, and their more fortunate fellows who had returned in glory from an expedition to the land. For nearly an hour the turbulence of a general movement was heard, issuing from the deep recesses of the frigate, and the boisterous sounds of hoarse merriment were listened to

---

① squadron:(空军或海军的)中队。

by the officers in indulgent silence; but all these symptoms of unbridled humor ceased by the time the morning repast was ended, when the regular sea-watch was set, and the greater portion of those whose duty did not require their presence on the vessel's deck, availed themselves of the opportunity to repair the loss of sleep sustained in the preceding night. Still no preparations were made to put the ship in motion, though long and earnest consultations, which were supposed to relate to their future destiny, were observed by the younger officers to be held between their captain, the first lieutenant, and the mysterious Pilot. The latter threw many an anxious glance along the eastern horizon, searching it minutely with his glass, and then would turn his impatient looks at the low, dense bank of fog, which, stretching across the ocean like a barrier of cloud, entirely intercepted the view towards the south. To the north and along the land the air was clear, and the sea without a spot of any kind; but in the east a small white sail had been discovered since the opening of day, which was gradually rising above the water, and assuming the appearance of a vessel of some size. Every officer on the quarter-deck[1] in his turn had examined this distant sail, and had ventured an opinion on its destination and character; and even Katherine, who with her cousin was enjoying, in the open air, the novel beauties of the ocean, had been tempted to place her sparkling eye to a glass, to gaze at the stranger.

"It is a collier[2]," Griffith said, "who has hauled from the land in the late gale, and who is luffing up to his course again. If the wind holds here in the south, and he does not get into that fog-bank, we can stand off for him and get a supply of fuel before eight bells are struck."

"I think his head is to the northward, and that he is steering off the wind," returned the Pilot, in a musing manner, "If that Dillon succeeded in getting his express far enough along the coast, the alarm has been spread, and we must be wary. The convoy[3] of the Baltic trade is in the North Sea, and news of our presence could easily have been taken off to it by some of the cutters that line the coast, I could wish to get the ship as far south as the Helder!"

"Then we lose this weather tide!" exclaimed the impatient Griffith; "surely we have the cutter as a lookout! besides, by beating into the fog, we shall lose the enemy, if enemy it be, and it is thought meet for an American frigate to skulk from her foes!"

The scornful expression that kindled the eye of the Pilot, like a gleam of sunshine lighting for an instant some dark dell and laying bare its secrets, was soon lost in the usually quiet look of his glance, though he hesitated like one who was struggling with his passions before he answered:

"If prudence and the service of the States require it, even this proud frigate must

---

①   quarter-deck:后甲板。

②   collier:运煤船。

③   convoy:(尤指有士兵护送的)车队,船队。

retreat and hide from the meanest of her enemies. My advice, Captain Munson, is, that you make sail, and beat the ship to windward, as Mr. Griffith has suggested, and that you order the cutter to precede us, keeping more in with the land."

The aged seaman, who evidently suspended his orders only to receive an intimation of the other's pleasure, immediately commanded his youthful assistant to issue the necessary mandates to put these measures in force. Accordingly, the Alacrity, which vessel had been left under the command of the junior lieutenant of the frigate, was quickly under way; and, making short stretches to windward, she soon entered the bank of fog, and was lost to the eye. In the mean time the canvas of the ship was loosened, and spread leisurely, in order not to disturb the portion of the crew who were sleeping; and, following her little consort, she moved heavily through the water, bearing up against the dull breeze.

The quiet of regular duty had succeeded to the bustle of making sail; and, as the rays of the sun fell less obliquely on the distant land, Katherine and Cecilia were amusing Griffith by vain attempts to point out the rounded eminences which they fancied lay in the vicinity of the deserted mansion of St. Ruth. Barnstable, who had resumed his former station in the frigate as her second lieutenant, was pacing the opposite side of the quarter-deck, holding under his arm the speaking-trumpet, which denoted that he held the temporary control of the motions of the ship, and inwardly cursing the restraint that kept him from the side of his mistress. At this moment of universal quiet, when nothing above low dialogues interrupted the dashing of the waves as they were thrown lazily aside by the bows of the vessel, the report of a light cannon burst out of the barrier of fog, and rolled by them on the breeze, apparently vibrating with the rising and sinking of the waters.

"There goes the cutter!" exclaimed Griffith, the instant the sound was heard.

"Surely," said the captain, "Somers is not so indiscreet as to scale his guns, after the caution he has received!"

"No idle scaling of guns is intended there," said the Pilot, straining his eyes to pierce the fog, but soon turning away in disappointment at his inability to succeed—"that gun is shotted, and has been fired in the hurry of a sudden signal! —can your lookouts see nothing, Mr. Barnstable?"

The lieutenant of the watch hailed the man aloft, and demanded if anything were visible in the direction of the wind, and received for answer that the fog intercepted the view in that quarter of the heavens, but that the sail in the east was a ship, running large, or before the wind. The Pilot shook his head doubtingly at this information, but still he manifested a strong reluctance to relinquish the attempt of getting more to the southward. Again he communed with the commander of the frigate, apart from all other ears; and while they yet deliberated, a second report was heard, leaving no doubt that the Alacrity was firing signal-guns for their particular attention.

"Perhaps," said Griffith, "he wishes to point out his position, or to ascertain ours; believing that we are lost like himself in the mist."

"We have our compasses!" returned the doubting captain; "Somers has a meaning in what he says!"

"See!" cried Katherine, with girlish delight, "see, my cousin! see, Barnstable! how beautifully that vapor is wreathing itself in clouds above the smoky line of fog! It stretches already into the very heavens like a lofty pyramid!"

Barnstable sprang lightly on a gun, as he repeated her words:

"Pyramids of fog! and wreathing clouds! By heaven!" he shouted, "'tis[①] a tall ship! Royals, skysails, and studdingsails all abroad! She is within a mile of us, and comes down like a racehorse, with a spanking breeze, dead before it! Now know we why Somers is speaking in the mist!"

"Ay," cried Griffith, "and there goes the Alacrity, just breaking out of the fog, hovering in for the land!"

"There is a mighty hull under all that cloud of canvas, Captain Munson," said the observant but calm Pilot: "it is time, gentlemen, to edge away to leeward."

"What, before we know from whom we run!" cried Griffith; "my life on it, there is no single ship King George owns but would tire of the sport before she had played a full game of bowls with—"

The haughty air of the young man was daunted by the severe look he encountered in the eye of the Pilot, and he suddenly ceased, though inwardly chafing with impatient pride.

"The same eye that detected the canvas above the fog might have seen the flag of a vice-admiral fluttering still nearer the heavens," returned the collected stranger; "and England, faulty as she may be, is yet too generous to place a flag-officer in time of war in command of a frigate, or a captain in command of a fleet. She knows the value of those who shed their blood in her behalf, and it is thus that she is so well served! Believe me, Captain Munson, there is nothing short of a ship of the line under that symbol of rank and that broad show of canvas!"

"We shall see, sir, we shall see," returned the old officer, whose manner grew decided, as the danger appeared to thicken; "beat to quarters, Mr. Griffith, for we have none but enemies to expect on this coast."

The order was instantly issued, when Griffith remarked, with a more temperate zeal:

"If Mr. Gray be right, we shall have reason to thank God that we are so light of heel!"

---

① 'tis: 即 it is,古诗用语。

The cry of "a strange vessel close aboard the frigate" having already flown down the hatches, the ship was in an uproar at the first tap of the drum. The seamen threw themselves from their hammocks, and lashing them rapidly into long, hard bundles, they rushed to the decks, where they were dexterously stowed in the netting, to aid the defences of the upper part of the vessel. While this tumultuous scene was exhibiting, Griffith gave a secret order to Merry, who disappeared, leading his trembling cousins to a place of safety in the inmost depths of the ship.

The guns were cleared of their lumber and loosened. The bulkheads were knocked down, and the cabin relieved of its furniture; and the gun-deck exhibited one unbroken line of formidable cannon, arranged in all the order of a naval battery ready to engage. Arm-chests[1] were thrown open, and the decks strewed with pikes, cutlasses, pistols, and all the various weapons for boarding. In short, the yards were slung, and every other arrangement was made with a readiness and dexterity that were actually wonderful, though all was performed amid an appearance of disorder and confusion that rendered the ship another Babel during the continuance of the preparations. In a very few minutes everything was completed, and even the voices of the men ceased to be heard answering to their names, as they were mustered at their stations, by their respective officers. Gradually the ship became as quiet as the grave; and when even Griffith or his commander found it necessary to speak, their voices were calmer, and their tones more mild than usual. The course of the vessel was changed to an oblique line from that in which their enemy was approaching, though the appearance of flight was to be studiously avoided to the last moment. When nothing further remained to be done, every eye became fixed on the enormous pile of swelling canvas that was rising, in cloud over cloud, far above the fog, and which was manifestly moving, like driving vapor, swiftly to the north. Presently the dull, smoky boundary of the mist which rested on the water was pushed aside in vast volumes, and the long taper spars that projected from the bowsprit of the strange ship issued from the obscurity, and were quickly followed by the whole of the enormous fabric to which they were merely light appendages. For a moment, streaks of reluctant vapor clung to the huge floating pile; but they were soon shaken off by the rapid vessel, and the whole of her black hull became distinct to the eye.

"One, two, three rows of teeth!" said Boltrope, deliberately counting the tiers of guns that bristled along the sides of the enemy; "a three-decker! Jack Manly would show his stern to such a fellow, and even the bloody Scotchman would run!"

"Hard up with your helm, quartermaster!" cried Captain Munson; "there is indeed no time to hesitate, with such an enemy within a quarter of a mile! Turn the hands up, Mr.

---

① Arm-chests: 军械箱。

Griffith, and pack on the ship from her trucks to her lower studdingsail-booms. Be stirring, sir, be stirring! Hard up with your helm! Hard up, and be damn'd to you!"

The unusual earnestness of their aged commander acted on the startled crew like a voice from the deep, and they waited not for the usual signals of the boatswain and drummer to be given, before they broke away from their guns, and rushed tumultuously to aid in spreading the desired canvas. There was one minute of ominous confusion, that to an inexperienced eye would have foreboded the destruction of all order in the vessel, during which every hand, and each tongue, seemed in motion; but it ended in opening the immense folds of light duck which were displayed along the whole line of the masts, far beyond the ordinary sails, overshadowing the waters for a great distance, on either side of the vessel. During the moment of inaction that succeeded this sudden exertion, the breeze, which had brought up the three-decker, fell fresher on the sails of the frigate, and she started away from her dangerous enemy with a very perceptible advantage in point of sailing.

"The fog rises!" cried Griffith; "give us but the wind for an hour, and we shall run her out of gunshot!"

"These nineties are very fast off the wind," returned the captain, in a low tone, that was intended only for the ears of his first lieutenant and the Pilot; "and we shall have a struggle for it."

The quick eye of the stranger was glancing over the movements of his enemy, while he answered:

"He finds we have the heels of him already! he is making ready, and we shall be fortunate to escape a broadside! Let her yaw a little, Mr. Griffith; touch her lightly with the helm; if we are raked, sir, we are lost!"

The captain sprang on the taffrail of his ship with the activity of a younger man, and in an instant he perceived the truth of the other's conjecture.

Both vessels now ran for a few minutes, keenly watching each other's motions like two skillful combatants; the English ship making slight deviations from the line of her course, and then, as her movements were anticipated by the other, turning as cautiously in the opposite direction, until a sudden and wide sweep of her huge bows told the Americans plainly on which tack to expect her. Captain Munson made a silent but impressive gesture with his arm, as if the crisis were too important for speech, which indicated to the watchful Griffith the way he wished the frigate sheered, to avoid the weight of the impending danger. Both vessels whirled swiftly up to the wind, with their heads towards the land; and as the huge black side of the three-decker[①], checkered with its triple batteries, frowned full upon

---

① the three-decker: 三层甲板船。

her foe, it belched forth a flood of fire and smoke, accompanied by a bellowing roar that mocked the surly moanings of the sleeping ocean. The nerves of the bravest man in the frigate contracted their fibres, as the hurricane of iron hurtled by them, and each eye appeared to gaze in stupid wonder, as if tracing the flight of the swift engines of destruction. But the voice of Captain Munson was heard in the din, shouting while he waved his hat earnestly in the required direction:

"Meet her! meet her with the helm, boy! meet her, Mr. Griffith, meet her!"

Griffith had so far anticipated this movement as to have already ordered the head of the frigate to be turned in its former course, when, struck by the unearthly cry of the last tones uttered by his commander, he bent his head, and beheld the venerable seaman driven through the air, his hat still waving, his gray hair floating in the wind, and his eye set in the wild look of death.

"Great God!" exclaimed the young man, rushing to the side of the ship, where he was just in time to see the lifeless body disappear in the waters that were dyed in its blood; "he has been struck by a shot! Lower away the boat, lower away the jolly-boat, the barge, the tiger, the—"

"'Tis useless," interrupted the calm, deep voice of the Pilot; "he has met a warrior's end, and he sleeps in a sailor's grave! The ship is getting before the wind again, and the enemy is keeping his vessel away."

The youthful lieutenant was recalled by these words to his duty, and reluctantly turned his eyes away from the bloody spot on the waters, which the busy frigate had already passed, to resume the command of the vessel with a forced composure.

"He has cut some of our running-gear," said the master, whose eye had never ceased to dwell on the spars and rigging of the ship; "and there's a splinter out of the maintopmast that is big enough for a fid! He has let daylight through some of our canvas too; but, taking it by-and-large, the squall has gone over and little harm done. Didn't I hear something said of Captain Munson getting jammed by a shot?"

"He is killed!" said Griffith, speaking in a voice that was yet husky with horror—"he is dead, sir, and carried overboard; there is more need that we forget not ourselves, in this crisis."

"Dead!" said Boltrope, suspending the operation of his active jaws for a moment, in surprise; "and buried in a wet jacket! Well, it is lucky 'tis no worse; for damme if I did not think every stick in the ship would have been cut out of her!"

With this consolatory remark on his lips, the master walked slowly forward, continuing his orders to repair the damages with a singleness of purpose that rendered him, however uncouth as a friend, an invaluable man in his station.

Griffith had not yet brought his mind to the calmness that was so essential to discharge the duties which had thus suddenly and awfully devolved on him, when his elbow was lightly touched by the Pilot, who had drawn closer to his side.

"The enemy appear satisfied with the experiment," said the stranger; "and as we work the quicker of the two, he loses too much ground to repeat it, if he be a true seaman."

"And yet as he finds we leave him so fast," returned Griffith, "he must see that all his hopes rest in cutting us up aloft. I dread that he will come by the wind again, and lay us under his broadside; we should need a quarter of an hour to run without his range, if he were anchored!"

"He plays a surer game—see you not that the vessel we made in the eastern board shows the hull of a frigate? 'Tis past a doubt that they are of one squadron, and that the expresses have sent them in our wake. The English admiral has spread a broad clew, Mr. Griffith; and, as he gathers in his ships, he sees that his game has been successful."

The faculties of Griffith had been too much occupied with the hurry of the chase to look at the ocean; but, startled at the information of the Pilot, who spoke coolly, though like a man sensible of the existence of approaching danger, he took the glass from the other, and with his own eye examined the different vessels in sight. It is certain that the experienced officer, whose flag was flying above the light sails of the three-decker, saw the critical situation of his chase, and reasoned much in the same manner as the Pilot, or the fearful expedient apprehended by Griffith would have been adopted. Prudence, however, dictated that he should prevent his enemy from escaping by pressing so closely on his rear as to render it impossible for the American to haul across his bows and run into the open sea between his own vessel and the nearest frigate of his squadron. The unpractised reader will be able to comprehend the case better by accompanying the understanding eye of Griffith, as it glanced from point to point, following the whole horizon. To the west lay the land, along which the Alacrity was urging her way industriously, with the double purpose of keeping her consort abeam, and of avoiding a dangerous proximity to their powerful enemy. To the east, bearing off the starboard bow of the American frigate, was the vessel first seen, and which now began to exhibit the hostile appearance of a ship of war, steering in a line converging towards themselves, and rapidly drawing nigher; while far in the northeast was a vessel as yet faintly discerned, whose evolutions could not be mistaken by one who understood the movements of nautical warfare.

"We are hemmed in effectually," said Griffith, dropping the glass from his eye; "and I know not but our wisest course would be to haul in to the land, and, cutting everything light adrift, endeavor to pass the broadside of the flag-ship."

"Provided she left a rag of canvas to do it with!" returned the Pilot. "Sir, 'tis an idle hope! She would strip your ship in ten minutes, to her plank shears. Had it not been for a lucky wave on which so many of her shot struck and glanced upwards, we should have nothing to boast of left from the fire she has already given; we must stand on, and drop the three-decker as far as possible."

"But the frigates?" said Griffith, "What are we to do with the frigates?"

"Fight them!" returned the Pilot, in a low determined voice; "fight them! Young man, I have borne the stars and stripes aloft in greater straits than this, and even with honor! Think not that my fortune will desert me now."

"We shall have an hour of desperate battle!"

"On that we may calculate; but I have lived through whole days of bloodshed! You seem not one to quail at the sight of an enemy."

"Let me proclaim your name to the men!" said Griffith; "'twill quicken their blood, and at such a moment be a host in itself."

"They want it not," returned the Pilot, checking the hasty zeal of the other with his hand. "I would be unnoticed, unless I am known as becomes me. I will share your Danger, but would not rob you of a tittle of your glory. Should we come to grapple," he continued, while a smile of conscious pride gleamed across his face, "I will give forth the word as a war-cry, and, believe me, these English will quail before it!"

Griffith submitted to the stranger's will; and, after they had deliberated further on the nature of their evolutions, he gave his attention again to the management of the vessel. The first object which met his eye on turning from the Pilot was Colonel Howard, pacing the quarter-deck with a determined brow and a haughty mien, as if already in the enjoyment of that triumph which now seemed certain.

"I fear, sir," said the young man, approaching him with respect, "that you will soon find the deck unpleasant and dangerous; your wards are—"

"Mention not the unworthy term!" interrupted the colonel. "What greater pleasure can there be than to inhale the odor of loyalty that is wafted from yonder floating tower of the king? —And danger! you know but little of old George Howard, young man, if you think he would for thousands miss seeing that symbol of rebellion leveled before the flag of his majesty."

"If that be your wish, Colonel Howard," returned Griffith, biting his lip as he looked around at the wondering seamen who were listeners, "you will wait in vain; but I pledge you my word that when that time arrives you shall be advised, and that your own hands shall do the ignoble deed."

"Edward Griffith, why not this moment? This is your moment of probation —submit to the clemency of the crown, and yield your crew to the royal mercy! In such a case I would remember the child of my brother Harry's friend; and believe me, my name is known to the ministry. And you, misguided and ignorant abettors of rebellion! Cast aside your useless weapons, or prepare to meet the vengeance of yonder powerful and victorious servant of your prince."

"Fall back! back with ye, fellows!" cried Griffith, fiercely, to the men who were gathering around the colonel, with looks of sullen vengeance. "If a man of you dare approach him, he shall be cast into the sea."

The sailors retreated at the order of their commander; but the elated veteran had continued to pace the deck for many minutes before stronger interests diverted the angry glances of the seamen to other objects.

Notwithstanding the ship of the line was slowly sinking beneath the distant waves, and in less than an hour from the time she had fired the broadside, no more than one of her three tiers of guns was visible from the deck of the frigate, she yet presented an irresistible obstacle against retreat to the south. On the other hand, the ship first seen drew so nigh as to render the glass no longer necessary in watching her movements. She proved to be a frigate, though one so materially lighter than the American as to have rendered her conquest easy, had not her two consorts continued to press on for the scene of battle with such rapidity. During the chase, the scene had shifted from the point opposite to St. Ruth, to the verge of those shoals where our tale commenced. As they approached the latter, the smallest of the English ships drew so nigh as to render the combat unavoidable. Griffith and his crew had not been idle in the intermediate time, but all the usual preparations against the casualties of a sea-fight had been duly made, when the drum once more called the men to their quarters, and the ship was deliberately stripped of her unnecessary sails, like a prize-fighter about to enter the arena, casting aside the encumbrances of dress. At the instant she gave this intimation of her intention to abandon flight, and trust the issue to the combat, the nearest English frigate also took in her light canvas in token of her acceptance of the challenge.

"He is but a little fellow," said Griffith to the Pilot, who hovered at his elbow with a sort of fatherly interest in the other's conduct of the battle, "though he carries a stout heart."

"We must crush him at a blow," returned the stranger; "not a shot must be delivered until our yards are locking."

"I see him training his twelves upon us already; we may soon expect his fire."

"After standing the brunt of a ninety-gun ship," observed the collected Pilot, "we shall not shrink from the broadside of a two-and-thirty."

"Stand to your guns, men!" cried Griffith, through his trumpet—"not a shot is to be fired without the order."

This caution, so necessary to check the ardor of the seamen, was hardly uttered, before their enemy became wrapped in sheets of fire and volumes of smoke, as gun after gun hurled its iron missiles at their vessel in quick succession. Ten minutes might have passed, the two vessels sheering close to each other every foot they advanced, during which time the crew of the American were compelled, by their commander, to suffer the fire of their adversary, without returning a shot. This short period, which seemed an age to the seamen, was distinguished in their vessel by deep silence. Even the wounded and dying, who fell in every part of the ship, stifled their groans, under the influence of the severe discipline, which gave a character to every man, and each movement of the vessel; and those officers who were required to speak were heard only in the lowest tones of resolute preparation. At length the ship slowly entered the skirts of the smoke that enveloped their enemy; and Griffith heard the man who stood at his side whisper the word "Now".

"Let them have it!" cried Griffith, in a voice that was heard in the remotest parts of the ship.

The shout that burst from the seamen appeared to lift the decks of the vessel, and the affrighted frigate trembled like an aspen with the recoil of her own massive artillery, that shot forth a single sheet of flame, the sailors having disregarded, in their impatience, the usual order of firing. The effect of the broadside on the enemy was still more dreadful; for a death-like silence succeeded to the roar of the guns, which was only broken by the shrieks and execrations that burst from her, like the moanings of the damned. During the few moments in which the Americans were again loading their cannon, and the English were recovering from their confusion, the vessel of the former moved slowly past her antagonist, and was already doubling across her bows, when the latter was suddenly, and, considering the inequality of their forces, it may be added desperately, headed into her enemy. The two frigates grappled. The sudden and furious charge made by the Englishman, as he threw his masses of daring seamen along his bowsprit, and out of his channels, had nearly taken Griffith by surprise; but Manual, who had delivered his first fire with the broadside, now did good service, by ordering his men to beat back the intruders, by a steady and continued discharge. Even the wary Pilot lost sight of their other foes, in the high daring of that moment, and smiles of stern pleasure were exchanged between him and Griffith as both comprehended, at a glance, their advantages.

"Lash his bowsprit to our mizzenmast[①]," shouted the lieutenant, "and we will sweep his decks as he lies!"

Twenty men sprang eagerly forward to execute the order, among the foremost of whom were Boltrope and the stranger.

"Ay, now he's our own!" cried the busy master, "and we will take an owner's liberties with him, and break him up—for by the eternal—"

"Peace, rude man," said the Pilot, in a voice of solemn remonstrance; "at the next

---

① mizzenmast:【海】后桅。

instant you may face your God; mock not his awful name!"

The master found time, before he threw himself from the spar on the deck of the frigate again, to cast a look of amazement at his companion, who, with a steady mien, but with an eye that lighted with a warrior's ardor, viewed the battle that raged around him, like one who marked its progress to control the result.

The sight of the Englishmen rushing onward with shouts and bitter menaces warmed the blood of Colonel Howard, who pressed to the side of the frigate, and encouraged his friends, by his gestures and voice, to come on.

"Away with ye, old croaker!" cried the master, seizing him by the collar; "away with ye to the hold, or I'll order you fired from a gun."

"Down with your arms, rebellious dog!" shouted the colonel, carried beyond himself by the ardor of the fray; "down to the dust, and implore the mercy of your injured prince!"

Invigorated by a momentary glow, the veteran grappled with his brawny antagonist; but the issue of the short struggle was yet suspended, when the English, driven back by the fire of the marines, and the menacing front that Griffith with his boarders presented, retreated to the forecastle of their own ship, and attempted to return the deadly blows they were receiving, in their hull, from the cannon that Barnstable directed. A solitary gun was all they could bring to bear on the Americans; but this, loaded with cannister, was fired so near as to send its glaring flame into the very faces of their enemies. The struggling colonel, who was already sinking beneath the arm of his foe, felt the rough grasp loosen from his throat at the flash, and the two combatants sunk powerless on their knees facing each other.

"How, now, brother!" exclaimed Boltrope, with a smile of grim fierceness; "some of that grist has gone to your mill, ha!"

No answer could, however, be given before the yielding forms of both fell to the deck, where they lay helpless, amid the din of the battle and the wild confusion of the eager combatants.

Notwithstanding the furious struggle they witnessed, the elements did not cease their functions; and, urged by the breeze, and lifted irresistibly on a wave, the American ship was forced through the water still further across the bows of her enemy. The idle fastenings of hemp and iron were snapped asunder like strings of tow, and Griffith saw his own ship borne away from the Englishman at the instant that the bowsprit of the latter was torn from its lashings, and tumbled into the sea, followed by spar after spar, until nothing of all her proud tackling was remaining, but the few parted and useless ropes that were left dangling along the stumps of her lower masts. As his own stately vessel moved from the confusion she had caused, and left the dense cloud of smoke in which her helpless antagonist lay, the eye of the young man glanced anxiously toward the horizon, where he now remembered he had more foes to contend against.

"We have shaken off the thirty-two most happily!" he said to the Pilot, who followed his motions with singular interest; "but here is another fellow sheering in for us, who shows as many ports as ourselves, and who appears inclined for a closer interview; besides, the hull of the ninety is rising again, and I fear she will be down but too soon!"

"We must keep the use of our braces and sails," returned the Pilot, "and on no account close with the other frigate; we must play a double game, sir, and fight this new adversary with our heels as well as with our guns."

"'Tis time then that we were busy, for he is shortening sail, and as he nears so fast we may expect to hear from him every minute; what do you propose, sir?"

"Let him gather in his canvas," returned the Pilot; "and when he thinks himself snug, we can throw out a hundred men at once upon our yards, and spread everything alow and aloft; we may then draw ahead of him by surprise; if we can once get him in our wake, I have no fears of dropping them all."

"A stern chase is a long chase," cried Griffith, "and the thing may do! Clear up the decks, here, and carry down the wounded; and, as we have our hands full, the poor fellows who have done with us must go overboard at once."

This melancholy duty was instantly attended to, while the young seaman who commanded the frigate returned to his duty with the absorbed air of one who felt its high responsibility. These occupations, however, did not prevent his hearing the sounds of Barnstable's voice calling eagerly to young Merry. Bending his head towards the sound, Griffith beheld his friend looking anxiously up the main hatch, with a face grimed with smoke, his coat off, and his shirt bespattered with human blood. "Tell me, boy," he said, "is Mr. Griffith untouched? They say that a shot came in upon the quarter-deck that tripped up the heels of half a dozen."

Before Merry could answer, the eyes of Barnstable, which even while he spoke was scanning the state of the vessel's rigging, encountered the kind looks of Griffith, and from that moment perfect harmony was restored between the friends.

"Ah! you are there, Griff, and with a whole skin, I see," cried Barnstable, smiling with pleasure; "they have passed poor Boltrope down into one of his own storerooms! If that fellow's bowsprit had held on ten minutes longer, what a mark I should have made on his face and eyes!"

"'Tis perhaps best as it is," returned Griffith; "but what have you done with those whom we are most bound to protect?"

Barnstable made a significant gesture towards the depths of the vessel, as he answered:

"On the cables; safe as wood, iron, and water can keep them—though Katherine has had her head up three times to—"

A summons from the Pilot drew Griffith away; and the young officers were compelled to forget their individual feelings, in the pressing duties of their stations. The ship which the American frigate had now to oppose was a vessel of near her own size and equipage; and when Griffith looked at her again, he perceived that she had made her preparations to assert her equality in manful fight.

Her sails had been gradually reduced to the usual quantity, and, by certain movements on her decks the lieutenant and his constant attendant, the Pilot, well understood that she only wanted to lessen her distance a few hundred yards to begin the action.

"Now spread everything," whispered the stranger.

Griffith applied the trumpet to his mouth, and shouted in a voice that was carried even to his enemy: "Let fall-out with your booms—sheet home—hoist away of everything!"

The inspiring cry was answered by a universal bustle; fifty men flew out on the dizzy heights of the different spars, while broad sheets of canvas rose as suddenly along the masts as if some mighty bird were spreading its wings. The Englishman instantly perceived his mistake, and he answered the artifice by a roar of artillery. Griffith watched the effects of the broadside with an absorbing interest, as the shot whistled above his head; but when he perceived his masts untouched, and the few unimportant ropes only that were cut, he replied to the uproar with a burst of pleasure. A few men were, however, seen clinging with wild frenzy to the cordage, dropping from rope to rope like wounded birds fluttering through a tree, until they fell heavily into the ocean, the sullen ship sweeping by them in cold indifference. At the next instant the spars and masts of their enemy exhibited a display of men similar to their own, when Griffith again placed the trumpet to his mouth, and shouted aloud:

"Give it to them; drive them from their yards, boys; scatter them with your grape—unreeve their rigging!"

The crew of the American wanted but little encouragement to enter on this experiment with hearty good will, and the close of his cheering words were uttered amid the deafening roar of his own cannon. The Pilot had, however, mistaken the skill and readiness of their foe; for, notwithstanding the disadvantageous circumstances under which the Englishman increased his sail, the duty was steadily and dexterously performed.

The two ships were now running rapidly on parallel lines, hurling at each other their instruments of destruction with furious industry, and with severe and certain loss to both, though with no manifest advantage in favor of either. Both Griffith and the Pilot witnessed with deep concern this unexpected defeat of their hopes; for they could not conceal from themselves that each moment lessened their velocity through the water, as the shot of their enemy stripped the canvas from the yards, or dashed aside the lighter spars in their terrible progress.

"We find our equal here!" said Griffith to the stranger. "The ninety is heaving up again like a mountain; and if we continue to shorten sail at this rate, she will soon be down upon us!"

"You say true, sir," returned the Pilot, musing; "the man shows judgment as well as spirit; but—"

He was interrupted by Merry, who rushed from the forward part of the vessel, his whole face betokening the eagerness of his spirit, and the importance of his intelligence.

"The breakers!" he cried, when nigh enough to be heard amid the din; "we are running dead on a ripple, and the sea is white not two hundred yards ahead."

The Pilot jumped on a gun, and bending to catch a glimpse through the smoke, he shouted, in those clear, piercing tones that could be even heard among the roaring of the cannon; "Port, port your helm! we are on the Devil's Grip! pass up the trumpet, sir; port your helm, fellow; give it them, boys—give it to the proud English dogs!" Griffith unhesitatingly relinquished the symbol of his rank, fastening his own firm look on the calm but quick eye of the Pilot, and gathering assurance from the high confidence he read in the countenance of the stranger. The seamen were too busy with their cannon and their rigging to regard the new danger; and the frigate entered one of the dangerous passes of the shoals, in the heat of a severely contested battle. The wondering looks of a few of the older sailors glanced at the sheets of foam that flew by them, in doubt whether the wild gambols of the waves were occasioned by the shot of the enemy, when suddenly the noise of cannon was succeeded by the sullen wash of the disturbed element, and presently the vessel glided out of her smoky shroud, and was boldly steering in the centre of the narrow passages. For ten breathless minutes longer the Pilot continued to hold an uninterrupted sway, during which the vessel ran swiftly by ripples and breakers, by streaks of foam and darker passages of deep water, when he threw down his trumpet, and exclaimed:

"What threatened to be our destruction has proved our salvation! Keep yonder hill crowned with wood one point open from the church tower at its base, and steer east by north; you will run through these shoals on that course in an hour, and by so doing you will gain five leagues of your enemy, who will have to double their tail."

The moment he stepped from the gun, the Pilot lost the air of authority that had so singularly distinguished his animated form, and even the close interest he had manifested in the incidents of the day became lost in the cold, settled reserve he had affected during his intercourse with his present associates. Every officer in the ship, after the breathless suspense of uncertainly had passed, rushed to those places where a view might be taken of their enemies. The ninety was still steering boldly onward, and had already approached the two-and-thirty, which lay a helpless wreck, rolling on the unruly seas that were rudely tossing her on their wanton billows. The frigate last engaged was running along the edge of the ripple, with her torn sails flying loosely in the air, her ragged spars tottering in the breeze, and everything above her hull exhibiting the confusion of a sudden and unlooked-for check to her progress. The exulting taunts and mirthful congratulations of the seamen, as they gazed at the English ships, were, however, soon forgotten in the attention that was required to their own vessel. The drums beat the retreat, the guns were lashed, the wounded again removed, and every individual able to keep the deck was required to lend his assistance in repairing the damages of the frigate and securing her masts.

The promised hour carried the ship safely through all the dangers, which were much lessened by daylight; and by the time the sun had begun to fall over the land, Griffith, who had not quitted the deck during the day, beheld his vessel once more cleared of the confusion of the chase and battle, and ready to meet another foe. At this period he was summoned to the cabin, at the request of the ship's chaplain Delivering the charge of the frigate to Barnstable, who had been his active assistant, no less in their subsequent labors than in the combat, he hastily divested himself of the vestiges of the fight, and proceeded to obey the repeated and earnest call.

▶扩展阅读

1. Benter, B. Sea Brothers: *The Tradition of American Sea Fiction from Moby Dick to the Present*. Philadelphia: University of Pennsylvania Press, 1988.

2. Clark, R. Ed. *James Fenimore Cooper: New Critical Essays*. London: Vision and Barngs & Boble, 1985.

3. Person, L. Ed. *A Historical Guide to James Fenimore Cooper*. New York: Oxford University, Press, 2007.

4. Philbrick, T. *James Fenimore Cooper and the Development of American Sea Fiction*. Cambridge, MA: Cambridge University Press, 1961.

5. Verhoeven, W. M. Ed. *James Fenimore Cooper: New Historical and Literary Contexts*. Amsterdam: Rodopi B. V., 1993.

▶学习参考网站

1. http://external.oneonta.edu/cooper/

2. http://www.jamesfenimorecooper.com/

3. http://www.csustan.edu/english/reuben/pal/chap3/cooper.html

【陈 岑 编注】

18. Ralph Waldo Emerson: "Seashore"

拉尔夫·瓦尔多·爱默生（Ralph Waldo Emerson，1803—1882），美国哲学家、文学家、诗人，美国超验主义运动的主要代表，强调人的价值，提倡个人绝对自由和社会改革。爱默生出身于马萨诸塞州波士顿的一个牧师家庭。在他 8 岁左右父亲去世，爱默生在母亲、姑姑等女性长辈的帮助和影响下成长。9 岁时，他就读于波士顿拉丁学校。该校成立于 1635 年，是美国第一所公立学校，许多社会名流都把儿女送到该校学习。14 岁他就读于哈佛学院（Harvard College），在校期间，他阅读了大量英国浪漫主义作家的作品，丰富了思想，开阔了视野。毕业后他曾执教两年，之后进入哈佛神学院，担任基督教唯一神教派牧师并开始布道。

1832 年以后，爱默生游历欧洲各国，结识了浪漫主义先驱华兹华斯和柯尔律治，尤其是与卡莱尔结下了深厚的友谊。他们的思想对爱默生日后超验主义思想体系的形成产生了很大影响。爱默生回到波士顿后，经常和他的朋友梭罗、霍桑、玛格丽特等人举行小型聚会，探讨神学、哲学和社会学问题。这种聚会当时被称为"超验主义俱乐部"，爱默生也自然而然地成为超验主义的领袖。1840 年爱默生任超验主义刊物《日晷》（*The Dial*）的主编，进一步宣扬超验主义思想。后来他把自己的演讲汇编成书，这就是著名的《论文集》（*Essays*）。《论文集》第一辑于 1841 年出版，包括《论自助》《论超灵》《论补偿》《论爱》《论友谊》等 12 篇论文。爱默生的《论文集》宣扬了人要信赖自我的主张。除《论文集》之外，爱默生的作品还有《论自然》（*Nature*）、《代表人物》（*Representative Men*）、《英国人的特性》（*English Traits*）、《诗集》（*Poems*）等。爱默生轻视纯理论的探索，信奉自然的神性，认为自然是超灵的外衣，存在于人和上帝之间，是通向真理的途径。在文章中，爱默生反复提及他的超灵哲学（over-soul），强调个人与自然关系的重要性。他的诗歌、散文独具特色，注重思想内容而没有过分华丽的辞藻，行文犹如格言，哲理深入浅出，说服力强，形成了典型的"爱默生风格"。有人评价他的文字说："爱默生似乎只写警句。"

爱默生一生几乎见证了美国整个 19 世纪的变化和发展。他出生时的美国缺乏统一的政体，更没有相对一致的意识形态。在他去世的时候，美国不但因为南北战争而统一，经济发展加速，它的文化也正在走出欧洲影响的笼罩，民族性格逐渐鲜明起来。他本人的思想对美国国民的积极影响功不可没。

爱默生笔下的世界具有多重意义，每件事物似乎都有隐藏的含义，他说："特殊的自然现

象象征着特殊的精神现象。"在诗作《海岸》("Seashore")中,作为大自然化身的海洋被赋予
了深刻的象征意义。海洋容纳百川,物藏丰富,蕴藏着无穷的能量与智慧。全诗将海洋拟人
化,以第一人称"我"的形式来倾听海洋的声音并展开丰富的遐想。诗歌第一节中的"我"好
像听到海洋以斥责的口吻批评朝圣者姗姗来迟,海洋列数了它带给人类的诸多贡献和启迪。
诗节中重复出现的设问句型起到了强调作用,加强的语气凸显出海洋毋庸置疑的力量。诗
歌第二节一开始就赞美大海如六月玫瑰般美丽,如七月彩虹般清新。诗人展开联想,将海洋
比喻成六月的玫瑰、陆地的清洁工、人类的灵药等以展示海洋的神奇和富有。诗歌的第三
节,诗人向读者展现了海洋的另一面:它拥有毁灭与重塑的能量,能将安第斯山脉击碎,也能
重新改造人类社会。诗的最后一节描写了海洋诡谲的一面。至此,诗人从不同侧面描写了
自己眼中的海洋。《海岸》虽然只是一首短诗,但爱默生的超验主义思想却能从中窥见一斑。

Seashore

I heard or seemed to hear the chiding Sea
Say, Pilgrim, why so late and slow to come?
Am I not always here, thy summer home?
Is not my voice thy music, morn and eve?
My breath thy healthful climate in the heats,
My touch thy antidote, my bay thy bath?
Was ever building like my terraces①?
Was ever couch magnificent as mine?
Lie on the warm rock-ledges, and there learn
A little hut suffices like a town.
I make your sculptured architecture vain,
Vain beside mine. I drive my wedges home,
And carve the coastwise mountain into caves.
Lo! here is Rome and Nineveh② and Thebes③,
Karnak④ and Pyramid and Giant's Stairs
Half piled or prostrate⑤; and my newest slab

① terrace:梯田;平台。
② Nineveh:尼尼微(古代东方奴隶制国家亚述的首都,遗址在今伊拉克北部的摩苏尔[Mosul]附近)。
③ Thebes:古底比斯(或译忒拜)城,位于尼罗河谷上、下埃及之间,绝佳的地理位置,使它成为中古时期历代王国的首都,历史悠久更胜于开罗。
④ Karnak:卡纳克神庙,位于尼罗河中游的卢克索。
⑤ prostrate:俯卧的;拜倒的。

Older than all thy race.

Behold the Sea,

The opaline①，the plentiful and strong，

Yet beautiful as is the rose in June，

Fresh as the trickling rainbow of July；

Sea full of food，the nourisher of kinds，

Purger of earth，and medicine of men；

Creating a sweet climate by my breath，

Washing out harms and griefs from memory，

And，in my mathematic ebb and flow，

Giving a hint of that which changes not.

Rich are the sea-gods：—who gives gifts but they？

They grope the sea for pearls，but more than pearls：

They pluck Force thence，and give it to the wise.

For every wave is wealth to Daedalus②，

Wealth to the cunning artist who can work

This matchless strength. Where shall he find，O waves！

A load your Atlas shoulders cannot lift？

I with my hammer pounding evermore

The rocky coast，smite Andes③ into dust，

Strewing my bed，and，in another age，

Rebuild a continent of better men.

Then I unbar the doors：my paths lead out

The exodus④ of nations：I disperse

Men to all shores that front the hoary main.

I too have arts and sorceries；

Illusion dwells forever with the wave.

I know what spells are laid. Leave me to deal

With credulous and imaginative man；

For，though he scoop my water in his palm，

A few rods off he deems it gems and clouds.

---

① opaline：蛋白石的；乳白色的

② Daedalus：代达罗斯，希腊神话中著名的建筑师和雕刻家，曾为克里特国王建造迷宫。

③ Andes：安第斯山脉(南美洲西部)，科迪勒山系的主干，是全世界最长的山脉。

④ exodus：大批地离去。

Planting strange fruits and sunshine on the shore,

I make some coast alluring, some lone isle,

To distant men, who must go there, or die.

▶扩展阅读

1. Allen, G. W. *Waldo Emerson*. New York: Viking Press, 1981.

2. Buell, L. *Emerson*. Cambridge, MA: The Belknap Press of Harvard University Press, 2003.

3. Gura, P. F. *American Transcendentalism: A History*. New York: Hill and Wang, 2007.

4. Myerson, J. *A Historical Guide to Ralph Waldo Emerson*. New York: Oxford University Press, 2000.

5. Packer, B. L. *The Transcendentalists*. Athens, GA: University of Georgia Press, 2007.

▶学习参考网站

1. http://www.transcendentalists.com/lemerson.html

2. http://plato.stanford.edu/entries/emerson/

【吴琳华　编注】

19. Edgar Allan Poe: "The City in the Sea"

埃德加・爱伦・坡（Edgar Allan Poe，1809—1849），美国诗人、小说家、文艺评论家，现代侦探小说的创始人，生于波士顿，父母为流浪艺人。坡两岁时母亲病故，后被一名弗吉尼亚州里士满的富商约翰・爱伦收养。17 岁时，坡的养父将其送入弗吉尼亚大学，但他因欠下一笔赌债而辍学。坡返回里士满后，跟养父反目成仇，始终没有和解。之后，坡在巴尔的摩、里士满、纽约与费城以卖文为生，过着极为拮据的生活。作为自由撰稿人，他先后为几家杂志社供稿，也曾受雇于若干期刊，其中包括《南方文学使者》（*Southern Literary Messenger*）。1836 年，坡与 13 岁的表妹弗吉尼亚・克莱姆结婚，十年后妻子死于肺病。坡因此受到严重打击，无可救药的酗酒使其身心受到严重损害，最终于 1849 年 10 月去世。

坡的作品主要由三部分组成：诗歌、小说和评论文章。其中诗歌与小说的成就突出，评论虽不乏独到见解，但除《写作的哲学》（*The Philosophy of Composition*，1846）和《诗歌原理》（*The Poetic Principle*，1850）外，多系偶感而发。坡一生写了大量短篇小说，风格怪异离奇，细致入微的心理和意识刻画使他的小说充满恐怖气氛。著名短篇小说有《厄舍府的倒塌》（"The Fall of the House of Usher"，1839）、《黑猫》（"The Black Cat"，1843）、《泄密的心》（"The Tell-Tale Heart"，1843）等。此外，坡还被誉为"侦探小说鼻祖"。1841 年 4 月，他成为《格雷厄姆杂志》（*Graham's Magazine*）的编辑，首次发表推理小说。1841 年发表的《莫格街谋杀案》（"Murders in the Rue Morgue"）被公认为最早的侦探小说。在创作过程中，爱伦・坡执着于他的"效果论"，他强调，"在短篇小说这种文艺形式当中，每一个事件，每一个细节描写，甚至每一个字句，都应该收到某种统一的效果，某种预想的效果，或某种印象主义的效果"。坡所说的效果，就是运用精雕细琢的语言，巧妙的细节描写，表现他心目中永恒的主题：美和美的幻灭、死亡的恐怖、忧郁的窒息，以及对怪异现象的疑惧。坡将这种"效果论"也运用到了他的诗歌当中，如《乌鸦》（"The Raven"，1845）。坡曾声称《乌鸦》是严格按照这一理论创作而成的。除此之外，其著名的诗歌还有《帖木儿》（"Tamerlane"，1827）、《致海伦》（"To Helen"，1831）、《安娜贝尔李》（"Annabel Lee"，1849）等。

《海中之城》（"The City in the Sea"，1831）呈现的是一座死神统治下的海城情景。该诗背景神秘怪诞，语调低沉，诗句中融入了诸多哥特式文学作品的元素。诗歌前两节对海中之城"神祠""宫殿""塔尖"和"雕塑"的描写为诗歌蒙上了一层梦境和幻觉的色彩。正如坡在第一节中写道："那里的圣坛、宫殿和城堡/（被时间侵蚀的城堡不会颤动）/与我们这里的全然不一样。"而诗歌的第三、四节则将诗歌的基调从"神秘怪诞"转向了"恐怖窒息"。"敞口的坟墓""身佩珠宝的死者""血红的海浪"以及"不属于人世的呻吟"等词语都很好地营造了诗歌恐怖的气氛。在这种令人紧张恐怖的气氛中,读者仿佛只敢低声吟诵以免吵醒了这座罪恶之城。在诗的最后,坡写道:海水正在逐渐变红。红色是火的颜色,也是血的颜色,恶魔的颜色。这更是将全诗神秘恐怖的气氛推向了制高点。诗中用到了诸多的修辞手法,如在第一节中诗人用了多个对比来突出海中之城的寂静和黑暗;死神至高无上的地位和海水的臣服,来自天堂的希望之光和"令人毛骨悚然的大海"的光芒,仿佛整个海城都顺从地在天空下沉睡和等待。诗歌中还大量采用拟人手法来增加艺术感染力,如"海水"顺从地匍匐在天空之下;"死神"傲然地俯视一切;"时间"孱弱地呼吸着,气若游丝。这一切将海城作为一个罪恶之城和死亡之城的面貌描写得淋漓尽致。另外,坡向来主张运用规则的韵律,他认为真正的诗歌是"用韵律创造美"。《海中之城》也不例外,诗中随处可见诸如尾韵、头韵、类韵、和音等多种押韵手法,这些手法的使用渲染并加强了诗歌的恐怖和忧郁色彩。

▶

The City in the Sea[①]

Lo[②]! Death has reared himself a throne

In a strange city lying alone

Far down within the dim West,

Where the good and the bad and the worst and the best

Have gone to their eternal rest.

There shrines and palaces and towers

(Time-eaten towers that tremble not!)

Resemble nothing that is ours.

Around, by lifting winds forgot,

Resignedly beneath the sky

The melancholy waters lie.

No rays from the holy heaven come down

On the long night-time of that town;

But light from out the lurid sea

---

① The City in the Sea:该诗初稿名为《毁灭之城》("The Doomed City"),写于 1831 年。1836 年,该诗修改后以《罪恶之城》("The City of Sin")发表在《南方文学信使》上。后来,几经修改,最终于 1845 年以《海中之城》("The City in the Sea")为名刊登于《美国评论》(American Review)。

② Lo:〈古〉看,瞧。

Streams up the turrets① silently—
Gleams up the pinnacles far and free—
Up domes—up spires—up kingly halls—
Up fanes—up Babylon-like② walls—
Up shadowy long-forgotten bowers
Of sculptured ivy and stone flowers—
Up many and many a marvelous shrine
Whose wreathéd friezes intertwine
The viol③, the violet, and the vine.
So blend the turrets and shadows there
That all seem pendulous in the air,
While from a proud tower in the town
Death looks gigantically down.

There open fanes and gaping graves
Yawn level with the luminous④ waves;
But not the riches there that lie
In each idol's diamond eye—
Not the gaily-jeweled dead
Tempt the waters from their bed;
For no ripples curl, alas!
Along that wilderness of glass—
No swellings tell that winds may be
Upon some far-off happier sea—
No heavings hint that winds have been
On seas less hideously serene.

But lo, a stir is in the air!
The wave—there is a movement there!
As if the towers had thrust aside,
In slightly sinking, the dull tide—
As if their tops had feebly given

---

① turret：角楼；炮塔。
② Babylon：古代巴比伦王国首都，巴比伦城；罪恶之都。
③ viol：中世纪的六弦提琴。
④ luminous：明亮的；发光的。

A void① within the filmy Heaven.
The waves have now a redder glow—
The hours are breathing faint and low—
And when, amid no earthly moans,
Down, down that town shall settle hence,
Hell, rising from a thousand thrones,
Shall do it reverence.

▶扩展阅读

1. Ackroyd, P. *Poe*: *A Life Cut Short*. London: Chatto & Windus, 2008.

2. Krutch, J. W. *Edgar Allan Poe*: *A Study in Genius*. New York: Alfred A. Knopf, 1926.

3. Poe, H. L. *Edgar Allan Poe*: *An Illustrated Companion to His Tell-Tale Stories*. New York: Metro Books, 2008.

4. Quinn, A. H. *Edgar Allan Poe*: *A Critical Biography*. New York: Appleton-Century-Crofts, 1941.

5. Silverman, K. *Edgar A. Poe*: *Mournful and Never-Ending Remembrance*. New York: Harper Perennial, 1991.

▶学习参考网站

1. http://www.poemuseum.org/index.php
2. http://en.wikipedia.org/wiki/Edgar_Allan_Poe
3. http://www.online-literature.com/poe/

【吴琳华　编注】

---

① void：空隙；空间。

20. Richard Henry Dana Jr.: *Two Years Before the Mast*

理查德·亨利·达纳(Richard Henry Dana Jr.，1815—1882)，1815 年 8 月 1 日出生于美国马萨诸塞州坎布里奇。他的父亲理查德·亨利·达纳(Richard Henry Dana Sr.)是一位评论家和诗人，因此他也被称为小理查德·亨利·达纳。1831 年，达纳就读于哈佛大学，然而在大学第三年开学前夕，他不幸患了麻疹，引发眼膜炎，视力严重下降，以致无法学习。为了更好地康复身体，达纳于 1834 年 8 月 14 日在波士顿登上了开往加利福尼亚(当时隶属墨西哥)的"朝圣者"号双桅帆船。这次航海历时两年，海上经历不仅让他的身体得以康复，而且让出身望族的他了解了水手的艰辛生活，增加了他对下层人民的同情。更重要的是，这次航行成就了他的代表作《两年水手生涯》(*Two Years Before the Mast*，1840)。1836 年，达纳回到波士顿，次年 12 月他重返哈佛大学法学院深造，成为同学中的佼佼者，并于 1838 年 6 月毕业。此后，他专攻海洋法，之后成为一名律师。1840 年，他在波士顿开设了自己的工作室。同年，达纳出版了《两年水手生涯》，此书在英美两国一经发行，就好评如潮。书中对航海细节的描述可以与笛福的荒岛描写相媲美。达纳的儿子后来在该书再版的序言中，引用了父亲的老船友杰克·斯图尔特的话，称赞这本书语言朴实，描写精确，细节翔实："我已经读了一遍又一遍。这一切都浮现在我的眼前，就好像是刚刚发生的一样。"英国作家劳伦斯(D. H. Lawrence)认为达纳的这部作品具有"伟大而绝望的风格"。美国约翰·霍普金斯大学英文系教授桑德奎斯特(Eric J. Sundquist)也评价说："在塑造盎格鲁—美洲人对加利福尼亚及其墨西哥裔人的想象作品中，达纳的《两年水手生涯》最为重要。"

达纳亲历的水手生活对他的文学创作产生了巨大影响，他的主要著作有《两年水手生涯》、《海员之友》(*The Seaman's Friend*，1841)、《往返古巴》(*To Cuba and Back*，1841)、《激动时代的演讲》(*Speeches in Stirring Times*，1910，去世后出版)、《个人小传》(*An Autobiographical Sketch*，1815—1841，回忆录，去世后出版)。在两年的商船航海岁月中，达纳目睹了海员遭受鞭打的屈辱和船上恶劣的生活环境。他发誓要揭露商船上水手的不公正待遇，呼吁社会改善普通海员的生活条件。《两年水手生涯》出版后，他接着又发表了非虚构类作品《海员之友》。此书堪称一本水手的法律指南，很长一段时间都被看成一部水手法律权利和责任的参考书。《两年水手生涯》和《海员之友》这两本书的出版令达纳名声大噪。

达纳的海上经历令他对苦难者和被压迫者产生了极大的同情，他青年时代表现出的勇敢、无私和公正的性格,始终贯穿于他漫长而卓越的律师生涯。在积累了多年处理涉及海员权利案件的法律实践经验后,他加入自由土地党,开始积极参与到废奴运动之中。美国内战期间,达纳担任美联邦检察官。在《逃亡奴隶法》执行期间,他曾作为法律顾问为逃亡奴隶辩护,因此遭到攻击。1856 年,达纳开始了英国之旅,他在当时英国的律师界和文学界享有盛誉。三年后,由于过度劳累,他的身体每况愈下,于是他开始环游世界。1878 年,他与家人一起搬至罗马,却不幸感染流感,于 1882 年 1 月 6 日去世,死后葬于罗马新教公墓。

《两年水手生涯》讲述了达纳自己的航海经历,书中不仅对船上制度、水手生活进行了详尽的描写,更对沿岸的风土人情进行了生动的介绍。除此之外,达纳还着重描述了水手们遭受的不公待遇,试图以此推动建立海事改革制度。达纳详尽地描写了水手的日常工作,包括升帆降帆、检修保养、装配索具、擦拭甲板及值班守夜。他的文笔自然朴素,向读者展示了水手生活的真实画面。比如,瑞典人山姆和约翰所遭受的鞭打、坡因特康塞普申地区的干燥大风、圣巴巴拉的婚宴舞曲、圣佩德罗的葬礼、"阿勒特"号的好望角环行等,这些栩栩如生的描写已成为世界文学中令人难忘的场景。以下选段取自《两年水手生涯》的第三十四章,作者描述了水手们危险而忙碌的船上工作,海上的天气变化及水手的应对策略。商船从南纬跨越到北纬,随着纬度变化,不同风景呈现在读者面前。

▶**Chapter 34**

Narrow Escapes—The Equator—Tropical Squalls—A Thunder Storm

The same day, I met with one of those narrow escapes①, which are so often happening in a sailor's life. I had been aloft② nearly all the afternoon, at work, standing for as much as an hour on the fore top-gallant③ yard, which was hoisted up, and hung only by the tie; when, having got through my work, I balled up my yarns, took my serving-board in my hand, laid hold deliberately of the top-gallant rigging, took one foot from the yard, and was just lifting the other, when the tie parted, and down the yard fell. I was safe, by my hold upon the rigging, but it made my heart beat quick. Had the tie parted one instant sooner, or had I stood an instant longer on the yard, I should inevitably have been thrown violently from the height of ninety or a hundred feet, overboard; or, what is worse, upon the deck. However, "a miss is as good as a mile"④; a saying which sailors very often have occasion to use. An escape is always a joke on board ship. A man would be ridiculed who should make a serious matter of it. A sailor knows too well that his life hangs upon a thread, to wish to be always reminded of it; so, if a man has an escape, he keeps it to himself, or makes a joke of

---

① narrow escapes:死里逃生。
② aloft:在空中。
③ top-gallant:上桅的。top-gallant yard:上桅桁。top-gallant forecastle:船首楼。
④ a miss is as good as a mile:失之毫厘,谬之千里。

it. I have often known a man's life to be saved by an instant of time, or by the merest chance,—the swinging of a rope,—and no notice taken of it. One of our boys, when off Cape Horn[①], reefing topsails of a dark night, and when there were no boats to be lowered away, and where, if a man fell overboard he must be left behind,—lost his hold of the reef-point, slipped from the foot-rope, and would have been in the water in a moment, when the man who was next to him on the yard caught him by the collar of his jacket, and hauled him up upon the yard, with— "Hold on, another time, you young monkey, and be d—d to you!"— and that was all that was heard about it.

Sunday, August 7th. Lat. 25° 59′ S., long. 27° 0′ W. Spoke the English bark Mary-Catherine, from Bahia, bound to Calcutta. This was the first sail we had fallen in with, and the first time we had seen a human form or heard the human voice, except of our own number, for nearly a hundred days. The very yo-ho-ing[②] of the sailors at the ropes sounded sociably upon the ear. She was an old, damaged-looking craft, with a high poop and top-gallant forecastle, and sawed off square, stem and stern, like a true English "tea-wagon," and with a run like a sugar-box. She had studding-sails out alow and aloft, with a light but steady breeze, and her captain said he could not get more than four knots out of her and thought he should have a long passage. We were going six on an easy bowline.

The next day, about three P. M., passed a large corvette-built ship, close upon the wind, with royals and skysails set fore and aft, under English colors. She was standing south-by-east, probably bound round Cape Horn. She had men in her tops, and black mast-heads; heavily sparred[③], with sails cut to a T[④], and other marks of a man-of-war. She sailed well, and presented a fine appearance; the proud, aristocratic-looking banner of St. George, the cross in a blood-red field, waving from the mizzen[⑤]. We probably were as fine a sight, with our studding-sails spread far out beyond the ship on either side, and rising in a pyramid to royal studding-sails and sky-sails, burying the hull in canvas, and looking like what the whale-men on the Banks, under their stump top-gallant masts, call "a Cape Horn-er under a cloud of sail."

Friday, August 12th. At daylight made the island of Trinidad, situated in lat. 20° 28′S., long. 29° 08′W. At twelve M., it bore N. W. 1/2 N., distant twenty-seven miles. It was a beautiful day, the sea hardly ruffled by the light trades, and the island looking like a small blue mound rising from a field of glass.

---

① Cape Horn:合恩角。位于南美洲最南端,以 1616 年绕过此角的荷兰航海家斯豪滕(Willem Corneliszoon Schouten)的出生地霍恩命名。

② yo-ho:唷吼。英语中的特殊感叹词,表达开心、惊喜、惊讶等情绪。

③ heavily sparred:圆杆上挂满了帆索。

④ with sails cut to a T:船帆切成一个 T 形。

⑤ mizzen:后桅的纵帆。

Such a fair and peaceful-looking spot is said to have been, for a long time, the resort of a band of pirates, who ravaged the tropical seas.

Thursday, August 18th. At three P. M., made the island of Fernando Naronha, lying in lat. 3° 55′ S., long. 32° 35′ W.; and between twelve o'clock Friday night and one o'clock Saturday morning, crossed the equator, for the fourth time since leaving Boston, in long. 35° W.; having been twenty-seven days from Staten Land—a distance, by the courses we had made, of more than four thousand miles.

We were now to the northward of the line, and every day added to our latitude. The Magellan Clouds①, the last sign of South latitude, were sunk in the horizon, and the north star, the Great Bear, and the familiar signs of northern latitudes, were rising in the heavens.

Next to seeing land, there is no sight which makes one realize more that he is drawing near home, than to see the same heavens, under which he was born, shining at night over his head. The weather was extremely hot, with the usual tropical alternations of a scorching sun and squalls of rain; yet not a word was said in complaint of the heat, for we all remembered that only three or four weeks before we would have given nearly our all to have been where we now were. We had plenty of water, too, which we caught by spreading an awning②, with shot thrown in to make hollows. These rain squalls came up in the manner usual between the tropics.—A clear sky; burning, vertical sun; work going lazily on, and men about decks with nothing but duck trowsers, checked shirts, and straw hats; the ship moving as lazily through the water; the man at the helm resting against the wheel, with his hat drawn over his eyes; the captain below, taking an afternoon nap; the passenger leaning over the taffrail③, watching a dolphin following slowly in our wake; the sailmaker mending an old topsail on the lee side of the quarter-deck; the carpenter working at his bench, in the waist; the boys making sinnet; the spun-yarn④ winch whizzing round and round, and the men walking slowly fore and aft with their yarns.—A cloud rises to windward, looking a little black; the sky-sails are brailed down; the captain puts his head out of the companion-way, looks at the cloud, comes up, and begins to walk the deck.—The cloud spreads and comes on;—the tub of yarns, the sail, and other matters, are thrown below, and the sky-light and booby-hatch put on, and the slide drawn over the forecastle.— "Stand by the royal halyards;"—the man at the wheel keeps a good weather helm, so as not to be taken aback. The squall strikes her. If it is light, the royal yards are clewed down, and the ship keeps on

---

① Magellan Clouds:即 Magellanic Clouds,麦哲伦云,南半球肉眼可见的两个云雾状天体,分为大小麦哲伦云。

② awning:遮阳篷。

③ taffrail:船尾栏杆。

④ spun-yarn:麻丝绞绳的。

her way; but if the squall takes strong hold, the royals are clewed up, fore and aft; light hands lay aloft and furl them; top-gallant yards clewed down, flying-jib[①] hauled down, and the ship kept off before it,—the man at the helm laying out his strength to heave the wheel up to windward. At the same time a drenching rain, which soaks one through in an instant. Yet no one puts on a jacket or cap; for if it is only warm, a sailor does not mind a ducking; and the sun will soon be out again. As soon as the force of the squall has passed, though to a common eye the ship would seem to be in the midst of it,— "Keep her up to her course, again!"— "Keep her up, sir," (answer);— "Hoist away the top-gallant yards!"— "Run up the flying jib!"— "Lay aloft, you boys, and loose the royals! "—and all sail is on her again before she is fairly out of the squall; and she is going on in her course. The sun comes out once more, hotter than ever, dries up the decks and the sailors' clothes; the hatches are taken off; the sail got up and spread on the quarter-deck; spun-yarn winch set a whirling again; rigging coiled up; captain goes below; and every sign of an interruption is removed.

These scenes, with occasional dead calms, lasting for hours, and sometimes for days, are fair specimens of the Atlantic tropics. The nights were fine; and as we had all hands all day, the watch were allowed to sleep on deck at night, except the man at the wheel, and one look-out on the forecastle. This was not so much expressly allowed, as winked at. We could do it if we did not ask leave. If the look-out was caught napping, the whole watch was kept awake.

We made the most of this permission, and stowed ourselves away upon the rigging, under the weather rail, on the spars, under the windlass[②], and in all the snug corners; and frequently slept out the watch, unless we had a wheel or a look-out. And we were glad enough to get this rest; for under the "all hands" system, out of every other thirty-six hours, we had only four below; and even an hour's sleep was a gain not to be neglected. One would have thought so, to have seen our watch, some nights, sleeping through a heavy rain. And often have we come on deck, and finding a dead calm and a light, steady rain, and determined not to lose our sleep, have laid a coil of rigging down so as to keep us out of the water which was washing about decks, and stowed ourselves away upon it, covering a jacket over us, and slept as soundly as a Dutchman between two feather beds.

For a week or ten days after crossing the line, we had the usual variety of calms, squalls, head winds, and fair winds;—at one time braced sharp upon the wind, with a taut bowline, and in an hour after, slipping quietly along, with a light breeze over the taffrail, and studding-sails out on both sides;—until we fell in with the north-east trade-winds;

---

① flying-jib：船首三角帆。
② windlass：起锚机，用于收、放锚和锚链，通常安装在船舶首艉部主甲板上，供舰船起抛锚系缆时用。

which we did on the afternoon of

Sunday，August 28th，in lat. 12° N. The trade-wind clouds had been in sight for a day or two previously，and we expected to take them every hour. The light southerly breeze，which had been blowing languidly during the first part of the day，died away toward noon，and in its place came puffs from the north-east，which caused us to take our studding-sails in and brace up；and in a couple of hours more，we were bowling gloriously along，dashing the spray far ahead and to leeward，with the cool，steady north-east trades，freshening up the sea，and giving us as much as we could carry our royals to. These winds blew strong and steady，keeping us generally upon a bowline，as our course was about north-north-west；and sometimes，as they veered a little to the eastward，giving us a chance at a main top-gallant studding-sail；and sending us well to the northward，until—

Sunday，Sept. 4th，when they left us，in lat. 22° N.，long. 51° W.，directly under the tropic of Cancer.

For several days we lay "humbugging about①" in the Horse latitudes②，with all sorts of winds and weather，and occasionally，as we were in the latitude of the West Indies—a thunder storm. It was hurricane month，too，and we were just in the track of the tremendous hurricane of 1830，which swept the North Atlantic，destroying almost everything before it. The first night after the tradewinds③ left us，while we were in the latitude of the island of Cuba，we had a specimen of a true tropical thunder storm. A light breeze had been blowing directly from aft during the first part of the night which gradually died away，and before midnight it was dead calm，and a heavy black cloud had shrouded the whole sky. When our watch came on deck at twelve o'clock，it was as black as Erebus④；the studding-sails were all taken in，and the royals furled；not a breath was stirring；the sails hung heavy and motionless from the yards；and the perfect stillness，and the darkness，which was almost palpable，were truly appalling. Not a word was spoken，but every one stood as though waiting for something to happen. In a few minutes the mate came forward；and in a low tone，which was almost a whisper，told us to haul down the jib. The fore and mizen top-gallant sails were taken in，in the same silent manner；and we lay motionless upon the water，with an uneasy expectation，which，from the long suspense，became actually painful. We could hear the captain walking the deck，but it was too dark to see anything more than one's hand before the face. Soon the mate came forward again，and gave

---

① humbugging about：窃窃私语。

② Horse latitudes：南北纬 30°—35°无风，又称"马纬度"。一种说法表明：由于无风，水手们基本不需要工作，于是他们就会拿着稻草填充的马在甲板上游行，游行结束后，水手们会把草马扔下船。后来，人们就把这个无风的 30°纬度叫作"马纬度"。

③ tradewinds：信风，又称贸易风，指的是在低空从副热带高压带吹向赤道低气压带的风。

④ Erebus：厄瑞玻斯，是希腊神话中的神，代表着冥土的黑暗。

an order, in a low tone, to clew up the main top-gallant sail; and so infectious was the awe and silence, that the clewlines and buntlines were hauled up without any of the customary singing out at the ropes. An English lad and myself went up to furl it; and we had just got the bunt up, when the mate called out to us, something, we did not hear what,—but supposing it to be an order to bear-a-hand, we hurried, and made all fast, and came down, feeling our way among the rigging. When we got down we found all hands looking aloft, and there, directly over where we had been standing, upon the main top-gallant-mast-head, was a ball of light, which the sailors name a corposant (corpus sancti), and which the mate had called out to us to look at. They were all watching it carefully, for sailors have a notion that if the corposant rises in the rigging, it is a sign of fair weather, but if it comes lower down, there will be a storm. Unfortunately, as an omen, it came down, and showed itself on the top-gallant yard-arm. We were off the yard in good season, for it is held a fatal sign to have the pale light of the corposant thrown upon one's face. As it was, the English lad did not feel comfortably at having had it so near him, and directly over his head. In a few minutes it disappeared, and showed itself again on the fore top-gallant yard; and after playing about for some time, disappeared again; when the man on the forecastle pointed to it upon the flying-jib-boom-end[①]. But our attention was drawn from watching this, by the falling of some drops of rain and by a perceptible increase of the darkness, which seemed suddenly to add a new shade of blackness to the night. In a few minutes, low, grumbling thunder was heard, and some random flashes of lightning came from the south-west. Every sail was taken in but the topsails, still, no squall appeared to be coming. A few puffs lifted the topsails, but they fell again to the mast, and all was as still as ever. A moment more, and a terrific flash and peal broke simultaneously upon us, and a cloud appeared to open directly over our heads and let down the water in one body, like a falling ocean. We stood motionless, and almost stupefied; yet nothing had been struck. Peal after peal rattled over our heads, with a sound which seemed actually to stop the breath in the body, and the "speedy gleams" kept the whole ocean in a glare of light. The violent fall of rain lasted but a few minutes, and was succeeded by occasional drops and showers; but the lightning continued incessant for several hours, breaking the midnight darkness with irregular and blinding flashes. During all which time there was not a breath stirring, and we lay motionless, like a mark to be shot at, probably the only object on the surface of the ocean for miles and miles. We stood hour after hour, until our watch was out, and we were relieved, at four o'clock. During all this time, hardly a word was spoken; no bells were struck, and the wheel was silently relieved. The rain fell at intervals in heavy showers, and we stood drenched through and blinded by the flashes,

---

① flying-jib-boom-end：艏斜杆末端。

which broke the Egyptian darkness with a brightness which seemed almost malignant；while the thunder rolled in peals，the concussion of which appeared to shake the very ocean. A ship is not often injured by lightning，for the electricity is separated by the great number of points she presents，and the quantity of iron which she has scattered in various parts. The electric fluid ran over our anchors，top-sail sheets and ties；yet no harm was done to us. We went below at four o'clock，leaving things in the same state. It is not easy to sleep，when the very next flash may tear the ship in two，or set her on fire；or where the deathlike calm may be broken by the blast of a hurricane，taking the masts out of the ship. But a man is no sailor if he cannot sleep when he turns-in，and turn out when he's called. And when，at seven bells，the customary "All the larboard① watch, ahoy？" brought us on deck，it was a fine，clear，sunny morning，the ship going leisurely along，with a good breeze and all sail set.

▶扩展阅读

1. Adams，C. F. *Richard Henry Dana*：*A Biography*. Wentworth Press，2019.

2. Dana，R. H. & Allston，W. *Lectures on Art*，*and Poems*. Franklin Classics Trade Press，2018.

3. Gidmark，J. B. Ed. *Encyclopedia of American Literature of the Sea and Great Lakes*. Westport，CT：Greenwood Pub Group，2000.

4. Bender，B. *Sea-Brothers*：*The Tradition of American Sea Fiction from Moby-Dick to the Present*. Philadelpha，PA：University of Pennsylvania Press，1988.

▶学习参考网站

1. https://pennyspoetry.fandom.com/wiki/Richard_Henry_Dana

2. https://www.nps.gov/people/richard-henry-dana-jr.htm

3. https://www.bartleby.com/23/

【王松林　朱慧琳　编注】

---

① larboard：左舷。从船尾向船头看，左边是左舷。

21. Walt Whitman:
"O Captain! My Captain!" and Others

沃尔特·惠特曼(Walt Whitman，1819—1892)，19 世纪美国诗人，出身于纽约长岛的一个农民家庭，父亲是英国血统，母亲是荷兰血统。在惠特曼近 4 岁时，全家搬到布鲁克林，虽然父亲以做木匠维持家庭生活，但家庭财力十分有限，所以他只在布鲁克林公立学校接受了六年的初等教育。11 岁时惠特曼开始独立谋生，他给布鲁克林一些著名律师做办公室助手，在此期间，他一边工作，一边自学，获得了文学、音乐、历史、地理、考古等方面广博的知识。1831 年，惠特曼在一家出版工人阶级报纸《爱国者》(Patriot)的报社做学徒，他不仅继续学习各类知识，还学到了排字、印刷等技能。之后，由于不愿在农场工作，他选择了乡村小学教师这一职业，并一直持续到 1841 年。1842—1843 年，惠特曼不断地在各家报社间更换工作。1845 年，也许是由于经济收入不稳定，他离开纽约，回到了布鲁克林。1846 年初，他担任《布洛克林鹰报》(Brooklyn Eagle)的编辑。他因在该报发表反对奴隶制度的文章，于 1848 年 1 月被解雇。后来他还担任过另一家报纸的主编，终因政见不合而离开新闻界。惠特曼早期所写的内容很多都是模仿一些带伤感情调的诗歌、随笔和短篇故事，学界普遍认为这些作品成就不高。离开报界后，从 1850 年开始，他一面从事体力劳动，一面专心于文学创作，并不断发表自由体诗歌，这些诗歌成了他的经典之作《草叶集》(Leaves of Grass，1855)初版内容的一部分。

惠特曼从小就与海洋结下了亲密的情缘。在谈到大海与其诗歌创作的关系时，他曾写道："当我看到一只船在海上扬帆行驶的时候，我想把它那模样描写出来……我感到必须写一部书来表现这样的流动，这个神秘的主题。后来我渐渐意识到……那是海滩，它将成为我作品中的一种无形的力量，一个对于我是渗透一切的象征和记号。"《草叶集》中有许多描写海洋、航海和水手的诗句，都写得生动传神而充满感情，其中流露出的诗人的胸怀也如大海般"辽阔博大，包罗万象"。

以下四首诗中，《啊，船长！我的船长！》("O Captain! My Captain"，1865)选自《林肯总统纪念集》(Memories of President Lincoln，1865)。林肯总统遇刺之后，惠特曼写了三首悼诗，其中最为人们熟知的就是这首《啊，船长！我的船长！》。这首诗的结构和韵律考究，在以自由体为特征的《草叶集》中比较少见。该诗把内战中的美国比作海上航行的船只，而林肯总统则是指引这艘船劈波斩浪、驶向海岸的船长。然而在船顺利靠岸时，这位船长却倒下了。岸上的人们在欢呼庆祝，胜利的旗帜在为他飘扬，然而他却倒在那里，人们急切而深沉的呼唤也不能让他再站立起来。作者通过岸上的热闹场面和甲板上的冰冷场面的强烈对比,表达了对"船长"之死的无比沉痛之情。在《草叶集》中,《海流集》(*Sea-Drift*,1855)是惠特曼描写海洋和以海洋为背景的一组诗,《在船上的舵轮旁》("Aboard at a Ship's Helm",1867)和《为所有的海洋和所有的船只歌唱》("Song for All Seas, All Ships",1873)是其中的两首。《在船上的舵轮旁》是一首抒情短诗,作者以素描的方式为读者展开了一个场景,接着又情不自禁地进入这个场景,注视着舵手,和他一起听着警告的钟声,看着他避开危险,继续前进。《为所有的海洋和所有的船只歌唱》把海洋、世界和人类融入一体进行歌唱。他歌唱海洋偏爱那些"从不为命运和死亡所震慑"的少数人,这是一首献给各民族勇敢的船长和水手们的赞歌。

《海上带有客舱的船上》("In Cabin'd Ships at Sea",1871)选自《铭言集》(*Inscriptions*,1871),诗歌生动地体现了诗人与大海和船只的因缘。诗中的大海代表了民众,诗人要把他的诗歌喻为海上航行的一叶扁舟,他要把自己的歌声"带给所有的水手和他们的船",通篇诗歌洋溢着乐观自信的情绪。

▶

O Captain! My Captain!

O Captain[①]! My Captain! our fearful trip is done,

The ship has weathered every rack, the prize we sought is won,

The port is near, the bells I hear, the people all exulting,

While follow eyes the steady keel, the vessel grim and daring;

But O heart! heart! heart!

O the bleeding drops of red,

Where on the deck my Captain lies,

Fallen cold and dead.

O Captain! my Captain! rise up and hear the bells;

Rise up—for you the flag is flung—for you the bugle trills,

For you bouquets and ribboned wreaths—for you the shores a-crowding,

For you they call, the swaying mass, their eager faces turning;

Here Captain! dear father!

This arm beneath your head!

It is some dream that on the deck,

You've fallen cold and dead.

---

① Captain:船长,这首诗中这一单词均被大写,特指林肯总统。

My Captain does not answer, his lips are pale and still;

My father does not feel my arm, he has no pulse nor will;

The ship is anchored safe and sound, its voyage closed and done;

From fearful trip the victor ship comes in with object won;

Exult O shores, and ring O bells!

But I, with mournful tread,

Walk the deck my Captain lies,

Fallen cold and dead.

▶

Aboard at a Ship's Helm

Aboard at a ship's helm,

A young steersman steering with care.

Through fog on a sea-coast dolefully ringing,

An ocean-bell—O a warning bell, rock'd by the waves.

O you[①] give good notice indeed, you bell by the sea-reefs ringing,

Ringing, ringing, to warn the ship from its wreck-place.

For as on the alert O steersman, you mind the loud admonition,

The bows turn, the freighted ship tacking speeds away under her gray sails,

The beautiful and noble ship with all her precious wealth speeds

away gayly and safe.

But O the ship, the immortal ship! O ship aboard the ship!

Ship of the body, ship of the soul, voyaging, voyaging, voyaging.

---

① you：即警告的钟声，此处作者转变了叙述的对象。

▶

Song for All Seas, All Ships

Today a rude brief recitative,
Of ships sailing the seas, each with its special flag or ship-signal,
Of unnamed heroes in the ships—of waves spreading and spreading
far as the eye can reach,
Of dashing spray, and the winds piping and blowing,
And out of these a chant for the sailors of all nations,
Fitful, like a surge.

Of sea-captains young or old, and the mates, and of all intrepid sailors,
Of the few, very choice, taciturn, whom fate can never surprise nor
death dismay①.
Pick'd sparingly without noise by thee old ocean, chosen by thee,
Thou sea that pickest and cullest the race in time, and unitest nations,
Suckled by thee, old husky nurse②, embodying thee,
Indomitable, untamed as thee.

(Ever the heroes on water or on land, by ones or twos appearing,
Ever the stock preserv'd and never lost, though rare, enough for
seed preserv'd.)

Flaunt out O sea your separate flags of nations!
Flaunt out visible as ever the various ship-signals!
But do you reserve especially for yourself and for the soul of man
one flag above all the rest,
A spiritual woven signal for all nations, emblem of man elate above death,
Token of all brave captains and all intrepid sailors and mates,
And all that went down doing their duty,
Reminiscent of them, twined from all intrepid captains young or old,
A pennant③ universal, subtly waving all time, o'er all brave sailors,
All seas, all ships.

---

① whom fate can never surprise nor death dismay：他们从不畏惧命运和死亡。

② old husky nurse：即大海，在惠特曼的诗里，大海常被比喻为老母亲，这里则比喻为乳母。

③ pennant：三角旗，即前面提到的"one flag above all the rest"（一面高于其他一切的旗帜）。

▶

In Cabin'd Ships at Sea

In cabin'd ships at sea,

The boundless blue on every side expanding,

With whistling winds and music of the waves, the large imperious waves,

Or some lone bark buoy'd on the dense marine,

Where joyous full of faith, spreading white sails,

She① cleaves the ether mid the sparkle and the foam of day, or under
many a star at night,

By sailors young and old haply will I, a reminiscence of the land, be read,

In full rapport at last.

Here are our thoughts, voyagers' thoughts,

Here not the land, firm land, alone appears, may then by them be said,

The sky o'er arches here, we feel the undulating deck beneath our feet,

We feel the long pulsation, ebb and flow of endless motion,

The tones of unseen mystery, the vague and vast suggestions of the
briny world, the liquid-flowing syllables,

The perfume, the faint creaking of the cordage, the melancholy rhythm,

The boundless vista and the horizon far and dim are all here,

And this is ocean's poem.

Then falter not O book, fulfil your destiny,

You not a reminiscence of the land alone,

You too as a lone bark cleaving the ether, purpos'd I know not
whither, yet ever full of faith,

Consort to every ship that sails, sail② you!

Bear forth to them folded my love, (dear mariners, for you I fold it
here in every leaf;)

Speed on my book! spread your white sails my little bark athwart the
imperious waves,

Chant on, sail on, bear o'er the boundless blue from me to every sea,

This song for mariners and all their ships.

---

① She:这里作者用"她"指航行在海面上的船。

② sail:航行,它的主语是本节第一句中的"book",在这里,作者把自己的诗集比作船只,在海上航行。

▶扩展阅读

1. Allen，E. A. & Allen，G. W. *Walt Whitman as a Man，Poet，and Legend with a Checklist of Whitman Publications* 1945—1960. Literary Licensing，LLC，2011.

2. Allen，G. W. *The Solitary Singer：A Critical Biography of Walt Whitman*. Chicago：University of Chicago Press，1985.

3. Allen，G. W. *A reader's Guide to Walt Whitman*. New York：Syracuse University Press，1970.

4. Akers，P. *The Principle of Life：A New Concept of Reality Based on Walt Whitman's "Leaves of Grass."* New York：Vantage Press，1992.

5. Beach，C. *The Politics of Distinction：Whitman and the Discourses of Nineteenth-Century America*. Athens，GA：The University of Georgia Press，1996.

6. Pearce，R. H. Ed. *Whitman：A Collection of Critical Essays*. New Jersey：Prentice-Hall，1962.

▶学习参考网站

1. http：//whitmanarchive.org/biography/walt_whitman/index.html♯origins

2. http：//www.blackcatpoems.com/w/walt_whitman.html

3. http：//www.poets.org/poet.php/prmPID/126

【王亚妮　编注】

22. Herman Melville: *Moby Dick*

赫尔曼·麦尔维尔(Herman Melville,1819—1891),出身于纽约一个有名望的家庭。他的祖父和外祖父都是美国独立战争时期的英雄,也是麦尔维尔作品中某些人物的素材。他的父亲曾经是一位成功的商人,从事进口贸易,但后来破产了。麦尔维尔 11 岁时丧父,他不得不中途辍学,边工作,边自学。他在银行当过职员,跟哥哥做过皮毛生意,在叔叔的农场工作过,还在乡村学校教过书。1839 年他在"圣劳伦斯"号商船上当水手,第一次远洋到英国利物浦。这次经历给他的系列航海小说提供了素材。回国后,麦尔维尔去了当时的西部,即现在的中西部地区寻找工作。当时,航运是重要的交通工具,他在密西西比河上的旅行经历也反映在他后来创作的小说中。1840 年他再次出海,成为捕鲸船上的一员。后来他加入了美国海军,离家多年后才返回家乡。他讲述的航海故事很受亲朋好友的欢迎,这激发起他创作的念头。27 岁时,他的小说《泰比》(*Typee*,1846)经过一番周折,先在英国出版,随即又在美国出版。这部小说的成功鼓舞了麦尔维尔继续创作。次年他结婚成家,还出版了第二部小说《欧穆》(*Omoo*,1847)。这两部小说及后来出版的《玛迪》(*Mardy*,1849)被看作他的"波尼利西亚系列"。但后一部小说的社会反响不及前两部。这三部小说都反映了他的航海知识和经历。1849 发表的《雷德本》(*Redburn*)既是一部海洋小说,也是一部成长小说。1851 年《白鲸》出版。撰写这部小说时,麦尔维尔不仅发挥了自己的航海经历,还去图书馆查阅了很多关于捕鲸业知识的书籍。遗憾的是,这部知识面广、思想深刻的小说在他有生之年并没有引起应有的关注,一个世纪后其魅力才逐步被世界各国的读者发现和挖掘,成为他最著名的小说。在麦尔维尔生前,不仅他的《白鲸》被忽视,后来的两部小说《皮埃尔》(*Pierre*,1852)和《骗子》(*The Confidence Man*,1857)也没能达到他预期的社会效果。这使他面临生存困境,失望的麦尔维尔不得不放弃写作,在纽约海关工作了 20 年。虽然他还发表了一些诗歌,但都没有给他带来足够的声誉和经济利益。他的后半生在默默无闻中度过。小说《比利·巴德》(*Billy Budd*,1886)在他去世之后被整理出版。麦尔维尔的作品还有《白外套》(*White-Jacket*,1850)、《伊莎雷尔·波特》(*Israel Potter*,1855)等小说。

《白鲸》的叙述者是一位名叫以实玛利的年轻人。他迷恋大海,在小说一开头就讲述了他要出海的种种理由。在海滨小镇南塔克特,由于囊中羞涩,他被迫和一位名叫魁魁格的土著人共住一间客房,共睡一张大床。他很快发现魁魁格虽然模样吓人,行动有些怪异,但却是一位心地善良、纯朴、忠厚的"野人",而且还是出色的标枪手。他们两人很快成为好朋友,

并决定一起签约,登上一艘名叫"皮阔德"的捕鲸船。在起航前,他们听到了关于这艘船船长的种种传闻。起航后好几天,大家都不见船长出舱,因此都对他充满好奇。

随着亚哈船长的出现,他的航海目标逐渐暴露:由于亚哈曾经被一条名叫莫比·迪克的白色巨头鲸咬掉一条腿,他一心想要报仇,杀死白鲸,讨回尊严。这头白鲸身体庞大、力大无比,而且神出鬼没,很多捕鲸者都知道它,并对它心存敬畏,能够征服这头白鲸被看作至高无上的荣誉。亚哈船长虽然装了一条假腿,但气势逼人,善于调动大家的激情和鼓舞大家的士气。在他的激励和胁迫之下,全船人跟他一起与白鲸展开了三天的殊死较量。他们从大船上放下几艘捕鲸小艇,桨手们负责划艇,标枪手们狠狠地刺杀白鲸。但这头白鲸难以对付,它顽强地抵抗人类的攻击,受伤之后,它潜伏到大船底下,不等小艇上的人赶来,便疯狂地咬破了"皮阔德"号,致使大船沉没,断了捕鲸者回家的路。气急败坏的亚哈船长率领众人与白鲸决一死战,结果同归于尽。桨手以实玛利早早被抛出小船,被路过的船只救起,从而幸免于难,成为唯一的幸存者。

《白鲸》中有大量关于鲸类的知识和航海术语,人物性格多样,其深邃的思想、丰富的象征、精彩的故事、生动的叙事和多重主题等吸引了无数的读者与评论者。自 20 世纪以来,对《白鲸》的研究持续不断,其中小说主题、人与自然、人与命运、人性瑕疵、社会等级及种族问题等都是研究热点。以下选段分别选自小说第一章、第二十八章、第一百三十五章和尾声。第一章介绍了该小说中的两位主要人物——叙述者以实玛利和亚哈船长;第二十八章讲述的是以实玛利对亚哈的印象;第一百三十五章叙述了全船人与白鲸进行殊死较量的惊心动魄的场面。

▶Chapter 1

Loomings

Call me Ishmael[①]. Some years ago—never mind how long precisely—having little or no money in my purse, and nothing particular to interest me on shore, I thought I would sail about a little and see the watery part of the world. It is a way I have of driving off the spleen and regulating the circulation. Whenever I find myself growing grim about the mouth; whenever it is a damp, drizzly November in my soul; whenever I find myself involuntarily pausing before coffin warehouses, and bringing up the rear of every funeral I meet; and especially whenever my hypos[②] get such an upper hand of me, that it requires a strong moral principle to prevent me from deliberately stepping into the street, and methodically knocking people's hats off—then, I account it high time to get to sea as soon as I can. This is

---

① Ishmael:以实玛利,基督教圣经中的人物。亚伯拉罕(Abraham)的妻子撒拉(Sarah)没有孩子,但她渴望有个儿子。于是,她把自己的使女夏甲(Hagar)给了亚伯拉罕为妾。夏甲和亚伯拉罕生下以实玛利。之后,撒拉生下了自己的儿子以撒(Isaac),遂把夏甲和以实玛利母子赶出家门。以实玛利有 12 个儿子成了部落酋长。

② hypos:疑病(症)。

my substitute for pistol and ball. With a philosophical flourish Cato[①] throws himself upon his sword; I quietly take to the ship. There is nothing surprising in this. If they but knew it, almost all men in their degree, some time or other, cherish very nearly the same feelings towards the ocean with me.

There now is your insular city of the Manhattoes, belted round by wharves as Indian isles by coral reefs—commerce surrounds it with her surf. Right and left, the streets take you waterward. Its extreme downtown is the battery, where that noble mole is washed by waves, and cooled by breezes, which a few hours previous were out of sight of land. Look at the crowds of water-gazers there.

Circumambulate the city of a dreamy Sabbath[②] afternoon. Go from Corlears Hook to Coenties Slip, and from thence, by Whitehall, northward. What do you see? —Posted like silent sentinels all around the town, stand thousands upon thousands of mortal men fixed in ocean reveries. Some leaning against the spiles; some seated upon the pier-heads; some looking over the bulwarks glasses! of ships from China; some high aloft in the rigging, as if striving to get a still better seaward peep. But these are all landsmen; of week days pent up in lath and plaster—tied to counters, nailed to benches, clinched to desks. How then is this? Are the green fields gone? What do they do here?

But look! here come more crowds, pacing straight for the water, and seemingly bound for a dive. Strange! Nothing will content them but the extremest limit of the land; loitering under the shady lee of yonder warehouses will not suffice. No. They must get just as nigh the water as they possibly can without falling in. And there they stand—miles of them—leagues. Inlanders all, they come from lanes and alleys, streets and avenues, —north, east, south, and west. Yet here they all unite. Tell me, does the magnetic virtue of the needles of the compasses of all those ships attract them thither?

Once more. Say you are in the country; in some high land of lakes. Take almost any path you please, and ten to one it carries you down in a dale, and leaves you there by a pool in the stream. There is magic in it. Let the most absent-minded of men be plunged in his deepest reveries—stand that man on his legs, set his feet a-going, and he will infallibly lead you to water, if water there be in all that region. Should you ever be athirst in the great American desert, try this experiment, if your caravan happen to be supplied with a metaphysical professor. Yes, as every one knows, meditation and water are wedded for

---

① Cato:加图,全名为 Marcus Porcius Cato Uticensis(95BC—46BC),是罗马共和国末期的政治家以及斯多葛哲学的追随者。他因清廉和坚韧的品质、尤其是与恺撒长期的冲突而为人所知。在公元前 46 年的塔普苏斯(Thapsus)战役失败后自尽身亡。

② Sabbath:安息日,主日。大部分基督徒把安息日定在星期日,犹太教徒和部分基督徒定在星期六,穆斯林定在星期五。

ever.

But here is an artist. He desires to paint you the dreamiest, shadiest, quietest, most enchanting bit of romantic landscape in all the valley of the Saco. What is the chief element he employs? There stand his trees, each with a hollow trunk, as if a hermit and a crucifix were within; and here sleeps his meadow, and there sleep his cattle; and up from yonder cottage goes a sleepy smoke. Deep into distant woodlands winds a mazy way, reaching to overlapping spurs of mountains bathed in their hill-side blue. But though the picture lies thus tranced, and though this pine-tree shakes down its sighs like leaves upon this shepherd's head, yet all were vain, unless the shepherd's eye were fixed upon the magic stream before him. Go visit the Prairies in June, when for scores on scores of miles you wade knee-deep among Tiger-lilies—what is the one charm wanting? —Water there is not a drop of water there! Were Niagara but a cataract of sand, would you travel your thousand miles to see it? Why did the poor poet of Tennessee, upon suddenly receiving two handfuls of silver, deliberate whether to buy him a coat, which he sadly needed, or invest his money in a pedestrian trip to Rockaway Beach? Why is almost every robust healthy boy with a robust healthy soul in him, at some time or other crazy to go to sea? Why upon your first voyage as a passenger, did you yourself feel such a mystical vibration, when first told that you and your ship were now out of sight of land? Why did the old Persians hold the sea holy? Why did the Greeks give it a separate deity[①], and own brother of Jove? Surely all this is not without meaning. And still deeper the meaning of that story of Narcissus, who because he could not grasp the tormenting, mild image he saw in the fountain, plunged into it and was drowned. But that same image, we ourselves see in all rivers and oceans. It is the image of the ungraspable phantom of life; and this is the key to it all.

Now, when I say that I am in the habit of going to sea whenever I begin to grow hazy about the eyes, and begin to be over conscious of my lungs, I do not mean to have it inferred that I ever go to sea as a passenger. For to go as a passenger you must needs have a purse, and a purse is but a rag unless you have something in it. Besides, passengers get sea-sick— grow quarrelsome—don't sleep of nights—do not enjoy themselves much, as a general thing;—no, I never go as a passenger; nor, though I am something of a salt, do I ever go to sea as a Commodore, or a Captain, or a Cook. I abandon the glory and distinction of such offices to those who like them. For my part, I abominate all honorable respectable toils, trials, and tribulations of every kind whatsoever. It is quite as much as I can do to take care of myself, without taking care of ships, barques, brigs, schooners, and what not. And as for going as cook, —though I confess there is considerable glory in that, a cook being a sort of

---

① deity：这里指罗马神话朱庇特(Jove)[统治诸神主宰一切的主神]的兄弟——海神尼普顿(Neptune)。

officer on ship-board—yet, somehow, I never fancied broiling fowls;—though once broiled, judiciously buttered, and judgmatically salted and peppered, there is no one who will speak more respectfully, not to say reverentially, of a broiled fowl than I will. It is out of the idolatrous dotings of the old Egyptians upon broiled ibis and roasted river horse, that you see the mummies of those creatures in their huge bakehouses the pyramids.

No, when I go to sea, I go as a simple sailor, right before the mast, plumb down into the fore-castle, aloft there to the royal mast-head. True, they rather order me about some, and make me jump from spar to spar, like a grasshopper in a May meadow. And at first, this sort of thing is unpleasant enough. It touches one's sense of honor, particularly if you come of an old established family in the land, the Van Rensselaers, or Randolphs, or Hardicanutes. And more than all, if just previous to putting your hand into the tar-pot, you have been lording it as a country schoolmaster, making the tallest boys stand in awe of you. The transition is a keen one, I assure you, from a schoolmaster to a sailor, and requires a strong decoction of Seneca and the Stoics to enable you to grin and bear it. But even this wears off in time.

What of it, if some old hunks of a sea-captain orders me to get a broom and sweep down the decks? What does that indignity amount to, weighed, I mean, in the scales of the New Testament? Do you think the archangel Gabriel[①] thinks anything the less of me, because I promptly and respectfully obey that old hunks in that particular instance? Who ain't a slave? Tell me that. Well, then, however the old sea-captains may order me about—however they may thump and punch me about, I have the satisfaction of knowing that it is all right; that everybody else is one way or other served in much the same way—either in a physical or metaphysical point of view, that is; and so the universal thump is passed round, and all hands should rub each other's shoulder-blades, and be content.

Again, I always go to sea as a sailor, because they make a point of paying me for my trouble, whereas they never pay passengers a single penny that I ever heard of. On the contrary, passengers themselves must pay. And there is all the difference in the world between paying and being paid. The act of paying is perhaps the most uncomfortable infliction that the two orchard thieves entailed upon us. But being paid, —what will compare with it? The urbane activity with which a man receives money is really marvellous, considering that we so earnestly believe money to be the root of all earthly ills, and that on no account can a monied man enter heaven. Ah! how cheerfully we consign ourselves to perdition!

Finally, I always go to sea as a sailor, because of the wholesome exercise and pure air of the fore-castle deck. For as in this world, head winds are far more prevalent than winds

---

① the archangel Gabriel:指天使长加百利,他是上帝的使者。

from astern (that is, if you never violate the Pythagorean maxim), so for the most part the Commodore on the quarter-deck gets his atmosphere at second hand from the sailors on the forecastle. He thinks he breathes it first; but not so. In much the same way do the commonalty lead their leaders in many other things, at the same time that the leaders little suspect it. But wherefore it was that after having repeatedly smelt the sea as a merchant sailor, I should now take it into my head to go on a whaling voyage; this the invisible police officer of the Fates, who has the constant surveillance of me, and secretly dogs me, and influences me in some unaccountable way—he can better answer than any one else. And, doubtless, my going on this whaling voyage, formed part of the grand programme of Providence that was drawn up a long time ago. It came in as a sort of brief interlude and solo between more extensive performances. I take it that this part of the bill must have run something like this:

"Grand Contested Election for the Presidency of the United States."

　　"WHALING VOYAGE BY ONE ISHMAEL."

　　"BLOODY BATTLE IN AFGHANISTAN."

Though I cannot tell why it was exactly that those stage managers, the Fates, put me down for this shabby part of a whaling voyage, when others were set down for magnificent parts in high tragedies, and short and easy parts in genteel comedies, and jolly parts in farces—though I cannot tell why this was exactly; yet, now that I recall all the circumstances, I think I can see a little into the springs and motives which being cunningly presented to me under various disguises, induced me to set about performing the part I did, besides cajoling me into the delusion that it was a choice resulting from my own unbiased freewill and discriminating judgment.

Chief among these motives was the overwhelming idea of the great whale himself. Such a portentous and mysterious monster roused all my curiosity. Then the wild and distant seas where he rolled his island bulk; the undeliverable, nameless perils of the whale; these, with all the attending marvels of a thousand Patagonian sights and sounds, helped to sway me to my wish. With other men, perhaps, such things would not have been inducements; but as for me, I am tormented with an everlasting itch for things remote. I love to sail forbidden seas, and land on barbarous coasts. Not ignoring what is good, I am quick to perceive a horror, and could still be social with it—would they let me—since it is but well to be on friendly terms with all the inmates of the place one lodges in.

By reason of these things, then, the whaling voyage was welcome; the great flood-gates of the wonder-world swung open, and in the wild conceits that swayed me to my purpose, two and two there floated into my inmost soul, endless processions of the whale, and, mid most of them all, one grand hooded phantom, like a snow hill in the air.

▶Chapter 28

Ahab

For several days after leaving Nantucket, nothing above hatches was seen of Captain Ahab. The mates regularly relieved each other at the watches, and for aught that could be seen to the contrary, they seemed to be the only commanders of the ship; only they sometimes issued from the cabin with orders so sudden and peremptory, that after all it was plain they but commanded vicariously. Yes, their supreme lord and dictator was there, though hitherto unseen by any eyes not permitted to penetrate into the now sacred retreat of the cabin.

Every time I ascended to the deck from my watches below, I instantly gazed aft to mark if any strange face were visible; for my first vague disquietude touching the unknown captain, now in the seclusion of the sea, became almost a perturbation. This was strangely heightened at times by the ragged Elijah's[①] diabolical incoherences uninvitedly recurring to me, with a subtle energy I could not have before conceived of. But poorly could I withstand them, much as in other moods I was almost ready to smile at the solemn whimsicalities of that outlandish prophet of the wharves. But whatever it was of apprehensiveness or uneasiness—to call it so—which I felt, yet whenever I came to look about me in the ship, it seemed against all warrantry to cherish such emotions. For though the harpooneers, with the great body of the crew, were a far more barbaric, heathenish, and motley set than any of the tame merchant-ship companies which my previous experiences had made me acquainted with, still I ascribed this—and rightly ascribed it—to the fierce uniqueness of the very nature of that wild Scandinavian vocation in which I had so abandonedly embarked. But it was especially the aspect of the three chief officers of the ship, the mates, which was most forcibly calculated to allay these colourless misgivings, and induce confidence and cheerfulness in every presentment of the voyage. Three better, more likely sea-officers and men, each in his own different way, could not readily be found, and they were every one of them Americans; a Nantucketer, a Vineyarder, a Cape man. Now, it being Christmas when the ship shot from out her harbor, for a space we had biting Polar weather, though all the time running away from it to the southward; and by every degree and minute of latitude which we sailed, gradually leaving that merciless winter, and all its intolerable weather behind us. It was one of those less lowering, but still grey and gloomy enough mornings of the transition, when with a fair wind the ship was rushing through the water with a vindictive sort of leaping and melancholy rapidity, that as I mounted to the deck at the call of

---

① Elijah：以实玛利在航行前见过的人，他曾预言"皮阔德"号的厄运。

the forenoon watch, so soon as I levelled my glance towards the taffrail, foreboding shivers ran over me. Reality outran apprehension; Captain Ahab stood upon his quarter-deck.[①]

There seemed no sign of common bodily illness about him, nor of the recovery from any. He looked like a man cut away from the stake, when the fire has overrunningly wasted all the limbs without consuming them, or taking away one particle from their compacted aged robustness. His whole high, broad form, seemed made of solid bronze, and shaped in an unalterable mould, like Cellini's cast Perseus.[②] Threading its way out from among his grey hairs, and continuing right down one side of his tawny scorched face and neck, till it disappeared in his clothing, you saw a slender rod-like mark, vividly whitish. It resembled that perpendicular seam sometimes made in the straight, lofty trunk of a great tree, when the upper lightning tearingly darts down it, and without wrenching a single twig, peels and grooves out the bark from top to bottom, ere running off into the soil, leaving the tree still greenly alive, but branded. Whether that mark was born with him, or whether it was the scar left by some desperate wound, no one could certainly say. By some tacit consent, throughout the voyage little or no allusion was made to it, especially by the mates. But once Tashtego's senior, an old Gay-Head Indian among the crew, superstitiously asserted that not till he was full forty years old did Ahab become that way branded, and then it came upon him, not in the fury of any mortal fray, but in an elemental strife at sea. Yet, this wild hint seemed inferentially negatived, by what a grey Manxman insinuated, an old sepulchral man, who, having never before sailed out of Nantucket, had never ere this laid eye upon wild Ahab. Nevertheless, the old sea-traditions, the immemorial credulities, popularly invested this old Manxman with preternatural powers of discernment. So that no white sailor seriously contradicted him when he said that if ever Captain Ahab should be tranquilly laid out—which might hardly come to pass, so he muttered—then, whoever should do that last office for the dead, would find a birth-mark on him from crown to sole.

So powerfully did the whole grim aspect of Ahab affect me, and the livid brand which streaked it, that for the first few moments I hardly noted that not a little of this overbearing grimness was owing to the barbaric white leg upon which he partly stood. It had previously come to me that this ivory leg had at sea been fashioned from the polished bone of the sperm whale's jaw. "Aye, he was dismasted off Japan," said the old Gay-Head Indian once; "but like his dismasted craft, he shipped another mast without coming home for it. He has a quiver of 'em."

I was struck with the singular posture he maintained. Upon each side of the Pequod's

---

① quarter-deck:(高级船员或军官所在的)后甲板区。

② Cellini's cast Perseus:一座珀尔修斯(希腊神话中的英雄)的青铜像,出自意大利雕塑家本维努托·切利尼 (Benvenuto Cellini)之手。

quarter deck, and pretty close to the mizzen shrouds, there was an auger hole, bored about half an inch or so, into the plank. His bone leg steadied in that hole; one arm elevated, and holding by a shroud; Captain Ahab stood erect, looking straight out beyond the ship's ever-pitching prow. There was an infinity of firmest fortitude, a determinate, unsurrenderable wilfulness, in the fixed and fearless, forward dedication of that glance. Not a word he spoke; nor did his officers say aught to him; though by all their minutest gestures and expressions, they plainly showed the uneasy, if not painful, consciousness of being under a troubled master-eye. And not only that, but moody stricken Ahab stood before them with a crucifixion in his face; in all the nameless regal overbearing dignity of some mighty woe.

Ere long, from his first visit in the air, he withdrew into his cabin. But after that morning, he was every day visible to the crew; either standing in his pivot-hole, or seated upon an ivory stool he had; or heavily walking the deck. As the sky grew less gloomy; indeed, began to grow a little genial, he became still less and less a recluse; as if, when the ship had sailed from home, nothing but the dead wintry bleakness of the sea had then kept him so secluded. And, by and by, it came to pass, that he was almost continually in the air; but, as yet, for all that he said, or perceptibly did, on the at last sunny deck, he seemed as unnecessary there as another mast. But the Pequod was only making a passage now; not regularly cruising; nearly all whaling preparatives needing supervision the mates were fully competent to, so that there was little or nothing, out of himself, to employ or excite Ahab, now; and thus chase away, for that one interval, the clouds that layer upon layer were piled upon his brow, as ever all clouds choose the loftiest peaks to pile themselves upon.

Nevertheless, ere long, the warm, warbling persuasiveness of the pleasant, holiday weather we came to, seemed gradually to charm him from his mood. For, as when the red-cheeked, dancing girls, April and May, trip home to the wintry, misanthropic woods; even the barest, ruggedest, most thunder-cloven old oak will at least send forth some few green sprouts, to welcome such glad-hearted visitants; so Ahab did, in the end, a little respond to the playful allurings of that girlish air. More than once did he put forth the faint blossom of a look, which, in any other man, would have soon flowered out in a smile.

▶**Chapter 135**

The Chase—Third Day

The morning of the third day dawned fair and fresh, and once more the solitary night-man at the fore-mast-head was relieved by crowds of the daylight look-outs, who dotted every mast and almost every spar.

"D'ye see him?" cried Ahab; but the whale was not yet in sight.

"In his infallible wake, though; but follow that wake, that's all. Helm there; steady, as thou goest, and hast been going. What a lovely day again! were it a new-made world, and made for a summer-house to the angels, and this morning the first of its throwing open to them, a fairer day could not dawn upon that world. Here's food for thought, had Ahab time to think; but Ahab never thinks; he only feels, feels, feels; THAT'S tingling enough for mortal man! to think's audacity. God only has that right and privilege. Thinking is, or ought to be, a coolness and a calmness; and our poor hearts throb, and our poor brains beat too much for that. And yet, I've sometimes thought my brain was very calm—frozen calm, this old skull cracks so, like a glass in which the contents turned to ice, and shiver it. And still this hair is growing now; this moment growing, and heat must breed it; but no, it's like that sort of common grass that will grow anywhere, between the earthy clefts of Greenland ice or in Vesuvius lava. How the wild winds blow it; they whip it about me as the torn shreds of split sails lash the tossed ship they cling to. A vile wind that has no doubt blown ere this through prison corridors and cells, and wards of hospitals, and ventilated them, and now comes blowing hither as innocent as fleeces. Out upon it! —it's tainted. Were I the wind, I'd blow no more on such a wicked, miserable world. I'd crawl somewhere to a cave, and slink there. And yet, 'tis a noble and heroic thing, the wind! who ever conquered it? In every fight it has the last and bitterest blow. Run tilting at it, and you but run through it. Ha! a coward wind that strikes stark naked men, but will not stand to receive a single blow. Even Ahab is a braver thing—a nobler thing than THAT. Would now the wind but had a body; but all the things that most exasperate and outrage mortal man, all these things are bodiless, but only bodiless as objects, not as agents. There's a most special, a most cunning, oh, a most malicious difference! And yet, I say again, and swear it now, that there's something all glorious and gracious in the wind. These warm Trade Winds, at least, that in the clear heavens blow straight on, in strong and steadfast, vigorous mildness; and veer not from their mark, however the baser currents of the sea may turn and tack, and mightiest Mississippies of the land swift and swerve about, uncertain where to go at last. And by the eternal Poles! these same Trades that so directly blow my good ship on; these Trades, or something like them—something so unchangeable, and full as strong, blow my keeled soul along! To it! Aloft there! What d'ye see?"

"Nothing, sir."

"Nothing! and noon at hand! The doubloon goes a-begging! See the sun! Aye, aye, it must be so. I've oversailed him. How, got the start? Aye, he's chasing ME now; not I, HIM—that's bad; I might have known it, too. Fool! the lines—the harpoons he's towing. Aye, aye, I have run him by last night. About! about! Come down, all of ye, but the regular look outs! Man the braces!"

Steering as she had done, the wind had been somewhat on the Pequod's quarter, so that now being pointed in the reverse direction, the braced ship sailed hard upon the breeze as she rechurned the cream in her own white wake.

"Against the wind he now steers for the open jaw," murmured Starbuck to himself, as he coiled the new-hauled main-brace upon the rail. "God keep us, but already my bones feel damp within me, and from the inside wet my flesh. I misdoubt me that I disobey my God in obeying him!"

"Stand by to sway me up!" cried Ahab, advancing to the hempen basket. "We should meet him soon."

"Aye, aye, sir," and straightway Starbuck did Ahab's bidding, and once more Ahab swung on high.

A whole hour now passed; gold-beaten out to ages. Time itself now held long breaths with keen suspense. But at last, some three points off the weather bow, Ahab descried the spout again, and instantly from the three mast-heads three shrieks went up as if the tongues of fire had voiced it.

"Forehead to forehead I meet thee, this third time, Moby Dick! On deck there! —brace sharper up; crowd her into the wind's eye. He's too far off to lower yet, Mr. Starbuck. The sails shake! Stand over that helmsman with a top-maul! So, so; he travels fast, and I must down. But let me have one more good round look aloft here at the sea; there's time for that. An old, old sight, and yet somehow so young; aye, and not changed a wink since I first saw it, a boy, from the sand-hills of Nantucket! The same! —the same! —the same to Noah as to me. There's a soft shower to leeward. Such lovely leewardings! They must lead somewhere—to something else than common land, more palmy than the palms. Leeward! the white whale goes that way; look to windward, then; the better if the bitterer quarter. But good bye, good bye, old mast-head! What's this? —green? aye, tiny mosses in these warped cracks. No such green weather stains on Ahab's head! There's the difference now between man's old age and matter's. But aye, old mast, we both grow old together; sound in our hulls, though, are we not, my ship? Aye, minus a leg, that's all. By heaven this dead wood has the better of my live flesh every way. I can't compare with it; and I've known some ships made of dead trees outlast the lives of men made of the most vital stuff of vital fathers. What's that he said? he should still go before me, my pilot; and yet to be seen again? But where? Will I have eyes at the bottom of the sea, supposing I descend those endless stairs? and all night I've been sailing from him, wherever he did sink to. Aye, aye, like many more thou told'st direful truth as touching thyself, O Parsee; but, Ahab, there thy shot fell short. Good-bye, mast-head—keep a good eye upon the whale, the while I'm gone. We'll talk to-morrow, nay, to-night, when the white whale lies down there, tied by head and tail."

He gave the word; and still gazing round him, was steadily lowered through the cloven blue air to the deck.

In due time the boats were lowered; but as standing in his shallop's stern, Ahab just hovered upon the point of the descent, he waved to the mate, —who held one of the tackle-ropes on deck—and bade him pause.

"Starbuck!"

"Sir?"

"For the third time my soul's ship starts upon this voyage, Starbuck."

"Aye, sir, thou wilt have it so."

"Some ships sail from their ports, and ever afterwards are missing, Starbuck!"

"Truth, sir: saddest truth."

"Some men die at ebb tide; some at low water; some at the full of the flood;—and I feel now like a billow that's all one crested comb, Starbuck. I am old;—shake hands with me, man."

Their hands met; their eyes fastened; Starbuck's tears the glue.

"Oh, my captain, my captain! —noble heart—go not—go not! —see, it's a brave man that weeps; how great the agony of the persuasion then!"

"Lower away!" —cried Ahab, tossing the mate's arm from him. "Stand by the crew!"

In an instant the boat was pulling round close under the stern.

"The sharks! the sharks!" cried a voice from the low cabin-window there; "O master, my master, come back!"

But Ahab heard nothing; for his own voice was high-lifted then; and the boat leaped on.

Yet the voice spake true; for scarce had he pushed from the ship, when numbers of sharks, seemingly rising from out the dark waters beneath the hull, maliciously snapped at the blades of the oars, every time they dipped in the water; and in this way accompanied the boat with their bites. It is a thing not uncommonly happening to the whale-boats in those swarming seas; the sharks at times apparently following them in the same prescient way that vultures hover over the banners of marching regiments in the east. But these were the first sharks that had been observed by the Pequod since the White Whale had been first descried; and whether it was that Ahab's crew were all such tiger-yellow barbarians, and therefore their flesh more musky to the senses of the sharks—a matter sometimes well known to affect them,—however it was, they seemed to follow that one boat without molesting the others.

"Heart of wrought steel!" murmured Starbuck gazing over the side, and following with his eyes the receding boat—"canst thou yet ring boldly to that sight? —lowering thy keel among ravening sharks, and followed by them, open-mouthed to the chase; and this the critical third day? —For when three days flow together in one continuous intense pursuit; be sure the first is the morning, the second the noon, and the third the evening and the end of that thing—be that end what it may. Oh! my God! what is this that shoots through me, and leaves me so deadly calm, yet expectant, —fixed at the top of a shudder! Future things swim before me, as in empty outlines and skeletons; all the past is somehow grown dim. Mary, girl! thou fadest in pale glories behind me; boy! I seem to see but thy eyes grown wondrous blue. Strangest problems of life seem clearing; but clouds sweep between—Is my journey's end coming? My legs feel faint; like his who has footed it all day. Feel thy heart, —beats it yet? Stir thyself, Starbuck! —stave it off—move, move! speak aloud! —Masthead there! See ye my boy's hand on the hill? —Crazed; —aloft there! —keep thy keenest eye upon the boats: —"

"Mark well the whale! —Ho! again! —drive off that hawk! see! he pecks—he tears the vane" —pointing to the red flag flying at the main-truck—"Ha! he soars away with it! —Where's the old man now? see'st thou that sight, oh Ahab! —shudder, shudder!"

The boats had not gone very far, when by a signal from the mast-heads—a downward pointed arm, Ahab knew that the whale had sounded; but intending to be near him at the next rising, he held on his way a little sideways from the vessel; the becharmed crew maintaining the profoundest silence, as the head-beat waves hammered and hammered against the opposing bow.

"Drive, drive in your nails, oh ye waves! to their uttermost heads drive them in! ye but strike a thing without a lid; and no coffin and no hearse can be mine:—and hemp only can kill me! Ha! ha!"

Suddenly the waters around them slowly swelled in broad circles; then quickly upheaved, as if sideways sliding from a submerged berg of ice, swiftly rising to the surface. A low rumbling sound was heard; a subterraneous hum; and then all held their breaths; as bedraggled with trailing ropes, and harpoons, and lances, a vast form shot lengthwise, but obliquely from the sea. Shrouded in a thin drooping veil of mist, it hovered for a moment in the rainbowed air; and then fell swamping back into the deep. Crushed thirty feet upwards, the waters flashed for an instant like heaps of fountains, then brokenly sank in a shower of flakes, leaving the circling surface creamed like new milk round the marble trunk of the whale.

"Give way!" cried Ahab to the oarsmen, and the boats darted forward to the attack; but maddened by yesterday's fresh irons that corroded in him, Moby Dick seemed combinedly possessed by all the angels that fell from heaven. The wide tiers of welded tendons overspreading his broad white forehead, beneath the transparent skin, looked knitted together; as head on, he came churning his tail among the boats; and once more flailed them apart; spilling out the irons and lances from the two mates' boats, and dashing in one side of the upper part of their bows, but leaving Ahab's almost without a scar.

While Daggoo and Queequeg were stopping the strained planks; and as the whale swimming out from them, turned, and showed one entire flank as he shot by them again; at that moment a quick cry went up. Lashed round and round to the fish's back; pinioned in the turns upon turns in which, during the past night, the whale had reeled the involutions of the lines around him, the half torn body of the Parsee was seen; his sable raiment frayed to shreds; his distended eyes turned full upon old Ahab.

The harpoon dropped from his hand.

"Befooled, befooled!" —drawing in a long lean breath—"Aye, Parsee! I see thee again. —Aye, and thou goest before; and this, THIS then is the hearse that thou didst promise. But I hold thee to the last letter of thy word. Where is the second hearse? Away, mates, to the ship! those boats are useless now; repair them if ye can in time, and return to me; if not, Ahab is enough to die—Down, men! the first thing that but offers to jump from this boat I stand in, that thing I harpoon. Ye are not other men, but my arms and my legs; and so obey me. —Where's the whale? gone down again?"

But he looked too nigh the boat; for as if bent upon escaping with the corpse he bore, and as if the particular place of the last encounter had been but a stage in his leeward voyage, Moby Dick was now again steadily swimming forward; and had almost passed the ship,—which thus far had been sailing in the contrary direction to him, though for the present her headway had been stopped. He seemed swimming with his utmost velocity, and now only intent upon pursuing his own straight path in the sea.

"Oh! Ahab," cried Starbuck, "not too late is it, even now, the third day, to desist. See! Moby Dick seeks thee not. It is thou, thou, that madly seekest him!"

Setting sail to the rising wind, the lonely boat was swiftly impelled to leeward, by both oars and canvas. And at last when Ahab was sliding by the vessel, so near as plainly to distinguish Starbuck's face as he leaned over the rail, he hailed him to turn the vessel about, and follow him, not too swiftly, at a judicious interval. Glancing upwards, he saw Tashtego, Queequeg, and Daggoo, eagerly mounting to the three mast-heads; while the oarsmen were rocking in the two staved boats which had but just been hoisted to the side, and were busily at work in repairing them. One after the other, through the port-holes, as he sped, he also caught flying glimpses of Stubb and Flask, busying themselves on deck among bundles of new irons and lances. As he saw all this; as he heard the hammers in the broken boats; far other hammers seemed driving a nail into his heart. But he rallied. And now marking that the vane or flag was gone from the main-mast-head, he shouted to Tashtego, who had just gained that perch, to descend again for another flag, and a hammer and nails, and so nail it to the mast.

Whether fagged by the three days' running chase, and the resistance to his swimming in the knotted hamper he bore; or whether it was some latent deceitfulness and malice in him: whichever was true, the White Whale's way now began to abate, as it seemed, from the boat so rapidly nearing him once more; though indeed the whale's last start had not been so long a one as before. And still as Ahab glided over the waves the unpitying sharks accompanied him; and so pertinaciously stuck to the boat; and so continually bit at the playing oars, that the blades became jagged and crunched, and left small splinters in the sea, at almost every dip.

"Heed them not! those teeth but give new rowlocks to your oars. Pull on! 'tis the better rest, the shark's jaw than the yielding water."

"But at every bite, sir, the thin blades grow smaller and smaller!"

"They will last long enough! pull on! —But who can tell"—he muttered—"whether these sharks swim to feast on the whale or on Ahab? —But pull on! Aye, all alive, now—we near him. The helm! take the helm! let me pass," —and so saying two of the oarsmen helped him forward to the bows of the still flying boat.

At length as the craft was cast to one side, and ran ranging along with the White Whale's flank, he seemed strangely oblivious of its advance—as the whale sometimes will— and Ahab was fairly within the smoky mountain mist, which, thrown off from the whale's spout, curled round his great, Monadnock hump; he was even thus close to him; when, with body arched back, and both arms lengthwise high-lifted to the poise, he darted his fierce iron, and his far fiercer curse into the hated whale. As both steel and curse sank to the socket, as if sucked into a morass, Moby Dick sideways writhed; spasmodically rolled his nigh flank against the bow, and, without staving a hole in it, so suddenly canted the boat over, that had it not been for the elevated part of the gunwale to which he then clung, Ahab would once more have been tossed into the sea. As it was, three of the oarsmen—who foreknew not the precise instant of the dart, and were therefore unprepared for its effects— these were flung out; but so fell, that, in an instant two of them clutched the gunwale again, and rising to its level on a combing wave, hurled themselves bodily inboard again; the third man helplessly dropping astern, but still afloat and swimming.

Almost simultaneously, with a mighty volition of ungraduated, instantaneous swiftness, the White Whale darted through the weltering sea. But when Ahab cried out to the steersman to take new turns with the line, and hold it so; and commanded the crew to turn round on their seats, and tow the boat up to the mark; the moment the treacherous line felt that double strain and tug, it snapped in the empty air!

"What breaks in me? Some sinew cracks! —'tis whole again; oars! oars! Burst in upon him!"

Hearing the tremendous rush of the sea-crashing boat, the whale wheeled round to present his blank forehead at bay; but in that evolution, catching sight of the nearing black hull of the ship; seemingly seeing in it the source of all his persecutions; bethinking it—it may be—a larger and nobler foe; of a sudden, he bore down upon its advancing prow, smiting his jaws amid fiery showers of foam.

Ahab staggered; his hand smote his forehead. "I grow blind; hands! stretch out before me that I may yet grope my way. Is't night?"

"The whale! The ship!" cried the cringing oarsmen.

"Oars! oars! Slope downwards to thy depths, O sea, that ere it be for ever too late, Ahab may slide this last, last time upon his mark! I see: the ship! the ship! Dash on, my men! Will ye not save my ship?"

But as the oarsmen violently forced their boat through the sledge-hammering seas, the before whale-smitten bow-ends of two planks burst through, and in an instant almost, the temporarily disabled boat lay nearly level with the waves; its half-wading, splashing crew, trying hard to stop the gap and bale out the pouring water.

Meantime, for that one beholding instant, Tashtego's mast-head hammer remained suspended in his hand; and the red flag, half-wrapping him as with a plaid, then streamed itself straight out from him, as his own forward-flowing heart; while Starbuck and Stubb, standing upon the bowsprit beneath, caught sight of the down-coming monster just as soon as he.

"The whale, the whale! Up helm, up helm! Oh, all ye sweet powers of air, now hug me close! Let not Starbuck die, if die he must, in a woman's fainting fit. Up helm, I say— ye fools, the jaw! the jaw! Is this the end of all my bursting prayers? all my life-long fidelities? Oh, Ahab, Ahab, lo, thy work. Steady! helmsman, steady. Nay, nay! Up helm again! He turns to meet us! Oh, his unappeasable brow drives on towards one, whose duty tells him he cannot depart. My God, stand by me now!"

"Stand not by me, but stand under me, whoever you are that will now help Stubb; for Stubb, too, sticks here. I grin at thee, thou grinning whale! Who ever helped Stubb, or kept Stubb awake, but Stubb's own unwinking eye? And now poor Stubb goes to bed upon a mattrass that is all too soft; would it were stuffed with brushwood! I grin at thee, thou grinning whale! Look ye, sun, moon, and stars! I call ye assassins of as good a fellow as ever spouted up his ghost. For all that, I would yet ring glasses with ye, would ye but hand the cup! Oh, oh! oh, oh! thou grinning whale, but there'll be plenty of gulping soon! Why fly ye not, O Ahab! For me, off shoes and jacket to it; let Stubb die in his drawers! A most mouldy and over salted death, though;—cherries! cherries! cherries! Oh, Flask, for one red cherry ere we die!"

"Cherries? I only wish that we were where they grow. Oh, Stubb, I hope my poor mother's drawn my part-pay ere this; if not, few coppers will now come to her, for the voyage is up."

From the ship's bows, nearly all the seamen now hung inactive; hammers, bits of plank, lances, and harpoons, mechanically retained in their hands, just as they had darted from their various employments; all their enchanted eyes intent upon the whale, which from side to side strangely vibrating his predestinating head, sent a broad band of overspreading semicircular foam before him as he rushed. Retribution, swift vengeance, eternal malice were in his whole aspect, and spite of all that mortal man could do, the solid white buttress of his forehead smote the ship's starboard bow, till men and timbers reeled. Some fell flat upon their faces. Like dislodged trucks, the heads of the harpooneers aloft shook on their bull-like necks. Through the breach, they heard the waters pour, as mountain torrents down a flume.

"The ship! The hearse! —the second hearse!" cried Ahab from the boat; "its wood could only be American!"

Diving beneath the settling ship, the whale ran quivering along its keel; but turning under water, swiftly shot to the surface again, far off the other bow, but within a few yards of Ahab's boat, where, for a time, he lay quiescent.

"I turn my body from the sun. What ho, Tashtego! let me hear thy hammer. Oh! ye three unsurrendered spires of mine; thou uncracked keel; and only god-bullied hull; thou firm deck, and haughty helm, and Pole-pointed prow, —death-glorious ship! must ye then perish, and without me? Am I cut off from the last fond pride of meanest shipwrecked captains? Oh, lonely death on lonely life! Oh, now I feel my topmost greatness lies in my topmost grief. Ho, ho! from all your furthest bounds, pour ye now in, ye bold billows of my whole foregone life, and top this one piled comber of my death! Towards thee I roll, thou all-destroying but unconquering whale; to the last I grapple with thee; from hell's heart I stab at thee; for hate's sake I spit my last breath at thee. Sink all coffins and all hearses to one common pool! and since neither can be mine, let me then tow to pieces, while still chasing thee, though tied to thee, thou damned whale! THUS, I give up the spear!"

The harpoon was darted; the stricken whale flew forward; with igniting velocity the line ran through the grooves;—ran foul. Ahab stooped to clear it; he did clear it; but the flying turn caught him round the neck, and voicelessly as Turkish mutes bowstring their victim, he was shot out of the boat, ere the crew knew he was gone. Next instant, the heavy eye-splice in the rope's final end flew out of the stark-empty tub, knocked down an oarsman, and smiting the sea, disappeared in its depths.

For an instant, the tranced boat's crew stood still; then turned. "The ship? Great God, where is the ship?" Soon they through dim, bewildering mediums saw her sidelong fading phantom, as in the gaseous Fata Morgana; only the uppermost masts out of water; while fixed by infatuation, or fidelity, or fate, to their once lofty perches, the pagan harpooneers still maintained their sinking lookouts on the sea. And now, concentric circles seized the lone boat itself, and all its crew, and each floating oar, and every lance-pole, and spinning, animate and inanimate, all round and round in one vortex, carried the smallest chip of the Pequod out of sight.

But as the last whelmings intermixingly poured themselves over the sunken head of the Indian at the mainmast, leaving a few inches of the erect spar yet visible, together with long streaming yards of the flag, which calmly undulated, with ironical coincidings, over the destroying billows they almost touched;—at that instant, a red arm and a hammer hovered backwardly uplifted in the open air, in the act of nailing the flag faster and yet faster to the subsiding spar. A sky-hawk that tauntingly had followed the main-truck downwards from its natural home among the stars, pecking at the flag, and incommoding Tashtego there; this bird now chanced to intercept its broad fluttering wing between the hammer and the wood; and simultaneously feeling that etherial thrill, the submerged savage beneath, in his death-gasp, kept his hammer frozen there; and so the bird of heaven, with archangelic shrieks, and his imperial beak thrust upwards, and his whole captive form folded in the flag of Ahab, went down with his ship, which, like Satan, would not sink to hell till she had dragged a living part of heaven along with her, and helmeted herself with it.

Now small fowls flew screaming over the yet yawning gulf; a sullen white surf beat against its steep sides; then all collapsed, and the great shroud of the sea rolled on as it rolled five thousand years ago.

▶Epilogue

"AND I ONLY AM ESCAPED ALONE TO TELL THEE"

—Job.

The drama's done. Why then here does any one step forth? —Because one did survive the wreck.

It so chanced, that after the Parsee's disappearance, I was he whom the Fates ordained to take the place of Ahab's bowsman, when that bowsman assumed the vacant post; the same, who, when on the last day the three men were tossed from out of the rocking boat, was dropped astern. So, floating on the margin of the ensuing scene, and in full sight of it, when the halfspent suction of the sunk ship reached me, I was then, but slowly, drawn towards the closing vortex. When I reached it, it had subsided to a creamy pool. Round and round, then, and ever contracting towards the button-like black bubble at the axis of that slowly wheeling circle, like another Ixion I did revolve. Till, gaining that vital centre, the black bubble upward burst; and now, liberated by reason of its cunning spring, and, owing to its great buoyancy, rising with great force, the coffin life-buoy shot lengthwise from the sea, fell over, and floated by my side. Buoyed up by that coffin, for almost one whole day and night, I floated on a soft and dirge like main. The unharming sharks, they glided by as if with padlocks on their mouths; the savage sea-hawks sailed with sheathed beaks. On the second day, a sail drew near, nearer, and picked me up at last. It was the devious-cruising Rachel, that in her retracing search after her missing children, only found another orphan.

▶扩展阅读

1. Delbanco, A. *Melville, His World and Work*. New York: Knopf, 2005.

2. Hardwick, E. *Herman Melville*. New York: Viking, 2000.

3. Levine, R. *The Cambridge Companion to Herman Melville*. Cambridge: Cambridge University Press, 1998.

4. Martin, R. *Hero, Captain, and Stranger: Male Friendship, Social Critique, and Literary Form in the Sea Novels of Herman Melville*. Chapel Hill: University of North Carolina Press, 1986.

5. Renker, E. *Strike through the Mask: Herman Melville and the Scene of Writing*. Baltimore: Johns Hopkins University Press, 1998.

▶学习参考网站

1. http://melvillesociety.org/

2. http://www.mobydick.org/

3. http://www.melville.org/

4. http://www.literaryhistory.com/19thC/Melville.htm

【芮渝萍　编注】

23. Stephen Crane: "The Open Boat"

　　斯蒂芬·克莱恩(Stephen Crane，1871—1900)，美国小说家、诗人，20世纪自然主义先驱，出身于新泽西州纽瓦克一个虔诚的教徒家庭，父亲是牧师，母亲是牧师的女儿。克莱恩虽然是家庭中最小的一个，却是一个早熟的孩子，很小就开始写作，到16岁时已经发表多篇文章。1891年，他认为大学学习对他来说只是浪费时间，因此离开学校，开始记者和作家生涯。其实，1888—1892年，每个夏天他都在新泽西海滨新闻处工作，做哥哥唐利·克莱恩的助手。1892年他由于报道社会敏感问题而被迫离开新泽西前往纽约。1892年以美国贫民窟生活为原型的中篇小说《街头女郎玛吉》(*Maggie: A Girl of the Street*)完成，但出版社拒绝出版此书，克莱恩决定自费出版。1893年初，这部小说正式出版。虽然此书后来被评论家认为是美国文学中第一部自然主义作品，但在刚出版时公众反响平平。1894年小说《红色英勇勋章》(*The Red Badge of Courage*)分期连载，此书最终于1895年成书出版。这部小说对战争的场面描写细腻，常被认为是战争小说的杰出代表，它对主人公的心理及在战场上的本能反应作了生动细腻的描写。该小说出版之初就使克莱恩在国内获得了一定知名度，并最终为他赢得了国际声誉。1897年3月，克莱恩乘船来到英国，受到民众的热烈欢迎，英国作家约瑟夫·康拉德(Joseph Conrad)对他非常赏识。他又前往希腊，报道希腊和土耳其的战争。1898年，克莱恩的肺痨症状已十分明显，但由于负债累累，经济状况糟糕，他只能继续工作以维持生活。同年，他接受了一家杂志的邀请，去古巴采访美西战争。在经历了疾病与失业危机后，1899年，克莱恩再次回到英国与妻子泰勒相聚。同年秋，他的病情加重。1900年克莱恩去德国疗养，希望病情有所好转，但是，几个月后克莱恩就死于德国，后葬于美国新泽西州长青墓地。

　　克莱恩的诗歌创作十分丰富，他曾发表过《黑色骑手》(*The Black Riders and Other Lines*，1895)和《战争是仁慈的》(*War Is Kind*，1899)两部诗集。他的诗作大多采用自由诗体，不拘泥于传统的音节和韵律，风格简洁，常常通过寓言式的意象揭示生活的某个真理。

　　小说《海上扁舟》("The Open Boat"，1898)是克莱恩根据自己的亲身经历创作完成的。1896年新年前夕，克莱恩受命作为战地记者去古巴采访，轮船从杰克逊维尔出发，由于大雾，在驶出港口不到三英里的时候，撞在了沙洲上，致使船体受伤。虽然第二天船被拖出沙洲继续行进，但是到了五月港，船又遭搁浅，当天晚上，船上的锅炉房开始漏水，由于抽水机出故障，轮船停滞不前。第三天，船上的乘客乘救生艇离开轮船，克莱恩与其他三人也乘上了 10 英尺长的小船,他们在佛罗里达海域辗转了一天半,最终弃船游上了海滩。其间,一名加油工没能坚持到最后,溺亡于海中。返回杰克逊维尔后,克莱恩就这一灾难发表了一篇报道。之后,他又根据这一经历创作了这部著名的短篇小说,这也是他创作生涯中唯一的海洋小说。

《海上扁舟》描述了轮船失事后厨子、记者、加油工、船长在海上所经历的从希望到无助,再到无望的过程。最初,他们寄希望于厨子所说的蚊子湾灯塔北边的收容所,断定只要收容所的人看见他们就一定会出来营救他们。可是,等他们靠近那里之后却没有看到任何希望。船只能继续漂在海上。接着,他们又看到海边驾车的人向他们挥手,然而,那些人并没有把他们看成遇难者,所以也没有联系船只来救他们,希望又一次破灭。在筋疲力尽之际,他们从狂风浪尖上跳下小船,凭借自己的毅力游上海岸。但是加油工没能坚持到最后一刻。小说描写了面对大海时,人类的渺小与无助。但是小说也强调了船上四人之间的相互合作与扶持,以及他们游到岸边时,岸上的人对他们的帮助,所以小说也体现了克莱恩创作中的人文主义精神。以下选段出自《海上扁舟》第五章至小说结尾,描述了遇难的四人在海上如何度过漆黑的夜晚,战胜生理和心理极限,最终获救的过程。

▶Chapter 5

"PIE,"[1] said the oiler and the correspondent,agitatedly. "Don't talk about those things,blast you!"

"Well," said the cook, "I was just thinking about ham sandwiches, and—"

A night on the sea in an open boat is a long night. As darkness settled finally, the shine of the light, lifting from the sea in the south, changed to full gold. On the northern horizon a new light appeared, a small bluish gleam on the edge of the waters. These two lights were the furniture of the world. Otherwise there was nothing but waves.

Two men huddled in the stern[2], and distances were so magnificent in the dinghy that the rower was enabled to keep his feet partly warmed by thrusting them under his companions. Their legs indeed extended far under the rowing-seat until they touched the feet of the captain forward. Sometimes, despite the efforts of the tired oarsman, a wave came piling into the boat, an icy wave of the night, and the chilling water soaked them anew. They would twist their bodies for a moment and groan, and sleep the dead sleep once more, while the water in the boat gurgled about them as the craft rocked.

The plan of the oiler and the correspondent was for one to row until he lost the ability, and then arouse the other from his sea-water couch in the bottom of the boat.

---

① pie:在上一节末尾,厨子问加油工喜欢哪一种馅饼,此处是厨子的回答。

② stern:此处作为名词使用,意思为"船尾"。

The oiler plied the oars until his head drooped forward, and the overpowering sleep blinded him. And he rowed yet afterward. Then he touched a man in the bottom of the boat, and called his name. "Will you spell me for a little while?" he said, meekly.

"Sure, Billie," said the correspondent, awakening and dragging himself to a sitting position. They exchanged places carefully, and the oiler, cuddling down to the sea-water at the cook's side, seemed to go to sleep instantly.

The particular violence of the sea had ceased. The waves came without snarling. The obligation of the man at the oars was to keep the boat headed so that the tilt of the rollers would not capsize her, and to preserve her from filling when the crests rushed past. The black waves were silent and hard to be seen in the darkness. Often one was almost upon the boat before the oarsman was aware.

In a low voice the correspondent addressed the captain. He was not sure that the captain was awake, although this iron man seemed to be always awake. "Captain, shall I keep her[①] making for that light north, sir?"

The same steady voice answered him. "Yes. Keep it about two points off the port bow[②]."

The cook had tied a life-belt around himself in order to get even the warmth which this clumsy cork contrivance could donate, and he seemed almost stove-like when a rower, whose teeth invariably chattered wildly as soon as he ceased his labor, dropped down to sleep.

The correspondent, as he rowed, looked down at the two men sleeping under foot. The cook's arm was around the oiler's shoulders, and, with their fragmentary clothing and haggard faces, they were the babes of the sea, a grotesque rendering of the old babes in the wood.

Later he must have grown stupid at his work, for suddenly there was a growling of water, and a crest came with a roar and a swash into the boat, and it was a wonder that it did not set the cook afloat in his life-belt. The cook continued to sleep, but the oiler sat up, blinking his eyes and shaking with the new cold.

"Oh, I'm awful sorry, Billie," said the correspondent, contritely.

"That's all right, old boy," said the oiler, and lay down again and was asleep.

Presently it seemed that even the captain dozed, and the correspondent thought that he was the one man afloat on all the oceans. The wind had a voice as it came over the waves, and it was sadder than the end.

---

① her:指这只小船,英语文学中常用阴性"她"指代船只。

② two points off the port bow:保持在左舷两度。

There was a long, loud swishing astern of the boat, and a gleaming trail of phosphorescence, like blue flame, was furrowed on the black waters. It might have been made by a monstrous knife.

Then there came a stillness, while the correspondent breathed with the open mouth and looked at the sea.

Suddenly there was another swish and another long flash of bluish light, and this time it was alongside the boat, and might almost have been reached with an oar. The correspondent saw an enormous fin speed like a shadow through the water, hurling the crystalline spray and leaving the long glowing trail.

The correspondent looked over his shoulder at the captain. His face was hidden, and he seemed to be asleep. He looked at the babes of the sea. They certainly were asleep. So, being bereft of[①] sympathy, he leaned a little way to one side and swore softly into the sea.

But the thing did not then leave the vicinity of the boat. Ahead or astern, on one side or the other, at intervals long or short, fled the long sparkling streak, and there was to be heard the *whirroo* of the dark fin. The speed and power of the thing was greatly to be admired. It cut the water like a gigantic and keen projectile.

The presence of this biding thing did not affect the man with the same horror that it would if he had been a picnicker. He simply looked at the sea dully and swore in an undertone.

Nevertheless, it is true that he did not wish to be alone with the thing. He wished one of his companions to awaken by chance and keep him company with it. But the captain hung motionless over the water-jar and the oiler and the cook in the bottom of the boat were plunged in slumber.

▶Chapter 6

"If I am going to be drowned—if I am going to be drowned—if I am going to be drowned, why, in the name of the seven mad gods, who rule the sea, was I allowed to come thus far and contemplate sand and trees?"

During this dismal night, it may be remarked that a man would conclude that it was really the intention of the seven mad gods to drown him, despite the abominable injustice of it. For it was certainly an abominable injustice to drown a man who had worked so hard, so hard. The man felt it would be a crime most unnatural. Other people had drowned at sea since galleys swarmed with painted sails, but still—

---

① be bereft of:丧失,使失去。

When it occurs to a man that nature does not regard him as important, and that she feels she would not maim the universe by disposing of him, he at first wishes to throw bricks at the temple, and he hates deeply the fact that there are no bricks and no temples. Any visible expression of nature would surely be pelleted with his jeers.

Then, if there be no tangible thing to hoot he feels, perhaps, the desire to confront a personification and indulge in pleas, bowed to one knee, and with hands supplicant, saying: "Yes, but I love myself."

A high cold star on a winter's night is the word he feels that she says to him. Thereafter he knows the pathos of his situation.

The men in the dinghy had not discussed these matters, but each had, no doubt, reflected upon them in silence and according to his mind. There was seldom any expression upon their faces save the general one of complete weariness. Speech was devoted to the business of the boat.

To chime the notes of his emotion, a verse mysteriously entered the correspondent's head. He had even forgotten that he had forgotten this verse, but it suddenly was in his mind.

> "*A soldier of the Legion lay dying in Algiers*①;
> *There was lack of woman's nursing, there was dearth of woman's tears;*
> *But a comrade stood beside him, and he took that comrade's hand*
> *And he said: 'I shall never see my own, my native land.'*"

In his childhood, the correspondent had been made acquainted with the fact that a soldier of the Legion lay dying in Algiers, but he had never regarded the fact as important. Myriads of his school-fellows had informed him of the soldier's plight, but the dinning had naturally ended by making him perfectly indifferent. He had never considered it his affair that a soldier of the Legion lay dying in Algiers, nor had it appeared to him as a matter for sorrow. It was less to him than breaking of a pencil's point.

Now, however, it quaintly came to him as a human, living thing. It was no longer merely a picture of a few throes in the breast of a poet, meanwhile drinking tea and warming his feet at the grate; it was an actuality—stern, mournful, and fine.

The correspondent plainly saw the soldier. He lay on the sand with his feet out straight and still. While his pale left hand was upon his chest in an attempt to thwart the going of his

---

① A soldier of the Legion lay dying in Algiers：这是 19 世纪英国诗人卡罗琳·诺顿(Caroline Norton,1808—1877)于 1867 年写的一首民谣,名为《莱茵河上的宾根》(Bingen on the Rhine),讲述了一个濒临死亡的法国外籍兵团士兵的故事。他身处阿尔及尔,非常渴望回到自己的故乡德国莱茵河畔的宾根。

life, the blood came between his fingers. In the far Algerian distance, a city of low square forms was set against a sky that was faint with the last sunset hues. The correspondent, plying the oars and dreaming of the slow and slower movements of the lips of the soldier, was moved by a profound and perfectly impersonal comprehension. He was sorry for the soldier of the Legion who lay dying in Algiers.

The thing which had followed the boat and waited had evidently grown bored at the delay. There was no longer to be heard the slash of the cut-water, and there was no longer the flame of the long trail. The light in the north still glimmered, but it was apparently no nearer to the boat. Sometimes the boom of the surf rang in the correspondent's ears, and he turned the craft seaward then and rowed harder. Southward, someone had evidently built a watch-fire on the beach. It was too low and too far to be seen, but it made a shimmering, roseate reflection upon the bluff back of it, and this could be discerned from the boat. The wind came stronger, and sometimes a wave suddenly raged out like a mountain-cat and there was to be seen the sheen and sparkle of a broken crest.

The captain, in the bow, moved on his water-jar and sat erect. "Pretty long night," he observed to the correspondent. He looked at the shore. "Those life-saving people take their time."

"Did you see that shark playing around?"

"Yes, I saw him. He was a big fellow, all right."

"Wish I had known you were awake."

Later the correspondent spoke into the bottom of the boat.

"Billie!" There was a slow and gradual disentanglement. "Billie, will you spell me?"

"Sure," said the oiler.

As soon as the correspondent touched the cold comfortable sea-water in the bottom of the boat, and had huddled close to the cook's life-belt he was deep in sleep, despite the fact that his teeth played all the popular airs. This sleep was so good to him that it was but a moment before he heard a voice call his name in a tone that demonstrated the last stages of exhaustion. "Will you spell me?"

"Sure, Billie."

The light in the north had mysteriously vanished, but the correspondent took his course from the wide-awake captain.

Later in the night they took the boat farther out to sea, and the captain directed the cook to take one oar at the stern and keep the boat facing the seas. He was to call out if he should hear the thunder of the surf. This plan enabled the oiler and the correspondent to get respite together. "We'll give those boys a chance to get into shape① again," said the captain. They curled down and, after a few preliminary chatterings and trembles, slept once more the dead sleep. Neither knew they had bequeathed to the cook the company of another shark, or perhaps the same shark.

As the boat caroused on the waves, spray occasionally bumped over the side and gave them a fresh soaking, but this had no power to break their repose. The ominous slash of the wind and the water affected them as it would have affected mummies.

"Boys," said the cook, with the notes of every reluctance in his voice, "she's drifted in pretty close. I guess one of you had better take her to sea again." The correspondent, aroused, heard the crash of the toppled crests.

As he was rowing, the captain gave him some whiskey and water, and this steadied the chills out of him. "If I ever get ashore and anybody shows me even a photograph of an oar—"

At last there was a short conversation.

"Billie... Billie, will you spell me?"

"Sure," said the oiler.

▶**Chapter 7**

When the correspondent again opened his eyes, the sea and the sky were each of the gray hue of the dawning. Later, carmine and gold was painted upon the waters. The morning appeared finally, in its splendor with a sky of pure blue, and the sunlight flamed on the tips of the waves.

On the distant dunes were set many little black cottages, and a tall white wind-mill reared above them. No man, nor dog, nor bicycle appeared on the beach. The cottages might have formed a deserted village.

The voyagers scanned the shore. A conference was held in the boat. "Well," said the captain, "if no help is coming, we might better try a run through the surf right away. If we stay out here much longer we will be too weak to do anything for ourselves at all." The others silently acquiesced in this reasoning. The boat was headed for the beach. The correspondent wondered if none ever ascended the tall wind-tower, and if then they never looked seaward. This tower was a giant, standing with its back to the plight of the ants. It represented in a degree, to the correspondent, the serenity of nature amid the struggles of the individual—nature in the wind, and nature in the vision of men. She did not seem cruel to him, nor beneficent, nor treacherous, nor wise. But she was indifferent, flatly

① get into shape: 使身体好起来。

indifferent. It is, perhaps, plausible that a man in this situation, impressed with the unconcern of the universe, should see the innumerable flaws of his life and have them taste wickedly in his mind and wish for another chance. A distinction between right and wrong seems absurdly clear to him, then, in this new ignorance of the grave-edge, and he understands that if he were given another opportunity he would mend his conduct and his words, and be better and brighter during an introduction, or at a tea.

"Now, boys," said the captain, "she is going to swamp sure. All we can do is to work her in as far as possible, and then when she swamps, pile out and scramble for the beach. Keep cool now and don't jump until she swamps sure."

The oiler took the oars. Over his shoulders he scanned the surf. "Captain," he said, "I think I'd better bring her about, and keep her head-on to the seas and back her in."

"All right, Billie," said the captain. "Back her in." The oiler swung the boat then and, seated in the stern, the cook and the correspondent were obliged to look over their shoulders to contemplate the lonely and indifferent shore.

The monstrous inshore rollers heaved the boat high until the men were again enabled to see the white sheets of water scudding up the slanted beach. "We won't get in very close," said the captain. Each time a man could wrest his attention from the rollers, he turned his glance toward the shore, and in the expression of the eyes during this contemplation there was a singular quality. The correspondent, observing the others, knew that they were not afraid, but the full meaning of their glances was shrouded.

As for himself, he was too tired to grapple fundamentally with the fact. He tried to coerce his mind into thinking of it, but the mind was dominated at this time by the muscles, and the muscles said they did not care. It merely occurred to him that if he should drown it would be a shame.

There were no hurried words, no pallor, no plain agitation. The men simply looked at the shore. "Now, remember to get well clear of the boat when you jump," said the captain.

Seaward the crest of a roller suddenly fell with a thunderous crash, and the long white comber came roaring down upon the boat.

"Steady now," said the captain. The men were silent. They turned their eyes from the shore to the comber and waited. The boat slid up the incline, leaped at the furious top, bounced over it, and swung down the long back of the waves. Some water had been shipped and the cook bailed it out.

But the next crest crashed also. The tumbling boiling flood of white water caught the boat and whirled it almost perpendicular. Water swarmed in from all sides. The correspondent had his hands on the gunwale① at this time, and when the water entered at that place he swiftly withdrew his fingers, as if he objected to wetting them.

The little boat, drunken with this weight of water, reeled and snuggled deeper into the sea.

"Bail her out, cook! Bail her out," said the captain.

"All right, captain," said the cook.

"Now, boys, the next one will do for us, sure," said the oiler. "Mind to jump clear of the boat."

The third wave moved forward, huge, furious, implacable. It fairly swallowed the dingey, and almost simultaneously the men tumbled into the sea. A piece of life-belt had lain in the bottom of the boat, and as the correspondent went overboard he held this to his chest with his left hand.

The January water was icy, and he reflected immediately that it was colder than he had expected to find it off the coast of Florida. This appeared to his dazed mind as a fact important enough to be noted at the time. The coldness of the water was sad; it was tragic. This fact was somehow mixed and confused with his opinion of his own situation that it seemed almost a proper reason for tears. The water was cold.

When he came to the surface he was conscious of little but the noisy water. Afterward he saw his companions in the sea. The oiler was ahead in the race. He was swimming strongly and rapidly. Off to the correspondent's left, the cook's great white and corked back bulged out of the water, and in the rear the captain was hanging with his one good hand to the keel of the overturned dinghy.

There is a certain immovable quality to a shore, and the correspondent wondered at it amid the confusion of the sea.

It seemed also very attractive, but the correspondent knew that it was a long journey, and he paddled leisurely. The piece of life-preserver lay under him, and sometimes he whirled down the incline of a wave as if he were on a hand-sled.

But finally he arrived at a place in the sea where travel was beset with difficulty. He did not pause swimming to inquire what manner of current had caught him, but there his progress ceased. The shore was set before him like a bit of scenery on a stage, and he looked at it and understood with his eyes each detail of it.

As the cook passed, much farther to the left, the captain was calling to him, "Turn over on your back, cook! Turn over on your back and use the oar."

"All right, Sir!" The cook turned on his back, and, paddling with an oar, went ahead

---

① gunwale: 舷缘, 船舷的上缘。

as if he were a canoe.

Presently the boat also passed to the left of the correspondent with the captain clinging with one hand to the keel. He would have appeared like a man raising himself to look over a board fence, if it were not for the extraordinary gymnastics of the boat. The correspondent marvelled that the captain could still hold to it.

They passed on, nearer to shore—the oiler, the cook, the captain—and following them went the water-jar, bouncing gayly over the seas.

The correspondent remained in the grip of this strange new enemy—a current. The shore, with its white slope of sand and its green bluff, topped with little silent cottages, was spread like a picture before him. It was very near to him then, but he was impressed as one who in a gallery looks at a scene from Brittany or Algiers.

He thought: "I am going to drown? Can it be possible? Can it be possible? Can it be possible?" Perhaps an individual must consider his own death to be the final phenomenon of nature.

But later a wave perhaps whirled him out of this small deadly current, for he found suddenly that he could again make progress toward the shore. Later still, he was aware that the captain, clinging with one hand to the keel of the dinghy, had his face turned away from the shore and toward him, and was calling his name. "Come to the boat! Come to the boat!"

In his struggle to reach the captain and the boat, he reflected that when one gets properly wearied, drowning must really be a comfortable arrangement, a cessation of hostilities[①] accompanied by a large degree of relief, and he was glad of it, for the main thing in his mind for some moments had been horror of the temporary agony. He did not wish to be hurt.

Presently he saw a man running along the shore. He was undressing with most remarkable speed. Coat, trousers, shirt, everything flew magically off him.

"Come to the boat," called the captain.

"All right, captain." As the correspondent paddled, he saw the captain let himself down to bottom and leave the boat. Then the correspondent performed his one little marvel of the voyage. A large wave caught him and flung him with ease and supreme speed completely over the boat and far beyond it. It struck him even then as an event in gymnastics, and a true miracle of the sea. An overturned boat in the surf is not a plaything to a swimming man.

The correspondent arrived in water that reached only to his waist, but his condition did not enable him to stand for more than a moment. Each wave knocked him into a heap, and the under-tow pulled at him.

---

① a cessation of hostilities: 休战，停战。

Then he saw the man who had been running and undressing, and undressing and running, come bounding into the water. He dragged ashore the cook, and then waded toward the captain, but the captain waved him away, and sent him to the correspondent. He was naked, naked as a tree in winter, but a halo was about his head, and he shone like a saint. He gave a strong pull, and a long drag, and a bully heave at the correspondent's hand. The correspondent, schooled in the minor formulae, said: "Thanks, old man." But suddenly the man cried: "What's that?" He pointed a swift finger. The correspondent said: "Go."

In the shallows, face downward, lay the oiler. His forehead touched sand that was periodically, between each wave, clear of the sea.

The correspondent did not know all that transpired afterward. When he achieved safe ground he fell, striking the sand with each particular part of his body. It was as if he had dropped from a roof, but the thud was grateful to him.

It seems that instantly the beach was populated with men with blankets, clothes, and flasks, and women with coffee-pots and all the remedies sacred to their minds. The welcome of the land to the men from the sea was warm and generous, but a still and dripping shape was carried slowly up the beach, and the land's welcome for it could only be the different and sinister hospitality of the grave.

When it came night, the white waves paced to and fro in the moonlight, and the wind brought the sound of the great sea's voice to the men on shore, and they felt that they could then be interpreters.

▶扩展阅读

1. Benfey, C. *The Double Life of Stephen Crane*. New York: Knopf, 1992.

2. Bergon, F. *Stephen Crane's Artistry*. New York: Columbia University Press, 1975.

3. Knapp, B. L. *Stephen Crane*. New York: Ungar Publishing Co., 1987.

4. Weatherford, R. M. "Introduction". *Stephen Crane: The Critical Heritage*. New York: Routledge, 1997.

5. Wertheim, S. & Sorrentino, P. M. *The Crane Log: A Documentary Life of Stephen Crane, 1871—1900*. New York: G. K. Hall & Co., 1994.

▶学习参考网站

1. http://www.wsu.edu/~campbelld/crane/index.html

2. http://www.skmatic.com/crane.php

【王亚妮　编注】

24. Mary Heaton Vorse:
"The Wallow of the Sea"

　　玛丽·希顿·沃斯（Mary Heaton Vorse，1874—1966），美国作家、诗人，出身于纽约市一个富裕家庭，在马萨诸塞州阿姆赫斯特市长大。她的父亲是一位文学教师，母亲从前夫那里继承了巨额家产。她从小跟随父母旅行，见多识广，受到很好的教育。1896 年她进入纽约艺术学生联盟系统学习绘画，但却发现自己缺乏绘画天赋。在学习期间，她结识了几位后来成为妇女运动重要领袖人物的朋友。玛丽自己也积极参与女性教育、女性经济独立、女性选举权、生育控制等女性运动。她还积极投身于和平运动、儿童福利、安居工程等公益事业。她两次结婚，两次守寡。她的第一任丈夫名叫阿尔伯特·沃斯，是哈佛大学的毕业生，喜爱文学，从事新闻工作。玛丽受丈夫影响，开始写作，并发现自己的写作才能远远胜过绘画能力，便立志成为作家。阿尔伯特不幸于 1910 年因脑出血去世。她的第二任丈夫名叫约瑟夫·奥布莱恩，也是一位新闻工作者，婚后三年便去世了。

　　玛丽·希顿·沃斯创作了一系列小说、诗歌和各种题材的文章。她的作品包括《家的心脏》（*The Heart of the House*，1906）、《游艇驾驶员的妻子》（*The Breaking-In of a Yachtsman's Wife*，1908）、《小小人》（*The Very Little Person*，1911）、《一位妇人的自传》（*The Autobiography of an Elderly Woman*，1911）、《心的家园》（*The Heart's Country*，1913）、《普雷斯顿一家人》（*The Prestons*，1918）、《定居》（*I've Come to Stay*，1919）、《成长之旅》（*Growing Up*，1920）、《男人和钢铁》（*Men and Steel*，1921）、《弗雷卡的拳头》（*Fraycar's Fist*，1923）、《时间与城镇》（*Time and the Town*，1942）等。她在《麦克卢尔杂志》（*McClure's Magazine*）、《亚特兰大月刊》（*Atlantic Monthly*）、《纽约客》（*The New Yorker*）、《哈珀斯周刊》（*Harper's Weekly*）、《新共和周刊》（*New Republic*）和《妇女家庭杂志》（*Ladies' Home Journal*）等著名刊物上发表小说和文章 400 多篇。她的作品一度受到读者的喜爱。

　　玛丽·希顿·沃斯对 20 世纪初和大萧条时期劳工阶层声势浩大的罢工游行做过一系列深度报道。在 88 岁高龄时，她在汽车工人联合会（UAW）领袖的陪伴下参加联合会成立 25 周年纪念日，被授予 UAW 社会正义勋章。出席这次活动的贵宾还有第一夫人埃莉娜·罗斯福，著名作家厄普顿·辛克莱（Upton Sinclair）等。

　　《汹涌的海》（"The Wallow of the Sea"）是玛丽·希顿·沃斯发表在《哈珀斯周刊》上的一篇短篇小说。故事的叙述者回顾了 15 岁时遇到的一位与众不同的人，她叫迪尔达。迪尔达是一位年轻迷人的吉卜赛女郎。她的行为方式和对待爱情的态度开启了年轻的叙述者认知世界的大门。爱情与金钱，哪个更重要？这个问题困扰了无数的女孩。迪尔达不加掩饰的直率性格，一次次地震惊了年轻的叙事者。海洋在这篇小说中起着重要的作用，是检验个人成长和考验个人勇气的场所。不成熟的约翰尼必须到波涛汹涌的海上去接受考验，才能成为真正的男子汉。勇敢的迪尔达不仅让约翰尼迅速成长起来，也极大地促进了年轻的叙述者的认知发展。作者把迪尔达刻画成一个具有异质文化性格的吉卜赛女郎，她的美貌、直率、活力和勇敢不仅为她赢得了爱情，还赢得了财富。三位不同性格、不同背景和不同年龄的男人爱上了她，她嫁给了年轻贫寒的约翰尼，得到了年老体迈的康伯伊留给她的遗产。

▶

The Wallow of the Sea

After twenty years I saw Deolda Costa again, Deolda who, when I was a girl, had meant to me beauty and romance. There she sat before me, large, mountainous, her lithe gypsy body clothed in fat. Her dark eyes, beautiful as ever, still with a hint of wildness, met mine proudly. And as she looked at me the old doubts rose again in my mind, a cold chill crawled up my back as I thought what was locked in Deolda's heart. My mind went back to that night twenty years ago, with the rain beating its devil's tattoo① against the window, when all night long I sat holding Deolda's hand while she never spoke or stirred the hours through, but stared with her crazy, smut-rimmed eyes out into the storm where Johnny Deutra was. I heard again the shuttle of her feet weaving up and down the room through the long hours.

It was a strange thing to see Deolda after having known her as I did. There she was, with her delight of life all changed into youngsters and fat. There she was, heavy as a monument, and the devil in her divided among her children—though Deolda had plenty of devil to divide. My first thought was: "Here's the end of romance. To think that you once were love, passion, and maybe even carried death in your hand—and when I look at you now!"

Then the thought came to me, "After all, it is a greater romance that she should have triumphed completely, that the weakness of remorse has never set its fangs in her heart." She had seized the one loophole that life had given her and had infused her relentless courage into another's veins.

---

① tattoo：连续急促的敲击声。"...the rain beating its devil's tattoo against the window"意思是沉重的雨滴不断地敲击着窗户。

I was at the bottom of[①] Deolda Costa's coming to live with my aunt Josephine Kingsbury, for I had been what my mother called "peaked," and was sent down to the seashore to visit her. And suddenly I, an inland child, found myself in a world of romance whose very colors were changed. I had lived in a world of swimming green with faint blue distance; hills ringed us mildly; wide, green fields lapped up to our houses; islands of shade trees dotted the fields.

My world of romance was blue and gray, with the savage dunes glittering gold in the sun. Here life was intense. Danger lurked always under the horizon. Lights, like warning eyes, flashed at night, and through the drenching fog, bells on reefs talked to invisible ships. Old men who told tales of storm and strange, savage islands, of great catches of fish, of smuggling, visited my aunt. Then, as if this were merely the background of a drama, Deolda Costa came to live with us in a prosaic enough fashion, as a "girl to help out."

If you ask me how my aunt, a decent, law-abiding woman—a sick woman at that—took a firebrand like Deolda into her home, all I would be able to answer is: If you had seen her stand there, as I did, on the porch that morning, you wouldn't ask the question. The doorbell rang and my aunt opened it, I tagging behind. There was a girl there who looked as though she were daring all mankind, a strange girl with skin tawny, like sand on a hot day, and dark, brooding eyes. My aunt said:

"You want to see me?"

The girl glanced up slowly under her dark brows that looked as if they had been drawn with a pencil.

"I've come to work for you," she said in a shy, friendly fashion. "I'm a real strong girl."

No one could have turned her away, not unless he were deaf and blind, not unless he were ready to murder happiness. I was fifteen and romantic, and I was bedazzled just as the others were. She made me think of dancing women I have heard of, and music, and of soft, starlit nights, velvet black. She was more foreign than anything I had ever seen and she meant to me what she did to plenty of others—romance. She must have meant it to my aunt, sick as she was and needing a hired girl. So when Deolda asked, in that soft way of hers:

"Shall I stay?"

"Yes," answered my aunt, reluctantly, her eyes on the girl's lovely mouth.

While she stood there, her shoulders drooping, her eyes searching my aunt's face, she still found time to shoot a glance like a flaming signal to Johnny Deutra, staring at her agape. I surprised the glance, and so did my aunt Josephine, who must have known she was in for nothing but trouble. And so was Johnny Deutra, for from that first glance of Deolda's that

---

① be at the bottom of:指某事的根源(或起因、导火索)。

dared him, love laid its heavy hand on his young shoulders.

"What's your name, dear?" my aunt asked.

"Deolda Costa," said she.

"Oh, you're one-armed Manel's girl. I don't remember seeing you about lately."

"I been working to New Bedford①. My father an' mother both died. I came up for the funeral. I—don't want to go back to the mills—" Then sudden fury flamed in her. "I hate the men there!"she cried. "I'd drown before I'd go back!"

"There, there, dear," my aunt soothed her. "You ain't going back—you're going to work for Auntie Kingsbury."

That was the way Deolda had. She never gave one any chance for an illusion about her, for there was handsome Johnny Deutra still hanging round the gate watching Deolda, and she already held my aunt's heart in her slender hand.

My aunt went around muttering, "One-armed Manel's girl!" She appealed to me: "She's got to live somewhere, hasn't she?"

I imagine that my aunt excused herself for deliberately, running into foul weather by telling herself that Deolda Was her "lot," something the Lord had sent her to take care of.

"Who was one-armed Manel?" I asked, tagging after my aunt.

"Oh, he was a queer old one-armed Portygee who lived down along," said my aunt, "clear down along under the sand dunes in a green-painted house with a garden in front of it with as many colors as Joseph's coat. Those Costas lived 'most any way." Then my aunt added, over her shoulder: "They say the old woman was a gypsy and got married to one-armed Manel jumping over a broomstick. And I wouldn't wonder a mite if 'twas true. She was a queer looking old hag with black, piercing eyes and a proud way of walking. The boys are a wild crew. Why, I remember this girl Deolda, like a little leopard cat with blue-black shadows in her hair and eyes like saucers, selling berries at the back door!"

My uncle Ariel, Aunt Josephine's brother, came in after a while. As he took a look at Deolda going out of the room, he said:

"P—hew! What's that?"

"I told you I was sick and had to get a girl to help out—what with Susie visiting and all," said my aunt, very short.

"Help out? Help out! My lord! *help out*! What's her name—Beth Sheba②?"

Now this wasn't as silly as it sounded. I suppose what Uncle Ariel meant was that Deolda made him think of Eastern queens and Araby. But my attention was distracted by the

---

① New Bedford:新贝德福,美国马萨诸塞州东南部港口城市。原是捕鲸港口,现仍为重要渔港。

② Beth Sheba:示巴,圣经故事中大卫王引诱了她,她后来成为以色列人的女王。

appearance of two wild-looking boys with a green-blue sea chest which served Deolda as a trunk. I followed it to her room and started making friends with Deolda, who opened the trunk, and I glimpsed something embroidered in red flowers.

"Oh, Deolda, let me see. Oh, let me see!" I cried.

It was a saffron shawl all embroidered with splotchy red flowers as big as my hand. It made me tingle as it lay there in its crinkly folds, telling of another civilization and other lands than our somber shores. The shawl and its crawling, venomous, alluring flowers marked Deolda off from us. She seemed to belong to the shawl and its scarlet insinuations.

"That was my mother's," she said. Then she added this astounding thing: "My mother was a great dancer. All Lisbon went wild about her. When she danced the whole town went crazy. The bullfighters and the princes would come—"

"But how—?" I started, and stopped, for Deolda had dropped beside the chest and pressed her face in the shawl, and I remembered that her mother was dead only a few days ago, and I couldn't ask her how the great dancer came to be in Dennisport in the cabin under the dunes. I tiptoed out, my heart thrilled with romance for the gypsy dancer's daughter.

When my aunt was ready for bed there was no Deolda. Later came the sound of footsteps and my aunt's voice in the hall outside my room.

"That you, Deolda?"

"Yes'm."

"Where were you all evening?"

"Oh, just out under the lilacs."

"For pity's sake! Out under the lilacs! What were you doing out there?"

Deolda's voice came clear and tranquil. "Making love with Johnny Deutra."

I held my breath. What can you do when a girl tells the truth unabashed.

"I've known Johnny Deutra ever since he came from the Islands, Deolda," my aunt said, sternly. "He'll mean it when he falls in love."

"I know it," said Deolda, with a little breathless catch in her voice.

"He's only a kid. He's barely twenty," my aunt went on, inexorably. "He's got to help his mother. He's not got enough to marry; any girl who married him would have to live with the old folks. Look where you're going, Deolda."

There was silence, and I heard their footsteps going to their rooms.

The next day Deolda went to walk, and back she came, old Conboy driving her in his motor. Old Conboy was rich; he had one of the first motors on the Cape, when cars were still a wonder. After that Deolda went off in Conboy's motor as soon as her dishes were done and after supper there would be handsome Johnny Deutra. We were profoundly shocked. You may be sure village tongues were already busy after a few days of these goings on.

"Deolda," my aunt said, sternly, "what are you going out with that old Conboy for?"

"I'm going to marry him," Deolda answered.

"You're *what*?"

"Going to marry him," Deolda repeated in her cool, truthful way that always took my breath.

"Has he asked you?" my aunt inquired, sarcastically.

"No, but he will," said Deolda. She looked out under her long, slanting eyes that looked as if they had little red flames dancing in the depths of them.

"But you love Johnny," my aunt went on.

She nodded three times with the gesture of a little girl.

"Do you know what you're headed for, Deolda?" said my aunt. "Do you know what you're doing when you talk about marrying old Conboy and loving that handsome, no-account[①] kid, Johnny?"

We were all three sitting on the bulkheads after supper. It was one of those soft nights with great lazy yellow clouds with pink edges sailing down over the rim of the sea, fleet after fleet of them. I was terribly interested in it all, but horribly shocked, and from my vantage of fifteen years I said.

"Deolda, I think you ought to marry Johnny."

"Fiddledeedee!" said my aunt. "If she had sense she wouldn't marry either one of 'em—one's too old, one's too young."

"She ought to marry Johnny and make a man of him," I persisted, for it seemed ridiculous to me to call Johnny Deutra a boy when he was twenty and handsome as a picture in a book.

My prim words touched some sore place in Deolda. She gave a brief gesture with her hands and pushed the idea from her.

"I can't," she said, "I can't do it over again. Oh, I can't—I can't. I'm afraid of emptiness—empty purses, empty bellies. The last words my mother spoke were to me. She said, '*Deolda, fear nothing but emptiness—empty bellies, empty hearts.*' She left me something, too."

She went into the house and came back with the saffron shawl, its long fringe trailing on the floor, its red flowers venomous and lovely in the evening light.

"You've seen my mother," she said, "but you've seen her a poor old woman. She had everything in the world once. She gave it up for love. I've seen what love comes to. I've seen my mother with her hands callous with work and her temper sharp as a razor edge nagging

---

① no-account:〈方〉没有用的,不足道的。

my father, and my father cursing out us children. She had a whole city in love with her and she gave up everything to run away with my father. He was jealous and wanted her for himself. He got her to marry him. Then he lost his arm and they were poor and her voice went. I've seen where love goes. If I married Johnny I'd go and live at Deutra's and I'd have kids, and old Ma Deutra would hate me and scream at me just like my mother used to. It would be going back, right back in the trap I've just come out of."

What she said gave me an entirely new vision of life and love. "They were married and lived happy ever afterward" was what I had read in books. Now I saw all at once the other side of the medal. It was my first contact, too, with a nature strong enough to attempt to subdue life to will. I had seen only the subservient ones who had accepted life.

Deolda was a fierce and passionate reaction against destiny. It's a queer thing, when you think of it, for a girl to be brought up face to face with the wreck of a tragic passion, to grow up in the house with love's ashes and to see what were lovers turned into an old hag and a cantankerous[①], one-armed man nagging each other.

My aunt made one more argument. "What makes you get married to any of 'em, Deolda?"

Now Deolda looked at her with a queer look; then she gave a queer laugh like a short bark.

"I can't stay here forever. I'm not going back to the mill."

Then my aunt surprised me by throwing her arms around Deolda and kissing her and calling her "my poor lamb", while Deolda leaned up against my aunt as if she were her own little girl and snuggled up in a way that would break your heart.

One afternoon soon after old Conboy brought Deolda home before tea time, and as she jumped out:

"Oh, all right!" he called after her. "Have your own way; I'll marry you if you want me to!"

She made him pay for this. "You see," she said to my aunt, "I told you I was going to marry him."

"Well, then come out motoring tonight when you've got your dishes done," called old Conboy.

"I'm going to the breakwater with Johnny Deutra tonight," said Deolda, in that awful truthful way of hers.

"You see what you get," said my aunt, "if you marry that girl."

"I'll get worse not marrying her," said Conboy. "I may die any minute; I've a high

---

① cantankerous: 脾气坏且抱怨不休的。

blood pressure, and maybe a stroke will carry me off any day. But I've never wanted anything in many years as I want to hold Deolda in my arms."

"Shame on you!" cried my aunt. "An old man like you!"

So things went on. Johnny kept right on coming. My aunt would fume about it, but she did nothing. We were all under Deolda's enchantment. As for me, I adored her; she had a look that always disarmed me. She would sit brooding with a look I had come to know as the "Deolda look." Tears would come to her eyes and slide down her face.

"Deolda," I would plead, "what are you crying about?"

"Life," she answered.

But I knew that she was crying because Johnny Deutra was only a boy. Then she would change into a mood of wild gayety, whip the shawl around her, and dance for me, looking a thousand times more beautiful than anyone I had ever seen. And then she would shove me out of the room, leaving me feeling as though I had witnessed some strange rite at once beautiful and unholy.

She'd sit mocking Conboy, but he'd only smile. She'd go off with her other love and my aunt powerless to stop her. As for Johnny Deutra, he was so in love that all he saw was Deolda. I don't believe he ever thought that she was in earnest about old Conboy.

So things stood when one day Capt. Mark Hammar came driving up with Conboy to take Deolda out. Mark was his real name, but Nick was what they called him, after the "Old Nick," for he was a devil if there ever was one, a big, rollicking devil—that is, outwardly. But gossips said no crueller man ever drove a crew for the third summer into the Northern Seas. I didn't like the way he looked at Deolda from the first, with his narrowed eyes and his smiling mouth. My aunt didn't like the way she signaled back to him. We watched them go, my aunt saying

"No good'll come of that!" And no good did.

All three of them came back excited and laughing. Old Conboy, tall as Mark Hammar, wide-shouldered, shambling like a bear, but a fine figure of an old fellow for all that; Mark Hammar, heavy and splendid in his sinister fashion; and between them Deolda with her big, red mouth and her sallow skin and her eyes burning as they did when she was excited.

"I'm saying to Deolda here," said Captain Hammar, coming up to my aunt, "that I'll make a better runnin' mate than Conboy." He drew her up to him. There was something alike about them; the same devil flamed out of the eyes of both of them. Their glances met like forked lightning. "I've got a lot more money than him, too," said Hammar, jerking his thumb toward Conboy. He roused the devil in Deolda.

"You may have more money," said she, "but you'll live longer! And I want to be a rich widow!"

"Stop your joking," my aunt said, sharply. "It don't sound nice."

"Joking?" says Captain Hammar, letting his big head lunge forward. "I ain't joking; I'm goin' to marry that girl."

My aunt said no more while they were there. She sat like a ramrod in her chair. That was one of the worst things about Deolda. We cover our bodies decently with clothes, and we ought to cover up our thoughts decently with words. But Deolda had no shame, and people with her didn't, either. They'd say just what they were thinking about.

After they left Deolda came to Aunt Josephine and put her arms around her like a good, sweet child.

"What's the matter, Auntie?" she asked.

"You—that's what. I can't stand it to hear you go on."

Deolda looked at her with a sort of wonder. "We were only saying out loud what every girl's thinking about when she marries a man of forty-five, or when she marries a man who's sixty-five. It's a trade—the world's like that."

"Let me tell you one thing," said my aunt. "You can't fool with Capt. Mark Hammar. It means that you give up your other sweetheart."

"That's to be seen," said Deolda in her dark, sultry way. Then she said, as if she was talking to herself: "Life—with him—would be interesting. He thinks he could crush me like a fly. —He can't, though—" And then all of a sudden she burst into tears and threw herself in my aunt's lap, sobbing: "Oh, oh! Why's life like this? Why isn't my Johnny grown up? Why—don't he—take me away—from them all?"

After that Captain Hammar kept coming to the house. He showed well enough he was serious.

"That black devil's hypnotized her," my aunt put it.

Deolda seemed to have some awful kinship to Mark Hammar, and Johnny Deutra, who never paid much attention to old Conboy, paid attention to him. Black looks passed between them, and I would catch "Nick" Hammar's eyes resting on Johnny with a smiling venom that struck fear into me. Johnny Deutra seldom came daytimes, but he came in late one afternoon and sat there looking moodily at Deolda, who flung past him with the air she had when she wore the saffron shawl. I could almost see its long fringes trailing behind her as she stood before him, one hand on her tilted hip, her head on one side.

It was a queer sort of day, a day with storm in the air, a day when all our nerves got on edge, when the possibility of danger whips the blood. I had an uncomfortable sense of knowing that I ought to leave Deolda and Johnny and that Johnny was waiting for me to go to talk. And yet I was fascinated, as little girls are; and just as I was about to leave the room I ran into old Conboy hurrying in, his reddish hair standing on end.

"Well, Deolda," said he, "Captain Hammar's gone down the Cape all of a sudden. He told me to tell you good-by for him. Deolda, for God's sake, marry me before he comes back! He'll kill you, that's what he'll do. It's not for my sake I'm asking you—it's for your sake!"

She looked at him with her big black eyes. "I believe you mean that, Conboy. I believe I'll do it. But I'll be fair and square with you as you are with me. You'd better let me be; you know what I'm like. I won't make you happy; I never pretended I would. And as for him killing me, how do you know, Conboy, I mightn't lose my temper first?"

"He'll break you," said Conboy. "God! but he's a man without pity! Don't you know how he drives his men? Don't you know the stories about his first wife? He's put some of his magic on you. You're nothing but a poor little lamb, Deolda, playing with a wolf, for all your spirit. There's nothing he'd stop at. Nothing," he repeated, staring at Johnny. "I wouldn't give a cent for that Johnny Deutra's life until I'm married to you, Deolda. I've seen the way Mark Hammar looks at him—you have, too. I tell you, Mark Hammar don't value the life of any man who stands in his way!" And the way the old man spoke lifted the hair on my head.

Then all of us were quiet, for there stood Captain Hammar himself.

"Why, Mark, I thought you'd gone down the Cape!" said Conboy.

"I lost the train," he answered.

"Well, what about that vessel you was going to buy in Gloucester?"

"I got to sail over," said Captain Hammar.

Conboy glanced out of the window. The bay was ringed around with heavy clouds; weather was making. Storm signals were flying up on Town Hill, and down the harbor a fleet of scared vessels were making for port.

"You can't go out in that, Mark," says Conboy.

"I've got the money," says Mark Hammar, "and I'm going to go. If I don't get down there that crazy Portygee'll have sold that vessel to some one else. It ain't every day you can buy a vessel like that for the price. He let me know about it first, but he won't wait long, and he's got to have the cash in his hands. He's up to some crooked work or he wouldn't 'a' sent the boy down with the letter; he'd 'a' sent it by post, or telegraphed even. He's let me know about it first, but he won't wait. It was getting the money strapped up that made me late. I had to wait for the old cashier to get back from his dinner."

"You and your money'll be in the bottom of the bay, that's where you'll be," said Conboy.

"If I'd taken in sail for every little bit o' wind I'd encountered in my life," said Mark Hammar, "I'd not be where I am now. So I just thought I'd come and run in on Deolda before I left, seeing as I'm going to marry her when I get back."

Johnny Deutra undid his long length from the chair. He was a tall, heavy boy, making up in looks for what he lacked in head. He came and stood over Mark Hammar. He said:

"I've had enough of this. I've had just enough of you two hanging around Deolda. She's my woman—I'm going to marry Deolda myself. Nobody else is going to touch her; so just as soon as you two want to clear out you can."

There was silence so that you could hear a pin drop. And then the wind that had been making hit the house like the blow of a fist and went screaming down the road. Deolda didn't see or hear; she was just looking at Johnny. He went to her.

"Don't you listen to 'em, Deolda. I'll make money for you; I'll make more than any of 'em. It's right you should want it. Tell 'em that you're going to marry me, Deolda. Clear 'em out."

That was where he made his mistake. *He* should have cleared them out. Now Captain Hammar spoke:

"You're quite a little man, ain't you, Johnny? Here's where you got a chance to prove it. You can make a hundred dollars tonight by taking the *Anita* across to Gloucester with me. We'll start right off."

Everyone was quiet. Then old Conboy cried out:

"Don't go, Mark. Don't go! Why, it's *murder* to tempt that boy out there."

At the word "murder" Deolda drew her breath in and clapped her hand over her mouth, her eyes staring at Johnny Deutra. "Nick" Hammar pretended he hadn't noticed. He sat smiling at Johnny.

"We-ll," he drawled. "How about it, Johnny? Goin'?"

Johnny had been studying, his eyes on the floor.

"I'll go with you," he said.

Then again for a half minute nobody spoke. Captain Hammar glared, letting us see what was in his dark mind. Old Conboy shrunk into himself and Deolda sat with her wild eyes going from one to the other, but not moving. We were all thinking of what old Conboy had said just before Captain Hammar had flung open the door. A sudden impulse seized me; I wanted to cry out: "Don't go, Johnny. He'll shove you overboard." For I knew that was what was in "Nick" Hammar's mind as well as if he had told me. A terrible excitement went through me. I wanted to fling myself at "Nick" Hammar and beat him with my fists and say, "He sha'n't go—he sha'n't, he sha'n't!" But I sat there unable to move or speak. Then suddenly into the frozen silence came the voice of "Nick" Hammar. This is what he said in his easy and tranquil way:

"Well, I'm goin' along. Are you coming, Conboy?" He spoke as though nothing had happened. "I'll meet you down at the wharf, Johnny, in a half hour. I'll leave you to say good-by to Deolda."

They went out, the wind blowing the door shut behind them.

Deolda got up and so did Johnny. They stood facing each other in the queer yellow light of the coming storm. They didn't notice my aunt or me.

"*You going*?" asked Deolda.

They looked into each other's eyes, and he answered so I could barely hear:

"Sure."

"*You know what he's thinking about*?" said Deolda.

Again Johnny waited before he answered in a voice hardly above a whisper:

"I can guess."

Deolda went up slowly to him and put one of her long hands on each of his shoulders. She looked deep into his eyes. She didn't speak; she just looked. And he looked back, as though trying to find out what she had in her heart, and as he looked a little flicker of horror went over his face. Then he smiled a slow smile, as though he had understood something and consented to it—and it was a queer smile to see on the face of a young fellow. It was as if the youth of Johnny Deutra had passed away forever. Then Deolda said to him:

"Good for you, Johnny Deutra!" and put out her hand, and he laid his in hers and they shook on it, though no word had passed between them. And all this time my aunt and I sat motionless on the haircloth sofa next to the wall. And I tell you as I watched them my blood ran cold, though I didn't understand what it was about. But later I understood well enough.

There never was so long an evening. The squall blew over and a heavy blow set in. I could hear the pounding of the waves on the outside shore. Deolda sat outside the circle of the lamp in a horrible tense quiet. My aunt tried to make talk, and made a failure of it. It was awful to hear the clatter of her voice trying to sound natural in the face of the whistle of the storm, and out wallowing in it the gasoline dory with its freight of hatred. I hated to go to bed, for my room gave on the sea, and it seemed as if the night and the tragedy which I had glimpsed would come peering in at me with ghastly eyes.

I had just got under the blanket when the door opened quietly.

"Who is that?" I asked.

"It's me—Deolda."

She went to the window and peered out into the storm, as though she were trying to penetrate its mystery. I couldn't bear her standing there; it was as if I could hear her heart bleed. It was as if for a while I had become fused with her and her love for Johnny Deutra and with all the dark things that had happened in our house this afternoon. I got out of bed and went to her and put my hand in hers. If she'd only cried, or if she'd only spoken I could have stood it; if she'd said in words what was going on inside her mind. But she sat there with her hand cold in mine, staring into the storm through all the long hours of the night.

Toward the end I was so tired that my mind went to sleep in that way your mind can when your body stays awake and everything seems far off and like things happening in a nightmare except that you know they're real. At last daylight broke, very pale, threatening, and slate colored. Deolda got up and began padding up and down the floor, back and forth, like a soul in torment.

About ten o'clock old Conboy came in.

"I got the license, Deolda," he said.

"All right," said Deolda, "all right—go away." And she kept on padding up and down the room like a leopard in a cage.

Conboy beckoned my aunt out into the entry. I followed.

"What ails her?" he asked.

"I guess she thinks she sent Johnny Deutra to his grave," said my aunt.

Conboy peered in the door at Deolda. Her face looked like a yellow mask of death with her black hair hanging around her.

"God!" he said, in a whisper. "*She cares*!" I don't believe it had dawned on him before that she was anything but a wild devil.

All that day the *Anita* wasn't heard from. That night I was tired out and went to bed. But I couldn't sleep; Deolda sat staring out into the dark as she had the night before.

Next morning I was standing outside the house when one of Deolda's brothers came tearing along. It was Joe, the youngest of one-armed Manel's brood, a boy of sixteen who worked in the fish factory.

"Deolda!" he yelled. "Deolda, Johnny's all right!"

She caught him by the wrist. "Tell me what's happened!"

"The other feller—he's lost."

"*Lost*?" said Deolda, her breath drawn in sharply. "Lost—how?"

"Washed overboard," said Joe. "See—looka here. When Johnny got ashore this is what he says." He read aloud from the newspaper he had brought, a word at a time, like a grammar-school kid:

With a lame propeller and driven out of her course, the *Anita* made Plymouth this morning without her Captain, Mark Hammar. John Deutra, who brought her in, made the following statement:

"'I was lying in my bunk unable to sleep, for we were being combed by waves again and again. Suddenly I noticed we were wallowing in the trough of the sea, and went on deck to see what was wrong. I groped my way to the wheel. It swung empty. Captain Hammar was gone, washed overboard in the storm. How I made port myself I don't know—'"

Here his reading was interrupted by an awful noise—Deolda laughing, Deolda laughing and sobbing, her hands above her head, a wild thing, terrible.

"Go on," my aunt told the boy. "Go home!" And she and Deolda went into the house, her laughter filling it with awful sound.

After a time she quieted down. She stood staring out of the window, hands clenched.

"Well?" she said, defiantly. "Well?" She looked at us, and what was in her eyes made chills go down me. Triumph was what was in her eyes. Then suddenly she flung her arms around my aunt and kissed her. "Oh," she cried, "kiss me, Auntie, kiss me! He's not dead, my Johnny—not dead!"

"Go up to your room, Deolda," said my aunt, "and rest." She patted her shoulder just as though she were a little girl, for all the thoughts that were crawling around our hearts.

When later in the day Conboy came, "Where's Deolda?" he asked.

"I'll call her," I said. But Deolda wasn't anywhere; not a sign of her. She'd vanished. Conboy and Aunt Josephine looked at each other.

"She's gone to him," said Conboy.

My aunt leaned toward him and whispered, "*What do you think*?"

"Hush!" said Conboy, sternly. "*Don't think*, Josephine! *Don't speak. Don't even dream*! Don't let your mind stray. You know that crew couldn't have made port in fair weather together. The strongest man won—that's all!"

"Then you believe—" my aunt began.

"Hush!" he said, and put his hand over her mouth. Then he laughed suddenly and slapped his thigh. "God!" he said. "Deolda—Can you beat her? She's got luck—by gorry, she's got luck! You got a pen and ink?"

"What for?" said my aunt.

"I want to write out a weddin' present for Deolda," he said. "Wouldn't do to have her without a penny."

So he wrote out a check for her. And then in two months old Conboy died and left every other cent to Deolda. You might have imagined him sardonic and grinning over it, looking across at Deolda's luck from the other side of the grave.

But what had happened wasn't luck. I knew that she had sent her Johnny out informed with her own terrible courage. A weaker woman could have kept him back. A weaker woman would have had remorse. But Deolda had the courage to hold what she had taken, and maybe this courage of hers is the very heart of romance.

I looked at her, stately, monumental, and I wondered if she ever thinks of that night when the wallow of the sea claimed Mark Hammar instead of Johnny Deutra. But there's one thing I'm sure of, and that is, if she does think of it the old look of triumph comes over her face.

▶扩展阅读

1. Garrison，D. *Mary Heaton Vorse：The Life of an American Insurgent*. Philadelphia：Texas University Press，1989.

2. Glenn，D. "Bohemian Rhapsodies：Mary Heaton Vorse's Labor Reportage". *Columbia Journalism Review*，2007.

3. Vorse，M. H. *A Footnote to Folly：Reminiscences of Mary Heaton Vorse*. New York：Farrar & Rinehart，1935.

4. Garrison，D. *Rebel Pen：The Writings of Mary Heaton Vorse*. New York：Monthly Review Press，1985.

5. Vorse，M. H. *The Autobiography of an Elderly Woman*. Boston：Houghton Mifflin Company，2007.

▶学习参考网站

1. http：//www.marxists.org/subject/women/authors/vorse/index.html

2. http：//www.spartacus.schoolnet.co.uk/USAvorse.htm

【芮渝萍　编注】

25. Ernest Hemingway:
The Old Man and the Sea

欧内斯特·海明威(Ernest Hemingway,1899—1961),美国小说家,早期为"迷惘的一代"的代表人物,1899 年出生在伊利诺伊州的芝加哥西部郊区橡树林镇。父亲是内科医生,母亲是多才多艺的音乐人。他是家里六个孩子中的老二。海明威从小跟随喜爱户外运动的父亲郊游、露营、钓鱼、捕猎。高中时期的海明威酷爱体育运动,成绩出色,常常给校报撰写稿件,还在校刊上发表诗歌和短篇小说。高中毕业后,在叔叔的帮助下他成为堪萨斯市一家报纸的新闻记者,虽然在此只工作了六个月,但这段经历对他的写作影响深远,新闻报道要求的简洁文风成为海明威作品的一大特色。第一次世界大战期间,他作为志愿者奔赴意大利,参加了红十字救护车队。他在前线受了重伤,受到了意大利政府的嘉奖。

海明威住院康复期间与一位美国护士产生恋情,这段经历反映在他的小说《永别了,武器》(*A Farewell to Arms*,1929)中。回到美国后,他为美国和加拿大的报纸写报道。1921 年海明威侨居巴黎,在那里他和格特鲁德·斯坦因(Gertrude Stein)、司各特·菲茨杰拉德(Scott Fitzgerald)等文人交往密切,被斯坦因称为"迷惘的一代"的一员。《太阳照常升起》(*The Sun Also Rises*,1926)是对这段侨居生活的写照。西班牙内战时期,他作为战地记者报道战事,并以这次战争为背景创作了《丧钟为谁而鸣》(*For Whom the Bell Tolls*,1940)。海明威喜欢旅行,他的足迹遍布北美、南美、欧洲、非洲等很多国家和地区,因此他的小说背景很多都不在美国。由于喜爱运动,他作品中不乏身强力壮的斗牛士、猎人、士兵等刚性十足的男子汉形象。海明威晚年因精神躁郁症等疾病自杀身亡。

海明威的文风具有鲜明的个性特色:句式明了、对话丰富、细节真实、措辞朴实无华,作品寓意深刻。海明威声称自己遵循"冰山原理"创作,即冰山八分之七隐没在水下,只有八分之一部分浮现在水面。

《老人与海》(*The Old Man and the Sea*,1952)是海明威后期创作中的杰作。故事发生在古巴哈瓦那的一个渔村。一位名叫圣地亚哥的老人出海 84 天没有捕到一条鱼,有人嘲笑他,有人同情他,而他的小徒弟马诺林则尽力帮助和安慰这位孤独不幸的老人。小徒弟的父亲认为老人开始背运,因此命令儿子跟别的船出海。但小徒弟却像他的师父一样,对别人的帮助带着一颗感恩的心,他每天都去海边迎接老人,帮他收拾渔具,给他鼓励和力所能及的帮助。老人也以坚定的信念坦然面对暂时的失利。第 85 天,他独自进入墨西哥湾深海处,一条巨大的马林鱼咬住了鱼钩，它拖着老人的小船游动了两天两夜。第三天老人和马林鱼都精疲力竭，老人把鱼拖到了船边，刺死了这条鱼。由于鱼太大，老人只能把它固定在船边。在返回的路上，马林鱼的血引来了众多鲨鱼，老人不得不跟鲨鱼进行搏斗，驱赶那些紧追不舍的鲨鱼。待老人回到岸边时，马林鱼已经被咬得只剩下骨架。该小说展示了这位饱经沧桑的老人对生活的态度。他贫穷但不卑贱，举止沉稳而优雅，苍老的身躯蕴藏着劳动者坚忍的力量。虽然长时间不走运，但是他仍以淡定的心态对待他人的议论，他相信自己还能捕到大鱼，相信自己的捕鱼经验和能力。他用行动和精神演绎了什么是真正的骄傲，什么是真正的失败。这部小说中的一句名言是"一个人可以被摧毁，但不能被打败"。评论者经常以此为例，阐释海明威作品中的硬汉子形象和"海明威式英雄"的精髓。不过，在古巴老人圣地亚哥的眼中，人与大海的关系并不是自然主义小说中的那种敌对关系，而是休戚相关、生死与共的和谐关系。《老人与海》蕴涵着深刻的海洋生态意识。

以下段落为《老人与海》的开头，它表现了圣地亚哥与徒弟马诺林之间的信任与友谊。男孩虽然不得不服从父亲，但他的言行表明他已经成长为一名善良、懂事、能干的青年。老人也多次表示在他眼里他已经是平等的伙伴，并让他做"两个渔夫之间"的事。他俩能像知心朋友一样讨论出海捕鱼。这部中篇小说是海明威最后创作的一部小说，曾获得普利策奖（The Pulitzer Prizes）。1954 年海明威被授予诺贝尔文学奖，这部中篇小说所起的作用功不可没。

He was an old man who fished alone in a skiff in the Gulf Stream and he had gone eighty-four days now without taking a fish. In the first forty days a boy had been with him. But after forty days without a fish the boy's parents had told him that the old man was now definitely and finally salao[①], which is the worst form of unlucky，and the boy had gone at their orders in another boat which caught three good fish the first week. It made the boy sad to see the old man come in each day with his skiff empty and he always went down to help him carry either the coiled lines or the gaff and harpoon and the sail that was furled around the mast. The sail was patched with flour sacks and，furled，it looked like the flag of permanent defeat.

The old man was thin and gaunt with deep wrinkles in the back of his neck. The brown blotches of the benevolent skin cancer the sun brings from its reflection on the tropic sea were on his cheeks. The blotches ran well down the sides of his face and his hands had the deep-creased scars from handling heavy fish on the cords. But none of these scars were fresh. They were as old as erosions in a fishless desert.

Everything about him was old except his eyes and they were the same color as the sea and were cheerful and undefeated.

---

① salao：〈西〉不幸。

"Santiago," the boy said to him as they climbed the bank from where the skiff was hauled up. "I could go with you again. We've made some money."

The old man had taught the boy to fish and the boy loved him.

"No," the old man said. "You're with a lucky boat. Stay with them."

"But remember how you went eighty-seven days without fish and then we caught big ones every day for three weeks."

"I remember," the old man said. "I know you did not leave me because you doubted."

"It was papa made me leave. I am a boy and I must obey him."

"I know," the old man said. "It is quite normal."

"He hasn't much faith."

"No," the old man said. "But we have. Haven't we?"

"Yes," the boy said. "Can I offer you a beer on the Terrace and then we'll take the stuff home."

"Why not?" the old man said. "Between fishermen."

They sat on the Terrace and many of the fishermen made fun of the old man and he was not angry. Others, of the older fishermen, looked at him and were sad. But they did not show it and they spoke politely about the current and the depths they had drifted their lines at and the steady good weather and of what they had seen. The successful fishermen of that day were already in and had butchered their marlin out and carried them laid full length across two planks, with two men staggering at the end of each plank, to the fish house where they waited for the ice truck to carry them to the market in Havana. Those who had caught sharks had taken them to the shark factory on the other side of the cove where they were hoisted on a block and tackle, their livers removed, their fins cut off and their hides skinned out and their flesh cut into strips for salting.

When the wind was in the east a smell came across the harbour from the shark factory; but today there was only the faint edge of the odour because the wind had backed into the north and then dropped off and it was pleasant and sunny on the Terrace.

"Santiago," the boy said.

"Yes," the old man said. He was holding his glass and thinking of many years ago.

"Can I go out to get sardines for you for tomorrow?"

"No. Go and play baseball. I can still row and Rogelio will throw the net."

"I would like to go. If I cannot fish with you, I would like to serve in some way."

"You bought me a beer," the old man said. "You are already a man."

"How old was I when you first took me in a boat?"

"Five and you nearly were killed when I brought the fish in too green and he nearly tore the boat to pieces. Can you remember?"

"I can remember the tail slapping and banging and the thwart breaking and the noise of the clubbing. I can remember you throwing me into the bow where the wet coiled lines were and feeling the whole boat shiver and the noise of you clubbing him like chopping a tree down and the sweet blood smell all over me."

"Can you really remember that or did I just tell it to you?"

"I remember everything from when we first went together."

The old man looked at him with his sun-burned, confident loving eyes.

"If you were my boy I'd take you out and gamble," he said. "But you are your father's and your mother's and you are in a lucky boat."

"May I get the sardines? I know where I can get four baits too."

"I have mine left from today. I put them in salt in the box."

"Let me get four fresh ones."

"One," the old man said. His hope and his confidence had never gone. But now they were freshening as when the breeze rises.

"Two," the boy said.

"Two," the old man agreed. "You didn't steal them?"

"I would," the boy said. "But I bought these."

"Thank you," the old man said. He was too simple to wonder when he had attained humility. But he knew he had attained it and he knew it was not disgraceful and it carried no loss of true pride.

"Tomorrow is going to be a good day with this current," he said.

"Where are you going?" the boy asked.

"Far out to come in when the wind shifts. I want to be out before it is light."

"I'll try to get him to work far out," the boy said. "Then if you hook something truly big we can come to your aid."

"He does not like to work too far out."

"No," the boy said. "But I will see something that he cannot see such as a bird working and get him to come out after dolphin."

"Are his eyes that bad?"

"He is almost blind."

"It is strange," the old man said. "He never went turtleing. That is what kills the eyes."

"But you went turtleing for years off the Mosquito Coast and your eyes are good."

"I am a strange old man."

"But are you strong enough now for a truly big fish?"

"I think so. And there are many tricks."

"Let us take the stuff home," the boy said. "So I can get the cast net and go after the sardines."

They picked up the gear from the boat. The old man carried the mast on his shoulder and the boy carried the wooden boat with the coiled, hard-braided brown lines, the gaff and the harpoon with its shaft. The box with the baits was under the stern of the skiff along with the club that was used to subdue the big fish when they were brought alongside. No one would steal from the old man but it was better to take the sail and the heavy lines home as the dew was bad for them and, though he was quite sure no local people would steal from him, the old man thought that a gaff and a harpoon were needless temptations to leave in a boat.

They walked up the road together to the old man's shack and went in through its open door. The old man leaned the mast with its wrapped sail against the wall and the boy put the box and the other gear beside it. The mast was nearly as long as the one room of the shack. The shack was made of the tough budshields of the royal palm which are called guano and in it there was a bed, a table, one chair, and a place on the dirt floor to cook with charcoal. On the brown walls of the flattened, overlapping leaves of the sturdy fibered guano there was a picture in color of the Sacred Heart of Jesus and another of the Virgin of Cobre①. These were relics of his wife. Once there had been a tinted photograph of his wife on the wall but he had taken it down because it made him too lonely to see it and it was on the shelf in the corner under his clean shirt.

"What do you have to eat?" the boy asked.

"A pot of yellow rice with fish. Do you want some?"

"No. I will eat at home. Do you want me to make the fire?"

"No. I will make it later on. Or I may eat the rice cold."

"May I take the cast net?"

"Of course."

There was no cast net and the boy remembered when they had sold it. But they went through this fiction every day. There was no pot of yellow rice and fish and the boy knew this too.

"Eighty-five is a lucky number," the old man said. "How would you like to see me bring one in that dressed out over a thousand pounds?"

"I'll get the cast net and go for sardines. Will you sit in the sun in the doorway?"

"Yes. I have yesterday's paper and I will read the baseball."

The boy did not know whether yesterday's paper was a fiction too. But the old man

---

① Virgin of Cobre: The patroness of Cuba,亦被称为"Our Lady of Charity of El Cobre",即古巴的守护神。

brought it out from under the bed.

"Perico gave it to me at the bodega," he explained. "I'll be back when I have the sardines. I'll keep yours and mine together on ice and we can share them in the morning. When I come back you can tell me about the baseball."

"The Yankees cannot lose."

"But I fear the Indians of Cleveland."

"Have faith in the Yankees my son. Think of the great DiMaggio[①]."

"I fear both the Tigers of Detroit and the Indians of Cleveland."

"Be careful or you will fear even the Reds of Cincinnati and the White Sax of Chicago."

"You study it and tell me when I come back."

"Do you think we should buy a terminal of the lottery with an eighty-five? Tomorrow is the eighty-fifth day."

"We can do that," the boy said. "But what about the eighty-seven of your great record?"

"It could not happen twice. Do you think you can find an eighty-five?"

"I can order one."

"One sheet. That's two dollars and a half. Who can we borrow that from?"

"That's easy. I can always borrow two dollars and a half."

"I think perhaps I can too. But I try not to borrow. First you borrow. Then you beg."

"Keep warm old man," the boy said. "Remember we are in September."

"The month when the great fish come," the old man said. "Anyone can be a fisherman in May."

"I go now for the sardines," the boy said.

When the boy came back the old man was asleep in the chair and the sun was down.

The boy took the old army blanket off the bed and spread it over the back of the chair and over the old man's shoulders. They were strange shoulders, still powerful although very old, and the neck was still strong too and the creases did not show so much when the old man was asleep and his head fallen forward. His shirt had been patched so many times that it was like the sail and the patches were faded to many different shades by the sun. The old man's head was very old though and with his eyes closed there was no life in his face. The newspaper lay across his knees and the weight of his arm held it there in the evening breeze. He was barefooted.

The boy left him there and when he came back the old man was still asleep.

---

① DiMaggio:迪马乔,即 Joseph Paul "Joe" DiMaggio(1914—1999),意大利籍美国人,棒球运动员。1955 年入选美国棒球名人堂。

"Wake up old man," the boy said and put his hand on one of the old man's knees.

The old man opened his eyes and for a moment he was coming back from a long way away. Then he smiled.

"What have you got?" he asked.

"Supper," said the boy. "We're going to have supper."

"I'm not very hungry."

"Come on and eat. You can't fish and not eat."

"I have," the old man said getting up and taking the newspaper and folding it. Then he started to fold the blanket.

"Keep the blanket around you," the boy said. "You'll not fish without eating while I'm alive."

"Then live a long time and take care of yourself," the old man said. "What are we eating?"

"Black beans and rice, fried bananas, and some stew."

The boy had brought them in a two-decker metal container from the Terrace. The two sets of knives and forks and spoons were in his pocket with a paper napkin wrapped around each set.

"Who gave this to you?"

"Martin. The owner."

"I must thank him."

"I thanked him already," the boy said. "You don't need to thank him."

"I'll give him the belly meat of a big fish," the old man said. "Has he done this for us more than once?"

"I think so."

"I must give him something more than the belly meat then. He is very thoughtful for us."

"He sent two beers."

"I like the beer in cans best."

"I know. But this is in bottles, Hatuey beer, and I take back the bottles."

"That's very kind of you," the old man said. "Should we eat?"

"I've been asking you to," the boy told him gently. "I have not wished to open the container until you were ready."

"I'm ready now," the old man said. "I only needed time to wash."

Where did you wash? the boy thought. The village water supply was two streets down the road. I must have water here for him, the boy thought, and soap and a good towel.

Why am I so thoughtless? I must get him another shirt and a jacket for the winter and some sort of shoes and another blanket.

"Your stew is excellent," the old man said.

"Tell me about the baseball," the boy asked him.

"In the American League it is the Yankees as I said," the old man said happily."

"They lost today," the boy told him.

"That means nothing. The great DiMaggio is himself again."

"They have other men on the team."

"Naturally. But he makes the difference. In the other league, between Brooklyn and Philadelphia I must take Brooklyn. But then I think of Dick Sisler[①] and those great drives in the old park."

"There was nothing ever like them. He hits the longest ball I have ever seen."

"Do you remember when he used to come to the Terrace?"

"I wanted to take him fishing but I was too timid to ask him. Then I asked you to ask him and you were too timid."

"I know. It was a great mistake. He might have gone with us. Then we would have that for all of our lives."

"I would like to take the great DiMaggio fishing," the old man said. "They say his father was a fisherman. Maybe he was as poor as we are and would understand."

"The great Sisler's father was never poor and he, the father, was playing in the Big Leagues when he was my age."

"When I was your age I was before the mast on a square rigged ship that ran to Africa and I have seen lions on the beaches in the evening."

"I know. You told me."

"Should we talk about Africa or about baseball?"

"Baseball I think," the boy said. "Tell me about the great John J. McGraw." He said Jota for J.

"He used to come to the Terrace sometimes too in the older days. But he was rough and harsh-spoken and difficult when he was drinking. His mind was on horses as well as baseball. At least he carried lists of horses at all times in his pocket and frequently spoke the names of horses on the telephone."

"He was a great manager," the boy said. "My father thinks he was the greatest."

"Because he came here the most times," the old man said. "If Durocher had continued to come here each year your father would think him the greatest manager."

---

① Sisler：西斯勒（Richard Alan Sisler，1920—1998），美国运动员，教练员，美国职业棒球联盟经理。Dick 为其绰号。

"Who is the greatest manager, really, Luque or Mike Gonzalez?"

"I think they are equal."

"And the best fisherman is you."

"No. I know others better."

"Que Va[①]," the boy said. "There are many good fishermen and some great ones. But there is only you."

"Thank you. You make me happy. I hope no fish will come along so great that he will prove us wrong."

"There is no such fish if you are still strong as you say."

"I may not be as strong as I think," the old man said. "But I know many tricks and I have resolution."

"You ought to go to bed now so that you will be fresh in the morning. I will take the things back to the Terrace."

"Good night then. I will wake you in the morning."

"You're my alarm clock," the boy said.

"Age is my alarm clock," the old man said. "Why do old men wake so early? Is it to have one longer day?"

"I don't know," the boy said. "All I know is that young boys sleep late and hard."

"I can remember it," the old man said. "I'll waken you in time."

"I do not like for him to waken me. It is as though I were inferior."

"I know."

"Sleep well old man."

The boy went out. They had eaten with no light on the table and the old man took off his trousers and went to bed in the dark. He rolled his trousers up to make a pillow, putting the newspaper inside them. He rolled himself in the blanket and slept on the other old newspapers that covered the springs of the bed.

He was asleep in a short time and he dreamed of Africa when he was a boy and the long golden beaches and the white beaches, so white they hurt your eyes, and the high capes and the great brown mountains. He lived along that coast now every night and in his dreams he heard the surf roar and saw the native boats come riding through it. He smelled the tar and oakum of the deck as he slept and he smelled the smell of Africa that the land breeze brought at morning.

Usually when he smelled the land breeze he woke up and dressed to go and wake the boy. But tonight the smell of the land breeze came very early and he knew it was too early in

---

① Que Va: 〈西〉一点也不,别客气。

his dream and went on dreaming to see the white peaks of the Islands rising from the sea and then he dreamed of the different harbours and roadsteads of the Canary Islands.

He no longer dreamed of storms, nor of women, nor of great occurrences, nor of great fish, nor fights, nor contests of strength, nor of his wife. He only dreamed of places now and of the lions on the beach. They played like young cats in the dusk and he loved them as he loved the boy. He never dreamed about the boy. He simply woke, looked out the open door at the moon and unrolled his trousers and put them on. He urinated outside the shack and then went up the road to wake the boy. He was shivering with the morning cold. But he knew he would shiver himself warm and that soon he would be rowing.

The door of the house where the boy lived was unlocked and he opened it and walked in quietly with his bare feet. The boy was asleep on a cot in the first room and the old man could see him clearly with the light that came in from the dying moon. He took hold of one foot gently and held it until the boy woke and turned and looked at him. The old man nodded and the boy took his trousers from the chair by the bed and, sitting on the bed, pulled them on.

The old man went out the door and the boy came after him. He was sleepy and the old man put his arm across his shoulders and said, "I am sorry."

"Qua Va," the boy said. "It is what a man must do."

They walked down the road to the old man's shack and all along the road, in the dark, barefoot men were moving, carrying the masts of their boats.

When they reached the old man's shack the boy took the rolls of line in the basket and the harpoon and gaff and the old man carried the mast with the furled sail on his shoulder.

"Do you want coffee?" the boy asked.

"We'll put the gear in the boat and then get some."

They had coffee from condensed milk cans at an early morning place that served fishermen.

"How did you sleep old man?" the boy asked. He was waking up now although it was still hard for him to leave his sleep.

"Very well, Manolin," the old man said. "I feel confident today."

"So do I," the boy said. "Now I must get your sardines and mine and your fresh baits. He brings our gear himself. He never wants anyone to carry anything."

"We're different," the old man said. "I let you carry things when you were five years old."

"I know it," the boy said. "I'll be right back. Have another coffee. We have credit here."

He walked off, bare-footed on the coral rocks, to the ice house where the baits were stored.

The old man drank his coffee slowly. It was all he would have all day and he knew that he should take it. For a long time now eating had bored him and he never carried a lunch. He had a bottle of water in the bow of the skiff and that was all he needed for the day.

The boy was back now with the sardines and the two baits wrapped in a newspaper and they went down the trail to the skiff, feeling the pebbled sand under their feet, and lifted the skiff and slid her into the water.

"Good luck old man."

"Good luck," the old man said. He fitted the rope lashings of the oars onto the thole pins and, leaning forward against the thrust of the blades in the water, he began to row out of the harbour in the dark. There were other boats from the other beaches going out to sea and the old man heard the dip and push of their oars even though he could not see them now the moon was below the hills.

Sometimes someone would speak in a boat. But most of the boats were silent except for the dip of the oars. They spread apart after they were out of the mouth of the harbour and each one headed for the part of the ocean where he hoped to find fish. The old man knew he was going far out and he left the smell of the land behind and rowed out into the clean early morning smell of the ocean. He saw the phosphorescence of the Gulf weed in the water as he rowed over the part of the ocean that the fishermen called the great well because there was a sudden deep of seven hundred fathoms where all sorts of fish congregated because of the swirl the current made against the steep walls of the floor of the ocean. Here there were concentrations of shrimp and bait fish and sometimes schools of squid in the deepest holes and these rose close to the surface at night where all the wandering fish fed on them.

In the dark the old man could feel the morning coming and as he rowed he heard the trembling sound as flying fish left the water and the hissing that their stiff set wings made as they soared away in the darkness. He was very fond of flying fish as they were his principal friends on the ocean. He was sorry for the birds, especially the small delicate dark terns that were always flying and looking and almost never finding, and he thought, the birds have a harder life than we do except for the robber birds and the heavy strong ones. Why did they make birds so delicate and fine as those sea swallows when the ocean can be so cruel? She is kind and very beautiful. But she can be so cruel and it comes so suddenly and such birds that fly, dipping and hunting, with their small sad voices are made too delicately for the sea.

He always thought of the sea as *la mar* which is what people call her in Spanish when they love her. Sometimes those who love her say bad things of her but they are always said as though she were a woman. Some of the younger fishermen, those who used buoys as floats for their lines and had motorboats, bought when the shark livers had brought much money, spoke of her as *el mar* which is masculine. They spoke of her as a contestant or a place or even an enemy. But the old man always thought of her as feminine and as something that gave or withheld great favours, and if she did wild or wicked things it was because she could not help them. The moon affects her as it does a woman, he thought.

He was rowing steadily and it was no effort for him since he kept well within his speed and the surface of the ocean was flat except for the occasional swirls of the current. He was letting the current do a third of the work and as it started to be light he saw he was already further out than he had hoped to be at this hour.

I worked the deep wells for a week and did nothing, he thought. Today I'll work out where the schools of bonito and albacore are and maybe there will be a big one with them.

Before it was really light he had his baits out and was drifting with the current. One bait was down forty fathoms. The second was at seventy-five and the third and fourth were down in the blue water at one hundred and one hundred and twenty-five fathoms. Each bait hung head down with the shank of the hook inside the bait fish, tied and sewed solid and all the projecting part of the hook, the curve and the point, was covered with fresh sardines. Each sardine was hooked through both eyes so that they made a half-garland on the projecting steel. There was no part of the hook that a great fish could feel which was not sweet smelling and good tasting.

The boy had given him two fresh small tunas, or albacores, which hung on the two deepest lines like plummets and, on the others, he had a big blue runner and a yellow jack that had been used before; but they were in good condition still and had the excellent sardines to give them scent and attractiveness. Each line, as thick around as a big pencil, was looped onto a green-sapped stick so that any pull or touch on the bait would make the stick dip and each line had two forty-fathom coils which could be made fast to the other spare coils so that, if it were necessary, a fish could take out over three hundred fathoms of line.

Now the man watched the dip of the three sticks over the side of the skiff and rowed gently to keep the lines straight up and down and at their proper depths. It was quite light and any moment now the sun would rise.

The sun rose thinly from the sea and the old man could see the other boats, low on the water and well in toward the shore, spread out across the current. Then the sun was brighter and the glare came on the water and then, as it rose clear, the flat sea sent it back at his eyes so that it hurt sharply and he rowed without looking into it. He looked down into the water and watched the lines that went straight down into the dark of the water. He kept them straighter than anyone did, so that at each level in the darkness of the stream there would be a bait waiting exactly where he wished it to be for any fish that swam there. Others let them drift with the current and sometimes they were at sixty fathoms when the fishermen thought they were at a hundred.

But, he thought, I keep them with precision. Only I have no luck any more. But who knows? Maybe today. Every day is a new day. It is better to be lucky. But I would rather be exact. Then when luck comes you are ready.

The sun was two hours higher now and it did not hurt his eyes so much to look into the east. There were only three boats in sight now and they showed very low and far inshore.

All my life the early sun has hurt my eyes, he thought. Yet they are still good. In the evening I can look straight into it without getting the blackness. It has more force in the evening too. But in the morning it is painful.

Just then he saw a man-of-war bird with his long black wings circling in the sky ahead of him. He made a quick drop, slanting down on his back-swept wings, and then circled again.

"He's got something," the old man said aloud. "He's not just looking."

He rowed slowly and steadily toward where the bird was circling. He did not hurry and he kept his lines straight up and down. But he crowded the current a little so that he was still fishing correctly though faster than he would have fished if he was not trying to use the bird.

The bird went higher in the air and circled again, his wings motionless. Then he dove suddenly and the old man saw flying fish spurt out of the water and sail desperately over the surface.

"Dolphin," the old man said aloud. "Big dolphin."

He shipped his oars and brought a small line from under the bow. It had a wire leader and a medium-sized hook and he baited it with one of the sardines. He let it go over the side and then made it fast to a ring bolt in the stern. Then he baited another line and left it coiled in the shade of the bow. He went back to rowing and to watching the long-winged black bird who was working, now, low over the water.

As he watched the bird dipped again slanting his wings for the dive and then swinging them wildly and ineffectually as he followed the flying fish. The old man could see the slight bulge in the water that the big dolphin raised as they followed the escaping fish.

The dolphin were cutting through the water below the flight of the fish and would be in the water, driving at speed, when the fish dropped. It is a big school of dolphin, he thought. They are widespread and the flying fish have little chance. The bird has no chance. The flying fish are too big for him and they go too fast.

He watched the flying fish burst out again and again and the ineffectual movements of the bird. That school has gotten away from me, he thought. They are moving out too fast and too far. But perhaps I will pick up a stray and perhaps my big fish is around them.

My big fish must be somewhere.

...

"If the others heard me talking out loud they would think that I am crazy," he said aloud. "But since I am not crazy, I do not care. And the rich have radios to talk to them in their boats and to bring them the baseball."

Now is no time to think of baseball, he thought. Now is the time to think of only one thing. That which I was born for. There might be a big one around that school, he thought. I picked up only a straggler from the albacore that were feeding. But they are working far out and fast. Everything that shows on the surface today travels very fast and to the north-east. Can that be the time of day? Or is it some sign of weather that I do not know?

He could not see the green of the shore now but only the tops of the blue hills that showed white as though they were snow-capped and the clouds that looked like high snow mountains above them. The sea was very dark and the light made prisms in the water. The myriad flecks of the plankton were annulled now by the high sun and it was only the great deep prisms in the blue water that the old man saw now with his lines going straight down into the water that was a mile deep.

The tuna, the fishermen called all the fish of that species tuna and only distinguished among them by their proper names when they came to sell them or to trade them for baits, were down again. The sun was hot now and the old man felt it on the back of his neck and felt the sweat trickle down his back as he rowed.

I could just drift, he thought, and sleep and put a bight of line around my toe to wake me. But today is eighty-five days and I should fish the day well.

Just then, watching his lines, he saw one of the projecting green sticks dip sharply.

"Yes," he said. "Yes," and shipped his oars without bumping the boat. He reached out for the line and held it softly between the thumb and forefinger of his right hand. He felt no strain nor weight and he held the line lightly. Then it came again. This time it was a tentative pull, not solid nor heavy, and he knew exactly what it was. One hundred fathoms down a marlin was eating the sardines that covered the point and the shank of the hook where the hand-forged hook projected from the head of the small tuna.

The old man held the line delicately, and softly, with his left hand, unleashed it from the stick. Now he could let it run through his fingers without the fish feeling any tension.

This far out, he must be huge in this month, he thought. Eat them, fish. Eat them. Please eat them.

How fresh they are and you down there six hundred feet in that cold water in the dark. Make another turn in the dark and come back and eat them.

He felt the light delicate pulling and then a harder pull when a sardine's head must have been more difficult to break from the hook. Then there was nothing.

"Come on," the old man said aloud. "Make another turn. Just smell them. Aren't they lovely? Eat them good now and then there is the tuna. Hard and cold and lovely. Don't be shy, fish. Eat them."

He waited with the line between his thumb and his finger, watching it and the other lines at the same time for the fish might have swum up or down. Then came the same delicate pulling touch again.

"He'll take it," the old man said aloud. "God help him to take it."

He did not take it though. He was gone and the old man felt nothing.

"He can't have gone," he said. "Christ knows he can't have gone. He's making a turn."

Maybe he has been hooked before and he remembers something of it.

Then he felt the gentle touch on the line and he was happy.

"It was only his turn," he said. "He'll take it."

He was happy feeling the gentle pulling and then he felt something hard and unbelievably heavy. It was the weight of the fish and he let the line slip down, down, down, unrolling off the first of the two reserve coils. As it went down, slipping lightly through the old man's fingers, he still could feel the great weight, though the pressure of his thumb and finger were almost imperceptible.

"What a fish," he said. "He has it sideways in his mouth now and he is moving off with it."

Then he will turn and swallow it, he thought. He did not say that because he knew that if you said a good thing it might not happen. He knew what a huge fish this was and he thought of him moving away in the darkness with the tuna held crosswise in his mouth.

At that moment he felt him stop moving but the weight was still there. Then the weight increased and he gave more line. He tightened the pressure of his thumb and finger for a moment and the weight increased and was going straight down.

"He's taken it," he said. "Now I'll let him eat it well."

He let the line slip through his fingers while he reached down with his left hand and made fast the free end of the two reserve coils to the loop of the two reserve coils of the next line. Now he was ready. He had three forty-fathom coils of line in reserve now, as well as the coil he was using.

"Eat it a little more," he said. "Eat it well."

Eat it so that the point of the hook goes into your heart and kills you, he thought.

Come up easy and let me put the harpoon into you. All right. Are you ready? Have you been long enough at table?

"Now!" he said aloud and struck hard with both hands, gained a yard of line and then struck again and again, swinging with each arm alternately on the cord with all the strength of his arms and the pivoted weight of his body.

Nothing happened. The fish just moved away slowly and the old man could not raise him an inch. His line was strong and made for heavy fish and he held it against his hack until it was so taut that beads of water were jumping from it. Then it began to make a slow hissing sound in the water and he still held it, bracing himself against the thwart and leaning back against the pull. The boat began to move slowly off toward the north-west.

The fish moved steadily and they travelled slowly on the calm water. The other baits were still in the water but there was nothing to be done.

"I wish I had the boy" the old man said aloud. "I'm being towed by a fish and I'm the towing bitt. I could make the line fast. But then he could break it. I must hold him all I can and give him line when he must have it. Thank God he is travelling and not going down."

What I will do if he decides to go down, I don't know. What I'll do if he sounds and dies I don't know. But I'll do something. There are plenty of things I can do.

He held the line against his back and watched its slant in the water and the skiff moving steadily to the north-west.

This will kill him, the old man thought. He can't do this forever. But four hours later the fish was still swimming steadily out to sea, towing the skiff, and the old man was still braced solidly with the line across his back.

"It was noon when I hooked him," he said. "And I have never seen him."

He had pushed his straw hat hard down on his head before he hooked the fish and it was cutting his forehead. He was thirsty too and he got down on his knees and, being careful not to jerk on the line, moved as far into the bow as he could get and reached the water bottle with one hand. He opened it and drank a little. Then he rested against the bow. He rested sitting on the un-stepped mast and sail and tried not to think but only to endure.

Then he looked behind him and saw that no land was visible. That makes no difference, he thought. I can always come in on the glow from Havana. There are two more hours before the sun sets and maybe he will come up before that. If he doesn't maybe he will come up with the moon. If he does not do that maybe he will come up with the sunrise. I have no cramps and I feel strong. It is he that has the hook in his mouth. But what a fish to pull like that. He must have his mouth shut tight on the wire. I wish I could see him. I wish I could see him only once to know what I have against me.

▶扩展阅读

1. Baker, C. *Hemingway: The Writer as Artist*. Princeton, NJ: Princeton University Press, 1972.

2. Mellow, J. R. *Hemingway: A Life Without Consequences*. New York: Houghton Mifflin, 1992.

3. Oliver, C. M. *Ernest Hemingway A to Z: The Essential Reference to the Life and Work*. New York: Checkmark, 1999.

4. Phillips，L. W. Ed. *Ernest Hemingway on Writing*. London：Grafton Books，1986.

5. Wagner-Martin，L. Ed. *A Historical Guide to Ernest Hemingway*. Oxford：Oxford University Press，2000.

▶学习参考网站

1. http：// www.timelesshemingway.com/

2. http：// www.lostgeneration.com/hrc.htm

3. http：// nobelprize.org/nobel_prizes/literature/laureates/1954/hemingway-bio.html

【芮渝萍　编注】

26. Rachel Louise Carson: The Sea Around Us

　　雷切尔·露易莎·卡森（Rachel Louise Carson，1907—1964），20 世纪美国著名的文学家、生态学家和环境保护主义者，出身于宾夕法尼亚州的一个普通农民家庭。童年的乡村生活培养了她对大自然的深厚感情。卡森中学毕业后进入宾夕法尼亚州女子学院文学系，业余时间喜爱诗歌创作。大学二年级时，她选修的生物学课程激发了她对大自然的浓厚兴趣。于是，大学三年级时她决定转系主修动物学。由于在大学表现突出，她被选为"科学俱乐部"的主席。1928 年大学毕业后，卡森进入约翰·霍普金斯大学攻读动物学，1932 年以优异成绩获得硕士学位；毕业后先后在霍普金斯大学和马里兰大学任教，并继续在马萨诸塞州的伍兹霍尔海洋生物实验室（Woods Hole Marine Biological Laboratory）攻读博士学位。1932 年她父亲去世，由于母亲需人赡养，她无力继续攻读学位，只得在渔业管理局（U.S. Bureau of Fisheries）找到一份兼职工作（后被正式聘用），以水生生物学家的身份为电台科普频道撰写文章。1941 年，她的第一部著作《在海风的下面》（*Under the Sea-Wind*）出版，该书以优美的文笔描写了海洋和海洋生物。不过，由于适逢第二次世界大战，此书未引起人们的注意。1951 年，《我们周围的海洋》（*The Sea Around Us*）一书由牛津大学出版，旋即引起轰动，并在很短的时间里就被翻译成数十种文字，卡森因此享誉世界，从此她辞去公职专门从事写作。1955 年她又出版了《海的边缘》（*The Edge of the Sea*）。这三部作品构成了她的"海洋三部曲"，奠定了卡森海洋传记作家和科普作家的地位。

　　但是，卡森最重要的作品是她的警世之作《寂静的春天》（*Silent Spring*，1962）。早在 20 世纪 40 年代，卡森和她的同事就开始关注滴滴涕（DDT）之类化学杀虫剂的滥用问题及美国政府的放任政策。卡森掌握了许多由于杀虫剂、除草剂过量使用导致野生生物濒临灭绝的证据，她撰文针对化学杀虫剂对人类和自然的危害提出警告，但她和其他一些科学家的声音受到利益集团的长期压制，相关文章几乎都被退稿，某些受到化工产品商支持的媒体还对她进行人身攻击，称她为"一个歇斯底里的女人"。于是，她决定写一本书。1962 年，《寂静的春天》在《纽约客》（*New Yorker*）上连载并很快风靡世界。这本书与她以往的作品不同，它直面社会问题，以大量有力的事实和科学依据揭露了滥用杀虫剂对生态的破坏与对人类健康的损害，抨击了技术至上主义和人类中心主义思想。著名散文家怀特（E. B. White）认为《寂静的春天》是一本"和《汤姆叔叔的小屋》一样的书——一本有助于改变潮流的书"。1963

年,卡森当选为美国艺术与文学院院士。在评价卡森时,学院主席卢·芒福德这样说:"作为一个有着伽利略和布丰一般庄重文风的科学家,她以科学的洞察和道德感情激发了我们的生命意识和自然意识,并预言了一种灾难性的可能,那就是我们目光短浅而技术性地征服自然可能毁掉我们赖以生存的资源。"

卡森曾在回忆中谈起,她儿时有两个梦想:一是观察所有与海洋有关的神奇事物,另一个是当作家。可以说,大海是卡森一生迷恋的对象。《我们周围的海洋》是卡森的成名作。这是一部叙述海洋的形成、特征及海洋生物链和海洋生态的作品。卡森以优美的文笔,描述了海洋生物从低级形态到高级形态的进化过程。她将大海看成一个有机的整体和系统,从生态整体论的角度阐述了海洋生物及其与生存环境的密切关系。从海水表面颜色的变化到海底深处地形的构造,从海洋生物的迁移到海水温度的变化和海水咸度的变化,作者笔下的海洋充满生机并呈现出整体性特征。作品语言充满诗意,叙述引人入胜。此书一经出版便好评如潮,《时代周刊》(Time)曾将其评为年度最杰出的作品,甚至有评论家将这本书称作"海的诗史"。《我们周围的海洋》获 1952 年美国国家图书奖并被拍成电影,获得奥斯卡最佳纪录片奖。

1964 年 4 月 14 日,卡森在马里兰州银泉镇(Silver Spring)因患乳腺癌去世,年仅 56 岁。临终前,她给好友多萝西·弗里曼写过一封信,表达了她对大海的眷恋之情,她说:"[我]最终归于大海——归于神圣的大洋,归于大洋里的海流,仿佛永远流动的时间之河,由始至终,由死到生。"以下选自《我们周围的海洋》的第一部分"大海母亲"(Mother Sea)的第一章和第三章,分别叙述了陆地及海洋的起源和四季变更中海洋生物的变化。

▶Chapter 1

The Grey Beginnings

And like earth was without form, and void;
and darkness was upon the face of the deep.

—GENESIS

BEGINNINGS are apt to be shadowy, and so it is with the beginnings of that great mother of life, the sea. Many people have debated how and when the earth got its ocean, and it is not surprising that their explanations do not always agree. For the plain and inescapable truth is that no one was there to see, and in the absence of eye-witness accounts there is bound to be a certain amount of disagreement. So if I tell here the story of how the young planet Earth acquired—an ocean, it must be a story pieced together from many sources and containing whole chapters the details of which we can only imagine. The story is founded on the testimony of the earth's most ancient rocks, which were young when the earth was young; on other evidence written on the face of the earth's satellite, the moon; and on hints contained in the history of the sun and the whole universe, of star-filled space. For although no man was there to witness this cosmic birth, the stars and the moon and the rocks were there, and, indeed, had much to do with the fact that there is an ocean.

The events of which I write must have occurred somewhat more than 2 billion years ago. As nearly as science can tell that is the approximate age of the earth, and the ocean must be very nearly as old. It is possible now to discover the age of the rocks that compose the crust of the earth by measuring the rate of decay of the radioactive materials. The oldest rocks found anywhere on earth—in Manitoba①—are about 2.3 billion years old. Allowing 100 million years or so for the cooling of the earth's materials to form a rocky crust, we arrive at the supposition that the tempestuous and violent events connected with our planet's birth occurred nearly two and a half billion years ago. But this is only a minimum estimate, for rocks indicating an even greater age may be found at any time.

The new earth, freshly torn from its parent sun, was a ball of whirling gases, intensely hot, rushing through the black spaces of the universe on a path and at a speed controlled by immense forces. Gradually the ball of flaming gases cooled. The gases began to liquefy, and Earth became a molten mass. The materials of this mass eventually became sorted out in a definite pattern: the heaviest in the centre, the less heavy surrounding them, and the least heavy forming the outer rim. This is the pattern which persists today—a central sphere of molten iron, very nearly as hot as it was two billion years ago, an intermediate sphere of semi-plastic basalt②, and a hard outer shell, relatively quite thin and composed of solid basalt and granite.

The outer shell of the young earth must have been a good—many millions of years changing from the liquid to the solid state, and it is believed that, before this change was completed, an event of the greatest importance took place—the formation of the moon. The next time you stand on a beach at night, watching the moon's bright path across the water, and conscious of the moon-drawn tides, remember that the moon itself may have been born of a great tidal wave of earthly substance, torn off into space. And remember that if the moon was formed in this fashion, the event may have had much to do with shaping the ocean basins and the continents as we know them.

There were tides in the new earth, long before there was an ocean. In response to the pull of the sun the molten liquids of the earth's whole surface rose in tides that rolled unhindered around the globe and only gradually slackened and diminished as the earthly shell cooled, congealed, and hardened. Those who believe that the moon is a child of earth say

① Manitoba：马尼托巴，位于加拿大中部的一个省。

② basalt：【地】玄武岩。

that during an early stage of the earth's development something happened that caused this rolling, viscid tide to gather speed and momentum and to rise to unimaginable heights. Apparently the force that created these greatest tides the earth has ever known was the force of resonance, for at this time the period of the solar tides had come to approach, then equal, the period of the free oscillation of the liquid earth. And so every sun tide was given increased momentum by the push of the earth's oscillation, and, each of the twice-daily tides was larger than the one before it. Physicists have calculated that, after 500 years of such monstrous, steadily increasing tides, those on the side towards the sun became too high for stability, and a great wave was torn away and hurled into space. But immediately, course, the newly created satellite became subject to physical laws that sent it spinning in an orbit of its own about the earth. This is what we call the moon. There are reasons for believing that this event took place after the earth's crust had become slightly hardened, instead of during its partly liquid state. There is to this day a great scar on the surface of the globe. This scar or depression holds the Pacific Ocean. According to some geophysicists, the floor of the Pacific is composed of basalt, the substance of the earth's middle layer, while all other oceans are floored with a thin layer of granite, which makes up most of the earth's outer layer. We immediately wonder what became of the Pacific's granite covering and the most convenient assumption is that it was torn away when the moon was formed. There is supporting evidence. The mean density of the moon is much less than that of the earth (3.3 compared with 5.5), suggesting that the moon took away none of the earth's heavy iron core, but that it is composed only of the granite and some of the basalt of the outer layers.

The birth of the moon probably helped shape other regions of the world ocean besides the Pacific. When part of the crust was torn away, strains must have been set up in the remaining granite envelope. Perhaps the granite mass cracked open on the side opposite the moon scar. Perhaps, as the earth spun on its axis and rushed on its orbit through space, the-cracks widened and the masses of granite began to drift apart, moving over a tarry, slowly hardening layer of basalt. Gradually the outer portions of the basalt layer became solid and the wandering continents came to rest, frozen into place with oceans between them. In spite of theories to the contrary, the weight of geologic evidence seems to be that the locations of the major ocean basins and the major continental land masses are today much the same as they have been since a very early period of the earth's history.

But this is to anticipate the story, for when the moon was "born there was no ocean. The gradually-cooling earth was enveloped in heavy layers of cloud, which contained much of the water of the new planet. For a long time its surface was so hot that no moisture could fall without immediately, being reconverted to steam. This dense, perpetually-renewed cloud covering must have been so thick that no rays of sunlight could penetrate it. And so the rough outline of the continents and the empty ocean basins were sculptured out of, the surface of the earth in darkness, in a Stygian① world of heated rock and swirling clouds and gloom.

As soon as the earth's crust cooled enough, the rains began to fall. Never have there been such rains since that time. They fell continuously, day and night, days passing into months, into years, into centuries. They poured into the waiting ocean basins, or, falling upon the continental masses, drained away to become sea.

That primeval ocean, growing in bulk as the rains slowly filled its basins, must have been only faintly salt. But the falling rains were the symbol of the dissolution of the continents. From the moment the rains began to fall, the lands began to be worn away and carried to the sea. It is an endless, inexorable process that has never stopped—the dissolving of the rocks, the leaching-out of their contained minerals, the carrying of the rock fragments and dissolved minerals to the ocean. And over the eons of time, the sea has grown ever more bitter with the salt of the continents.

In what manner the sea produced the mysterious and wonderful stuff called protoplasm② we cannot say. In its warm, dimly-lit waters the unknown conditions of temperature and pressure and saltiness must have been the critical ones for the creation of life from non-life. At any rate they produced the result that neither the alchemists with their crucibles nor modern scientists in their laboratories have been able to, achieve. Before the first living cell was created, there may have been many trials and failures. It seems probable that, within the warm saltiness of the primeval sea, certain organic substances were fashioned from carbon dioxide, sulphur, nitrogen, phosphorous, potassium, and calcium. Perhaps these were transition steps from which the complex molecules of protoplasm arose—molecules that somehow acquired the ability to reproduce themselves and begin the endless stream of life. But at present no one is wise enough to be sure.

Those first living things may have been simple micro organisms rather like some of the bacteria we know today—mysterious borderline forms that were not quite plants, not quite animals, barely, over the intangible line that separates the non-living from the living. It is doubtful that this first life possessed the substance chlorophyll, with which plants in sunlight transform lifeless chemical into the living stuff of their tissues. Little sunshine could enter their dim world, penetrating the cloud bank from which fell the endless rains. Probably the sea's first children lived on the organic substances then present in the ocean waters, or, like the iron and sulphur bacteria that exist today, lived directly on inorganic food.

All the while the cloud cover was thinning, the darkness of the nights alternated with

---

① Stygian:【希神】冥河(Styx)的,漆黑的。

② protoplasm:【生】原生质;原浆;细胞质。

palely-illumined days, and finally the sun for the first time shone through upon the sea. By this time some of the living things that floated in the sea must have developed the magic of chlorophyll. Now they were able to take the carbon dioxide of the air and the water of the sea and of these elements, in sunlight, build the organic substances they needed. So the first true plants came into being.

Another group of organisms, lacking the chlorophyll but needing organic food, found they could make a way of life for themselves by devouring the plants. So the first animals arose, and from that day to this, every animal in the world has followed the habit it learned in the ancient seas and depends, directly or through complex food chains, on the plants for food and life.

As the years passed, and the centuries, and the millions of years, die stream of life grew more and more complex. From simple, one-celled creatures, others that were aggregations of specialized cells arose, and then creatures with organs for feeding, digesting, breathing, reproducing. Sponges grew on the rocky bottom of the sea's edge and coral animals built their habitations in warm, clear waters. Jellyfish swam and drifted in the sea. Worms evolved, and starfish, and hard-shelled creatures with many-jointed legs, the arthropods. The plants, too, progressed, from the microscopic algae to branched and curiously-fruiting seaweeds that swayed with the tides and were plucked from the coastal rocks by the surf and cast adrift.

During all this time the continents had no life. There was little to induce living things to come ashore, forsaking their all-providing, all-embracing mother sea. The lands must have been bleak and hostile beyond the power of words to describe. Imagine a whole continent of naked rock, across which no covering mantle of green had been drawn—a continent without soil, for there was no land plants to aid in its formation and bind it to the rocks with their-roots. Imagine a land of stone, a silent land, except for the sound of the rains and winds that swept across it. For there was no living voice and no living thing moved over the surface of the rocks.

Meanwhile, the gradual cooling of the planet, which had first given the earth its hard granite crust, was progressing into its deeper layers; and as the interior slowly cooled and contracted, it drew away from the outer shell. This shell, accommodating itself to the shrinking sphere within it, fell into folds and wrinkles—the earth's first mountain ranges. Geologists tell us that there must have been at least two periods of mountain-building (often called "revolutions") in that dim period so long ago that the rocks have no record of it, so long ago that the mountains themselves have long since been worn away. Then there came a third great period of upheaval and readjustment of the earth's crust, about a billion years ago, but of all its majestic mountains the only reminders today are the Laurentian hills of eastern Canada, and a great shield of granite over the flat country around Hudson Bay.

The epochs of mountain building only served to speed up the processes of erosion by which the continents were worn down and their crumbling rock and contained minerals returned to the sea. The uplifted masses of the mountains were prey to the bitter cold of the upper atmosphere and under the attacks of frost and snow and ice the rocks cracked and crumbled away. The rains beat with greater violence upon the slopes of the hills and carried away the substance of the mountains in torrential streams. There was still no plant covering to modify and resist the power of the rains.

And in the sea, life continued to evolve. The earliest forms have left no fossils by which we can identify them. Probably they were soft-bodied, with no hard parts that could be preserved. Then, too, the rock layers formed in those early days have since been so altered by enormous heat and pressure, under the foldings of the earth's crust, that any fossils they might have contained would have been destroyed.

For the past 500 million years, however, the rocks have preserved the fossil record. By the dawn of the Cambrian period①, when the history of living things was first inscribed on rock pages, life in the sea had progressed so far that all the main groups of backboneless or invertebrate animals had been developed. But there were no animals with backbones, no insects or spiders, and still no plant or animal had been evolved that was capable of venturing on to the forbidding land. So for more than three-quarters of geologic time the continents were desolate and uninhabited, while the sea prepared the life that was later to invade them and make them habitable. Meanwhile, with violent tremblings of the earth and with the fire and smoke of roaring volcanoes mountains rose and wore away, glaciers moved to and fro over the earth, and the sea crept over the continents and again receded. It was not until Silurian time, some 350 million years ago, that the first pioneer of land life crept out on the shore. It was an arthropod, one of the great tribe that later produced crabs and lobsters and insects. It must have been something like a modern scorpion, but, unlike some of its descendants, it never wholly severed the ties that united it to the sea. It lived a strange life, half-terrestrial, and half-aquatic, something like that of the ghost crabs that speed along the beaches today, now and then dashing into the surf to moisten their gills.

Fish, tapered of body and stream-moulded by the press of running waters, were evolving in Silurian rivers②. In times of drought, in the drying pools and lagoons, the shortage of oxygen forced them to develop swim bladders for the storage of air. One form that possessed an air-breathing lung was able to survive the dry periods by burying itself in

---

① Cambrian period:【地】寒武纪。
② Silurian rivers:【地】志留纪(的)时期的河流。

mud, leaving a passage to the surface through which it breathed.

It is very doubtful that the animals alone would have succeeded in colonizing the land, for only the plants had the power to bring about the first amelioration of its harsh conditions. They helped make soil of the crumbling rocks, they held back the soil from the rains that would have swept it away, and little by little they softened and subdued the bare rock, the lifeless desert. We know very little about the first land plants, but they must have been closely related to some of the larger seaweeds that had learned to live in the coastal shallows, developing strengthened stems and grasping, root like holdfasts to resist the drag and pull of the waves. Perhaps it was in some coastal lowlands, periodically drained and flooded, that some such plants found it possible to survive, though separated from the sea. This also seems to have taken place in the Silurian period. The mountains that had been thrown up by the Laurentian revolution gradually wore away, and as the sediments were washed from their summits and deposited on the lowlands, great areas of the continents sank under the load. The seas crept out of their basins and spread over the lands. Life fared well and was exceedingly abundant in those shallow, sunlit seas. But with the later retreat of the ocean water into the deeper basins, many creatures must have been left stranded in shallow, land-locked bays. Some of these animals found means to survive on land. The lakes, the shores of the rivers, and the coastal swamps of those days were the testing grounds in which plants and animals either became adapted to the new conditions or perished.

As the lands rose and the seas receded a strange fish like creature emerged on the land, and over the thousands of years its fins became legs, and instead of gills it developed lungs. In the Devonian sandstone this first amphibian left its footprint.

On land and sea the stream of life poured on. New forms evolved, some old ones declined and disappeared. On land the mosses and the ferns and the seed plants developed. The reptiles for a time dominated the earth, gigantic, grotesque, and terrifying. Birds learned to live and move in the ocean of air. The first small mammals lurked inconspicuously in hidden crannies of the earth, as though in fear of the reptiles. When they went ashore the animals that took up a land life carried with them a part of the sea in their bodies, a heritage which they passed on to their children and which even today links each land animal with its origin in the ancient sea Fish, amphibian, and reptile, warm-blooded bird and mammal— each of us carries in our veins a salty stream in which the elements sodium, potassium, and calcium are combined in almost—the same proportions as in sea water. This is our inheritance from the day, untold millions of years ago, when a remote ancestors having progressed from the one-celled to the many-celled stage, first developed a circulatory system in which the fluid was merely the water of the sea. In the same way, our lime-hardened skeletons are a heritage from the calcium-rich oceans of Cambrian time. Even the protoplasm that streams within each cell of our bodies has the chemical structure impressed upon all living matter while life's first simple creatures were brought forth in the ancient sea. And as life itself began in the sea, so each of us begins his identical life in a miniature ocean within his mother's womb, and if the stages of his embryonic development, repeats the steps by which his race evolved, from gill-breathing inhabitants of a water world to creatures able to "live on land".

Some of the land animals later returned to the ocean. After perhaps 50 million years of land life, a number of reptiles entered the sea about 170 million years ago, in the Triassic period[①]. They were huge and formidable creatures. Some had oar like limbs by which they rowed through the water; some were web-footed, with long, serpentine necks. These grotesque monsters disappeared millions of years ago, but we remember them when we come upon a large sea turtle swimming many miles at sea, its barnacle-encrusted shell eloquent of its marine life. Much later, perhaps no more than 50 million years ago, some of the mammals, too, abandoned a land life for the ocean. Their descendants are the sea lions, seals, sea elephants and whales of today.

Among the land mammals there was a race of creatures that took to an arboreal existence. Their hands underwent remarkable development, becoming skilled in manipulating and examining objects, and along with this skill came a superior brain power that compensated for what these comparatively small mammals lacked in strength. At last, perhaps somewhere in the vast interior of Asia, they descended from the trees and became again terrestrial. The past million years have seen their transformation into beings with the body and brain and spirit of man.

Eventually man, too, found his way back to the sea. Standing on its shores, he must have looked but upon it with wonder and curiosity, compounded with an unconscious recognition of his lineage. He could not physically re-enter the ocean as the seals and whales had done. But over the centuries, with all the skill and ingenuity and reasoning powers of his mind, he has sought to explore and investigate even its most remote parts, so that he might re-enter it mentally and imaginatively.

He built boats to venture out on its surface. Later he found ways to descend to the shallow parts of its floor, carrying with him the air that, as a land mammal long unaccustomed to aquatic life he needed to breathe. Moving in fascination over the deep sea he could not enter, he found ways to probe its depths, he let down nets to capture its life, he invented mechanical eyes and ears that could re-create for his senses a world long lost, but a world that, in the deepest part of his subconscious mind, he had never wholly forgotten.

---

① Triassic period:【地】三叠纪[系]时期。

And yet he has returned to his mother sea only on her own terms. He cannot control or change the ocean as, in his brief tenancy of earth; he has subdued and plundered the continents. In the artificial world of his cities and towns, he often forgets the true nature of his planet and the long vistas of its history, in which the existence of the race of men has occupied a mere moment of time. The sense of all these things comes to him most clearly in the course of a long ocean voyage, when he watches day after day the receding rim of the horizon, ridged and furrowed by waves; when at night he becomes aware of the earth's rotation as the stars pass overhead; or when, alone in this world of water and sky, he feels the loneliness of his earth in space. And then, as never on land, he knows the truth that his world is a water world, a planet dominated by its covering mantle of ocean, in which the continents are but transient intrusions of land above the surface of the all encircling sea.

▶Chapter 3

The Changing Year

Thus with the year seasons return.
—MILTON

FOR the sea as a whole, the alternation of day and night, the passage of the seasons, the procession of the years, are lost in its vastness, obliterated in its own changeless eternity. But the surface waters are different. The face of the sea is always changing. Crossed by colours, lights and moving shadows, sparkling in the sun, mysterious in the twilight, its aspects and its moods vary hour by hour. The surface waters move with the tides, stir to the breath of the winds, and rise and fall to the endless, hurrying forms of the waves. Most of all, they change with the advance of the seasons. Spring moves over the temperate lands of our Northern Hemisphere in a tide of new life, of pushing green shoots and unfolding buds, all its mysteries and meanings symbolized in the northward migration of the birds, the awakening of sluggish amphibian life as the chorus of frogs rises again from the wet lands, the different sound of the wind which stirs the young leaves where a month ago it rattled the bare branches. These things we associate with the land, and it is easy to suppose that at sea there could be no such feeling of advancing spring. But the signs are there, and seen with understanding eye, they bring the same magical sense of awakening.

In the sea, as on land, spring is a time for the renewal of life. During the long months of winter in the temperate zones the surface waters have been absorbing the cold. Now the heavy water begins to sink, slipping down and displacing the warmer layers below. Rich stores of minerals have been accumulating on the floor of the continental shelf—some freighted down the rivers from the lands; some derived from sea creatures that have died and whose remains have drifted down to the bottom; some from the shells that once encased a diatom, the streaming protoplasm of a radiolarian, or the transparent tissues of a pteropod①. Nothing is wasted in the sea; every particle of material is used over and over again, first by one creature, then by another. And when in spring the waters are deeply stirred, the warm bottom water brings to the surf are a rich supply of minerals, ready for use by new forms of life.

Just as land plants depend on minerals in the soil for their growth, every marine plant, even the smallest, is dependent upon the nutrient salts or minerals in the sea water. Diatoms must have silica, the element of which their fragile shells are fashioned. For these and all other micro plants, phosphorous is an indispensable mineral. Some of these elements are in short supply and in winter may be reduced below the minimum necessary for growth. The diatom population must tide itself over this season as best it can. It faces a stark problem of survival, with no opportunity to increase, a problem of keeping alive the spark of life by forming tough protective spores against the stringency of winter, a matter of existing in a dormant state in which no demands shall be made on an environment that already withholds all but the most meager necessities of life. So the diatom holds their place in the winter sea, like seeds of wheat in a field under snow and ice, the seeds from which the spring growth will come.

These, then, are the elements of the vernal blooming of the sea: the "seeds" of the dormant plants, the fertilizing chemicals, the warmth of the spring sun. In a sudden awakening, incredible in its swiftness, the simplest plants of the sea begin to multiply. Their increase is of astronomical proportions. The spring sea belongs at first to the diatoms and to all the other microscopic plant life of the plankton. In the fierce intensity of their growth they cover vast areas of ocean with a living blanket of their cells. Mile after mile of water may appear red or brown or green, the whole surface taking on the colour of the infinitesimal grains of pigment contained in each of the plant cells. The plants have undisputed sway in the sea for only a short time. Almost at once their own burst of multiplication is matched by a similar increase in the small animals of the plankton. It is the spawning, time of the copepod and the glass worm, the pelagic shrimp and the winged snail. Hungry swarms of these little beasts of the plankton roam through the waters, feeding on the abundant plants and themselves falling prey to larger creatures. Now in the spring the surface waters become a vast nursery. From the hills and valleys of the continent's edge lying far below, and from the scattered shoals, and banks, the eggs or young of many of the

① pteropod:翼足目软体动物。

bottom animals rise to the surface of the sea. Even those which, in their maturity, will sink down to sedentary life on the bottom, spend the first weeks of life as freely swimming hunters of the plankton. So as spring progresses new batches of larval rise into the surface each day, the young of fishes and crabs and mussels and tube worms, mingling for a time with the regular members of the plankton.

Under the steady and voracious grazing, the grasslands of the surface are soon depleted. The diatoms become more arid more scarce, and with them the other simple plants. Still there are brief explosions of one or another form, when in a sudden orgy of cell division it comes to claim whole areas of the sea for its own. So, for a time each spring, the waters may become blotched with brown, jelly-like masses, and the fishermen's nets come up dripping a brown slime and containing no fish, for the herring have turned away from these waters as though in loathing of the viscid, foul-smelling algae. But in less time than passes between the full moon and the new, the spring flowering of Phaeocystis[①] is past and the waters have cleared again.

In the spring the sea is filled with migrating fishes, some of them bound for the mouths of great rivers, which they will, ascend to deposit their spawn. Such are the spring-run Chinooks[②] coming in from the deep Pacific feeding grounds to breast the rolling flood of the Columbia, the shad moving into the Chesapeake and the Hudson and the Connecticut, the alewives seeking a hundred coastal streams of New England, the salmon feeling their way to the Penobscot and the Kennebec. For months or years these fish have known only the vast spaces of the ocean. Now the spring sea and the maturing of their own bodies lead them back to the rivers of their birth.

Other mysterious comings and goings are linked with the advance of the year. Capelin gather in the deep, cold water of the Barents Sea, their shoals followed and preyed upon by flocks of auks, fulmars, and kittiwakes. Cod approach the banks of Lofoten, and gather off the shores of Iceland. Birds whose winter feeding territory may have encompassed the whole Atlantic or the whole Pacific converge upon some small island, the entire breeding population arriving within the space of a few days. Whales suddenly appear off the slopes of the coastal banks where the swarms of shrimp like krill are spawning, the whales having come from no one knows where, by no one knows what route.

With the subsiding of the diatoms and the completed spawning of many of the plankton animals and most of the fish, life in the surface waters slackens to the slower pace of midsummer. Along the meeting places of the currents the pale moon jelly Aurelia[③] gathers in

---

① Phaeocystis：棕囊藻。
② Chinooks：奇努克风（chinook wind），指春秋两季从海上吹向美国西北部海岸和加拿大西南海岸的湿暖西南风。
③ jelly Aurelia：海月水母。

thousands, forming sinuous lines or windrows across miles of sea, and the birds see their pale form shimmering deep down in the green water. By midsummer the large red jellyfish Cyanea① may have grown from the size of a thimble to that of an umbrella. The great jellyfish moves through the sea with rhythmic pulsations, trailing long tentacles and as likely as not shepherding a little group of young cod or haddock, which find shelter under its bell and travel with it.

A hard brilliant, coruscating phosphorescence often illuminates the summer sea. In waters where the protozoan Noctiluca② is abundant it is the chief source of this summer luminescence, causing fishes, squibs, or dolphins to fill the water with racing flames and to clothe themselves in a ghostly radiance. Or again the summer sea may glitter with a thousand-thousand moving pinpricks of light, like an immense swarm of fireflies moving through a dark wood. Such an effort is produced by a shoal of the brilliantly phosphorescent shrimp Meganyctiphanes③, a creature of cold and darkness and of the places where icy water rolls upward from the depths and bubbles with white ripplings at the surface.

Out over the plankton meadows of the North Atlantic the dry twitter of the phalaropes, small brown birds, wheeling and turning, dipping and rising, is heard for the first time since early spring. The phalaropes have nested on the arctic tundra's, reared their young, and now the first of them are returning to die sea. Most of them will continue south over the open water far from land, crossing the Equator into the South Atlantic. Here they will follow where the great whales lead, for where the whales are there also are the swarms of plankton on which these strange little birds grow fat.

As the fall advances, there are other movements, some in the surface, some hidden in the green depths that betoken—the end of summer. In the fog-covered waters of Bering Sea, down through the treacherous passes between the islands of—the Aleutian chain and southward into the open Pacific, the herds of fur seals are moving. Left behind are two small islands, treeless bits of volcanic soil thrust up into the waters: of Bering Sea. The islands are silent now, but for the several, months of summer they resounded with the roar of millions, of seals come ashore to bear and rear their young — all the fur seals of the eastern Pacific crowded into a few square miles of bare rock and crumbling soil. Now once more the seals turn south, to roam down along the sheer underwater cliffs of the continent's edge, where the rocky foundations fall away steeply into the deep sea. Here, in a blackness more absolute than that of arctic winter, the seals will find rich feeding as they swim down to prey

---

① jellyfish Cyanea：霞水母。
② the protozoan Noctiluca：原生夜光虫。
③ Meganyctiphane：大夜光虾。

on the fishes of this region of darkness.

Autumn comes to the sea with a fresh blaze of phosphorescence, when every wave crest is aflame. Here and there the whole surface may glow with sheets of cold fire, while below-schools of fish pour through the water like molten metal. Often the autumnal phosphorescence is caused by a fall flowering of the dinoflagellates, multiplying furiously in a short-lived repetition of their vernal blooming.

Sometimes the meaning of the glowing water is ominous. Off the Pacific coast of North America, it may mean that the sea is filled with the dinoflagellate Gonyaulax[①]—a minute plant that contains a poison of strange and terrible virulence. About four days after Gonyaulax comes to dominate the coastal plankton, some of the fishes and shellfish in the vicinity become toxic. This is because, in their normal feeding, they have strained the poisonous plankton out of the water. Mussels accumulate the Gonyaulax toxins in their livers, and the toxins react on the human nervous system with an effect similar to that of strychnine[②]. Because of these facts, it is generally understood along the Pacific coast that it is unwise to eat shellfish taken from coasts exposed to the open sea where Gonyaulax may be abundant, in summer or early fall. For generations before the white men came, the Indians knew this. As soon as the red streaks appeared in the sea and the waves began, to flicker at night with the mysterious blue-green fires, the tribal leaders forbade the taking of mussels until these warning signals should have passed. They even set guards at intervals along the beaches to warn inlanders who might come down for shellfish and be unable to read the language of the sea.

But usually the blaze and glitter of the sea, whatever it's meaning for those who produce it, implies no menace to man. Seen from the deck of a vessel in open ocean, a tiny, man-made observation point in the vast world of sea and sky, it has an eerie and unearthly quality. Man, in his vanity, subconsciously attributes a human origin to any light not of moon or stars or sun. Lights on the shore, lights moving over the water, mean lights kindled and controlled by other men, serving purposes understandable to the human mind. Yet here are lights that flash and fade away, lights that come and go for reasons meaningless to man, lights that have been doing this very thing over the eons of time in which there were no men to stir in vague disquiet.

On such a night of phosphorescent display Charles Darwin stood on the deck of the Beagle as she ploughed southward through the Atlantic off the coast of Brazil.

---

① the dinoflagellate Gonyaulax：膝沟藻属的腰鞭毛虫。
② strychnine：【药】士的宁（马钱子碱），一种中枢兴奋药物，乃国际奥委会禁用的中枢神经系统兴奋剂。

The sea from its extreme luminousness presented a wonderful and most beautiful appearance [he wrote in his diary]. Every part of the water which by day is seen as foam glowed with a pale light. The vessel drove before her bows two billows of liquid phosphorous, and in her wake was a milky train. As far as the eye reached the crest of every wave was bright; and from the reflected light, the sky just above the horizon was not so utterly dark as the rest of the Heavens. It was impossible to behold this plain of matter, as it were melted and consumed by heat, without being reminded of Milton's description of the regions of Chaos and Anarchy.①

Like the blazing colours of the autumn leaves before they wither and fall, the autumnal phosphorescence betokens the approach of whiter. After their brief renewal of life the flagellates and the other minute algae dwindle away to a scattered few; so do the shrimps and the copepods, the glass-worms and the comb jellies. The larvae of the bottom fauna have long since completed their development and drifted away to take up whatever existence is their lot. Even the roving fish schools have deserted the surface waters and have migrated into warmer latitudes or have found equivalent warmth in the deep, quiet waters along the edge of the continental shelf. There the torpor of semi-hibernation descends upon them and will possess them during the months of winter.

The surface waters now become the plaything of the winter gales. As the winds build up the giant storm waves and roar along their crests, lashing the water into foam and flying spray, it seems that life must forever have deserted this place. For the mood of the winter sea, read Joseph Conrad's description:

The greyness of the whole immense surface, the wind furrows upon the faces of the waves, the great masses of foam, tossed about and waving, like matted white locks, give to the sea in a gale an appearance of hoary age, lustreless, dull, without gleams, as though it had been created before light itself.②

But the symbols of hope are not lacking even in the greyness and bleakness of the winter sea. On land we know that the apparent lifelessness of winter is an illusion. Look closely at the bare branches of a tree, on which not the palest gleam of green can be discerned. Yet, spaced along each branch are the leaf buds, all the spring's magic of swelling green concealed and safely preserved under the insulating, overlapping layers. Pick off a piece of the rough bark of the trunk; there you will find hibernating insects. Dig down

---

① 选自《查尔斯·达尔文在英国皇家船舰"比格尔"号上的航行日记》,诺拉·巴洛主编,剑桥大学出版社,1934 年,第 107 页——原注。

② 选自康拉德:《大海如镜》,达博岱-佩奇出版社,1925 年肯特版,第 71 页——原注。

through the snow into the earth. There are the eggs of next summer's grasshoppers; there are the dormant seeds from which will come the grass, the herb, the oak tree.

So, too, the lifelessness, the hopelessness, the despair of the winter sea are an illusion. Everywhere are the assurances that the cycle has come to the full, containing the means of its own renewal. There is the promise of a new spring in the very iciness of the winter sea, in the chilling of the water, which must, before many weeks, become so heavy that it will plunge downward, precipitating the overturn that is the first act in the drama of spring. There is the promise of new life in the small plant like things that cling to the rocks of the underlying bottom, the almost formless polyps from which, in spring, a new generation of jellyfish will bud off and rise into the surface waters. There is unconscious purpose in the sluggish forms of the copepods hibernating on the bottom, safe from the surface storms, life sustained in then-tiny bodies by the extra store of fat with which they went into this winter sleep.

Already, from the grey shapes of cod that have moved, unseen by man, through the cold sea to their spawning places, the glassy globules of eggs are rising into the surface waters. Even in the harsh world of the winter sea, these eggs will begin the swift divisions by which a granule of protoplasm becomes a living fishlet[①].

Most of all, perhaps, there is assurance in the fine dust of life that remains in the surface waters, the invisible spores of the diatoms, needing only the touch of warming sun and fertilizing chemicals to repeat the magic of spring.

▶扩展阅读

1. Brooks, P. *The House of Life: Rachel Carson at Work*. Boston: Houghton Mifflin, 1972.

2. Carson, R. L. *Silent Spring*, New York: Mariner Books, 2002.

3. Carson, R. L. *The Sea Around Us*, Oxford: Oxford University Press, 1991.

4. Carson, R. L. *The Edge of the Sea*, New York: Mariner Books, 1998.

5. Lear, L. *Rachel Carson: Witness for Nature*. New York: Henry Holt, 1997.

6. Quaratiello, A. *Rachel Carson: A Biography*. New York: Amherst, 2010.

▶学习参考网站

1. http://en.wikipedia.org/wiki/Rachel_Carson

2. http://earthday.wilderness.org/hero/carson.pdf

3. http://www.bookrags.com/research/rachel-louise-carson-1907-1964-amer-enve-01/

【王松林　编注】

---

① fishlet: 小鱼。

27. David Hays & Daniel Hays: *My Old Man and the Sea*

　　大卫·海斯(David Hays,1930),是闻名于世的舞台设计大师。他于 1967 年创建了美国国家盲人剧院,是该剧院的首位艺术总监,担任此职长达 29 年。他让盲人的手势语成为一种聚光灯下的艺术,赢得世人瞩目。他长期在英国和美国从事戏剧工作,获得多所大学的荣誉博士学位。《主体聚光:导演与演员舞台灯光指导》(*Light on the Subject*:*Stage Lighting for Directors and Actors-and the Rest of Us*,1989)是他撰写的一部关于舞台灯光布局及效果的专著。1999 年他获得哈佛大学颁发的杰出校友的哈佛艺术勋章,成为第五位获得此项荣誉的人。在他之前获得此勋章的杰出人物有著名作家约翰·厄普代克(John Updike,1998)、摇滚女歌手邦妮·瑞特(Bonnie Raitt,1997)、民谣歌手皮特·西格(Pete Seeger,1996)和电影明星杰克·莱蒙(Jack Lemmon,1995)。《今天我是一个男孩》(*Today I Am a Boy*,2000)讲述了 67 岁的大卫回归犹太教的心路历程。

　　丹尼尔·海斯(Daniel Hays,1960),是大卫·海斯的儿子,在爱达荷州从事问题青年野外生存监督工作,擅长跆拳道,获得环境科学硕士学位,持有船长执照。他跟父亲共同创作了畅销回忆录《我的老爸与海》(*My Old Man and the Sea*,1995)。这部回忆录穿插了父子俩的叙事和两人撰写的一些航海日志,记载了两人一起穿越合恩角的冒险历程。他们航行的船只是两人共同建造的只有 25 英尺长的帆船。他们从康涅狄格出发,绕合恩角一圈后返回,历时 317 天,航行了 17000 英里。他们创下了美国人靠不足 30 英尺长的船穿越合恩角的纪录。在完成了这次难忘的航行之后,25 岁的丹尼尔返回学校,并成家立业。但他对大海的钟爱依然不减,后来他再次逃离了人类社会,买下了加拿大新斯科舍海岸附近的一座小岛,建造了一座小屋,带领妻子和继子居住到岛上,他们像鲁滨孙·克罗索一样过着自给自足的生活。丹尼尔的另外一本回忆录《鲸鱼岛上》(*On Whale Island*:*Notes From a Place I Never Meant to Leave*,2002)记载了这段经历。

　　《我的老爸与海》记载了他们沿着加勒比海向南,穿越巴拿马运河,经过加拉巴哥群岛和复活节岛,绕过合恩角,返回康涅狄格的航程。父子俩生动详细地记载了他们航海途中的种种冒险和两人之间的沟通交流、父子俩的内心世界和对这次航海的期盼。对两人来说这是一次发现之旅:发现自我,发现父子角色的变化,发现自然的力量。对儿子来说,是难忘的成年仪式。

所选章节根据每段开头所标示的日期记录了航海当天的所见所闻,所思所想。在所选前两节中,丹(丹尼尔)讲述了在"麻雀"号航行到第一百七十七天,快到达合恩角时他们突遭暴风雨袭击的整个过程。此时是南半球的冬季,天气变幻莫测,险峻的海域对大学毕业不久的丹尼尔来说是一次严峻的生死考验。当他们安然度过这段危险路程后,父子俩不约而同地举杯,悼念那些葬身在这里的勇敢的人们。同样一次危机,在父亲大卫的笔下,读者看到的更多的是一个成熟男人丰富的航海知识以及作为一位父亲的骄傲。他说道:"骑士中有半人半马,为什么我们航海人却没有一个称呼来指代半人半船呢?丹尼尔在那一刻就是其化身。"这充分体现了身为人父的大卫看到儿子成长后感到的骄傲。

航海过程中的重重危机以及危机后的平静与收获无疑改变了年轻的丹尼尔。所以在航海归来的那天,丹尼尔的日记里处处流露出他对"麻雀"号和航海生活的恋恋不舍,以及对陆地上人类生活的不适和疏离。选篇最后是丹尼尔结束航行,回家生活一周的日记。日记表明,一些曾经是他喜欢和熟悉的事物如今却令他感到生疏,甚至厌恶,这更加反衬出他对航海生活的热爱和留恋。

DAN

DAY 175. Dawn, three hundred miles west of Cape Horn. Full moon and angry oceans. When you think of these waves, imagine a big, green Mack truck[①] skidding at you sideways, with fifty bathtub loads of shaving cream on top. *Sparrow* bobs right over them. Last night, in a three-hour Force 8 gale[②], a big wave whomped us, filling the cockpit and finding leaks not yet tested. We've screwed boards over the portholes and have all sorts of lids, caps, and cloths lashed-to, stuffed-in, and wadded-around vents, chimneys, and deck fittings.

Icebergs! Hitting an iceberg in a gale is what I fear. One reason Cape Horn is so feared is that the gales are usually westerly. If you want to go west, against them, you must fight for every mile. Captain Bligh[③] spent thirty-one days in a gale, going just eighty-five miles, said, "Forget this!" turned tail (probably seasick and depressed), and went *all the way around the world* to get to Tahiti. At least we're going east. The gales are with us. Right now the roaring in the rigging is like the soundtrack from a bad dream. Even if you're moving well, it's unsettling. I imagine falling over and freezing. The water temperature is fifty degrees[④] or less, so quickly numbing. You cannot sail to windward in a real blow—right angles to the wind is about the best you can do. I discovered this trying to recover a sail bag.

---

① 美国的麦克货车(Mack truck),是赫赫有名的载重型卡车。1900年公司建立,其产品行销全世界。

② Force 8 gale:8级大风。

③ Captain Bligh:布莱(1754—1817),英国海军将领,"恩惠"号船长和地方长官。1789年舰艇上部分士兵叛乱,把他和忠于他的人放逐到一条小船上,几周之后他安全抵达帝汶岛,航行了近4000英里。

④ 50华氏度相当于10摄氏度。

Dad was changing jibs, and before he could smother the empty bag and stuff it below, it filled with wind with a bang like a pistol shot and almost yanked off his arm.

A troop of porpoises—around twenty-five—races with us. From the top of the waves, they leap eight feet in the air. I can see them in the water in the wave crests above us, silhouetted against the sky. They're called Chilean dolphins and are not supposed to be this far offshore.

Sleeping is hard, everything rattles and things fall on you (cats, books, clothes, Dads, pens, toys, flashlights, chopsticks, bowls, crackers—or everything from the spice rack, which escapes together and for no known reason). Exhaustion finally does it, but by then it's time to get up. Dad keeps clothes in the jam cupboard over his head so the jars won't rattle. The weather here is fast to change. I begin my watch at midnight, all bundles with my big furry hat almost covering my eyes, wearing thick mittens and baggy pants. Now it's short sleeves and bright at 0600. Although the temperature range here is like a northern Canadian summer, in the fifties and sixties, the wind is so strong that fifty degrees can feel freezing cold.

DAN

DAY 177. Barometer easing its angle of dive. Alter course to stay north of Diego Ramirez—can't risk approaching that rock in this visibility. Will go down Drake Passage between it and the Horn, angling up to the Horn. I'm disappointed—Cape Horn is the last land mass of South America, and Diego Ramirez is just a rock, covered by cold waves and the ultimate lonely place before Antarctica. Even so, it's land.

DAY 178. On January 6, just after I got our noon position and wrote the above, a gale clomped down on us—with Force 8 winds and gusts to Force 9. In the afternoon I came on deck and besides seeing that Dad was working hard at the tiller, the seas and sky looked furious. White streaks were smeared along the waves, the wind almost visible! Seas built and grew until it was necessary for us to look aft and steer down each wave, keeping the stern toward the following seas. Some waves were bigger than others—foaming and looking really mean. Graybeards. The automatic steering wouldn't work—the paddle was spending too much time out of the water. (The whole boat seemed to be spending too much time out of the water.) We took two-hour watches.

It's hard to see a wave (in photos, impossible). You see the mass of it—not much height—then you rise slowly as the water floods beneath you and you're on top. I was at the helm watching this really big one and suddenly I knew *Sparrow* hadn't risen and twenty feet of wave was straight up over us.

We surfed for a moment and fell off it to starboard, flat into the water. The boat didn't seem to tip over but the port rail rose up suddenly above me as I slid down. What I'd been standing on was above my shoulder level. I was in the ocean! The foaming waves I'd been looking at were at my chin. My tether was yanked tight as *Sparrow* came up level, surfed again, and fell over to port, the starboard deck and rail shooting up over my head. I kicked my legs and paddled for a moment in free water, then *Sparrow* righted and I was scooped on deck.

By the time all this happened, it had been thirty-six hours since I'd had a fix on the sun to establish our position. My dead reckoning put us near Diego Ramirez (fifty miles southwest of Cape Horn). But you can't steer accurately in a gale, so I was jumpy.

The gale broke up by 0100 and, with the moon full, there it was: a frozen wave at the end of the continent. A featureless gray hump. The Horn.

DAVID

My Horn passage started at 0700 on January 7. The sunrise had been ominous. The paddle that goes down into the water to work the self-steerer was jumping out as the stern lifted high. I jibed and the main sheet looped under the paddle, threatening to snap it off. I called for Dan and he held me by the heel like Achilles's mother as I went in headfirst for the line and cleared it. Dan was angry because I unclipped my tether, but it didn't stretch that far and I didn't want to take time to reclip it. "But we're not moving, Dan," I said weakly. I was glad he was angry because that meant he'd use the tether himself. We dismantled the Navik and steered by hand for the first time on this passage. Seas and wind built and it was a proper gale, going with us. We took in the jib; she flew with only a spot of mainsail exposed. Slocum's phrase repeated in my head: "Even while the storm raged at its worst, my ship was wholesome and noble." And *Sparrow* was magnificent: delicate but steady, swift and airy on the foam crest, strong and driving through the great valleys. She seemed born for this day.

At noon, Dan shifted course, visibility was down to a few hundred yards. Forget Diego Ramirez. If we didn't hit it we wouldn't see the Horn either. The Horn is three things: the rock itself, Drake Passage (the water in which you sail around it), and the whole idea of the passage. We were in the Passage, and surely we'd survive for the third. I settled for two out of three. At one that afternoon I asked Dan when we'd be off (if not crashed onto) the Horn and he said, "0100 tomorrow morning." The gale picked up and Dan steered, howling "Aaayippeeeeeee!" as we surfed down the long gray waves with their tops torn off and the spray racing us. It was quiet and dry below. I realized that Dan had hardly ever steered by tiller, but his skill was marvelous, undoubtedly honed by hours of handling the joystick in video-game parlors. He looked possessed. Horsemen have their centaurs, why don't we sailors have a name for the half-man, half-boat that Dan was at that moment?

Because we were hand-steering we changed to two-hour stints. During my early-evening watch, the gale stared to fly apart, moderating. This is the most dangerous time of a gale, because the puffs can be fierce after random lulls, and the wind can shoot at you suddenly from a different direction. At eight-thirty at night I was below making tea and lighting the evening lamp when *Sparrow* went down hard to starboard. Then bam! down to port. Without a horizon below, hanging on and standing not upright but with the angle of the boat, I only know that we were down because the water covering the porthole was not wave froth but solid green—I was looking straight down into the ocean. A felt bootliner that was drying knocked the lamp out of my hand and onto the bunk. The water roared, like a train running over us.

"OK, Dan?"

"I'm fine, Dad." His voice sounded subdued.

My eye was taken during this by the blue plastic cat pan, which was secured by cord on two sides. It jumped up, did a 180° turn and landed upside down, then leaped again and did a full 360° flip and landed face down again. It looked like a little girl in a blue dress, skipping rope. I thought of that calmly. The binoculars were in my berth with the oil lamp; their teak box had broken. It was the only thing we hadn't built ourselves. Everything else was in place. I didn't learn until he told me the next day that Dan had gone overboard.

The gale broke on my ten-to-midnight watch, and the moon, almost full, showed through the racing clouds as they tore apart: a slow film flicker. After my watch I was below, again making tea, and Dan called, "Dad, I think I see the Horn," and I was up on deck at ejection speed and there it was.

"How did you see it, Dan?"

"One wave didn't go down."

I'd never seen it but of course it was the Horn; its form must have been in my genes. The great rock sphinx, the crouching lion at the bottom of the world. The sea and the sky and the faintly outlined huge rock were all the same color—indigo, graded like the first three pulls of the same ink on a Japanese woodblock print. We embraced, then stood entranced. I went below and poured a finger of Kahlua for each of us (I oddly remembered a guest saying, "No, Leonora, the finger is held sideways, not straight down"). We toasted. I was about to say, "To the men who died here," when Dan said, "To the people died here." It was the only possible thing to say. There was the rock, after 2,500 miles of ocean, our first sighting, the rock itself.

"You said 0100, Dan, and here we are."

"Yes, but I was aiming for ten miles off."

"You can't be less than eight..." I was staggered by that. Two hundred and thirty miles in thirty-six hours without sky for sights, only our eyes on the compass and on our wake to judge speed, in full gale, in strong current, and with a course change in the middle, and his error was two miles. The Horn bore north and I stepped behind him. Few had rounded the Horn in a boat this small, and he was ahead of me.

We were in the Atlantic. I had a sudden craving for simple food, and made a plain omelette for us. Three eggs in the pan, one on the floor. Perfectly moist in the middle. Just a sprinkle of dill. It was getting light. Between us and the Horn, thousands of small petrels fluttered and dipped, like a vast spread of brown-and-white lace undulating a foot above the surface.

DAN

DAY 178. Morning, January 8. There is enough light by 0300 for us to take pictures. I'm too excited to sleep. To see land after twenty-four days at sea. I'd planned to put on my wet suit and swim away to get a picture of *Sparrow* in front of the Horn, but when we are actually there the thought raises the hairs on my teeth. Dad agrees. He had thought of going up to it—I guess for forty years—and neo he's too awed and wants to leave it to itself. It's not really his choice; the island won't be played with.

I had many pictures of what I thought rounding the Horn would look like. Usually *Sparrow* would be transformed into an old square-rigger and I'd be taking in the tallant as the seas crashed against us. But, in fact, I spend a good part of the morning annoyed that I can't get the little balls of instant milk to dissolve in my coffee.

In the Galapagos, I'd burned "Sparrow 1984" nicely into a teak board. I wanted to hang it up at Post Office Bay, but we didn't get there. I passed it up on deck before my watch, intending to throw it in the sea when we reached the Horn. It was swept overboard when the wave threw us on our side. The sea took it.

I realize how committed I am to this boat. Last night, when *Sparrow* fell and I was in the ocean, I thought only about her, not me. If I'd been rolling over in a car I'd have thought about whether I'd live or die. But in the water I wanted to get back on board to help *Sparrow* live on. I understand that without her I'd die, and that isn't the same as a wrecked car or a burned-down house that you walk away from. But there's a deep bonding and it can turn into love and purpose. Perhaps it explains why men could live a horribly hard life on the old sailing ships. In bad storms, they would put out to sea away from the dangers of land.

I can see myself on *Sparrow* in a harbor and someone rows up and says, "Is this the *Sparrow* that went around Cape Horn?" I'll say, "Yes," and be happy that they admire the boat and won't say, "I was there too."

DAVID

By 1000, on January 8, the Horn was in clear sight behind and already we'd bent our easterly course toward north. Suddenly, a sheet of hail about the size of capers hit me so hard in the back that I stumbled forward in the cockpit. Just out of a blue sky, or at least a broken sky, not a rain or storm sky. And with it came the strongest wind we'd had, over fifty knots (Force 10). The sea stayed flat but turned white—we were already in shelter from the Horn and its islands—and in less than a minute I clawed down the jib and had another tuck in the main, and then in fifteen minutes the williwaw was over. I mostly remember the petrels chattering under the bow when I went forward. I hoped Dan wasn't awakened, but he must have heard and felt that blast of hail.

Hours later, after dinner on the day we rounded the Horn, I watched a good sunset, with clouds by Poussin, saw more seabirds (our first grebes), and the first weed in the water. It was time to read E. B. White again, and I was feeling at peace. But it breezed up and we had bumpy and crooked water by dark.

DAN

DAY 317. The last day.

0500. I can feel Montauk, and I don't know if that's because I trust my navigation or if it's a feeling I have by itself. I know it's just over the curve of the earth.

Not wanting to round the point with a foul tide, I drift and sleep for a few hours. Then I put on too much sail and start beating toward home. The rail is constantly awash, but I don't care. *Sparrow* is crashing through waves, splashing sheets of spray twenty feet in all directions. I feel like a fluorescent light bulb trying to light. I want to just ease the sheet a bit and turn back to sea while there is still time, as at Fernando; but I'm out of chutney. Got to restock, at least.

Can I keep this dream going forever and never again face the consequences of human interaction? Where do I fit in and what do I do now? Am I still in my dad's shadow or can I go forward with this lead? Do I have my own permission? When will I know?

0700. Montauk. I sail close into the shore and tack up toward the point. The water is a frothy blue-green. It is different from any other water I've seen this past year.

1200. I pull out the radio and hear the voices of friends telling me to hurry up. There are seventy-five people waiting, and CBS can't wait past five o'clock. I cringe, then ease the sheet a wee bit, slowing down and sending CBS on their way.

As usual it's choppy—all of the ocean trying to squeeze into Long Island Sound by way of this point. I pick out familiar landmarks—the nuclear power plant, Race Rock, New London Ledge, New London Light. They all come out of the blur as they stood against the backdrop of imagination for so long.

Two motorboats covered with cameras churgle out and find me. I am circled and clicked at—talk about self-conscious! I haven't dealt with more than three people at a time for ten months, and suddenly through their lenses I am presenting myself to millions! It's quite clear that tonight everyone on earth will stop what they're doing and watch me on television.

I sail past my home, which stands on four iron legs over the familiar piece of rack, Hobb's Island. The water is deep up to the front porch and I am tempted to jump off. The monkey looks at it sideways.

The motorboats with their camera crews are gone now (setting up their "arrival shots," I imagine). I see Burr's dock a mile north. It looks crowded.

Out of the familiar scenery roars Dad in our launch, *Rozinante*. It needs paint. He's all smiles. We give each other a silent look of love—we don't even wave.

Dad motors off to catch lines at the dock. It's very quiet. The wind's gentle and northeast, my favorite wind.

A half mile to go.

NOTES MADE in the bathtub, first week home:

Giving someone my autograph, I spelled my name wrong. Home is finding your old key chain and having no idea whose it is. I forget what the keys do. I'll have to start over!

One year. I don't judge it by one more income tax return, or another twelve months of screaming TV commercials. I see it as more than six hundred sun sights and the Earth's gone around again. I wasn't here to watch changes take place at home, and sailing is such another world that the past year seems like a movie that just let out. I've been gorging myself on everything craved—women, driving too fast, loud music, bread, baths, and clean clothes. I'm surprised to again find that happiness doesn't come from how much I can consume. It was easy to think so all year—that all that stuff would make a difference. I forgot it's why I left.

My checkbook is...well, it just is. I can't remember how to use it. My ears buzz from loud Rolling Stones music, and last weekend I dented the front of my car by driving too far into some backwoods of Maine.

My desire to do more and go farther hasn't changed one bit. And I know it never will. I won't stuff desires, or whims, or fantasies away with reasons to justify why I shouldn't pursue them. Sometimes I feel like Tiger on his morning spaz run.

▶扩展阅读

1. Maytal，A. "Set Designer Founds Famed Theatre of the Deaf"，*The Harved Crimson*，June 03，2002.

2. Gewertz，K. "Hays to Receive the 1999 Harvard Arts Medal"，*Harvard Gazette*，April 08，1999.

▶学习参考网站

1. http：//www.mtexpress.com/2002/02-06-05/02-06-05hays.htm

2. http：//www.thecrimson.com/article/2002/6/3/set-designer-founds-famed-theatre-of/

3. http：//www.amazon.com/My-Old-Man-Sea-Father/product-reviews/

【芮渝萍　编注】